SLEDGEHAMMER: A ROCK & ROLL FABLE

Volume II

Jason Stuart

BURNT
BRIDGE

For Molly, God of the 80's

Acknowledgements

This book is for everyone who loves the 80's, that wild, bizarre, awful, wonderful decade full of sheer and utter nonsense — that cocaine-fueled fever dream of Reaganomics, Cold War hysteria, pop culture, and pumped sneakers.

Also: special thanks to my editors for sharpening and polishing this into the best it could be.

Thanks to my beta readers: Juliana, Charlie from Starkville, and Nick. Thank you so much for working through the early drafts of this with me.

And thanks to my daughter for making me want to show her the 80's we always wished we had.

Somewhere in the '80's...

Where it's dark in the city...

EPISODE I

"GOD BLESS THE CHILDREN OF THE BEAST"
–MÖTLEY CRÜE, 1983

THE BUTCHER–FRAMED BY THE ROARING fires of the great hearth–sliced bone and sinew, rending the flesh of the youngling, letting its blood flow into the dishes, the goblets, the chalice that would go to the master for his evening's repast. The howls and screams of the others sang as music to him while he went about his preparations.

Above, in the many storied layers of the tower, the master wandered through the unlit corridors of his cragged, moistened manor. That accursed and most malformed of all creation, the soulless one slumped upon his stone seat and peered out into the glimmering eyes of his proselytes. His horn, protruding out of his skull, had twisted and grown larger with age. He was so old now he no longer felt time. Yet it had snuck up on him once again. An ending loomed on the horizon. *His Eldar mother poured out this bitter cold,* heralding the doom she sowed. *Another* apocalypse. *For them.* Never he. Bound as he was. Be it drowning, burning, or just the endless, icy nothing. Always, he would remain. As was his curse. Undying. Ever-living.

"Where is my Evilyn?" he asked into the darkness. The titter of finger and toenails scattered across the wet stone floors. Candles lit themselves, just enough to cascade off her silhouette as she flowed into his arcade.

"I am here, my Lord." She dropped to one knee, bowing her head before him. The pomegranate-hued side of her opulent hair caught the dancing glow of the candle she'd lit with her own whispers.

"My Jester Queen." He ran his blood-hued and black-nailed fingers across her chin. "Tell me, is it Midsomar approaches?" His voice low, a warm growl.

"It is, my Lord." She bowed lower. "The preparations are set. The city is all in order."

"Yes, of course." He tired of this talk. So many of these. So tedious. All of it, the endless repetition. Long since maddening. But this time, if not something entirely new, at least something rare.

"Mother Night comes. The days shall shorten again," he muttered. "And then they shall come no more. For a time. For all things are thus. Ever changing. Ever the same. This isn't the first time she's tried to wake the dreamer. Nor shall it be the last."

Evilyn drew her gaze up to his eyes, those cold stones set in his large, horned head. The void within him bleeding out, pouring their emptiness into the room, into her.

"I'm bored. Let us amuse ourselves, in our readying for my solstice."

"Of course, My Prince. What do you wish?"

"Release some of my children."

"Your *children,* my Lord?"

He heard the tint in her voice. Some part of her former self remained. A residual. He would expunge that from her, this very night in fact. For he'd an appetite now.

"Let them play," he said. "But away from *my* city."

I

"GATOR HIDE"
—THE VANDALS, 1989

WALLY THE GAME WARDEN looked down at the pieces of what had been a boat—not a small one, neither. One of them big jobs these yups would get. A little money came their way, it'd be burnt a hole in their wallet before long, so they up and bought them the biggest, baddest Sunday fishing rig they could find. Probably some doctor or banker got himself a big payday under the Commie Ron days, the bastards. The Real American would see to all that. That's how Wally figured it.

The stinking reporter was late. He'd decided to come out and take another look at the wreckage. The drunks from the swamps had been up to their tall-telling again. Wasn't no nevermind. They'd been saying their nonsense for years in these parts, only difference is now somebody worth a dollar had lost a fancy toy, and it had made a stink all the way into town.

And here she come now, he thought, as the whirling rotors caught his eardrums off guard. The tops of the tall pines whipped back and forth as the whirlybird descended toward the sandy bald spot just off Cross Bayou at the Pearl River. He'd tried to get them to drive out and meet him at the station, but she'd insisted on bringing the noise of eight counties.

"Have you seen it?" she asked as she climbed down from the copter. The pilot stayed aboard, began scribbling in his charts. At least it wasn't too hot, but Wally still couldn't imagine wanting to sit behind all that glass with the sun coming on.

"What? The boogey monster? Lady, I been policing these bogs and swamps for coming up twenty years, and believe me, I've my count right. Ain't never seen as much as a 12-footer, much less something half the size of a football field out of fairy tales."

"What about that business east of here earlier this year?" She referred to the rumors of monsters and machines having attacked one of the towns nearby. Details of the event had been sparse, and stranger things had been reported in and around the city of New Orleans for years.

"Well that ain't neither here nor there."

He led the reporter to the riverbank. She looked over the shredded boat the same as he had done twice now, poking and prodding at it—wrote down a bunch of notes.

"Are these marks consistent with bites?" She pointed to the shreds and scrapes along the hull of the boat.

"The teeth would have to be at least—" he trailed off, holding up his thumb and index finger to estimate the size.

"I'd like to go upriver," she said. "Take a look at the area."

"Well, that'll take some doing." He scratched his head. "I'll have to requisition us a boat, and that'll be—"

"If this thing is half the size I've heard, I've no interest in being anywhere near it, much less right on top of it." She marched back toward her conveyance. "That's why I brought a chopper, sir."

* * *

Wally never cared much for being up high. He liked trucks and boats. And mostly having his own two feet planted on the ground. They followed the river up past Pearlington and nearly to the interstate and then turned back for another sweep. She scanned the area with a set of high-dollar binoculars. Wally just used the scope on his thirty-aught.

"There." She pointed her finger down at the water by Browns Island.

Wally aimed his rifle scope at her finger's direction. He ran up and down the water's edge as it trickled past the tiny island. He couldn't make out any...then he saw it. Or saw something. It was the rippling—the way the water moved, the swish and swirl of it. And to hell if it wasn't big... damn big.

"Get us in closer," she said to the pilot. He followed the order, and the chopper lurched down, hovering a few dozen feet above the water, too close for Wally's peace of mind.

She kept her eyes peeled on the water, following the motion of that heavy tail swishing back and forth until it disappeared.

"Where'd it go?" She looked at Wally.

He spied all around the river, toward either bank. Thing had gone under. Got spooked. Knew it was being hound-dogged, likely. Thing was smart. Too smart. Gave Wally a spider-up-his-back kind of gnaw.

"Let's go up a bit," he said. "I don't like this."

"No," she said. "Take us closer to where it went under."

The pilot followed suit, dipped them down again. She leaned out over the edge, aiming her eye for any sign of the fiend. Wally kept his eyes sharp and his rifle cocked.

The pilot saw it first. The mighty monster surged from the river, its gigantic snout the full length of Wally's pickup truck, snapping at their tiny fiberglass hull like it were a toy. The pilot lurched them to the side and out of the demon's reach.

The reporter fell forward, tumbling out of the copter. Wally's instinct kicked in. He let go his rifle and snatched her arm just before it left his reach, held her tight, wrenched her in his grip and hurled her back on the bird with them. The giant croc slammed its body back into the muddy brown of the Pearl, vanishing again beneath its rolling water. The reporter tried to scream but the air left her chest in raw fright. She set to heaving, hyperventilating.

The pilot needed no order. He skedaddled fast as spinning rotors could get them.

The reporter caught her breath. Wally stared off to where they'd been—still wrapping his mind around what he'd just seen, trying to decide the worst of it, the damn beast or the loss of his best rifle.

"We—" The reporter tried to find her words. "We've—We've gotta call the—someone. The army. The navy. Something. That...thing! That's the biggest—"

Wally tried to settle her down, get her to manage her breathing. The pilot cooked them away as fast as they could get.

"We've got to warn people. Call out the national guard." She calmed herself somewhat.

Wally shook his head over it. "I'll make the call." He looked east, toward the Bay. "I know a guy...who knows a girl."

II
"ECHO BEACH"
—MARTHA AND THE MUFFINS, 1980

WIND WHISPERED ACROSS the white sands of the south beach of Ile de Navire as the three girls and one off-duty vice cop lay out under the billowing clouds. Lydia Stiles, spiked black bangs as always, sported her pentacle-necked black bathing suit and avoided what little sun shined that day with her massive-brimmed hat, also black. Her on-again paramour, Bruce Nguyen, the former undercover high school cop she'd necked with after the Prom-pocalypse, had brought them all out on the Vice Squad's Scarab go-fast boat. Becky LeCroiseur stretched her already perfectly tan legs.

Quiet, sitting away to herself, that flame-red hair rippling in the gulf breeze, the one they called Molly Slater took it all in. The waves lapping at the far side of the small island calmed her constantly processing mind. There was still so much she didn't know. She soaked in the information. Some days she wished she could just plug a cord into the whole world and instantly know everything at once.

The decaying fortress loomed behind them, its red brick walls chipped away year by year as the encroaching waters threatened to swallow it in some not-distant future. She stared back at it, admiring the elegant simplicity of its design, archaic as it was. She had taken to noting old designs, cataloging and storing them for possible future use. She still went out to patrol the streets most nights, and more than a few daytimes. Her particular abilities had their uses.

She watched her friends pick at one another. Lydia, the best friend, almost scared the sun might bite her, teased at the boy, a man really, who harbored more affection for Lydia than he let on. His dilated eyes and quickened heartbeat betrayed him with every glance at her face. But the others didn't see these things. Becky, their foe-turned-friend, looked back at her with a knowing wink and a wry smile.

She admired them. Though their lives had exploded in the months prior, they adapted well. Resilient, these human creatures were. But, she knew she was not the same as them. She could never be like they were. Their lives, fragile, fleeting, precious because of that. She cherished them all the more. She found herself, in the back of her mind, wishing every nanosecond she could be one of them, to live and think, and love, and be as they were. But she knew she never would. And that was okay, too. She smiled as she thought of their kindness toward her, how they accepted her in spite of what she was, what she'd done. She loved them for that. If she *could* love.

Some squawking from the Scarab's radio sent Nguyen to investigate its message.

"So, how is our *other* friend doing?" Becky asked Lydia, though she glanced back at the redhead.

"Oh, Two-fer?" Lydia said. "She's good, I guess. Probably cruising the streets, keeping things even-keel, I don't know."

"You call her *Two-fer?*" Becky wrinkled her face. It didn't sound like the kindest name.

"Well, I mean sorta. She still hasn't really picked a name, but I was saying a shape-shifting android twin is like having two Molly's at once, so, you know, like a Two-fer." Lydia shrugged her shoulders, seeming fine with the moniker.

"She probably wouldn't like that name." Becky thought of her own decade and a half spent living with a false name she never chose nor wanted. She shuddered at the memory.

"She doesn't love it." The redhead finally spoke. It was the first thing she'd said all afternoon since they'd arrived.

Lydia looked back at the face of her best and oldest friend. She'd noticed how quiet she'd been. Lydia knew Molly still had a lot on her mind and had decided to let her be. But, now Lydia's face bore her curiosity. "How do you know she doesn't like it?" She squinted one eye. "I've never even said it when she was ar–" Lydia glared at the smirk on the redhead's face, "God damn it, Molly, or *you!*"

Becky held her belly laughing.

The android wearing Molly Slater's face laughed as well.

"How long have you, like... you know?" Lydia was less angry at the machine than she was worried for her friend. This wasn't the first time the *real* Molly had skipped on hanging out with them.

"I wish you would use a different look," Lydia said. "I mean–"

The android smirked and shifted her face and outfit to a mirror image of Lydia. "Not cool." Lydia glared.

Becky giggled, and the android shifted to her too, mimicking her darker tone and Big River brown hair she now sported.

"I will literally sue you." Becky's eyes lasered the machine wearing her face.

The Android shifted back to Molly's face, the only one she seemed comfortable with. She'd had her fun, but now looked across the gulf, staring into the horizon. She did want a name. She just didn't know which one. She wanted a lot of things.

"Hey." Nguyen made his way back, gathering his gear from the sand. "We gotta book. There's a situation. And we're gonna need the *other* one for this, I think."

"How did literally everyone know but me?" Lydia folded her arms in a pout.

Nguyen took out his wallet, flashing his gleaming silver shield. "Hi, girlfriend," he said. "I'm detective Bruce Nguyen. Have we met?"

Lydia slitted her eyes at him. He would be hearing more on this later.

III
"I STILL DREAM ABOUT YOU"
–JOAN JETT & THE BLACKHEARTS, 1988

HIGH ABOVE DOWNTOWN, sat upon her perch atop the Hancock building, The Sledgehammer watched her sleepy town. She reclined, stretched out across the ledge, waving her head back and forth to the calm sounds of Genesis. If she closed her eyes to Collins' voice, the whisper of the night air, the crunch of tires against the street, she could almost dream about the boy she still wanted to hold every day. Easton. Her Easton. Becky's Easton. Everyone's Easton. His sandy, curly locks that dangled from behind his ears with his sunglasses on his head. Even at night, he and Nguyen both wore them. All those nights she'd spent with the two of them. Putting things right. Making the world maybe some small amount better— or at least making themselves feel better about it.

But he was gone now. Not even a shadow. Not a single whisper on the wind of him tonight. She'd raged at first, in the weeks since his death at the hands of that... *thing*. But now it became a hollow sadness—an emptiness where he'd once been in her life, in all their lives.

The others coped as they should. His best friends, Becky and Nguyen, they leaned on each other. And both had become close with her own best friend, Lydia. She was glad for them. It's why she sent her robot twin to be with them most nights. *She* needed friends, too. To learn from, to observe, to show her how to be more like them. More human. Something Molly had come to accept she'd never been, nor ever be.

She was just The Hammer.

It was time to go to work. She felt him, ten blocks north. She'd honed her soul-hearing, as she called it now, to filter out all the noise and feel people's intents, their will, their conflicts, and their guilt. Among all their other emotions, it was interesting, the things a person felt just before committing a crime—the desperation, the fear, so thick it clawed at her mind. And a lot of hate, self-hate. This one was no different. She zeroed him from the rooftop, positioned, aimed her body at his exact spot with her mind (she'd gotten more accurate with her leaps). She closed her eyes and shot into the air.

The guy, the boy, couldn't have been any older than she was. He had a red jacket, but he wasn't a Mute—not yet. Their ranks had scattered across the gulf, broken, despondent. All thanks to her and her former foe, that goblin creature that had called itself Blake Elvis. But the kid was exactly what the gangs looked for. Young, broke, hungry, and desperate. His neck was cold, but his head poured sweat as he fidgeted with the .38 snubnose in his jacket pocket. His body twitched as he stumbled toward the all night Seven-Eleven. He lingered outside the door—the cashier eyeing him for the threat he very much was.

"You don't want to do this." Her voice, a warm wind on his icy back, sent a wave of calm into him. He turned to face her, her eyes. Like steel water looking all the way into him, into everything he ever was and ever had been, ever would be.

"I–I–."

"It's okay." She touched his shoulder—looked directly into his eyes. "You're gonna go home now, yeah?"

"Ye-yeah." He took his hand off the gun in his pocket. "I-I'm sorry."

"I know. It's okay. You're better than this. You're a good kid. I can see it. Yeah?"

"Yes. Yes, ma'am, Miss Sledgeh—"

"You can just call me Hammer." She smiled. He would be okay now. He handed her the gun from his pocket. She emptied the shells into her hand and handed it back to him. "Go hock it and buy some food. You need to eat more."

"Yeah, okay." He smiled back at her. She hugged him.

The shop clerk was on the phone inside. Molly felt his emotions, could almost read his lips. He hung up the phone and walked out with a sawed-off shotgun. His intent was steadier than the boy's had been.

"I done called the police." He aimed the barrels square at the boy's chest.

Molly stepped in between them, giving the clerk the same look she'd given the kid. The Clerk's heart dropped. He'd been ready to shoot. He'd almost wanted to. But she cold-stared him. She sent her will straight into his hardening heart.

"He's going home. He's done nothing wrong yet, and now he won't, will you kid?" she glanced back then turned to the clerk. "And neither will you. Now go put that back up. You won't need it tonight. I'm here. It's gonna be a nice, quiet night."

The clerk looked into her eyes. He believed her. Just like they all did. All she needed to do was look into them—speak calmly with intent. He lowered his gun, walked it back inside. The kid wandered into the night. The clerk came back outside, staring down at his shoes, not wanting to see her face from his own guilt.

"I did call the cops. They'll be on their way."

"They're already here." Molly had felt Nguyen and the girls blocks before they drove up. Nguyen was going to tell her something awful.

IV
"HOLY DIVER"
–DIO, 1983

THEY WAITED TILL FIRST LIGHT, a thing that vexed Molly The Hammer, since Wally the game warden said there was no use trying to track in the dead of night. For his human eyes, maybe, but hers saw just fine in the pitch. They saw a lot more besides. She saw colors they couldn't. Sometimes, she almost thought she saw sound. More than once recently, playing on her guitar (which she did less and less since the prom fiasco), she felt energy flowing out of her, or the guitar, or both. There was so much she still didn't know.

The reporter sat next to her in Wally's truck, stoic, unimpressed with the entirety of Molly. She'd taken a few photos the night before, as Molly and Nguyen had arrived. Molly's suit amusing her. "Kitschy," she'd said, snapping another photo as Molly came into view. They'd worked on it a lot in the weeks since. Nguyen had mail-ordered something called Kevlar, and they'd sewn patches all around her stretch denim pants and her cut-off jean jacket. He seemed to have a knack for this sort of life. They'd even made her a head wrap and eye mask she could pop on and tie back like a bandana. It helped cut down on her wardrobe malfunctions. It could take a bullet or two, and would hold up in a fire, which she'd learned the time she'd run into one last month downtown. Molly knew she looked a little calico. She didn't much care.

Lydia had insisted on coming out. It was a good thirty-minute drive through backroads and bottom swamps near the state line, the ground getting wetter and sloppier the closer they got to Big Muddy. When they turned off the paved roads into the wet red dirt, Lydia slowed her heavy diesel dually to a crawl, hit a switch on her updated dashboard, half alive with lights and stat readouts. Molly felt the truck lift itself higher as Lydia engaged the mud function on her tires.

"Twofer really did a number on this truck," she said to Molly, who hadn't asked. "I'm not gonna want to give it back when my brother gets out."

"Well, you've got some time," Molly had said. "Also, don't call her that."

"Yeah, I know."

The gator, or the croc, or whatever it was, (the only three who'd put eyeballs on it couldn't agree on species) looked to be headed south by southeast, according to the game warden. Molly deferred to his tracking ability, but something new stained the air now—a kind of menacing whisper. Almost a voice, but not out loud. Like it spoke only to her.

More than once she'd caught herself remembering that crazy preacher who'd called her the devil's child. Her red hair, same as his, the gangly creep had told her. *What if she was the devil's child?* She still had no idea what she was, where she came from, anything really. Some nights, she felt like she could hear the moans of the wandering dead, souls who hadn't found their way across. She hadn't told her friends. They'd been through enough. And she didn't want them to think... She didn't know what to think anymore. She tried to look only as far forward as the next job. The next wrong to right. The next monster to slay.

And now she had one. A full-blown monster. Straight out of Hell.

Wally the warden pulled the truck to a stop near a clearing not far from Bayou Caddy, near Ansley. The chopper hovered above them. Molly had told Lydia and Nguyen to hang back in the truck as she and the warden went out to inspect on foot. She didn't even like him being out in the brush with her. She could take a bite; he couldn't. Of course, he toted a Marlin lever gun that looked like it could drop a rhino—so long as he could Ethan Cord that sucker in a hurry, she hoped.

Wally walked her into the slog, pointing at this or that, naming off types of trees or plants that Molly forgot as soon as the sound was off the wind. She admired the way he cared so much about it—that he was proud of the work he did. There was something in that she respected—a kind of honor in it. She might have forgotten the names of the trees, but she'd remember his. Like she was keeping score or something.

They crept to the riverbank. Wally fingered the safety off his heavy rifle, and Molly cocked both her fists, ready to go. His feet, still moving forward, stopped making any sound at all. Like a snake, he slipped through the brush, Molly right on his heels, ready to maim anything that lurched for him.

She smelled it before he did. So awful she gagged from it, turned her head away from the knowledge of what it would be before they saw it. Rounding the next clearing, there it was—an old stilted fishing shack decimated into splinters and timber. Blood. Everywhere. A hand on the ground. A ring on its finger. Shreds of bloody, torn clothes. A nightmare in red and green before them.

"It's got the taste now." Wally shook his head and spat. He spun from side to side as though the yacht-sized demon would jump out at him. He tracked the prints, its talons each as long as Wally was tall. And Molly too. She'd noticed her increase in height over the last few months as her pants all stopped short at her ankles—replacing them one pair at a time. Whatever that was about.

"That's the sluice." Wally pointed to a smooth area on the ground, leading into the river, angled with the current. "He's swimming downriver, toward the coast," He aimed his rifle barrel into the horizon.

The two of them ran back to the truck, its radio already squawking, as was the reporter.

"T.C.'s in the air. He's got a make on it," she said. "He's southeast three miles and moving fast."

Molly looked at Wally, the knot already in his throat.

"He's headed for the beach," he said.

Nguyen and Lydia had run up and heard it all. Nguyen stared into the trees, the terror growing on his jawline. Molly looked at Lydia, who was just now seeing it for herself.

"The boat show!" Lydia said. "The festival on Lakeshore! There'll be hundreds!"

"There's no way we'll beat it there," Nguyen's face went stark white.

Molly glared at Lydia, a message sending and received all at once.

"I'm on it." Lydia ran to her truck, jumped on her radio's mic, and began jabbering fast as she could.

* * *

Lakeshore Beach popped with energy, alive with the crowds gathering for their annual Memorial Day boat and water stunt show. Go-fast cigarette boats twisted and turned in what little surf the barrier islands let through, most of it from their own wakes. The beach crowds thickened down the sand for half a mile as music boomed from a mainstage near the center of it all. The local high school water-sports team approached in formation. The boys formed the base on their water skis. The girls stood atop their shoulders, and more above them, forming a pyramid four levels high. Each held a ski rope attached to their towboat. The girl at the top held hers in one hand as she waved and smiled at the crowd all out to enjoy the day.

Their faces fell from elation to shock, then terror. She looked on in confusion, as did her teammates beneath her. Arms pointed, people running off the beach toward the highway, toward their cars. Kids screamed. Parents scooped them up and ran. The kids in the pyramid craned their necks behind them to see. And they saw.

The monster raced toward them. One of the go-fast boats capsized, turning too short to avoid it. Its massive, gigantic jaws opened up. It was less than a hundred yards behind them. The panic set in. The formation fell apart. Screams rang out as they tumbled down, chaotic, into the saltwater, the boat speeding away without them now. The girl from the top made no sound as the flaring white teeth came ever closer to her. There was no point.

Someone from the beach shouted at the top of his lungs as the sound of motorcycle exhaust split the air. "It's Her! It's the Sledgehammer!"

The Honda motorcycle shot off the highway, ramping a sand bank, soaring above the beach. From mid-air, its frame exploded, its parts re-arranging themselves around the body of its rider, molding and reforming, almost liquidly, into a metal warrior, then slammed to a landing, planting two massive steel feet into the sand and morphing both her arms into one giant cannon. She fired a blast thick as her own body right into the demon's mouth.

The monster shrieked as it bore the brunt of the heat-ray blast. It shut its scalded mouth before it could swallow the girl from the pyramid, and it veered off its course. A go-fast boat swept in and guys from the deck pulled her and two of her friends in. More boats sped up for the others.

The android defender on the beach fired again. Another blast slammed the reptilian creature in its side. It roared from the pain—smoking wounds appearing on its tank-like hide. It set its gaze upon its aggressor, slit its eyes and swam for her. She fired again. And again. It bore the brunt of the blasts but continued at her. The crowds from the beach scattered, fleeing fast as they could as the behemoth roared toward their savior.

The Metal Molly set her eyes to her foe as it gained ground on her—her blasts only enraging it further. A helicopter whir cut into the sound of the screams and the chaos as she reformed her arms into separate blades, razor-thin along each edge, and steeled herself for the fight coming at her. The beast sprinted at her as its legs hit the sand, her blade-arms taut and ready to slice as its jaws snapped shut—and stopped.

Just short of her reach, the android saw the monster struggle, wriggling its head and body, trying to lurch itself forward, snapping at her all the while. Then it slid backward, away from her. Its eyes in shock, it wrenched its head back to see what had stalled it.

Molly Slater had it by the tail. Her android twin, who deserved her own name, had bought her just enough time. The crowds watched from safe distance as the beast reeled from her grip on its tail. Molly wasn't letting go. She twirled, spinning herself, and soon the whole of the massive monster moved in unison with her in a whirlwind motion. With her momentum, Molly hurled it into deep water.

Molly turned to her partner. "Hold the beach."

Her twin sister formed a gun arm and cocked it.

Molly launched herself toward where she'd thrown the demon. Half a mile out, she'd sent it. It regained its position as she landed on its back with a fist slamming into its cinder-block scales. She bellowed blow after blow into it as it thrashed and writhed, flinging her off itself. It whipped its tail at her, batting her into the water. Then it charged, its jaws opening wide to swallow her whole.

Molly gripped two of its long teeth and planted her feet into its bottom jaw and held its mouth open. The monster pressed its muscles harder, trying to snap her shut in its mouth. Molly felt it clamping down harder, so she pressed herself further, her feet crunching its mandible bones.

"Not today, fuck-ugly," she yelled into the void of its throat.

"What are you?" Came a voice in her head. Some voice. Not her own.

"Who said that?" She lost focus and the Croc tossed her to one side, out of its mouth. It spun, whipping her with its tail, skipping her body across the surface of the water like a stone until she sank beneath. She dolphin-swam to the surface as the behemoth bore down on her. It clamped her again, plunging the two of them toward the depths of the great Gulf of Mexico. Molly raged against the roof of its mouth, shoving her fists through its soft gums, sending its cool blood gushing all over her. It began to gag and tried to swallow, and she kicked a tooth loose and used it to stabbed the monster's tongue. It reared in pain, and Molly shot out into the water like a bullet.

"You are some Fae-foe! A tormentor!" The voice in her head said again. *Where was it coming from?* Molly saw the eyes of the crocodile staring into her. Was it coming from him? Or her? Molly hadn't checked it for a package. Not that it mattered. She wanted to ask it something in return, but being underwater and all...

She answered back all the same. With her fists.

"Father!" the creature called out as she wailed into it. "Father!"

* * *

The sun's light on the beach faded into the west. The local news had come and gone. The beachgoers from the day fizzled. The reporter from New Orleans had arrived not long after Molly dive-bombed the monster from the chopper. She had Wally the game warden in tow. The android in the Sledgehammer suit stood sentry, her eyes diligent for any sign of renewed danger. Becky had joined them by now and stood by, watching. Lydia and Nguyen stared at the coastline, Lydia's dark eyes peering into the abyss of the horizon, waiting, watching, *praying* for any sign of her friend.

"Look, kid, I—" Wally the warden began to say, his eyes betraying his thoughts.

"Save it." Lydia ignored him and nodded to her android friend.

More minutes went by. Then an hour. The sun set. Nguyen cursed under his breath and turned away. The game warden swore and started for his truck. The reporter and the pilot made for the chopper. Lydia and Molly's sister stared all the same. Becky walked over and hugged Lydia, calling the Android to join in.

"No." Lydia shook out of the hug. "No." She folded her arms and stomped to the water's edge—staring into the darkening horizon.

"There!" the Android pointed into the distance across the water.

The reporter stopped the chopper from warming up and ran back to see. Wally ran to his truck for his rifle. He racked the lever, sending one of its buffalo-bore rounds into the chamber.

The Android's eyes became slits. Her arms melded into a giant plasma cannon again, warming up for a blast, the strange crystal cores buried deep in her chest powering all of it, all of her.

Out in the depths of the gulf, just beyond the edge of the sea shelf, Lydia finally saw it moving. Toward them. First just some shape. Then it rose further out of the water—its cold, staring, hateful eyes. Its leathery scales glinted in the rising moonlight. Lydia shook her head, refusing to believe what she saw. The monster continued its crawl out of the brackish water. Both Wally and the Android readied their shots. Nguyen came for Lydia to take her and Becky off the beach.

"Wait!" Lydia shouted. They all looked at her like she was crazy. "Just wait!"

The Android turned, shifted her eyes to a different mode.

"It's her!" The Android re-shifted her arms and formed a large spotlight, shining out into the gulf, right on the creature's head crawling out of the murk. As its head inched closer and drew higher out of the water, they saw an arm holding it by its lower jaw. The arm drew out of the water and joined the shoulder next to muddy locks of bright red hair. A ripped denim jacket, soaked and torn, filthy with algae, adorned a trudging slayer from the water. Her head hung grim, her expression flat and solemn.

Molly Slater carried the thing all the way to the beach, dropped it at the shoreline, and went right for Lydia's truck, grabbed a beer out of the ice chest and swallowed it in one gulp.

"Bet that'll be a story for your paper!" Lydia grinned at the reporter.

"Oh, it'll be something." She snapped a flash photo of the dead croc that still stretched a good 20 yards into the lapping gulf waters.

"I meant her." Lydia pointed at the beer-guzzling Sledgehammer, already smiling and laughing with her sister and Becky. "The Sledgehammer!" Lydia slammed her fist into her palm. She was so proud of her best friend she felt herself bursting.

"Her?" the reporter shrugged her shoulders and walked back to the chopper as it prepared for take-off. "I'm from NOLA, kid. I've seen a lot stranger things than that. You ever come to town." She handed Lydia a business card as she boarded the copter. "Look me up. I'll show you some wild stuff."

Lydia took the card as the lady climbed aboard and the chopper took off, rising into the sky. She flipped it over, squinted to see the letters in the hazy light. It had the paper, *New Orleans Register,* a desk phone number, and her name: Alex Charlton.

V
"THE PORK CHOP EXPRESS"
–JOHN CARPENTER, 1986

LYDIA STARED INTO THE ENGINE bay of what had once been a pristine quad cab GMC dually pickup truck. Her brother had left the heavy rig in her care when he went upstate to serve his time for working the family business. Very little of the truck had remained stock after he sank much of his proceeds from sales into the beast, but a few mods and some nitrous were nothing compared to what a super alien android had accomplished. For one, it no longer ran on diesel or any fossil fuel. Lydia didn't really understand any of it. It just ran. And like a bat out of hell, too. The tires no longer needed air. She could press a button and modify them for different terrains, including even the soupiest mudholes (not that Lydia was keen on mud-riding as many from her neck of the woods enjoyed).

"Of course!" she shouted. Her friend with the red hair popped her eyes at the random outburst. "Andi. It's perfect. It's a cute name, and it fits. I think she'll like this one!"

Her friend bobbed her head back and forth. Mulled it over.

"Actually, yeah. She wouldn't hate that one at all." She went back to tweaking the guitar she'd been tuning.

"Right. Because you're her again aren't you?" Lydia stared at the girl, dumbfounded at the resemblance. It was unnerving how well she could copy Molly, anyone for that matter, but she was especially good at Molly, even down to her mannerisms. It gave Lydia the creeps.

"I'm me, yes," Andi said.

"I mean her. You're you but pretending to be her." Lydia folded her arms. "You know what I mean. Where is she? I'm supposed to be hanging out with my best friend. No offense."

"None taken." She put down the guitar and stood up to go select one of Hoyt's machines to work on. She loved fixing the things he never got quite right. She admired humans who built things. It made her feel close to them.

"Well...?"

"She's with the hunter." Andi wound up the timer on a pen flashlight.

* * *

Molly slid the goblin's blade down the shoulder of the felled beast, separating hide from flesh, carving out another sliver in roughly the same shape as the one tanning on the ground behind her. Blake's creepy twin swords were the only thing that could cut her skin, so she always kept them with her. They came in handy for all sorts of things.

Wally the game warden had gotten the carcass hauled off the beach to a remote location up in the boons. She wanted a piece of her own before the "top men" came to cart it off to be studied. She finished slicing Wally a third section when Lydia's truck pulled up.

"Well that's gruesome." Lydia slammed her truck door.

Molly modeled the two dripping pieces of hide, one over each shoulder and crisscrossing her chest, flesh and coagulant oozing down her neon striped unitard. She smiled at Lydia shaking her head.

Lydia folded her arms at the sight. She knew Molly's fake smile when she saw it. The red drizzling down her uniform, the all-too-comfortable way she'd skinned the hide, too. Molly was getting worse by the day. Lydia knew she had to pull her back up somehow. "I hope to hell you brought spare clothes somewhere, because you ain't walking around The Quarter stinking of that, and I really don't want to turn around and go all the way back home again."

"Do what now?' Molly said just as Lydia hit her with the fire hose outside the station, the same one Wally used to knock the clumps of mud off his 4x4 after a long day in the bush. "Hey what the—" Molly writhed and shoved her palms to block the heavy spray, Lydia forming a smile at her friend's discomfort.

"Throw your gross-ass gator skin in the back and come on."

"Go where?" Molly said. "I'm not done with—"

Lydia hit her with the hose again.

* * *

The low-hanging cypress whizzed by them as Lydia rolled down the backroads toward Chef Menteur Highway. She had the windows down, blowing the reek off Molly as best she could. The further west she drove, the ground either side of the blacktop turned first to mush then marsh. The more manageable-sized cousins of Molly's recent kill darted from the slim shoulders back into the brownwater bogs. The Beastie Boys were cold-kicking it hard on her surround sound at a deafening roar, Lydia throwing poorly formed gang signs out her window as Molly glared from the passenger side. The full array across the truck's remade console looked to Molly like something out of science fiction, but, of course, so was *she* along with the author these modifications, Andi the Android Molly Copy. Molly also didn't hate the name Andi.

"Okay, but why, again, are we going to the city?" Molly furrowed her brow. She had been looking forward to making a gator stew out of the carcass. What could it hurt? As always, she was never exactly hungry but always wanted to eat.

"Because you need a break. I need a break. Because School's out. Forever. We're eighteen. We're free. And because I want a daiquiri and a hand grenade and some zydeco music and probably some gumbo. And because I said so."

"I've got summer school, though, remember?" Molly sighed.

"As if you even go." Lydia sneered, hit her blinker to take an exit.

"I do go." Molly stared off behind her. "Sometimes it still smells like him there."

"Okay, well, that was—" Lydia raked a tear off her eye and threw it out the window. "Look, I'm sorry. But we're still going. You need this. We need this. And *you* will be at summer school all day today. I already took care of it."

Lydia wheeled into a Truck Stop just before they crossed the Pontchartrain, her own rig catching the eye of the road-weary truckers, then doubly so when they saw the black-clad goth and soggy redhead exit its cab.

Inside the store, Lydia perused the tourist brochures, getting ideas for things to do in the city while Molly availed herself of the 2-dollar shower stalls. Looking around at the general dinginess of the place, Lydia decided Molly was a trooper.

She grabbed two or three interesting-looking brochures, some ghost tours, carriage rides, Lafitte's Blacksmith Shoppe, and one for an occult bookstore she really wanted to check out from the looks of it. Four extra-long Slim-Jims, two RC colas, and a moon pie later, she waited outside, watching two idiots and some dude dressed like Abe Lincoln cram themselves into a phone booth that seemed oddly placed.

Molly came out clean and fresh but still wore the drawn face of a girl going through the motions of a life rather than living it. The black jeans Lydia loaned her didn't look bad but stopped short at her ankles. Had Molly gotten that much taller? The t-shirt stock inside hadn't been updated in a minute—a few Manning shirts for sale, still some Commie Ron '84's on the rack (good riddance to that hack). Molly had settled on a neon pink "Gator Tours" iron-on tank top, which she then covered with her denim cut she was never without. She'd made the newest one reversible—normal on one side, the Sledgehammer colors on the other.

Back in the rig, they pushed further down the Chef Menteur, rolling through Little Vietnam. Cranking the windows down, Molly enjoyed the breeze on her face. The smells of the avenues lit across her, bringing her a smile. She could go for a big bowl of soup. Or maybe the whole pot. Signs littered the area, all the languages and styles blending together, the neon lights increasing the closer they got to the old city.

"Earth to Molly, Over," Lydia said into the mic of her CB radio. Andi had upgraded it to have a range of 300 miles, as well as a direct communication link between the truck and herself that worked by bouncing signals off radio towers into orbiting satellites in space or something that Lydia had mostly forgotten. Either way it all worked. Somehow.

Molly rolled her eyes at Lydia playing with her new gadgets. The truck had come to resemble something from a TV show more than anything that rolled off a Detroit assembly line. Molly stared into the dreary clouds hovering above the Central Business District as they cruised into the city proper. Rain spat at the windshield as they rolled up the windows, coming down harder now. It had been perfectly clear when they left the coast not two hours ago.

"Just listen to Ol' Lydia Stiles in the Slaughterhouse Silverado on a drab and drizzly morning. When some wild-eyed eighty-foot croc-monster tries to tear up your town?" Lydia winked at Molly. "You just introduce them to your old friend, The SledgeHammer! Yessir, she'll send them packing. Express Mail!"

Molly glared at Lydia for as long as she could without laughing. But she did laugh.

VI
"HOLIDAY"
—MADONNA, 1983

MOLLY STARED AT THE GRAY sky as Lydia haggled with the parking lot attendant. The rain had abated, but the clouds lingered. They'd each been to the city at least a dozen times before, rarely for more than a few hours. Molly's foster dad Hoyt had always insisted on leaving before dark. But the more she thought about it, she couldn't recall a single sunny day she'd ever seen in the city.

"Five freaking dollars! Can you believe this shit?" Lydia huffed and shoved her wallet back in her purse (more a black satchel with a chain for a strap and padlocks around it than an actual purse). "Where to first?"

"You're the boss of this trip, Bangs." Molly shrugged, looked down the street at a Lucky Dog cart. She could go for three of those.

"Hurricanes." Lydia marched toward the French Quarter.

* * *

The girls, to their credit, had only gotten distracted nine times by the randomness on the streets and the oddities in the shops. Lydia finished off her third daiquiri when they reached The Riverwalk. A spray-painted robot mime marched at them. A juggler tossed lit torches in the air as the sound of a half dozen musicians blended into a kaleidoscope of sound. Molly now wished they'd brought their own axes and amps. They could set up and make some good beer money.

"Bet you twenty dollars I can tell you where you got yo' shoes," a woman walked up to Molly and said. She had a cool twist-out hairdo reaching down past her shoulders. Her Detroit jersey shirt and long-johns undershirt were at least a size too big. She had an inside-out jacket tied around her waist, and some very last-decade jeans. She also had a broken-in pair of red Chuck Taylors that mirrored Molly's own (she'd opted for her purples today), so there was at least that.

"What about it? Twenty dollars. Come on, try me." She got close to Molly's face, which had the opposite of what may have been its intended effect, as Molly tried not to giggle. She was starting to have fun despite herself.

"No bet." Lydia stumbled into the mix. She tossed her empty cup at the can and missed, then pointed a finger almost at their new acquaintance. "Not our last rodeo in this city, got me?"

"First rodeo." Molly stabilized her friend, then looked at the girl running the hustle. Her outfit was worn but not dirty, and there was something behind her eyes. And her posture, her build told a different story than her clothes. "Sorry, I got to get her a glass of water."

The hustler moved to her next target, but Molly watched her from the side as she maneuvered Lydia toward a beignet shop further up.

The girls wandered toward Canal Street, deciding to catch a tour through the state-of-the-art aquarium. Lydia told Molly all about it, what she'd seen in the TV commercials back home, all the species they had, the mega tanks with some of the big boys. She also wanted to see the 3D movie about the Megalodons. She neglected to mention the hologram projector they'd installed out front of the 3D theater. When the sixty-foot shark made of light leaped out, jaws snapping at them, Molly cocked her fists and squared-up for the fight. Everyone around chuckled at the redhead girl in the cutoff jacket ready to pop off at the fake shark. Lydia was all the way on the ground laughing.

"Not cool, Lyd." Molly shoved her arms in her pockets as they grabbed tickets inside.

* * *

Three hours, ten shops, and a bowl of ice cream later, they found themselves further uptown. Coming out of the hat store, Lydia almost sober and sporting her new John Bull pulled low—nearly covering her eyes—Molly felt a ray of sun on her face for the first time since coming into town. The crowds on the street had thinned as they cruised through the CBD, wandering about with no real goal. Molly watched a man in a tailored suit glide past her, appearing to talk to himself (going on about a spike in the stock market) before she noticed a small device by his ear. She stared at him curiously, tracing the thin black cord run from his earpiece down into his pocket. His right hand scratched at his nose and she saw he had a small dark scar just before his knuckle. Under his slick leather shoes, he stood atop some device with a wheel on either side that seemed to move wherever he wanted it to go. He caught her staring and scowled back at her before he rolled into one of the newer high-rise buildings.

"I've seen those." Lydia nodded her head toward where Molly stared. "Japanese. It's like the future over there. I read about it in *Time.*"

The city had grown faster than it could keep up with these past dozen years. She remembered hearing the stories of the old New Orleans, the French Quarter, the jazz and the zydeco, all of it. It was before her time, of course, but she had imagined how it might have been. Of the few times she'd visited the city over the years, it seemed different each time—always bigger than the last, more buildings, taller ones, the skyline crowded now. The people had doubled, tripled. Every day more came, escaping the cold north. Global cooling sent people south in droves.

A scream rang out. Every face and eye turned toward the sound. Molly's eyes and ears zeroed on it—a runner, moving fast through the sparse crowd. He gripped a handbag, dodging and ducking passersby as he cooked away from them. From the origin of the event, a lady got to her feet, dusted herself, pointed in the runner's direction.

Molly turned to Lydia already face-coding her not to show off. Molly glanced around, spotted an overflowing trashcan and snagged a glass bottle from it. She squinted, locked on her target. Lydia pointed in the exact opposite direction and screamed out, "Hey, it's Bobby Hebert!" Everyone turned to see where Lydia pointed, and Molly let fly with the bottle. It spiraled better than if Hebert himself had tossed it and knocked the purse-snatcher out cold, sending him faceplanting into the sidewalk. Molly glanced around—seemed none had noticed her eighty-yard bullseye.

But one had.

Half a block behind them, leaning near an alleyway, the girl with the twist-out hair and the Detroit jersey shirt leered sideways at the feat she'd just witnessed. She narrowed her eyes, stepping out to follow along behind them but keeping her distance all the same.

THE GIRLS CRUISED DOWN DECATUR, Molly stopping Lydia from buying another hurricane. They passed by the old St. Louis Cathedral, its spires stabbing into the purpling afternoon sky, dwarfed now by the many high-rises surrounding the old part of the city. Between the tall business buildings and the almost constant cloud cover, it was a wonder the people here ever got any sun.

"Can you believe that guy?" Molly looked at Lydia backward dance-walking to the faint sounds of a jazz horn somewhere nearby. A stilt-walker cruised past them, his face dripping in red and white makeup as he stalked toward Canal street, waving down at the kids pointing up at him. "Broad daylight and everything?"

"They scared of the night, sha," a voice said from behind her. The girls turned and saw a lady working a table with a sign showing an open palm with an eye in the center. She laid out her candles and jewelry for sale—an older white lady with dreads (Molly recalled the biker gang she'd battled more than one time). The artists' alley was alive with more than a dozen such setups, the live painters and dancers busying themselves for a night's work to come. "They come out in the day. They try for what they can in the light."

"What are they scared of?" Molly looked into the woman, making her uncomfortable. She felt it. The longer Molly stood before her, arms folded, her questioning stare, the woman twitching and fidgeting.

"Him. They scared of Him." She never took her eyes off Molly's.

"Do you tell fortunes?" Lydia plopped herself on the little stool before the palm reader.

"Lydia." Molly scolded with a look.

"What? I've never done it."

"It's $5, child."

Molly folded her arms and stood in protest. Nothing about this gave her a good feeling. The tiny moment of sun earlier had faded back behind the incessant clouds. Her watch told her the day waned. The city gave her an ill feeling, much as it had the last time she'd visited with her dad, the day they came to shop for prom.

Lydia slapped out a crumpled bill from her purse. The lady took it as Lyd stretched out her hand, the lady tracing the lines with her crony fingers. It wasn't that Molly thought it was a scam—though it probably was—but that she herself was living proof that stranger things in the world turned out all too real.

"You feel left out." The reader stared Lydia in the eyes. "You want to belong, but you do not. Your family, your friends. You see yourself outside them."

Lydia shifted, her usual confident smirk fading into a flat line.

"Someone new has come into your life. They have set a path in motion for you. You will lose something. Something that connects you to your home."

"Lydia, that's enough. Let's go." Molly glared at the reader.

"No." Lydia kept her eyes locked on the reader's. "Finish it."

"Your lifeline is fractured." The reader continued to track Lydia's palm lines. She looked back to Lydia's face, a solemn expression washing across her own. "You will be betrayed. You shall dwell amongst the dead. You will be cast onto the corpse shore. I'm sorry."

"Whoah. Dark." Lydia took her hand back. She grinned and rolled her eyes, showing off her casual toughness as always, but Molly felt the tremor of fear running down her best friend's spine. She wanted to slap the craggy witch for doing this.

"Now do me." Molly laid her hand down on the reader's table, plopped her cash next to it with the other. She stared bullet holes in the woman's face.

The woman trembled as she took Molly's palm in her hand—Molly noting the same scar she'd seen on the yuppie earlier. As soon as their skin touched one another, Molly felt the shriek of terror race through the old woman who recoiled as if she'd been shot. She stared back at Molly's face, her eyes flooding, the water raining down her cheeks.

"I'm sorry." She shoved all her items back into her large sack as fast as she could. She raked with her whole arm to get them in. "I'm sorry. He made me. He made all of us. He promised he would—Please don't..." Her eyes tried to finish her plea but gave up. She left half her things on her table as she abandoned them, running off into the night.

"Psycho and a half." Lydia glanced back at Molly who kept her eyes lasered on the fleeing woman.

"We should go," Molly said.

Lydia whipped out another of her flyers she'd pulled from the truck stop that morning. "There's one more place I want to check out."

VIII
"PEOPLE ARE STRANGE"
—ECHO & THE BUNNYMEN, 1987

JUST A BLOCK OFF JACKSON SQUARE, Lydia led them using her tourist map—Molly groaned at how obvious the two of them had looked all day—to a joint called Dave's Occult Books & The Arcane. A horse carriage pulled up in front of it, the rider patting the hairy animal on his shoulder as he walked across to a pub for a break.

In front of the store, two wooden Indians stood guard inside a half circle of white powder—*salt?*—encased in what looked like plastic cement. Two large old faded mirrors with bars around them framed the front entrance. Lydia led them inside where an unremarkable man stood behind the counter with a warm smile.

"Welcome to Dave's Occult," he said. "You ladies in the market for anything in particular?"

"No, I don't think—"

Yes, sir." Lydia walked toward the counter. "We're looking for anything on supernatural powers, creatures from other worlds, alchemy, anything like that."

"Oh, I can get you all fixed up. Just let me finish these tabs right quick, I'll show you around.

"This was the main reason I wanted to come, well half the main reason. I also wanted you to have some fun." Lydia dropped her hand on Molly's shoulder. It felt dense in Lydia's hand and higher than before all this had started. Molly *was* taller now. "I thought maybe we could find out some clues as to who you are, where you came from."

Molly stared out the window to the street. A clique of people in expensive clothes had gathered outside, looking at the shop, though none venturing in. Frowns colored their faces as they stared inside. She turned and glanced around the place. It seemed about like any other small bookstore in The Quarter with some gris-gris and the odd dangling doll here, a polished metal skull there, and mirrors—lots of mirrors. He had them all over the shop, old ones too, the oxidation from the backing showing near the bottoms. Molly decided he must have a problem with thieves, though she wondered at the pawn shop value of his inventory.

Besides all the books, old and new, he had a smattering of odds and ends. There were oils in vials, used RC and Coke bottles with clear liquid marked "Holy Water," all kinds of salts, herbs, incense, crucifixes, fleur-de-lis, the works. And garlic. Knots of garlic in baskets hung from the ceiling. The place reeked of it.

Molly and Lydia weren't the only patrons in the store. Two younger girls, maybe fourteen, browsed the books in the back, whispering among themselves while Lydia neared them poking about the shelves. They amused Molly, the way they dressed, pouch belts around their wastes, silver jewelry dangling from their wrists, their sienna skin tone masked by their black hair. One wore a shirt with a helmet on it, though it didn't quite seem like the right shape as Molly recalled the logo from the city's team. And of course, Lydia, the expert on all things football and wrestling, observed it.

"Shouldn't that helmet be gold?" Lydia stared at the kid's shirt. Molly shook her head. Lydia could never just let a thing go. "That's like some kind of brown."

"It's not a Saints' helmet." The girl stood to her full height, looking Lydia in the eye. "And it's copper."

Molly shook her head and wandered toward the front. The door chimed as another customer walked in. He was big, over six and a half feet tall, his neck and shoulders bulging beneath the fabric of his shirt. He had dark amber skin and hazel eyes that didn't fail to notice hers looking back at him. She blushed and looked away but side-glanced him all the same. He was older, maybe fifty—the widow peaks in his salting hair reached back so far, the bit of hair he had left running across his scalp resembled a mohawk. Feathered earrings. Silver chains adorned his neck. Silver bracelets on his wrists and rings on nearly every finger. He wore a cutoff denim jacket not unlike her own, and his looked to have seen its share of battles as well. His face was tired, as was he. Molly couldn't help herself and reached in with her feelings. He was sad, frustrated, beaten, and alone. He was so terribly alone. Molly almost wanted to cry for him.

He walked to the counter and handed the clerk a cloth sack that jingled. Molly needed some air, swelling with the emotion she took in from the moment, from the day, the thought of her poor Easton flooding back to her, his smile as he lay dying in her arms just weeks ago. She glanced at Lydia comfortably arguing with fourteen-year-olds about football, or wrestling, or something equally inane.

She jingled out the door, across the salt line, and into the dingy, aromatic street. She wondered if she took up smoking would it mess with her abilities. It always seemed to calm other people down. The two girls exited the store right after her, scurrying home as they looked to the purpling sky.

"Les Grenouilles," a voice said as the kids moved up the street. "Good kids. Make this city proud, they do."

Molly turned to the voice and saw he sat in the driver's seat of the horse coach, a wide-brimmed straw farmer's hat pulled over his ebony face. He had a crutch leaned against the buckboard next to him, his clothes old, nearly threadbare. She'd seen him somewhere before. She knew it. Before she could think to say anything, the big man from inside walked out, looked intently at her one time, then glared at the carriage driver before he hurried off himself, like they were all late for a train.

Molly turned and glared into the driver's eyes. Now she remembered him. He had stood outside the window of the cafe the last time she'd been to the city, staring at her, like he knew her.

"Who are you?" She focused her gaze.

"I open the gates. I stand at the door. I am then and will be."

"I don't understand. What is this? Do you know me?"

"You will find him. Find him at the place of the wounded warrior. Seek him there. The forgotten soldier. You have to make him remember. He's needed now more than before. The darkness is coming. *She* is coming soon."

"Find who? What? Tell me how you know me."

"Remember: the power of the father restores the daughter. The power of the son destroys the mother."

"I don't know what that means. Stop talking like that and just say normal things—" Molly started to march toward the driver to shake him into making sense, but the door chime turned her head. Lydia walked out with a book in her hands and a smile on her face. Molly turned back to the carriage, but the driver was gone. *Had he ever been there?*

"Who was that big muscled dude in there?" Lydia fiddled with her book. "He looked just like Rocky Johnson but older."

Molly didn't know who that was but assumed it was some wrestler.

"Check this out." Lydia showed off the brown book with green leaf designs on the cover. "It's a grimoire, he told me. It's a spell book. Isn't that rad? Maybe I can learn some cool magic and fight badguys with you?"

Molly's Cascio watch beeped at her—seven o'clock, the time she'd set for them to leave and get back home. She pressed the button to shut it off, noting its digital face. She stared across the square, up at the spires of the great St. Louis Cathedral. She thought of Our Lady of the Gulf, all the times she walked by it back home, her first brutal battle with Blake's monsters. And it dawned on her for the first time all day in this city. The church bells never rang. None of them had.

"RHYTHM IS GONNA GET YOU"
—GLORIA ESTEFAN & MIAMI SOUND MACHINE, 1987

MOLLY HAD HER HANDS FULL wrangling a distracted Lydia darting off to every random sight or sound on the long walk through The Quarter back to the truck. Twice she tried to buy another hurricane before Molly took her wallet away. They made it back to Canal Street and started north toward the interstate, another eight blocks to the parking lot. If they didn't hurry, they'd be on the hook for another five bucks and Lydia would flip out.

Molly almost got her past the Canal Street Popeyes without incident, but another street hustler got in their faces. He had a deck of cards and told them to pick one. Molly tried waving him off, but he stayed right in her face. Her ire rose, but she didn't want to make it weird. She calmed herself (she'd been on edge all day in the city and didn't know why) and readied herself to do the trick where she just told people things and they did them. It didn't always work, and she was iffy with this guy already.

"Say, jack," a voice behind him said. "Leave them girls be. You ain't all that."

The man turned to see her, giving Molly and Lydia a fair view too. She had faded jeans and sported a Detroit letter jacket. She had a sweet face, at least ten years ahead of Molly or more. Bright auburn eyes. A head of twist-outs angling to her shoulders and a pair of Chuck Taylors Molly hadn't forgotten. She'd cleaned up, changed her clothes, and was all but a new person.

Molly eyed the woman as the cardsharp went on to his next mark.

"You following us?"

"Say what now?" The woman shrugged her shoulders, picked up three empty Jack Daniel's bottles, and began flipping them up and catching them. "I'm just a plain old person trying to make a buck or two. Ain't no thing. What about this?" She tossed the bottles higher, increasing her speed but catching them with practiced hands. "What you bet I can do four bottles? Five?"

"No bet." Molly pulled Lydia away from the spectacle, trying to get them moving again.

The juggler followed them, keeping her bottles going as she walked, a feat that did not fail to impress Molly. Humans could do some pretty amazing stuff when they wanted to. Especially Mick Mars.

"Come on, two bucks, and I'll go for six. You can't beat that. These babies are heavy too."

"Really, we're good."

She caught all her bottles and put them down, all but one "Okay, how about this? I throw this one right here as high as I can, and I bet you I catch it upside down on my flat palm."

"No way," Lydia said. Molly could have slapped her. "What do we get if you don't?"

The girl grinned an infectious grin from one ear to the other.

"Y'all's drinks are on me rest of the night."

Molly's face raced every code at light speed to Lydia but she had already heard "drinks" and slapped the hustler's hand for a deal. Somehow that sealed it. Molly didn't know why, but she was always careful what she agreed to, especially since Blake the darkboy creature and his so-called "debt." Whatever that had been about.

She reared back with the whiskey bottle several times, gearing herself up for what Molly already knew was another hustle, and now Lydia would be out however much money. In fact, it bothered her that no sum had been agreed to. The hustler reared back one last time and let fly with the bottle, shooting it into the sky. Between the dim evening and the lights up and down the street, Molly almost lost track of it as it flipped end over end, cresting, and plummeted back toward them. The sharp-eyed girl stuck her palm out and smiled at Molly. The bottle's neck, sure enough, slammed down on her flattened hand. And she *almost* had it... until it wobbled, went wild. She tried to save it but only flung it further out of her hand, flipping it right at Molly's face. Molly snatched it out of the air like it was in slow motion (because for her, of course, it was).

"Oh, snap!" The girl made a face like she was sorry. "Damn that was a catch, though. You play ball, girl?"

"Hey!" Lydia put her hands on her hips. "Bet's a bet."

"Yeah, you're right. I ain't backing out. Besides, I know the best place. Y'all like music? 'Course you do." She tossed her empty bottles in the nearby can and walked toward the street. "It's down the Irish Channel, though. We gotta cab it."

Molly walked behind Lydia, no talking her out of this now, the woman grinning and motioning them over. Molly got a lump in her gut like this was what she'd wanted the whole time.

"We got a ride. You can just jump in with us," Lydia said.

"Man, I was hoping you'd say that." The woman high-fived Lydia.

Molly sighed.

"PRINCESS OF THE NIGHT"
–SAXON, 1981

HER NAME WAS REGINA MURPHY LONG, so she told them on the ride through the city, all the while messing about with every knob and button on Lydia's augmented console. Or, just Murph for short, she said.

"What's this do?" She clicked a button on the broadband radio transmitter, a red light going off.

"Yeah, I'm here. What's up?" came Andi's scratchy voice over the radio. Lydia swatted the woman's hand away from her gear. Molly thought of her twin sister impersonating her back home as she scowled, glaring out the window at the darkened city. The clouds from the day had dissipated, the moon out in force, calling down to its night creatures. She felt... something she didn't like.

"Nothing, we're fine." Lydia held the mic, grimacing at their nosy new friend. "We're all fine here. How are you?"

"Uh... good. Becky wants to take me shopping, but I don't see the point since I can just simulate any–"

"Yeah that's great," Lydia said. "Sounds good. Just checking in. See you soon. Over."

"K. Over."

Molly chuckled, the first levity she'd felt since taking on the third wheel.

"Who was that?" Murph looked to each girl in turn for an answer. "Turn left up here. This is a nice rig. How you come by all this fancy setup in here? Y'all rob a Radio Shack or something?"

They turned off Napoleon onto Tchoupitoulas–the little cafes and bars alive with the night. Downtown back home had nothing on this place, and this wasn't even the busy part of town. Lydia wheeled into a parking spot not far from the venue, and they made their way toward the bar.

A batch of turbros from Tulane cruised by, laughing into their fists at the oddball trio of Lydia's all-black and spider-bangs, Molly's ripped denim, and the thirty-something in the letter jacket. Everyone headed for the same place they were, The Jester Queen with its big neon letters lit up out front. The place was a two-story yellow warehouse-looking joint with AC units in all the upstairs windows– already thick with drinkers and hecklers. There was a line to get in. No Dice at the door, just two big hairy-faced dudes that looked like they were half-dog. Molly remembered Blake's mutants and shuddered.

"This place used to be called Tipitina's." Murph walked them through the door, slapping a bill into a doorman's hand. Some of the fratbros whined about it, and Molly swore she heard one of the door guys growl. "But it got bought out by the Jareth Corporation. Old money family. Or was. Hostile takeovers. Corporate mergers. Lot of big money moving down here from New York. All this global cooling, and all that. Y'all buy that shit? I mean damn it's cold in Detroit, for sure, though."

Murph got them a round of shots and a table right in the center of everything. She glanced around the room, pausing her eyes on each point of exit, noting the staff and anyone taller than the average. Molly noticed her doing it because it's just what she had done as soon as they walked in. Murph held up her glass to toast, but Molly waved hers off.

"No?" Murph raised an eyebrow.

"Doesn't do much for me." Molly looked to the empty stage. No instruments up there tonight. It was a weeknight.

"Yo! Dig the strawberry red, sweetheart." Some college dude in a popped collar and a white jacket ogled at her. "Strawberry wine!!" He tried to sing out, already sheets to the wind. His buddy grabbed him.

"So, you're not from here, either?" Lydia noted the jacket again. "Because no one would be caught dead in that jacket anywhere within a hundred miles of the Dome."

Molly shook her head. Lydia took her sports so damn seriously. Between the wrestling, the football, and lately she was even getting into racing, for the maker's sake.

"Yeah, sure. My mom was from around here, but I'm from all over. Moved around a lot. Dallas. Compton. Flint. Rock City. All that. Always heard the stories. Came down here to see what this gumbo was all about, you know? Plus, like I said, just too damn cold up north now."

Murph ordered another round and was visibly irritated Molly wasn't drinking. She needn't waste her money since alcohol had no effect on Molly, but she couldn't exactly explain that to some random streetcon Lydia let tag along just for a couple of free shots. This whole thing stunk more by the minute as Molly stewed on it. She peeled her eyes at the four corners of the place again. Wall to wall with people, mostly college kids and other townies from nearby and the Carrollton and Uptown areas. A few that maybe looked like tourists, but none stuck out so bad as Molly and her companions, and she began to wonder if that was the point. Their table was conspicuously visible.

A shot of clear liquid slapped onto the table in front of Molly. Lydia's dark eyes zeroed on the turbro with the popped collar. His buddy backed him up as they'd mustered the courage to make their play. Murph laughed—a heavy, bombastic laugh that almost made Molly laugh with her. Molly really couldn't get a read on this woman. She reached in with her senses, but Murph was a rock. No emotion going out one way or another. Guarded. Practiced.

"Drink with me, Strawberry Wine!" The fratguy held up his glass in a toast, waiting for Molly to clink it. She shook her head. "What? You scared to drink? Can't take the heat?" He and his buddies laughed.

Molly's eyes turned to slits. Lydia's went wide as golfballs, telling her *no please don't* in their face-code, but it was already too late.

Molly jumped up, drew to her full height next to the guys.

"Your friend's tall." Murph looked at Lydia then smirked at the scene playing itself out, keeping one eye on the bartender and the doormen.

"Put some money on it, tough guys." Molly downed the shot, slammed it on the table—careful not to shatter it and the oak at the same time—then placed her palm on the guy's cheek, tapping him. "What do you say? Couple hundred says I drink you and your buddies under the table no sweat."

"Molly." Lydia stood up. Murph grinned and laughed that infectious laugh again. Molly giggled too.

"You're on, Strawberry!" The guy circled his finger in the air at the waitress, who Murph noticed made an eye at the bartender.

The bartender laid out a tray of shots, Everclear, as the fratbro requested. Molly shrugged as they lined them up, the guys laughing and ribbing each other. They each took a glass in their hands, the guy mock-toasting Molly as they bent their elbows and kicked them back. Lydia surveyed the scene, the indoor balconies crowded with people looking down toward the stage and dance floor not two yards from where Murph had seated them.

A woman appeared upstairs from a back room—late forties, gorgeous, head-to-toe money, sparkling, diamonds, the full nine. Her hair was two-tone, one half golden blonde, the other side darkened, almost lavender. Her face nearly doubled the light in the dimmed bar, but her eyes told a different story.

"Who's that?" Lydia nudged Murph's attention upward, careful not to point.

"Ah, yeah. That's the owner. Evilyn Jareth. Weird story. Old family. Had connections. Used to be a prosecutor back in the day, so I heard. Got disbarred. Lost most of the family business to Cain Capital. This is the only thing she had left. She fell pretty far." Murph took a pull off her beer. Lydia noted the woman's peering eyes again, surveying her fiefdom. She seemed interested in the little drinking contest Molly was going to win.

And win she did. Lydia admired her old friend, seeing her getting fired up, being playful as she turned up glass after glass. The boys rooted their guy on, chanting at him all the way. "Moose! Moose! Moose!" they called out. Lydia could barf. Of course, it would be over something like this, but Lydia was happy and relieved to see Molly finally relax and enjoy herself. She saw her crack at the corners of her mouth as she poured another one down, and the broad-shouldered boy started to wobble. It was the first time Lydia had seen her smile since prom night, when it all went to Hell in a fist-pounding psycho tank.

"You know a lot about this place for someone from Detroit." Lydia swigged her beer, tipping it to Molly as she downed another Everclear, the frat guy wobbling to either side now.

"Yeah, well, you pick up a lot on the streets. I ask around. Read the papers. Library's free, you know. Not just the bathrooms." Murph smirked, but she glanced at the balcony again, the sultry owner missing from her prior perch.

Lydia watched Murphy watch the room and began to see why Molly had been so edgy. She realized she had to do better to think like the partner of a hero, see the things unseen, expect trouble. Was that what she was now? A partner? A sidekick? She rolled that idea around in her head. She pulled out the grimoire from her bag, flipped through it, looking at the macabre drawings and incantations. Too bad it wasn't in English. Some weird language she couldn't pronounce. Not French or Spanish. She did a year of each back at Bay High—glad to see those days behind her. Poor Molly still had summer school. She did see one word she thought she recognized: *diafol*. Was that Irish or Welsh?

Murph got up to pat Molly on the back, the contest ending with her opponent carried out the door by his cohorts. Molly waved and blew a kiss to them as they walked out the door. Murph slid toward the front to get a glimpse out the windows, like she was waiting for something. Molly looked down at the bar at the last few untouched shot glasses, each brimming with its useless liquid.

"You sure know how to drink." The warm voice ran down Molly's back like coffee. She peered her eyes up from the glasses into the shadowed hazels of a woman with two-tone hair and a ten-thousand-dollar smile.

"I reckon." Molly folded her arms, glancing side to side for the previous bartender.

"How about I make you something special?" She winked at Molly, already shaking something in the tin. Molly shrugged. *Sure, what does it matter?* The woman poured out a milky liquid, cloudy vapor rising off the brim. "This shot be just as sweet as pie."

Molly took it in her fingers, raising the glass to the uncomfortably pretty woman with the smoky eyes that seemed to look right through her, into her. "What do we drink to?"

"To the great solstice pyre. Burning ever higher. Making music like the devil's choir." She raised her glass to toast.

"K, that's weird but whatever." Molly tossed hers back. She twisted her neck, squinted her eyes. *Woo that had some kick.* She shivered, shook her head to clear the haze. She felt warm, a little dizzy. Not bad, though. In fact, not bad at all.

"What was that?" Molly shivered again. Licked the last of it off her lips. "How much for another one?"

"You want *another*?" Jareth widened her eyes. "I like you. You're very interesting."

* * *

Lydia stuck her head in her book, fascinated by a sketching of a gateway into the "realm of mists" opposite a page of what she assumed was something about how such a thing worked. Maybe there was something in here to offer a clue on who or what Molly really was. Or maybe it was a waste of thirteen dollars. Murph dropped a fresh beer in front of her.

"Where'd your friend go?" Murph looked around the room. Lydia couldn't tell if she was really looking for Molly or... something else.

The lights throughout the bar dimmed as strobes illuminated the stage. A glitzy black dress, silver elbow-length gloves and sparkling half-lavender hair adorned the stage, a microphone in one hand and a martini glass in the other.

"A surprise performance for tonight, ladies and gentlemen. From the Baytown across the great Lake Ponchartrain, I give you—" Evilyn Jareth leaned over to Molly as she pounded her sneaks onto the stage. "What was your name again, kid?"

"Just call me Power Ballad." Molly half-tripped and stumbled taking the last step onto the stage. She glanced around the room, haze in her eyes, nothing but shapes and blur. She liked the sounds, though. The sounds of their feelings blended into one low, humming vibration flowing into her. She moved with it. The lady with the two-tone hair cranked up some electronic song machine. She'd explained it all to Molly over their third drink of whatever had made her feel so... *numb*. She liked it. It took the pain—the pain of losing him—away. Finally. Some new thing from Japan, the lady had said. All the new things were from Japan.

"It plays the music for you," Jareth had told her. "All you have to do is sing."

Molly belted into the mic for everyone to step inside and walk this way. The guitar chords pierced out into the neon bar signs. Molly ripped into Leppard's "Pour some Sugar On Me." She leaned all the way back, her shoulders nearly to the floor, then sprang back up, almost losing her balance as Jareth steadied her, joining in with her liquid voice for the chorus.

"Your friend's pissed up a tree." Murph nodded at the stage, then back at the front door. Bodies moved toward various exit points. Then she turned back to the spectacle before them. "I mean she's drunk as hell."

"Yeah, Molly doesn't really—" Lydia stopped herself not knowing how to explain the truth she was no longer sure of herself. She put her beer down, glanced sideways at their unknown companion, then around the room. *Okay, sidekick, you're on the clock.*

She watched the two of them go at the song like it owed them money. Molly always did have that smoky, raspy voice of someone older than her driver's license belied. And she put it to full use into the microphone, pouring her whole self into a drunken solo. Lydia recalled their first gig at that juke joint back home with the chicken wire stage.

Lydia wanted to laugh, sit back, relax, and enjoy the moment. Molly looked so happy up there. She deserved this. Molly saved everyone from eminent doom from a godawful maniac and she deserved to sing, and play, and have fun, and, yes, even have a drink for the dude's sake. But, Lydia knew it was all wrong.

Murph's attention diverted from the stage. She zeroed her eyes on the side exit. A couple of young guys, far drunker than the redhead on the stage, found themselves carried out the door by some thick-armed, volleyball-looking girls dressed like extras from *Nuke-Em High.* One of them, sporting a spiked mullet, peered back, a flash of red-eye as the strobe touched her face.

"Shit. I gotta go." Murph zipped her jacket, laid a twenty down on the table and headed for the door.

Molly was faster. She dropped the mic onto the stage mid-note, the screech of the feedback piercing the ears of the crowd. Lydia jumped up, shoving her book in her bag as she watched Molly bolt out the door like the place was on fire.

MURPHY RAN UP TCHOUPITOULAS, catching sight of the crew she'd made in the bar shoving the two young guys out the door. They split off into two groups, one in a black dodge, the other in a red Camaro. She beat her feet as best she could but knew she wasn't going to catch them. She'd completely blown the whole thing. The kid on the stage had caused enough distraction, they took their chance when they had it. She was ready to throw her hands up and start over when the redhead blew past her like she was standing still.

Molly raced up the street, the lights a blur in her head. She wobbled one way then the other. Her vision jumped, skipped across the night. Shapes came in and out of her head as she pounded her feet against the pavement. She veered left, almost fell down. Then she careened to the right and slammed into a pickup so hard she caved in the driver's side door. She got up, dusted herself off and started again. Murph caught up to her as Molly slammed into the side of a second car.

"Kid, you okay? Damn." Murph stared at the dent in the car's metal door. Molly tried to shake free and start her run again. She still sensed the fear, the confusion, the call for help that had reached out to her on the stage, but it faded fast.

"Hey, what the hell?" Lydia pulled up in her Silverado.

Murph shoved Molly into the back, climbing in behind her and into the shotgun seat.

"Can this thing move?" She aimed her finger at the rapidly disappearing Camaro lights up the street.

"Oh yeah." Lydia shoved her stick into gear and flipped her overdrive switch Andi had installed—bless that sweet Android's crystal heart. She roared her heavy beast up Tchoupitoulas Street into Irish Channel, moving toward the port. Murph's head hit the back of her seat when Lydia dropped the stick again.

"Damn, kid." Murph studied the array of lights across the truck's dash again. This thing wasn't stock, for sure. She glanced into the back to check out the power-drinker. Molly flailed from one side to the other as Lydia banked the curves in her heavy truck, the lights on the Camaro still in her line of sight.

"Mind telling me why we're following them?"

"Yeah, it's a bit of a tale. Short version is they took some kids out of the bar. I need to know where they're taking them."

"I'll handle this." Molly slurred her speech as she moved to the center of the back bench. Murph watched her grab a rolled bundle of heavy leather from the floorboard, reach in and pull out a wolf-pommeled blade, gleaming from the streetlights piercing in through the windows.

"What the fuck? A sword?" Murph eyed the blade like it was the strangest thing she'd seen all night.

"Yeah, Molly. Maybe put away the SUPER sharp stabby thing that can, you know, cut ALL of us." Lydia eyed her friend through the rear-view mirror.

Molly hiccupped, put the blade back with its twin, and stared out the windshield. She tried zeroing her vision several times but couldn't keep focus. She tried slowing her time, but she couldn't hold it. It would sputter and go again at normal speed, maybe faster. Something in her stomach flipped. *A new sense? No, she was going to vomit.*

Lydia gained on the Camaro, which had caught wind of being tailed. They banked a hard right into the neighborhoods, and Lydia followed suit, staying on them, inching away the gap. Josephine, then St. Thomas to Felicity. They zigged, and Lydia zagged along behind with her turbo-charged dually. They moved out of housing districts and into warehouses, high rises going up. New construction everywhere. Cranes and heavy equipment left overnight got in her way as the Camaro zipped through it all.

"Domnii Morții," Murph said. "At least I think that's who it is. Eastern-bloc gang that set up shop here years back."

"Commies?" Lydia banked onto Chippewa, then St. Andrew.

"Your guess is good as mine, but yeah. Or maybe Filles Perdues, but I don't know much about them yet. They seem new."

"I thought the gangs all left the city?" Lydia cut the wheel, dodging an oncoming van. She lost speed but cranked it back up. She still had the Camaro in sight. In the rearview, the redhead looked a little green. "My sorta-boyfriend used to live here. He said the gangs got run out years ago."

"Old gangs. New ones moved in. Domnii Morții started showing up maybe eight years back. Some others too. There, cut right!" Murph pointed.

Lydia banked, cutting a hard angle onto Constance Street, but didn't make it. She pinged her bumper against that of a Ford Pinto parked at the curb. She reversed and lurched back at it. The lights of the Camaro faded.

"They're getting away." Molly leaned forward, then collapsed into the back again.

Lydia gunned it down Constance but screeched to a halt at the first sign of the brass.

"What the fuck?" Murph's eyes widened at the sight of a marching procession coming at them. Horns, drums, flutes, all of it. Costumed revelers danced in the street. Sugar skulls adorned the faces of the musicians. One in the lead wore a top hat, long heavy black dreads snaking from underneath it. His hollow eyes stared through the windshield and into Molly's, like they saw someone they knew. More came, and more again. The street filled, out of nowhere, with the celebration, or whatever it was.

"Second line," Lydia said. "At this hour?"

"No. That's no second line. Chante-Toujours." Murph grimaced, breathing heavy. Lydia could tell she was uneasy. She'd only hopped in the truck to grab Molly before she got herself into real trouble. Then Murph had jumped in and started barking orders. It all came so fast, but now the questions traffic-jammed in her head.

"Oh god. Oh no no no." Murph shook her head. "No, this is bad."

More bodies came from behind their pickup, long dark coats, red splatter-painted cuffs and collars. They looked like they wore makeup too. Not skulls or anything, just pale white foundation and heavy on the eyeshadow. They stalked toward the second-line. The leaders of the procession produced blades, batons, chains. They balled their fists, brandished their weapons for the fight about to commence.

Another group arrived, some of them Asian-looking. Slicked black hair, black uniform-style shirts with toggle buttons. Rolled cuffs. Red sashes. They held back, watching the first two groups, not eager to join in.

"What the?" Murph noted the newcomers. "What the fuck are they doing here?"

"Who?"

"Hēishǒu Móguǐ. The Black Hands of the Demon. Showed up in Detroit years back. Before the F.R.E.D.'s drove them out."

"I'll handle this." Molly leaned up and slammed her fist into her palm like a booming door-slam. Murph twisted her head, ears ringing from the clap of it.

"Yeah, no, Drunky Smurf, why don't you sit down and NOT do anything like that at all because of... reasons." Lydia glared at her friend, face-coding her for *I will make you regret this forever if you don't calm your ass down.* Molly acquiesced to her friend's fierce look, for the time being. But she kept her eyes glued out the windshield as the main two groups marched at each other.

One long, dooming silence fell on the old street. The groups met each other in the dim valley formed by St. Mary's and St. Alphonsus, two gothic churches that loomed at each other as though they themselves were locked into some ancient duel, their stone faces darkening all beneath them. Then it lit off. Black jackets flew into the Creole crowd. Flashes of light reflected off blades. Crunches of ribs and forearms used to block. Thunks of bats and batons hitting skulls. A scream. Maybe two. The Hēishǒu Móguǐ joined the fray, getting their licks in. The scene became a maelstrom of war and blood. Molly ground her teeth, staring at Lydia through the rearview. Murph, the wildcard sitting in the cab beside them, stared helpless at the chaos.

Then the lights faded. All around the street, the lamp posts darkened as if something covered them. The shrieks stabbed the air, those sonic screams. Dozens, no, hundreds came as Lydia saw them now, or what little she could of them. Murph saw them too, as did Molly. Swarms flew in from everywhere, glomming onto the lamp posts outside the buildings, blocking out all the light. *Bats.* They clung to everything emitting any kind of radiance—even the truck's headlights. They slapped themselves onto Lydia's vehicle, covering her windshield, blocking the view forward. Then the screams started—from the brawlers on the street. Bloodcurdling hell-terror.

The girls panicked. Molly started out the door, having enough of playing the bystander. Murph grabbed her before she could hit the latch, and Lydia locked the doors, knowing that wouldn't stall Molly for long if she didn't want it to.

"Get us the fuck out of here, Kid," Murph shouted.

Lydia didn't have to be asked twice or nice. She floored it in reverse, twisting her neck to stare out the back window, trying not to mow down any black coats lingering behind her. Her vision was slim, the lights all gone, the reds of her brake lights barely showing her anything more than shapes. Then one shape in particular. A man. Dead in her path.

Lydia screamed and cut the wheel to avoid him. She whirled into a 180 turn, slamming her front end against another truck parked on the street. She looked again out the back window, where she was sure she'd seen a tall, dark figure. There'd been no thunk or thud. They hadn't felt anything touch her rig, not until it slammed against the other vehicle. Whatever she'd seen, or thought she had, vanished into the still swarming darkness.

The screams continued. More now than before.

She threw the truck into gear to get them away, but the tires spun in their tracks. She hit the turbo and still nothing.

"We're hung up," Murph yelled, noting the two trucks had caught together on impact. "Just book. Go now! Go!"

Murph rushed the girls out the door of the cab, bracing the wobbling Molly holding her cane swords as they all ran across the bleak street into an empty side alley.

XII

"DESCENT INTO MYSTERY"
–DANNY ELFMAN, 1989

THE GIRLS FLED DOWN the alleyway, Murph tucking them behind a dumpster as Molly retched and kept pulling herself away to try and run toward the danger. Lydia grabbed her and shoved her against the wall by the dumpster, out of sight of any other stragglers who might have fled the chaos.

"My truck!" Lydia tried to breathe, calm herself.

"We can't worry about that now. I have to get you guys safe. I can't lose you too." Murph reached behind her, under her Detroit jacket.

"What do you mean lose us too?" Lydia watched her as she pulled out a black Colt semi-auto pistol. "Dude. What the hell?"

"Just sit tight. I'll be back." Murph took off back the way they'd come, disappearing into the haze of the night.

Lydia steadied herself, looked to Molly who still wasn't fit for duty. Molly got up, braced herself on the brick wall behind her. She took her cut jean jacket off, flipped it inside out to reveal her rainbow logo on the back.

"Molly no," Lydia said, but Molly was already gone. "Guess I'll just stay here then. Alone. Great."

* * *

Molly, dizzy from the drink, slapping her head to clear it any way she could, ran into Constance Street, banked right and tore at the scene of the carnage ready to dole out justice to whatever needed it. She skidded her Converse to a halt, the lights having returned. Bodies lay strewn up and down the street, most groaning, ailing, still moving–blood-stained spots all about. Murph stood, gun drawn and gripped with both hands, pointed down and away. She shook her head at the redhead teenager in the flipped around jacket, then looked back up and down the scene again. Most of the brawlers had fled. Only the unlucky few lay prostrate on the ground.

Molly Slater, The Sledgehammer, surveyed the situation, looking for the threat. Murphy looked back at her, gun in her hand. Molly couldn't decide what to make of that and looked beyond her for the time being. The fallen gangs picked themselves up, some walking it off, others carried. None had any fight left in them. Molly sensed out with her feelings, reaching, searching. Fear. They were terrified. But not of her. They glanced all around themselves, looking to be sure *it* was gone.

Molly's eyes narrowed. Her blurred vision zeroed—a shape, that's all she saw, but it was enough. Flowing from building to building, rooftop to rooftop, flapping into the night air—nothing but a dark shadow that evaded all light.

"Kid, what the hell do you think you're—" Murph held her gun ready for anything, but she wasn't ready to see the kid leap into the night sky like gravity didn't exist. Murph's jaw dropped, hung open, and she stared into the disappearing denim dream.

Molly bounded onto the rooftops, following the flapping shape that moved as fast as she did. She hurled herself across one building to the next, her senses, reflexes still dizzy. She slammed into walls, missed her footing several times, busted onto her face. She got up, shot herself across the rooftops, toward the two old towering cathedrals, the great steeple of St. Mary's Assumption stabbing into the sky.

Molly caught herself before falling off the crumbling edge of the dilapidated building a block away from the church, staring at its crimson brickface. Above the gathering mist, the grim dark of the sticky night, far above her, she saw it, resting for a moment atop the high steeple, the thick milky air obscuring the form. She glared at the figure, its dark visage hidden from her, but she felt it gazing back at her. Molly looked dead at the thing staring at her, its wings flapping like a cape in the wind as it crouched, like some gargoyle, here in the forgotten parts of this gothic city. And in a wisp of fog it was gone. Vanished. She blinked, squinted. The haze in the air and inside her head messed with her vision, but Molly knew what she saw. And what she saw was a bat.

A bat the size of a man.

EPISODE 11

"MASTER OF PUPPETS"
—METALLICA, 1986

THE GOOD DOCTOR set about her work, the new proteins injected into the necrotic cells showing significant growth. If the catalyzation continued at pace, it would yield quite interesting results. The maggots crawling out of his eye sockets turned her stomach over. She scraped them away, put them in a dish. Could be useful for something later. She never liked to waste.

The screeching sound of rusted metal doors disturbed the doctor's work, followed by the pounding of heeled boots on the ailing metal floors of the abandoned facility. The noise told her the identity of her visitor long before she entered the makeshift laboratory and operating room—sealed off from the main area of the former power plant. For someone so bent on keeping her machinations secret from even the devil himself, her benefactor could wake the very dead on the table before her.

Evilyn Jareth burst into the room, eyes flared, staring directly into Dr. Bianca Tesche, then pulled a stiletto knife from her belt and stabbed the workshop table.

"Something wrong?" Dr. Tesche said.

"Tell me we are close, Bianca." Evilyn examined the fetid corpse on the table, noting its contracting musculature. "Tell me you can build what I need."

"I have something for you, something I think you'll like." Tesche walked to the other table, motioning Evilyn to join her. This cadaver dwarfed the first one. Its massive, hulking arms dangled from either side, its leg muscles, twitching and convulsing with new growth, bulged under the sheet draped over it. Wires and tubes protruded from underneath, some feeding it the chemical concoctions the doctor had devised, the others pumping its half-decayed body full of electricity.

Evilyn studied it with a smile as Tesche pulled the sheet to reveal the head— putrid, rotten eyes bulged and lips eaten away by nature long ago, its teeth bared into a permanent snarl, barely visible underneath the largest goalie's mask she'd ever seen. And next to him, resting under his arm, a forge-welded splitting axe twice the size any sane person would ever use.

"I needed something I could bolt onto him." Bianca noted Evilyn's gaze again at the goalie's mask. "If you want to have any kind of control, it's got to stay on, right?"

"And you're sure it's him? *The* Axe-man?" Evilyn admired the doctor's work, studied the blade of the axe.

"Don't touch that." The doctor swatted her employer's hand away before it touched the blade. "It's an alloy made with—you know what. And yes, I'm quite sure it's him. He speaks at times."

"Speaks?"

"Sort of. He just repeats a line from an old jazz tune over and over."

"Delicious. I just hope it works." Evilyn retreated to the front of the lab, slumped in a chair, twisting a strand of the purple side of her hair. "*He* was out last night. I saw him."

"Again?" Tesche joined her boss, making a note on her pad as she looked at the other subject. "That's not like him these days."

"Something's changed. New arrivals have altered the field."

"Is that good or bad... for us?"

Evilyn chewed at her fingernail, her upper lip curling, her teeth almost canine in the dim light of the old plant.

"I'm going to look into it." She spat her dead skin onto the floor.

I
"KNOW HOW"
—YOUNG MC, 1989

REGINA MURPHY LONG, Gina to some, Murphy or Murph to most others, brushed her thick black hair off her shoulder as she made her morning rounds. Wayne State cutoff sweater, tights with pink leg-warmers, she breathed steady as her Cons slapped the blacktop of the old city. Headphones pumped in the MC as she twirled and danced through her jog, turning up Canal away from the river. She faded and dodged skateboarders passing the Tchoup, shadow boxed two plucky girls in pigtails the other side of Magazine. She slap-fived a suited out-of-towner walking out of The Sheraton who held up his hand hailing a car. He wrinkled his face at her as she cruised toward St. Charles.

She picked up her speed and cut down Baronne, veered left at Gravier. She gazed up at the great structures rising above her, cranes atop half the buildings in the CBD. Cain Capital towered above her at Loyola and Gravier. Bank of America grew taller by the hour a few blocks away. Macy's had a footprint down south now. Not far behind her was the Germain Enterprises high-rise, soon to be demoted to the second tallest building in the city.

Froggering herself across Loyola, Murph backward-somersaulted into Duncan Plaza, cutting a perfect flip, not even losing her headphones in the move. Two yuppies with a fluffy dog gave her the golf clap, and she returned the gesture with a pirouette and half-bow. She jogged into the park, pausing at a gang of girls taking turns holding the jump rope for each other. Their giggles as they tripped themselves sent energy up her arms into her neck. She flinched it out, smiled back at them.

"Can you do it?" One of them pointed the end of the rope at her—a challenge. Murph grinned at them, tousled one's head, took the rope and flipped it backwards, then forwards, then alternated side-to-side, never missing a step. She cut loose at the end, holding the rope in both hands like a weapon, slinging the handles like airplane propellers, making a whirlwind of noise, then slung one end of the rope, letting it flow through her fingers like water, popping a pinecone off a nearby limb.

"Whoa!" the kids' eyes widened as she handed them the rope and jogged on.

She stopped for a breather and pulled her water bottle from her small backpack—along with her Kodak. She snapped a few shots at the scenery around her, then aimed her camera above her, at the looming face of the nearly finished Lili Tower.

It had been the talk of the town since she arrived. 90 stories high and it still wasn't complete. Its megalithic superstructure had already grown to the tallest in the rapidly growing southern city. Murph had seen the decline of Old Detroit, once the jewel of the Midwest, the beating heart of American Iron, now a near-frozen ruin of its former self, an ice-coated wasteland governed by the unforgiving steel of *those* machines. But this construction more than all the others held her fascination—its hexagonal shape, its great spires going up as its last 6 floors pyramidded into a large open shrine with six pillars holding up a crystalline kaleidoscope encased in a steel rim. In the center of all the pillars stood a large stone, ancient and brooding—like someone had plucked it from some other world and plopped it down in the heart of the Crescent City.

She racked the zoom on her lens, getting as close as she could to the doglike gargoyles glaring at everything beneath them. The whole structure was a dark gray steel, tinted windows, and still very much a mystery. It had yet to open to the public. Murph snapped a few more photos, lost herself for a moment in its allure, then shook her head out of it.

She jogged on through the city, back toward The Quarter, the old town. She preferred the Spanish-style architecture to the new steel gods of the CBD. She ducked past a pair of donut-eaters, giving them a mock-salute and a sweet smile they couldn't help but return. She hopped a right onto Bourbon, cruising through the early morning crazies and those still picking up the pieces from the night before. She took a breather, clocking her time outside the old Mr. Lee's Laundry at the 500 block, checking her pulse, slowing herself down, calming, hearing her father's voice, what he'd always said to her. *Breathe. Calm your heart. Focus.*

"Hey Murph!" The shaggy old, vaguely Asian man sat outside the laundry and laid out a few handmade ornaments and necklaces for sale, his left eye always looking off in some other direction while the right stayed trained on her at all times. "What about it, Murphy? How you doing today?"

"Not bad, Victor." Murph jogged in place to keep her heart rate up. She handed him a spare water from her bag and tucked a dollar into his cup. He bowed his head to her. "You made it all right last night?"

"Oh me? I'm always fine. This city and me, we understand each other." He switched eyes on her.

"Why don't you go stay at Germain's shelter? They'd give you a bed, something to eat for breakfast. Help you with a job."

"I have a job!" He insisted with his eyes. "I have an important job. Besides, I like this spot. This is all that's left here. Used to be a whole Chinatown. All up and down this block. Many families. Very strong. Now, not as much. Moved here, there, all over."

Murph zoned out on the old man's story as she scoped the notice board just above his head—mostly locals posting items for sale, wish lists, rooms to rent or services offered. A good rate on a plumber, she saw. But it was the missing teens she shivered at. She pulled one down to go over it. Sixteen. Kind of pretty. She shook her head, cursing herself for the debacle of the night before. She'd lost sight of the two young guys in the haze. She thought she'd finally had a lead. *Who's taking you? And why?* She asked in her mind for the thousandth time.

"You gonna search for those kids?" Victor shifted his tone, looking inside her. She paused her jogging, felt herself slip for a second, heard her father scold her.

"Who me?" Murph smirked, shrugged her shoulders. "Who I look like? The Shriners? Maybe if there's a reward."

"Ha! Very good." Victor grinned. "You don't fool me. You have a pure heart. I know you do."

"Yeah well." Murphy slipped another folded dollar into his cup. "Just keep that a secret for me, if you would."

"Bless you, Murphy." Victor pressed his palms together in front of his face, bowing again. "Among dragons, you are the princess!"

"Thanks, Vic." Murph picked up her legs again, getting her rhythm back. She never knew why the old man got her going like he did, sweet old geezer. She took a bow and started off.

"Remember, Murphy. You let me know if you ever need anything. If you have a problem, and no—"

"Yeah yeah, Victor." She jogged backward, waving him goodbye for the day. "I know who to call."

II
"RISE"
—PUBLIC IMAGE, LTD., 1986

LYDIA STARED OUT the window over the barely lit city already alive with the day. Construction crews worked atop the many buildings. Just like the bay back home, so many moved down, more every day. There was no end to jobs for those with the skills. It was hard to believe that this gothic southern party town was fast becoming a major city. All thanks to some weather.

She wrapped herself tighter in the white robe, sipping the tasty coffee already made when she woke in the California king bed in a guest room of some enormous suite. Molly slept dead to the world, a tale yet to be told and one that still unnerved Lydia. Their temporary lodging's benefactor remained missing for the morning.

Lydia cursed herself, the city, their new acquaintance, the world, the former president Commie Ron, and basically everything short of her red-haired best friend for the loss of her truck—rather her brother's truck. Everything got so out of control so fast, the melee in the streets, the bodies lying strewn about, several not moving, the truck still stuck in the wreckage and immobile. Murphy had shouted for them to make a run for it when the first sounds of sirens pierced the night air.

And they had, ducking down alleys and into the residentials, Molly tripping over herself, slurring her words all the while, mumbling something about a bat. There had been those, for sure. Lydia had never seen a single bat in her life, and suddenly an army of them. But something else—somewhere in the midst of the chaos, as they ran up Felicity, moving as fast as they could, avoiding police lights, Murph eyeing for a cab, Lydia swore she'd heard the low howl of something. Like a wolf.

"Think fast." Murph flung a brown bag at Lydia's face which caught it as much as her hands did. "Got you guys some breakfast."

Lydia scowled as she inspected the bag. Bagels with cheese. *Where is this person even from? Bagels?*

"She up yet?" Murph poured herself a cup of coffee.

The sound of retching from the bathroom down the hall answered the question. Both Lydia and Murph wrinkled their faces as it continued several moments. Then a faucet ran, along with an audible "Fuck." through the bathroom door.

Lydia chuckled through her frustration. Molly finally joined the living, trudging toward the kitchen. Lydia offered her the bag. Molly inspected it and almost hurled again. Murph poured a tall glass of O.J., topped it with a shot of Stolichnaya, and slid it at Molly as she slumped onto the stool at the bar.

"Hair of the dog."

Molly studied the glass, its bright color mocking her throbbing head. Lydia's already pissed but grinning face didn't lighten Molly's mood either.

"Not sure if this helps, but I'll try anything." Molly downed it.

"First hangover?" Murph checked her watch, took a bite of her bagel and put the juice up. "Thought you two were seasoned."

"Look, we just need to get my truck and get back home." Lydia folded her arms. None of this gave her a warm or fuzzy. The street rat act. The unexplained chase. The three-gang brawl. The bats. The fact that they didn't stay for the cops. Then this place. A two-bedroom suite at the top of the Windsor Court?

"That's probably not going to happen." Murph looked Lydia in the eye, a hint of empathy but not much. Lydia wanted to punch her—with Molly's fist. "See, either the gangs got it after we left, or the cops did. And I don't know which is worse in this town. The day cops are weird. And the night cops... They're weirder."

"How do you know that?" Lydia looked at the bagels again. Still nope.

"Because she's a secret cop." Molly stifled a gulp of juice trying to come back up the pipe. "Aren't you?"

Lydia looked at Molly who shook her head. They both glared at Murphy.

"You got good instincts, kid."

"Not my first time with secret cops." Molly grabbed a bagel, then the whole bag.

"Fine. Sure. Detroit P.D. Twelve years on the force. Detective. Had a partner and a pension and the full nine. Till *the company* came in. Bought the whole city, including the police. Turned most of us out of a job. Replaced us with the F.R.E.D.s."

"Freds?" Lydia raised an eyebrow.

"Free Roaming Enforcement Drones. Big ugly fuck you robots. Kill you over a damn glitch in their mainframe, y'ain't careful. Y'all ain't ever seen those? Lucky you. World's changing, kid. Anyway. That's half of it. The other half is my partner got iced. I don't have all the pieces together yet, but it all tracks back to here, this city, that joint last night, missing kids, gangs, some cult, and the rest I don't know. I've been on the ground here a couple months. This place is creep factor 900. I get a bad feeling every night I go out. The streets are clean as a whistle. The streetcars move like clockwork. Business runs on rails. But kids like you come here. They don't always come back. No reports. No police files. No stories in the paper. Like it never happened. Like they were never here. I'm telling you. This town is weird."

Molly's face grew grim, not just from the hangover from whatever had gotten *her* drunk, already a strong argument in Murph's favor for weirdness. But then their lives had been nonstop weird since last October. Why should this be any different?

"Okay. I showed you mine. Now you show me yours." Murph pointed her eyebrows at the girls, namely Molly who wolfed down the last of the bagels. Lydia started to change her mind on them but lost her shot.

Molly looked back at Lydia, then to Murph, then Lydia again. Lydia shrugged and rolled her eyes, their face-code for *might as well; who cares?* Molly downed the rest of her second glass of juice, then squeezed the glass, bursting it to shards. Murph jumped back, clenching her fists, putting herself into a defensive stance. Molly grabbed the biggest jagged piece of glass in her hand and put it against her left wrist.

"Kid, no!" Murph leapt forward, but Molly was already slicing it back and forth. Murph's eyes grew three feet wide. There was no blood. Not a drop.

Then Molly ate the glass.

"Where's my jacket?" Molly crunched, gulped the shards down her throat. Lydia shook her head at Molly on the jazz again. Her hangover must be wearing off quick. Just like everything worked a little different with her.

Lydia tossed Molly her denim cut from their pile of clothes on the floor. Molly reversed it, showing off her colors. Her rainbow hammer insignia. She copped a look at the cop.

"I'll be damned." Murph stared at it, the pieces clicking together in her mind. "You're the Baytown Badass. I heard about you. Thought that shit was made up."

"I sometimes think that too." Molly slipped off her jacket and slumped on the couch.

"Is this your super suit?" Murph inspected the denim with a grimace. "Needs work."

"Yeah yeah." Molly rolled her eyes. "So what now? How do we find these people that got your partner?"

"You're volunteering to help?" Murph lifted an eyebrow. "I won't say I couldn't use a—whatever you are."

"So, we're doing *this* now?" Lydia asked. "Can I use your phone? I have to make a call."

Murph nodded to the phone on the wall in the corner, and Lydia made her way to it. Molly stared out the window from the top floor penthouse, a lavish and spacious affair now that she gathered it in with a sober mind. All the modern appliances. There'd even been two toilets in the bathroom she'd used earlier; she hadn't been sure which one to ralph in. She figured it out when one of them shot water in her face.

"Yeah, it's sorta complicated... you're gonna have to go to her summer school classes," Lydia spoke into the phone across the room. "Uh huh... Yeah... I don't know."

Molly watched Lydia roll her eyes into the phone receiver. Murph walked back into the giant master bedroom for a shower. Molly peaked through the crack in the door, saw her lift her shirt off, a tattoo of some Asian letters ran down her back —Molly didn't know any other languages, save a hint of French. Murph turned and caught her staring and pushed the door shut.

"Yeah, now that you mention it, a tracking system does sound like a *great* idea. Wish we'd thought of that before!" Lydia spoke louder into the phone.

Murph rejoined them in a bathrobe, looking at Molly then at Lydia.

"We're gonna need you to cover for—well, a while I guess." Lydia twisted he cord in her fingers. "Until we let you know."

"Who's she talking to?" Murph looked to Molly.

"My sister. Sorta. Long story." Molly sighed.

"Yeah, I got a few of those. Long stories, not sisters." She tossed a towel at both of them. "Get cleaned up."

Lydia caught her towel, still on the phone with Andi. "Also... Can you do *me* a little? At least go tell my dad and brothers... I don't know. Tell them I got a job down here or something."

"Actually, yeah." Murph smiled a devilish grin. "That's an idea."

THE GIRLS' NEWLY MADE friend pulled up in front of the Windsor Court behind the wheel of a 1985 Ferrari Mondial convertible redder than Molly's hair. She had the top down as the girls jumped into the tan leather seats. Lydia had thrown a fit upstairs about wearing Murph's "human clothes" as she'd put it.

"Girl, you look like Paul Bearer had a daughter." Murph had tossed a pair of blues and a checkered shirt at the spiked bangs with too much mascara. "And wipe off half that shit on your face."

Molly made do with her own outfit and a solid blue overshirt left unbuttoned, shoving her SledgeHammer cut into a backpack she snaked out of the closet. The wind whipped through their hair as they did the stop-n-go all the way up Canal toward the interstate.

"So, you gotta explain the car, the penthouse, all of it." Molly squinted at Murph's easy grin as she one-handed the wheel.

"Yeah, how's a cop from out of town get digs and wheels like this?"

"Yeah, that." She shrugged, held up one hand. "So, you see... I sorta took a security gig for this writer when I got down here. Some lady named Riz. Bigshot, I think. I don't know. I didn't read her books. Needed someone to watch over the place, run errands, that sort of deal. Using the car's sort of a perk."

Lydia gave Molly a look from the backseat. It was code for *Bullshit.*

* * *

A tornado of paper and bodies dodging each other in the narrow through-spaces defined the mail room at the bottom floor of the Germain Enterprises building, everyone scurrying off to one place or the next with carts full of parcels and envelopes. Despite most of the suits upstairs having those new portable telephones, the world of the 80's still ran on old dead tree. Stacks of it all around the area buried what may have once been furniture. Somewhere underneath the chaos, a supervisor shouted commands at the flurry of underlings.

"Murph, is that you? The hell you been? I barely saw you yesterday." He shifted a stack of papers to reveal all five feet of himself, his horseshoe hair standing straight up.

"De Palma!" Murph hugged the little guy, and Molly felt his mood soften against his own wishes. "Did I miss a single drop yesterday? Did I?"

"Well..." De Palma wrinkled an eye at her.

"Besides, brass up top had me running the company car out to the club again. Some suit's wife. You know they can't stand the guys driving their wives around."

De Palma laughed, then gave the once over to her new companions.

"Who's the new blood?"

"HR sent these down. New recruits. Wanted me to show 'em the ropes. They're moving me to permanent motor pool."

"Says who? Why'm I just hearing of this?"

"Look man." Murph rubbed his balding head. "I don't make the rules."

* * *

Murph did make the rules. She walked Molly and Lydia through the motions of their first cart delivery, Lydia grouching the whole time and tugging at her *normie clothes.* Molly soaked it in, watching and cataloging everything and everyone around her. She admired the way Murph seemed to flow through the halls of the massive building, pointing out every section and division, what they did, and often what they didn't do.

"This place is a giant maze. They're into everything from marshmallows to missile defense systems. There's almost 20,000 people that work in this building, and Germain owns nine other buildings in this city alone. Last year this company borrowed more money than the entire state of Florida did. Then they earned triple that amount back."

Murph ducked them into a corner office on the 66th floor, pulled the cart inside and shut the blinds. She opened a tall storage bin and pulled out a black double-breasted business suit and began peeling her outfit off.

"Look away if you're squeamish." She turned to spare them at least the frontal.

Lydia wilded her eyes and looked out the tall windows onto the city. Molly stared at the tattoo on Murph's back again, the lines of the characters drawing her in. She finally looked to Lydia who shook her head at all of it.

"Told you this place is a mess." Murph slipped out of her jeans and into the slacks and slid on her business heels. "They don't even know who's coming or going. Chain of command is all over the place. You could work here a month and not even know who your boss is."

Murph finished the change. Molly and Lydia looked back at a whole new person. They blinked their eyes at the sharpness of her outfit, the way her face seemed to transform along with it. She drew her lips tight, narrowed her eyes. She touched up her makeup with a kit from her purse.

A woman burst in with a stack of papers.

"Oh, sorry, Ms. Gina." She laid them on the desk, eyeing Molly and Lydia up and down.

"Don't mind them, Doralee." Murph clicked her makeup kit shut and waved the girls out of the office along with their mail cart. "This is my niece from out of town. I helped get her get a job in the mail room. She's headed for the board room one day."

Murph and the secretary laughed as Molly and Lydia squelched their confusion into mere stares.

"Your niece?" Doralee stared at Molly, then at Murph.

"Yeah, well, she's adopted." Murph winked. "So, girls, it was good saying hi, but I've got a stack of reports here, and you've got your rounds to do. You got those down pat now, right?" She winked at them. "I'll explain later," she whispered, away from the secretary.

Murph eased them out of her office and closed the door. Molly heard her pick up the phone and start arguing with someone about billing invoices. Lydia face-coded her with a glare. None of this made any sense.

IV
"SOMETIMES THE GOOD GUYS FINISH FIRST"
—PAT BENATAR, 1987

MURPHY, NOW GINA HAMMOND since she was in *suit mode*, pored over the billing reports. Germain Enterprises wasn't her first choice, but Cain Capital was locked down tighter than a steel drum floating off the old Marcello docks down at the port. Germain's company had hired her on the spot for the mail room, which is exactly where she wanted to be. Two weeks on the job, she had the lay of the building down to a science, the ins and outs, comings and goings of all the suits, their schedules, layoffs, new hires, clients, subsidiaries, all of it. She knew on Monday who would be fired on Friday. There were as many vacant executive offices on any given day as there were actual suits bothering to show up to work. A number of the senior execs worked graveyard hours, which seemed off to her. She'd noted their names and added them to her list to check out.

Moving into one of the vacant offices had been easy enough. A few bogus memos, a requisition for a secretary from the pool, a shredded division closure order sent down to HR, and she was all set. She wasn't the only woman at the junior executives table during meetings (usually held evenings instead of mornings), but she was the only black woman, so she played it conservative. *Listen, learn, and observe,* she reminded herself—her father's teachings stuck with her. She still heard his voice in her head after all these years—a hard man. But she missed him.

Germain himself was the most elusive. According to accounts, he was around her age. Never present for any meetings, though, and barely mentioned. An heir, she'd found out. Had the majority of shares since his parents left it all to him in a trust. Happy enough to let the board do as they wished, he lived a life of luxury. Must be nice, she figured. Billionaire playboy jet-setting around the world. What a life.

His company was a mess. It's like no one really understood or even cared about turning a profit. Murph had picked up a thing or two from running the same long con back in Rock City on AllCorp—the American division of Volund-Yöndemoni—at least until they *purchased* the police department from the city and canceled her op. This was before they canned the whole force and started dumping the FREDs on the streets, turning the city into a hellhole. She ground her teeth thinking about it.

Over a third of Germain's revenue got redirected into various R&D projects, most redacted and off the books. The entire division had been moved offsite to an undisclosed location. Much of the rest, after overhead and salaries, went into various philanthropic projects all around the city. He funded parks, venues, festivals, libraries, museums, social programs, homeless shelters, blood drives, and a robust jobs program. Three companies were most responsible for much of the city's growth over the last decades: Cain Capital, Germain Enterprises, and the old JarethCo—now owned by Cain. Everyone from up north was looking for a place to escape the creeping cold, and competition in the south was fierce. Atlanta rivaled Old New York, Dallas had doubled, and Miami was a Metropolis. NOLA struggled to keep its quintessential character. Murph recalled when she arrived, every person she met on the street, chatted with over a drink, even half the bums— all transplants. She could walk the city all day and not meet a single native. All the big money companies moved their operations somewhere south. Like sharks to the smell of blood. Only London remained of the old northern metros—ruled by the iron hand of the Iron Lady herself. Murph hated Thatcher maybe more than she had Commie Ron.

Burning the day and night at both ends, she power-napped at her desk sometimes. Her dreams haunted her. Baskin' face, her old partner. Bloodied and screaming. He'd gone down to look for his daughter who'd come to NOLA, like all the others, looking for work. Her calls became scarce, he'd said in his own weekly call to Murph. Then they cut off altogether. She'd begged him to wait for her. But he said he couldn't wait another day, much less a month for her to get out. She cursed under her breath, just thinking about it—how much she hated AllCorp. One day she'd go back to Detroit. She'd take the fight home. She punched the palm of her hand thinking about those walking tanks on her old neighborhood streets.

* * *

"I just want you to understand what you're getting into." Murph laid the photos out on the coffee table of the penthouse for the two kids. That's what they were. A couple of kids in the city for a good time, have their palms read, drink a hand grenade, and go back with a tale or two. Now they stared, solemn-eyed, into the faces of death. Photos from the file Baskin sent her, his field notebook, slam full of scribblings and sketches, most of it she couldn't make out. Like a logbook of him slowly losing his mind. She could only imagine the rage tinged with terror as he crawled deeper into the abyss of whatever haunted this town.

The redhead took it in stride, like she'd been through this ringer before. The raven-haired kid in the black makeup held her gut with her hand. She pitied them, superpowers or no. Murph knew what she signed up for when she joined the academy. Heard her father's voice in her head railing against it. How he always wanted to protect her, coddle her, hide her away from the world like his precious secret. She knew he'd wanted a boy—someone to carry on the line. He'd said as much over the years with his sad eyes when he looked at her: *Zuìzhōng Lóng.* Some times he looked like his heart tore in half as he called her that.

"It's some kind of nihilist death cult is what I've come up with." Murph poured herself a drink, offered the bottle to the teens, the red waving it off. Lydia grabbed it by the neck and poured it down her throat. Murph's eyes widened at the gulp. "Domnii Morţii, the gang from the other night—they're connected to it, maybe the root of it. I thought I had it zeroed to that bar I took you to, but maybe not. Nothing in this weird city ever makes sense."

Molly's mind wandered to the vacuum cleaner robot that wheeled into the room, beeping if it got close to a wall. She double-blinked at it and fidgeted her head. Every day in the city showed her some new thing she'd never heard of but just seemed totally normal to everyone here. Other than her android twin, Molly didn't trust machines—precisely because of her twin, as it were. She looked at Lydia taking her second shot right off the bottle. *Poor Lyd. She deserves better than this.* Molly knew she should send her home where she'd be safe from whatever this was shaping up to be. But the truth is she wanted Lydia with her.

"What do you mean death cult?" Lydia put the bottle down and looked over the photos again. Murph's old partner, Baskin, bloated and morbid after he'd floated out of the Pontchartrain, chunks of him missing—like they'd been eaten by something. A story as old as the city itself, going as far back as the LaFitte days. A city full of old legends and half-forgotten myths. *The Forgotten Soldier?* Where had Molly heard that? Who was the man in the straw hat? And the telepathic crocodile? Had that been real, or did she imagine it?

Murph laid out more photos. Kids this time, most no older than Molly and Lydia, many younger. Lydia shivered at them, Molly stone-faced. Like they'd been carved up in some ritual, like something out of ancient history. Disemboweled. Torn apart. Their limbs gone. Their necks looked hacked away, chunks of flesh missing. Their guts just gaping cavities. Eyes ripped from their sockets. And their skin, their faces, drained, wrinkled. Like someone drank them to death.

The robot dinged to vacuum under their feet.

V
"WALKING ON SUNSHINE"
–KATRINA & THE WAVES, 1983

MOLLY TOOK TO THE TEDIUM of the mailroom like a familiar blanket. She missed the long lazy nights at Tracey's Treasure Box, her old job back home, Tracey's elaborate outfits, never the same one twice. She pined for her senior year, before it all fell apart in an instant. Skateboarding to school in the gray hours of dawn, a wink from a cute boy driving with his top down. Stupid face-code games with Lydia during Civics class. Hoyt and Clair, her foster parents she'd finally let love her. She longed for it all. It seemed so far away now, though only left behind a few days ago. But maybe she'd never really been there. At least not in a long time.

Lydia hated the job, hated the whole corporation. "I hate anyone who wears a suit to work." She shoved envelopes into her cart for their rounds. "You know, this isn't what I envisioned it would be when I got to team up with you fighting the badguys. This is just lame."

The girls took their full carts by Murph's office so she could sift through them for *intel*. After that, they hit the hallways, going on their separate routes, but always finding a way to meet every so often for a break. The work was surprisingly simple. They could each clear a cart in less than thirty minutes where the other mail guys might take two hours. The key was to either look busy or not be seen at all. They would hang out in the back stairwells together or take the service elevator to the roof and goof around, staring at the gray skyline of the city.

"I don't mind this." Molly stood on one hand, balanced herself on her fingertips, picking them off the ground one by one until she stood, perfectly balanced, on the tip of her index finger.

"You're a showoff." Lydia looked around the empty roof atop the city, the second tallest building on the horizon. The new Lili tower climbed into the clouds across from them, its glaring gargoyle carvings sending a shiver down her back. "Get down before someone sees you." Lydia stared back at the gargoyle, wondering if it already had.

* * *

The employee cafeteria was top notch. Germain's employees ate like royalty. Lydia grabbed two apples and a Greek yogurt to go along with her risotto. Molly piled everything on her plate. She had a steak, a baked potato, two hoagies, a taco bowl, and seven clusters of grapes. It was all-included. They could take as much as they wanted, so Molly took.

And she ate.

"Jesus, Mol, they're staring." Lydia glanced around, watching the eyes and snickers and pointing fingers. *Maybe the food was why Molly had gotten so tall.* Lydia figured Molly must have grown four inches since last fall. They were once the same height, but now Lydia stood on tiptoes to meet her eye to eye.

"Let 'em." Molly tore into her steak with her bare hands. They only had a 30-minute lunch, all the food in the world but no time to eat it. She had to get it in while she could. They sat and laughed with each other and munched their food, Molly enjoying the view out the 20th floor cafeteria windows. "I'm sorry about your truck. But, honestly, other than that, I'm kinda having a good time. I missed... I don't know. Us, I guess."

Molly Smiled. So did Lydia.

"I am too, mostly." Lydia snaked a French fry from Molly's tray. Like they were back at Bay High. It wasn't the worst day.

"Oh my god!" someone screamed. "He's gonna jump!"

Molly's eyes zeroed, out the windows, across the block. A man crept out onto the ledge of the Cain building. He kept looking down, fidgeting. Like he was working up the last of his courage.

"You gotta–" Lydia turned, but Molly was already gone.

* * *

Out on the ledge, the man trembled, fidgeting. He peered over the edge, staring down at the street forty stories below. He retracted, bracing his arms against the wall behind him. Tears welled and dripped from the corners of his eyes. Somewhere a freighter's foghorn blew. Birds squawked. He looked over the edge again—still the same.

A neon-striped leotard strolled around the corner of the building. Hands shoved in the pockets of a spray-painted denim cutoff jacket. Wild red hair flowed out above a cheap Mardi Gras mask.

"Wh-what?" he stared at her—focusing on the mask.

"Oh sorry, pal." Molly paused her walk. "I was just out for a stroll. Usually don't meet people up here."

"Y-you... what?"

"Sorry." Molly reached out her hand to introduce herself. "You can call me Sledgehammer. Or Just Hammer. Or S.H. Any of those, really. I'm not picky."

"Th-the mask!" he pointed at it.

"Oh yeah, you like it?" Molly adjusted it on her face, gave him a pose.

"It's not one of *hers*. Who are you? Who sent you? I won't go back. I won't let them make me into—" He peered over the ledge again, more resolve on his lips this time.

Molly reached for him.

"Whoa, pal, what's that about?"

"I won't let them turn me. Those—things. Bloodsuckers. Ghouls. Wolves. I won't. I'd rather die."

"Okay, man. Just breathe. Just calm down."

"You're *not* one of them?" He stared into her eyes. They stared back into him. She flowed out her soul-hearing power to calm him—ease his mind. It worked, but he fought it. Of all her abilities, this remained the biggest mystery to her, how she felt their emotions, could sometimes push back into them. It only worked on the decent ones, those who had some goodness left in them. Others were too far gone. They only had hate, fear, or sickness left in them. Those she had to resort to hands and fists. But this one? He had goodness in him. She felt it. But so much fear. It poured out of him in buckets. He was scared to death.

"Just come on back with me, and you can tell me all about it." She said it again with her eyes. She reached out her hand. He took it.

Molly walked the trembling man through the same window he'd climbed out. She took him through the hallways of the 4-Leaf offices, one of the numerous sub-companies in the Cain Capital building. He shook as he walked by his staring colleagues, many of them slitting their eyes at him, and *her.* Molly didn't like what she felt from this place.

Security guards stomped off the elevator. His fear shot to the roof again, boiling his mind. He gripped her hand tight, like a boy clinging to his mother, begging her for safety.

"No! No, I won't let them turn me!"

"Ma'am, we'll take him from here." A guard glared at her.

Molly sluiced the poor man's terror from her brain and looked into the guard. Nothing. He felt nothing. Nor the others with him. Like dolls or objects.

"I'll walk him down."

"Ma'am, this employee needs medical attention." He reached for the man's arm. "We will deliver him to the authorities so he can—"

"I didn't ask. I told you." Molly's jaw tightened and her fist clenched.

The guards didn't try their luck.

VI
"CHARIOTS OF PUMPKINS"
–JOHN CARPENTER, 1982

MURPHY TAPPED HER FOOT, arms folded, looking out the window of her appropriated corner office. She glanced down at the girls with a side-eye. Molly sensed Murph's irritation at the spectacle of the ordeal, but at the same time she couldn't argue with saving the man's life.

"We're going to have to talk about some ground rules later, but obviously not here." Murph looked around her office, goosebumps forming on her skin. "I swear some days I think these walls have ears. Half the people up here give me the heebs."

Murph swapped her outfit and walked the girls down to the mail room so they could punch their cards. Molly and Lydia hung up their work shirts and headed to the parking garage across the street. Murph had her head in a two-inch thick file of financial reports she'd snaked from upstairs. She tossed her satchel and the other folders she'd grabbed into a milk crate she kept in the trunk.

Molly felt a shiver down her spine and turned. Far off at the opposite end of the garage, she felt its source. She ambled toward the sensation, her stomach churning the closer she got to it.

"Mol, what the hell?" Lydia jogged to her.

Molly clocked her eyes on the car—some old Ford Pinto. But the man at the wheel—wearing a Mardi Gras mask—it was *him,* the same man she'd saved earlier. She moved forward, eager to speak to him but realized she wasn't dressed for the occasion. She paused and thought better of it. Him being in the mask felt odd, the way he'd reacted to hers before. Then, almost as if he saw her, even recognized her, he picked up a gas can and dumped the fuel all over himself. Murph joined them to see what was going on. She tried to grasp Molly's shoulder, but Molly bolted toward him. She was still thirty feet away when he lit the Zippo and burst into flames. The interior of the cab turned bright orange and yellow. Flames licked out the windows.

Molly's heart sank. She felt what Murph had felt earlier. This place, this whole town, it was sick.

* * *

Back at Murph's suite—she'd whisked them home before the cops showed, again—the girls shared a drink in silence. Molly tossed one back in solidarity.

"What was that about?" Lydia poured herself another rum. Molly stared out the long window at the purpling city skyline, her stomach in knots. She could vomit. But a rage grew inside her. A seed sprouting. Whatever plagued this place, she would cure it. The cries and sorrows of ten thousand victims of some unsaid horror infected her mind. She tried to soften them, to quiet them enough she could think. But she wouldn't forget them. She would avenge them.

"Your guess is as good as mine at this point. The J-Queen was my first real lead, and we blew that one. I thought they worked out of there, but if they did, they won't now, not anytime soon. We're back to zero." Murph pulled off her work shirt, leaving just her black tank on as she walked toward her bedroom.

"Then there's Hēishǒu Móguǐ." Murph returned, slipping into a tight hooded pullover, wrapping a pouch belt around her waist. "Them being here changes things."

"Who are they?" Lydia stared at her glass, contemplating a third shot.

"They're a doomsday cult. Old world shit. Ancient prophecies and demon worship. It's all fucked. From the lay of this town, I'd say they're just the latest in a stack of such crazies. But then—" Murph stared at Molly's cherry red hair, bright eyes, and little brown freckles. She shook her head. "You kind of change the color of the water I'm used to drinking, so what the fuck do I know?"

"There was this reporter." Lydia fished out her wallet.

"Do what?" Murph reached for the card Lydia produced.

"She told me to find her if we ever came to town. She said she'd *seen things.*"

"Yeah, I bet." Murph studied the card. "I know this chick. She writes for the fishwrapper."

"The what?" Molly wrinkled a brow. Actually, fish sounded good right about then.

"Yeah it's all kooky shit. Conspiracy mumbo jumbo. Giant wolves and that bit. But, hell, it's worth a shot."

Murph and Lydia's voices melted into a single noise. Molly's body wandered to the tall windows. Her eyes, welling with liquid, stared at the neon of The Crescent City, if it still was that. The handful of people she'd met at the office building were all from anywhere else—Brooklyn, Toronto, London, Paris, a few Eastern Blockers, accents thick, right out of a bad movie. She saw that poor man again, his blank face in the car as he doused himself—the terror on his face out on the ledge. The mask—he'd pointed at her mask, then he had one on himself.

The Forgotten Soldier, Molly almost whispered aloud. The man in the straw hat flashed across her mind. *Who—what was he? What was she? What was happening?* It scratched at her mind. Was she the forgotten soldier? Maybe the sickness swallowing this city held some secret of who and where she came from. One thing she did know—this place kept its secrets tight. But she would break it. She smashed her fist into her palm as loud as a clap, jolting the other two from their conversation.

"I'm going out there." Molly went for her satchel with her gear.

"Not in that loud-ass nonsense, you ain't." Murph snatched the denim cut from her, rolled her eyes and tossed it away. She walked into her room and pulled some clothes from a bag on the floor in her closet. She walked back out, tossed a set of black tights and another hoodie like the one she had on. "You're working with the pros now, kid. Got to dress the part. I don't need rainbows flashing across the sky giving away my position."

"Hey what about me?" Lydia held out her hands, looking at the clothes in Molly's arms.

"You bulletproof?" Murph glanced back.

"Well, no, but—"

"You got one of these?" Murph whipped out her Colt and racked the slide to chamber a round, flicked the safety and put it back.

"Well, no, but—"

"Then you can monitor coms." Murph plunked a heavy radio down on the counter, switched it on. "Just fine from here."

"Yeah but—" Lydia sighed.

VII

"THE KILLING MOON"
—ECHO & THE BUNNYMEN, 1983

MURPH TOOK MOLLY OUT for the nightbeat, each with an earpiece and Lydia back at the penthouse on a three-way. Molly hopped a building just off Bourbon and took the eye in the sky, the moonlight glinting off her eyes, the rest of her a shadow. Murphy walked the crowds as a gray-man, watching the slicks and the pickpockets.

"What are we looking for?" Molly's voice cracked in the earpiece.

"Young, drunk, stupid, and lost." Murph came back over the radio.

Molly thought of her and Lydia their first night in town. *Idiots,* she cursed herself. Her getting drunk still confused her. She couldn't recall much of how it happened. She remembered the shots with the turbros, but after that everything was a blur until...the bat. She knew she saw something on the steeple that night.

Molly eagle-eyed Murph doing her thing, pro that she was, the way she slid through the crowds, stalked behind a mark. She heard her talking to a few here and there, bumming a cig or a light or both, anything to get them talking. Molly would zero them as soon as Murph made contact. She admired how Murph could smell a lie as fast as Molly sensed it—it was something else. More than once, Molly caught herself drifting back to the days with Easton and Nguyen, two baby cops making their rounds, letting her neon-striped-self tag along as they tagged the badguys. Molly felt at home again here. Sometimes, if she half closed her eyes...

"Don't look back, but you've got a tail on your six." Molly's voice rang in Murph's ear. She'd just shot the bull with a couple of working girls making the rounds. She gave them a nod and moved on toward the river.

"Give me the skinny." Murph kept her eyes forward, letting Molly give her the layout.

"Four guys. Black jackets. They've been on you a minute. Just following. Like they're watching."

Murph took a turn, then another, weaving away from the crowds and the nightlife. She moved out of the lights, down an empty street off the main drag. She crept past a couple closed-up antique shops and a cafe long done for the day. A busted streetlight. A cat scuttled about somewhere not far off. Whispers as the black jackets turned down the same street.

"Boys, now y'all can't be walking—" Murph turned to face them, flashing a smile that washed off her face just as fast. They wore tang suits—heavy toggle buttons. Cropped bowl haircuts. Black claw tattoos on their hands.

Then the knives came out.

Whatever smart quip Murph had started to say was long gone off her lips. She hadn't told her fists to present themselves–they just had. Their eyes–trained, hollow, wrong–stared back at her, through her, into the night behind her.

A sound of thunder exploded everyone's focus, all but the one who'd made it. Murph flinched, shook her head out of her haze. She'd never frozen like that before. She collected herself as she watched the kid go to work. Molly flung two down the alleyway in an instant, sending them for a long nap. A quick one went at her with his knife like a machine gun, cutting up her tights and hoodie before she picked him up by his hair and–*slapped him?* She slapped him right across his face like some boy being scolded at a bar. *Who was this chick?* Murph lost the plot for a second. Molly dropped the stabby one and moved to the last one standing. He muttered out a long string of Mandarin as she grabbed him by the throat.

"Wait." Murph gained her wits again. She pulled out the Colt and pointed it at the goon, not that she needed it after seeing the kid work. Not a scratch on her, though she needed new clothes.

"Why are you here? Why are you in New Orleans?" Murph jammed the gun in his cheek. She caught Molly's eyes on the gun. "What do you know about the dead kids? Talk, you piece of shit."

Murph gouged the barrel further into his cheek, Molly wincing at her. The man muttered out another long string of Chinese.

"Tell me why you're here." Murph's face grew hot, her hand too, tingling and numb at the same time.

He looked at Molly, then at Murph. "Xuǎn yīgè."

Those words seared through Murph's mind. She blinked, cocked the hammer on her gun and pulled the trigger...into Molly's closed fist around the barrel. The Red's eyes looked back at her, into her, staring into her soul, judging her.

The sirens said it was time to go. Molly popped the man in the face, putting him down for a snooze, grabbed Murph around the waist, and launched them both onto the building next to them, out of sight.

* * *

Back at the Penthouse, the dark-haired kid eyeballed the two of them walk through the door silent. Murph went straight for the liquor, pouring herself a tall glass, her hand still shaking. Murphy could do without them both for a moment. *No, you can't,* she told herself. *Especially now.*

"Want to tell me what that was about?" Molly folded her arms, giving her that judgy little snot look again. "What did he say to you?"

"I look like I fucking speak Chinese?" Murph gulped her whiskey and went to her room. She flung her black clothes off, put on something light and fluffy to make herself feel normal again, like a person. She slept like hell that night.

* * *

The next days were quiet. No more black Tang suits, thank the gods. They went out again and came back with less to show than before. She saw how Red looked at her, looked *to* her. She didn't know what to make of it, so she shook it off. Kids always had their shit to work through. Heavens knew she certainly had at that age. Probably a boy. Or a long-gone daddy. Or both. She saw her own eighteen-year-old self, alone against the world. Signing on the dotted line for the academy. Determined prove to the old man she didn't need anyone's protection. Stupid, naive kid. Murph shook her head. *Kids.*

"You're a detective." Molly looked at her on their way to the garage after a workday, Murph still in her business getup this time, another stack of papers to sort through later that night.

"That's what my shield said, yeah." Murph didn't look up from her stack.

"What's the wounded warrior mean?"

Lydia gave the face code for *huh?*

"The what?" Murph looked back at her.

"The place of the wounded warrior. Something a guy said when I got here. Been itching at me."

"Shit I don't know. Don't talk to weirdos in the French Quarter, kid."

"Now she tells us." Lydia folded her arms and sank into the back seat. Murph frowned at the sidekick. She'd wanted to send that one home, better safe than sorry, but she'd proved herself handy on the mini-Nagra and was quick to call out local cop movements from the scanner. Not a bad little dispatcher. Still, Murph didn't like liabilities. The battering ram redhead was an asset, the other one not as much.

"Maybe the V.A." Murph tossed her hands up. "That's my best guess."

* * *

Back at the Penthouse, Molly went to gear up in her new all-blacks, but Murph only poured herself a juice and grabbed a donut from the counter, still in her executive suit.

"Yeah, look, we're gonna have to raincheck it this time." Murph bit her donut, checked her watch. "Y'all stay put. Order a pie and watch some tube or something. I'm gonna try that news chick you mentioned. Got a sit-down with her in ten, so I gotta bolt." Murph grabbed her keys and gulped the rest of the pastry. "Don't do..." she looked back at the blank stares of the teen brigade, shook her head at them. "Just don't."

THE MUSTY OFFICES OF *The Register* were exactly what Murph expected. Bunch of suspender-clad mustaches cranked-up on black coffee and all wearing bad ties. Stacks of old papers, file folders, and black and white photos littered every desk and corner of the floor. Someone in the back, behind a glass door yelled at some other silhouette about expenses, something about not paying for novelty teeth. Cigars and cigarettes lit the room more than the few buzzing lamp bulbs. A fly flitted about on a half-eaten sandwich that looked a week old, sitting on a desk with no one at it.

"Who you hear to see?" a mustache mouthed at her as she cruised through the bullpen, or what pretended to be one. There was a big picture of a blurry UFO on the wall, for crying out loud. Stranger things, Murph allowed to herself, thinking of her redheaded friend.

"I already found her." Murph said, spying the set of legs propped up on a desk in the far corner, face buried behind an issue of the same rag on the sign out front.

"Oh, of course." Mustache laughed. "Got a big lead on a ghost story? Monsters from the deep? Invisible flying cars? Or the bat!" He walked off laughing, his buddies slapping his back as they poured more coffee. This whole place wreaked of it. Murph could go for a cup.

"Yo, 'Lex!" Murph folded her arms, waited for the paper to bend down and reveal a face. Not what she expected. A set of glasses, sure, but that was about the only *pencil-neck* aspect of her. The rest was business casual and not bad looking. Blonde hair in a ponytail. Pinched cheeks. A light in her eye that showed Murph this town hadn't murdered her soul. *Yet.*

"I know you?" Alex wrinkled her brow.

"Tell me a story." Murph turned a chair around and sat backwards in it, deciding she would like this woman already.

* * *

Alex Charlton took Murph through the paces—gave her the rundown on half the unsolveds in the city's last ten years. The kind of stuff that made Old Detroit look like *Family Ties* if any of it was true. *If.* Those wild eyes lit up every time she switched gears to the next tall tale. Murph nodded and followed along with it, much as she could. Alex talked like a machine gun going off, sucking back cigarettes and coffee, herself every bit the newshound as any of the others.

"And that's not even the weirdest thing." Alex stamped out her cigarette and motioned for Murph to follow her into the back archives. She pulled out a set of microfiches and stuck one in, rolled through the film until she saw what she wanted—a blemish on the film. A story from that issue blurred and gone—illegible—like it may as well have not happened.

"A hundred or more like this." Alex lit another coffin nail and plugged in the next fiche. She scrolled through a dozen more just like the first. Gaps everywhere. Some had front page leads blurred out. "All over the course of about five years, going back to about '78."

"So, what's that about?" This wasn't on Murph's wish list of info on this town, but now it wasn't *not* on it either. That was the worst about this place. Like a damn Hydra. Soon as she chased down one decent lead, it turned into two new ones, even more confusing and strange.

"You tell me." Alex let the cigarette hang so far out of her mouth Murph didn't know how it stayed put other than sheer will. "And it ain't just this rag. *The Times* is the same way. Every paper in town. Even the damn *Advertiser* and the pennies. Back issues blotted out, sliced up, or just outright missing."

Murph's neck hair stood up, and that often meant they had eavesdroppers. Her senses always went haywire in this town. No place ever felt safer than any other. Something kept clawing at her mind, had been ever since she got here, double now that the Red showed up. Those words from the Tang suit still echoed in her head. She needed some air.

"Take a walk with me." Murph nodded at the door.

Alex grabbed her jacket and smokes.

* * *

"The Jester Queen?" Alex rubbed her chin. "That's an interesting angle. Jareth's an old family here. Sad story if you ain't heard it. She was a good prosecutor but got busted working with a vigilante, according to some hushed whispers I dug up. But that's all before my time."

"So, you're not local either?"

"Nah. I followed a wild goose chase here about six years back. Looking for the moving castle."

"Say what?" Murph hadn't heard that one yet.

"Yeah. Some Romanian Count moving a whole damn castle brick by brick to the middle of the swamp out past Belle Chasse. I ran it down. Thought it was connected to some illuminati thing. Devil worship. Cults. That sort of thing."

Now the woman was speaking Murph's language. Devil worship? Cults? Sounded like the same crap that took down her partner. The Black Hands being in town now? Couldn't be a coincidence. *Moving Castle?* Wasn't even the weirdest thing this week.

"This count. He got a name?" Murph raised an eyebrow.

"Sardo," was all she got out of her mouth before Murph's neck hairs went ice cold.

Murph front-kicked Alex into the brick wall of the building next to them. Her other leg planted on the ground and launched herself airborne into a backflip as the car crashed into another one parked at the curb. Murph's body crested the flip and landed like a cat on the hood of the offending vehicle.

Some maniac burst from the driver's seat holding a wheel gun pointed at Alex. Murph flipped down, kicked it from his hands, then reverse-roundhoused him in the head, knocking him stupid. He had an eye-mask on like some badguy in an old film reel.

"No!" he shouted, his body twitching, fidgeting. "You can't stop it. Can't stop what's to become. We are the night. I will arise. She will return. I will be reborn into the eternal darkness!" He stammered out as he backed away from Murphy.

"Yo, dude, look out for the—"

A delivery truck crunched the man underneath itself, mincing his bones before its brakes could go to work. Murph grimaced and turned away from the sight. She looked to Alex, barely shaken up. Too cranked on caffeine and nicotine and this damn town to still care.

"Some moves." She pursed her lips and wrinkled her brow at Murph.

"Yeah, well, a couple karate classes at the YMCA, you can learn a lot." Murph shrugged.

Alex nodded.

They did the usual dance. The blue boys showed, along with the meat wagon. They took their statements, gave Murphy the stare. She'd had nothing but the runaround from the local constabulary since she got here. Never in her years had she seen this much piss aimed at a fellow badge. Just one more thing on the list of wrongs in the Big Easy. Alex kept to the bare skinny, tightlipped like a pro. Murphy *did* like this one.

Headed back to the newsroom, Alex finished dumping the lowdown on her. Said it wasn't the first "random accident" or maniac in a mask she'd had come at her. It *was* the first one to go lethal with it, Alex admitted. She gave Murph more new leads than she could chase in a month if she worked double time. Maybe the kids could do a few, but she didn't love the idea of cutting them loose on their own.

"That's a lot to run down." Murph sighed, but she was up to it. *For Baskin,* she told herself. But not just him. The Black Hands made it even more personal.

"Be nice if you could get into the Germain party." Alex shrugged, fishing out her smokes.

"The what?" Murph looked at her sideways.

"Oh yeah. All of them will be there. Fucking mayor, commissioner, D.A., every wig in town, all the investors of every major project. The who's who love their hobnobs. Germain's putting it on at his penthouse. Dude's a recluse but loves his soirees, I hear. If you knew anyone high up enough with his outfit, maybe you could score some invites."

Murph grinned. "Yeah. I think I know someone."

VIII
"SUICIDE IS PAINLESS"
—EASTERN IMAGES, 1985

LYDIA STARED UP at the gothic majesty of the Lili Tower as it ruled the night sky with its old-world style. The looming gargoyles were a bit on the nose, even for her. Lydia wasn't quick to be creeped out, never had been, and especially since some goblin tried to demolish her town with undead automatons and a monster army. But that building sent a windy chill down her back as they walked down Gravier.

They'd taken the streetcar most of the way. Molly had insisted they go tonight. Lydia started to object, reiterating Murph's orders but then remembered that she didn't follow anyone's orders and besides she wasn't a huge fan of *Murph* to begin with. She didn't trust her. She trusted Molly, and Molly seemed to trust Murph, so that was something. But Lydia kept her doubts.

They got to the medical district, Molly noting the X she'd drawn on her tacky city map they sell to tourists in the junk shops and bodegas. Molly looked across the street, the soulless gray concrete building facing her. The closer she got, the more she felt it. So much pain, hurt, and loss whispered at her. It weighed her down, her steps slowing as they got nearer. Lydia sensed Molly's unease.

"Look, why do we need to be here?" She glanced around. There was a cool-looking bar just up Freret, probably a med student hangout. It had some arcade games near the front window. "Let's just grab a beer and then bail. This is making you weird again. I hate when you're weird."

"Look, I just have to, all right." Molly glanced toward the bar Lydia stared at. Was it only a week since they got here? Felt like longer. Time always felt longer to her now. Days crawled by, each one its own small lifetime in her mind. When she closed her eyes, she tried to picture Easton, but he faded more each time. She tried to picture her old self, her old life. But it waned with every blink. "You go grab a drink. I won't be long."

"You don't know that." Lydia shook her head. "You're always ditching me. Again. And I mean, I know—it's just—I don't know. You know?"

"Yeah. I know." Molly hugged her friend.

* * *

Inside, the bureaucracy of it slammed into Molly like her android twin's metal fists. Fluorescent lights flickered enough to drive anyone mad that wasn't already. Visitors slouched in the waiting area, along with walk-in patients and the ones who'd thought ahead by making an appointment, only to wait all the same.

"Help you?" a lady at the front didn't look up as Molly approached the window.

"Yeah I don't know, I–" Molly looked around again. She felt something. She was in the right place. She knew it.

"Visiting or patient?" The lady wrinkled her mouth at Molly.

"I don't–I'm looking for someone I don't–he was a soldier."

"Baby, they're all soldiers here." She shook her head, shuffled her papers and sighed. "It's the V.A."

"Yeah, I know I–" It wasn't lost on Molly how she must look. And she knew she couldn't very well say a mystery man in a straw hat told her a riddle and she came here and, oh yeah, she was a super-powered weirdo from whichever god knows where. Molly certainly couldn't remember and–*that was it.* "Forgotten. Forgets."

"What? Kid, you gotta make some sense."

"He can't remember. He was a soldier. He fought in the war. He was a hero." She said that last part and was sure of it. She looked into the nurse's eyes. The nurse was tired, busy, and more than a little annoyed, but she wasn't a bad person. "Just help me find him. Please. Take me to him."

The nurse looked into Molly's eyes, and that thing happened, whatever it was that she did to them.

"Okay, kid. I believe you. I'll get someone to take you down." She grabbed her phone and dialed a number. "Yeah, get me an orderly. I think I got someone here for The Colonel. Yeah, you heard me. Yes. *That* Colonel."

* * *

His name was Colonel John Carthage. He'd fought in basically every war since he'd been born. He signed up with the Army Air Corps right out of high school during the big one, as the orderly told her on the long walk through the endless repeating hallways. He'd been a dogfighter over the western theater. Won a batch of medals. Dropped ordnance all across Korea. Took his commission after that. Worked with special operations. Saw some action again in Vietnam. Led a recon crew into the jungles.

"Found something," the orderly said. He seemed to know about all there was to know about this guy–like he was a fan. "Went bonkers after that. They said he got shell-shocked. Might've been zapped with them space rays or something, man. You know they got all kind of stuff they never tell us about." He stared at Molly as he said it.

He was one of *those* guys. Molly wanted to roll her eyes, but then, *she* was right in front of him, a walking talking big super top secret thing herself. Might as well let him believe. He might be right.

"Did you bring me my Cabbage Patches?" The Colonel demanded as she walked into his room. He stood on top of his dresser, his eyes wild and cocked at her.

"I'm sorry." Molly turned to the orderly who looked uneasy.

"I need my Cabbage Patches!" The Colonel shouted and stamped his foot on the dresser. "They told me they would send them. I have to have them! I can't sleep here without them. They sing away the ghosts." He stared right into Molly's eyes. "They know I'm here."

Molly felt his pain, his confusion. She sucked it all into herself. She reached to calm him with her mind, her voice.

"Oh man, he's off his meds again. He's not safe now." The orderly pulled Molly back, but she pushed him away.

"It's okay. I can help him." She walked into his room. The Colonel retreated further across his dresser, pressing his palms into the ceiling, his breaths short and fast.

"I gotta get The Sergeant. Don't go near him." The orderly ran down the hallway to the nearest nurse station.

Molly eased forward, her hand stretched out, her mind sending soothing energy into The Colonel. She felt it penetrate him, felt him coming back at her with his fear, his confusion.

"It's okay." Molly stepped forward. "I'm never going to hurt you."

"I know that." The Colonel sat down on the dresser. He smiled. "I've waited so long, you know?" He started to well up, his face stifling a quiver. "I did bad things. I hurt people. I'm sorry. I thought I had to. I—" He started to cry as Molly got to him.

She took him in her arms and helped him down toward his bed. She held his head and let him bleed his pain into her. This wasn't what she thought she would find, but it was why she'd come. She knew that now.

"I know." She patted his head with her hands. "I know."

The orderly came back, followed by *The Sergeant.* He was big as the door. He wore the same scrubs as anyone else on the staff, but where they found his size was beyond her. His arms were thick and lithe like wrought iron. His wrists each sported a silver chain bracelet, along with one around his neck. His face hid behind a salted beard, and his hair, widow peaks so far back in his head, almost like a *mohawk.* Molly recognized him—the same man from the bookshop. It couldn't be coincidence. Her life had stopped letting her believe in such things.

"It's you." She stared at him, her eyes arresting his. He looked away from her, back to the orderly.

"Thought you said he was manic again." The Sergeant said at the orderly, small as a child next to the tree trunk man. Lydia was right. He did look like one of her wrestlers, just older—worn down but still dangerous.

"He—he was." The orderly seemed more nervous at The Sergeant than The Colonel.

"Go on, kid. I'll take it from here." The Sergeant patted the orderly on the head and sent him off, his mood, his whole demeanor softening, becoming a different man. "Who are you?" He put his eyes on Molly, his sternness hiding something from her.

"I—I was supposed to come here. I can't explain why. A guy in a straw hat, he..." Molly found herself dumbly emptying her guts in the moment. She caught herself and pulled back, but she'd let out more than she meant to.

"Legba." The big man breathed a long, slow breath and nodded gently at her. He hadn't flinched when she described the strange man on the horse carriage, the riddle, all of it. The Sergeant shook his head, sat down in the chair next to The Colonel's bed. The Colonel stared at him, a whole conversation passing between the two of them unsaid, unknown to anyone else except for Molly. She felt enough of it to know it had happened. They shared the secret The Sergeant held from her.

"I think I'm supposed to find you. Both of you, maybe. I don't—" Molly looked around the room for something, anything.

"I'm gonna give you a piece of advice kid, the best you've ever gotten in your life." The Sergeant studied Molly as she busied about the room on her hunt. "Get the hell out of this town as fast and as far as you can."

Molly glanced back at him; his head hung down in that moment. He slipped for just a second and she felt his *shame*. He drowned in it. Just as quick as he slipped, he bottled it back up, became stern again. The Colonel looked at his friend, asking a question with his eyes.

Molly found something in a box against the far wall, an old baseball. "Look, I know I'm here for a reason. I can help with whatever's happening here."

"No." The Sergeant sighed. "You can't. And the ones who can *won't*."

Molly gripped the ball, showed it to The Colonel. "Is this terribly precious to you?"

The Colonel shook his head like he'd never seen it before.

"Look kid, I'm telling you—"

Molly crunched the baseball in her hand, crumpling it and dropping the pieces beneath her. She stared into both men's eyes. She nodded to each of them again.

"I'm supposed to be here. I don't know why, but I am. Tell me that I can't help you." Molly looked at the Sergeant, locking her jaw. "Tell me you've ever seen anything like that before."

The Sergeant sighed. "I can tell you're new here."

* * *

Outside the hospital, up the street in the walk-up bar, Lydia sipped her drink and ran her fingers across the arcade games. She let out a breath, wishing Molly would hurry, not that it mattered. Soon as she got done with this weirdness, it would be another night of her and their new friend running around town playing ninjas while she sat in the apartment listening to their radios and making tapes of dumb thugs spouting nonsense. Lydia felt very small.

She looked at the games. They had a Mrs. Pac-Man, a racing game, and some poker games. Over in the corner was one of those make-a-wish games with the bust of a genie inside, like a creepy puppet. If you got your coin in his mouth, he'd grant your wish. She looked into its dead eyes—the lights were off, probably busted or not plugged in—and sighed.

"I wish I could be more like Molly." She knocked her knuckle against the glass case holding the genie inside. "I wish I had a power, or...something." Lydia righted herself, gathered up her shoulders again. She'd make something of the night and have another drink. A group of girls at the bar looked at her. She'd noticed them walk in, their rad punk style, studded leather, black lace, chokers, the works. They'd been hard to miss. Their ringleader—a platinum blonde with spiked bangs, hair cropped short in front, and flowing long out the back—gave Lydia a full up-down inspection.

"Hey, kid." She nodded to Lydia. "I'm Étoile. What's your name?"

IX
"WILD THING"
—TONE LOC, 1989

THE LAST THING LYDIA WANTED to do was go work a full eight-hour shift doing her mail rounds. Sure, the job paid more than she'd ever seen in her short life so far, but, hell, she was just out of high school, and it was summer. She should be sleeping in, hanging out with a black-haired beautiful police boy—or maybe not— she still hadn't told him she'd gone to his least favorite city and had exactly what he always said would happen...*happen.* She'd given up on getting her brother's truck back. She could save up, get a new one, get Andi to fix it up again. Poor Andi, Lydia thought to herself. Back home playing doppleganger for Molly with no one but Becky as a friend and coach, and that was poor company on a good day. She'd called and checked on her twice this week, lied and said everything was fine. Andi mentioned working a case with Nguyen—*her* Nguyen—and Lydia felt a tinge of jealousy...toward a robot. Now this town really was getting to her.

At least she'd finally met someone cool, something she hadn't mentioned to the dynamic duo.

"Nix the uniforms for today." Murph poured them a coffee as Molly shrugged and tossed her work shirt in the hamper. Lydia made hers a double and thanked the gods she wasn't going to wander boring halls passing out memos all day. But, she sighed because it surely meant Murph had a worse job planned for them.

"What's up, boss?" Molly sat on the barstool and spun herself to make eye contact with Lydia. She'd been down after her mystery meeting in the VA but was peppy enough this morning.

"Shopping. What size gowns you girls wear? We're going to a party tonight."

* * *

In the time the girls had known her, they'd seen already a half a dozen versions of Murphy Long, but they'd yet to see the woman that exited the master bedroom of the deluxe suite of the Windsor. Already tall, the six-inch stilettos put her well over even Molly's height (though Molly had gained at least another half inch since they got here). Her sparkling red gown set the room on fire and her onyx eyes reflected the lights, twinkling like the first stars in the night. Her hair flowed down like a black river draping her face—made up to show off her every feature.

Lydia gulped and found herself almost jealous again. Between the super-powered cherry-hair and now the perfect-ten rogue cop, she was definitely the squeaky third wheel. Murph opted to put Lydia in a pants suit, having her play the role of the driver. In fairness, it was the sharpest outfit Lydia had ever worn and worth more than she would clear in a month at the new job. Plus, it meant she got to drive that slick Ferrari, so she didn't complain.

* * *

The Royal St. Charles had been purchased and remodeled some years back by one Mr. Jack Germain, billionaire, playboy, and general philanthropic venture capitalist. He made the top three floors his personal in-town penthouse. His parties were the toast of the city, and he had them often. Murph told them as much as she knew on the drive up Canal, all while watching Lydia's lead foot like a hawk.

The three of them exited the red Ferrari like power brokers, the girls falling in line behind Murphy. Lydia wanted to hate it—she did—but the car, the suit, a full-on ballroom party full of the richest people she could imagine, it was all so far out. She tried not to trip on herself. She couldn't wait to tell Étoile. They'd hit it off over their drink the other night. Lydia had showed her the grimoire she bought at the bookshop the first night in town, and Étoile even knew how to read some of the words.

"Guy sounds like a winner." Molly took it all in, walking through the foyer into the main lobby toward the elevators. They were directed to the express elevator, Germain having requested it for the guests this evening.

"That's a way to put it. Guy shows up maybe ten years back, walks into a major inheritance left dormant for years. Orphaned as a kid, apparently. You almost feel bad for the guy. Almost." Murph nodded to the elevator attendant to take them to the top.

"What's he like?" Molly hung on that word: *orphan.*

"Search me. He's hardly ever around—lets the board run the business, do whatever they want. He's a night owl from what I've heard. I've never even seen the guy." Murph took them off the elevator and into the wolves' den.

* * *

The spectacle left Molly dumbstruck. She'd seen wealth up close and personal with Blake back home, Becky even, but not like this. She saw men's watches worth more than her parents' house. Women's jewelry that cost more than half a block. The buffet spread would make a small country blush. And they gambled it all away like it was water. Roulette tables. Craps. Blackjack. A whole mini casino set up just for the occasion. The floor-to-ceiling tinted windows on the opposite wall gave a god's eye view over the city. People of every age and some seemingly ageless flitted and flirted about. Wives, husbands, marriages, all meaningless words at a thing like this.

Murph called out the key players. She'd made some dummy clutch purses, each with a wireless lav mic in them. The girls could conveniently *misplace* them where Murph thought she could glean the most info.

"There's the mayor, chief of police next to him. The Executive VP of Cain Capital behind us." She pointed discreetly, directing Lydia to the mark. "Far corner is some Hollywood bigwigs, don't know 'em all, but the fat one's name is Weinstein."

They mingled, smiling and fawning as Murph taught them to do. "Just defer, no matter what they say," she'd told them on the way over. "For chrissakes, don't break anything, or anyone." She'd aimed that comment at Molly. They were there just for intel, she insisted. She kept pointing out the guests. The D.A. was in tow, a bunch of billionaires, New York real estate moguls, she said, one she mentioned even had his own private island.

"And that's—" Murph raised an eyebrow, curling her lip. "The governor of Arkansas and his wife. The hell are they doing here?"

* * *

Murph targeted her girls like a battalion commander. Lydia, acting as her attaché, got away with carrying the larger bag, holding most of their spy gear. Molly had mentioned it must have cost a fortune.

"Yeah but not mine." Murph had chuckled. "If you think about it, we're just giving it right back to Germain since it came out of his expense account. Guy's so loaded he won't even notice."

"Which one is he?" Molly craned her neck to look around the vast array of suits and gowns. They blurred into one another.

"You know I've never even laid eyes on the guy. Why don't you poke around and find out. And kid—" Murph stressed at Molly with her eyes.

"Yeah yeah. I got it. Don't break anything."

Molly wandered, noticing Murph ingratiate herself next to the mayor and police chief at the roulette table. The woman was smooth as butter. Not ten seconds and she had the mayor's eyes locked to her while the police chief's wife stared bolts into her back. Molly wondered if Murph was entirely on the up-and-up, but she'd felt a deep core of decency in the woman. The night in the alley gave Molly pause about her. But, whatever else she was and may have done, Murph had never gone all the way over the edge.

Making her way toward the long windows, Molly gazed down on the city. They were easily three times the height of the Windsor up here. The town really did look small. The newer buildings going up would be even taller, especially the Lili, the one Murph talked about. From the corner of her eye, Molly caught that governor dude scoping her which was just *ew, no.* He cackled with that private island guy Murph mentioned, but his eye slimed onto her everywhere she went.

Watching him instead of herself, trying to evade his gaze, Molly bumped into some guy in a tux. They were all in tuxes, but his was different—not as lavish but better cut. He had the figure for it, too. Tall but not huge. Muscled, she could tell from bracing herself against his arm, but again not outlandish. He had sharp features to his face. He looked maybe thirty but could be a great-looking forty. He looked as confused and out of place as she felt.

"Oh sorry, clumsy me." Molly tried to fake giggle, but she was terrible at it. It only made her more buffoonish in the moment. He had interesting eyes. Serious. Sad.

"No, no, not at all." He smiled. He was not something she hated looking at. "Entirely my fault. Can I get you a drink?"

Molly noticed he already had one in his hand, a dark red wine. Molly knew squat about wines.

"Oh, um. That's okay. Doubt I need another one, you know?" She chuckled. That one was involuntary. Why did this guy give her goosebumps? *She* didn't get goosebumps. *Stay on the mission, Molly,* she told herself. "Say, you wouldn't know which of these dudes is Jack Germain, would you?"

Dudes? God on skates, Molly, what are you 12 again? She shook her head. She wanted to crawl away and blush and hide. This was... *no not like Easton.* Not like that. But something. She took a breath.

"Yeah, I don't think any of these *dudes* is him." He smiled again. That devilish smile.

"Yeah thanks. Sorry again." Molly bailed. She zipped across the ballroom to escape her embarrassment. Of course, the one cute guy at this weird rich people party and she would shove her whole entire foot right in her face and besides why was she even looking at new dudes anyway? The whole point here was to be sad and miss the one she loved and lost and this was just weird and wrong and now that guy was looking at her again and she split off down a hallway.

* * *

"Well, your honor, I think you should bet it all. You can always raise taxes a little if you lose, right?" Murph laughed with the mayor as she took a swig of her martini. Lydia, the good little actress it turned out, hit her with another one, three olives on a toothpick and everything. Unbeknownst to the marks, Lydia had been pouring them out in the bathroom and filling them with water. Murph played quite the lush.

"You better watch this one, Mayor. She'll have her hand in the emergency fund before the night's over." The D.A. cackled as he bet his chips on black. The Chief of Police hesitated. "Come on, De Gras, time to live dangerously." He munched a cigar as he grinned at Murph and gave her a wink.

She winked right back and curled the corner of her lips into a thin smile.

"So, you ran for election on reform, I hear." Murph teased her glass some. "What sort of plans you have in mind?" Her eyes danced with his, getting him drunker than the double Scotch in his left hand.

The mayor got quiet. The Police Chief narrowed his eyes. The D.A. calmed him with a touch on his shoulder and laughed it off.

"I heard an odd rumor just yesterday about some old vigilante. What's that about?"

A pin dropped at that. Even the jocular D.A. got quiet.

"I–" The Mayor looked around the room, then to his two compatriots. "I have no comment on that. I've taken measures to make this town safer than it's ever been. If you'll excuse me." He took off toward the restrooms, leaving his chips on the table. The D.A.'s winsome humor returned, but the Police Chief kept his eye on her.

"Haven't I seen you before?" He squinted, getting a read on her face.

"Oh, I'm sure you have," Murphy said more to his wife than The Chief. That sorted that problem *right* out. Every time. His wife whisked that man away faster than he could clear his head of the image Murphy knew good and well she put there. Men were so damn easy; Murph laughed to herself.

Deftly leaving a clutch at the table, she made her way through the room again. Caught the chief sneaking another glare her way before he got into a chat with a uniform blue that came in from the hallway outside. That could be something. Murph found Lydia and ordered her to that corner with her eyes. *Now, where was the damn redhead?* She gave her *one* job.

Kids.

* * *

Molly found herself in the paintings adorning the long hallway toward the opposite wing of the massive Penthouse. It was like an entire mansion atop a high rise. She'd had a pretty terrible experience with wealth before, but she tried to remind herself that was an anomaly. They weren't all a bunch of goblin-like monsters out to bend this world to their evil will, surely.

Whoever this Germain guy was, he sure had better taste than Blake had. These were great paintings. She'd even seen some of them in books. Old stuff. Statues on pedestals. Busts of maidens, warriors, kings. Hanging tapestries. She felt lost in it. Like it told a story of the world from the very beginning.

"There you are." Murph's voice woke Molly from her reverie. "The hell you doing down here? We're on the clock, Red." Murph took her by the arm and started to drag her back to the party, but they both got distracted by the open door where they stood.

"I don't know if we should–"

Murph's sneer cut Molly's sentence off before it could make her feel any dumber than she already did. She did a quick glance around and slipped in behind her sly companion.

Murph's cynical, seen-it-all eyes widened when they walked into the long room. A mural on the wall depicted a massive squidlike monster wrecking ships at sea. Across both sides of the room stood armored statues of varying sizes, all large men, some bordering on gigantic. Murph stared at them one by one, as did Molly, calling them out by the placards in front of them.

"Nimrod. Samson. Heracles?" Murph tilted her head at that one. A gargantuan of a man, draped in a lion's skin—a club nearly as big as himself braced in his arms. Murph looked at Molly who just shrugged. "Surely not *The*—you know."

The statues continued. Bellerophon. A more primitive and gruesome one in matted fur and ill-fitted iron armor. Sigurd, its placard read. The one next to it, similar, bigger even, labeled Beowulf.

They were so caught up in staring at the fascinating statues and their all-too-real armor and accoutrements, they didn't notice the man standing behind them, admiring them as much as they admired the *art*, if they could call it that.

"And how do you say this one?" Murph pointed down at its placard with her foot. "Leo-Nid-ass?"

"Leonidas." The man moved toward them as he said it. Molly turned, ice crawling like a spider down her spine to her legs—the same man she'd bumped into earlier. The one with the hot coffee eyes and the way-too-confident smile. "It's Spartan." He looked at Molly.

"How's that?" Murph folded her arms. Molly felt her tensing up, not liking being caught off guard. But, this guy *was* arresting. There was—Molly couldn't put her finger on it—something about him.

"He was king of Sparta. A hero, some say. But every man's hero is another's villain. He stood against an empire. He lost. But then all empires lose, eventually. Just like all heroes eventually die."

"And you are?" Murph squinted her eyes at the guy.

"Oh. Right. Sorry. Jack Germain." He offered his hand and smiled. Like that lost boy Molly first bumped into.

"Are you sure?" Molly folded her arms. She didn't love games like this.

"Well, I said it wasn't any of *those* dudes out there, didn't I?" He smiled at her again and winked.

"Wow. In the very flesh." Murph put a hand on her hip. *Was she trying to flirt with him?* And why did that bother Molly so much? "Regina Hammond." She put her hand in his and shook it like a man, her grip impressing him from the look on his face. "VP in Development. Ms. Slater here is my assistant. You're our boss."

"Well, boss is a bit far. I usually leave the day to day stuff to—"

"Sir." Came the voice of one of the servants at the doorway of the war room, or whatever this place was. "Some of the guests are beginning to depart."

"Oh, right. Well, that's—who?" He appeared lost in his thoughts for a moment, looking first at Murph, then Molly, then back to Murph.

"Mayor Mainotte and Chief De Gras, sir. Also, your friends from Arkansas."

"Right." Germain looked back at the girls. "I've got to see about a thing. You two enjoy the party. Maybe run into you again later." He winked at Molly.

He was out the door as quickly as he'd slipped in, leaving the two of them more confused than when he arrived.

"What was that about?" Murph squinted, then looked at Molly who threw her shoulders up. "And who even has a room like this? The fuck?"

X
"SHAKEDOWN"
—BOB SEGAR, 1987

MURPH SLID OUT OF HER DRESS in the front seat of the car like she'd done it a thousand times. Molly didn't want to know how to acquire that skill. She sat in the back, struggling not to rip through the sequin gown and get into her black tights. She understood the clandestine thing, she did, but it just put a crimp in her whole raison d'etre. Molly *wanted* people to see her, to see hope, to see something good. Something they could believe in.

Murph had the mini Nagra in her lap that had been running the whole evening in the car, steady reeling its tape back and forth listening for...something. Molly shoved her arm too hard through the tight knit shirt and ripped the sleeve off. Murph shook her head.

"Okay, got something." She played the tape. Muffled voices. Clinking glasses. She turned the volume up.

"Tell me what's up?" The Chief's voice came across muffled, but it was him.

"Got a tip. Something's going down at the old power plant."

"So, why's that warrant pulling me out of a meeting with the mayor?"

"Filles Purdue, Loups-Garous." the other voice said.

"The devil will have my head if we don't get down there. Come on, let's go."

Murph turned off the tape as Molly ripped off the other sleeve to match.

"Loup-Garous?" Molly looked at Lydia.

"Yeah." Murph switched off the radio and shook her head at Molly's destroyed outfit. "I swear, kid. Loups-Garous. Remnants of an old gang called The Red Mutants. Got run out of town years ago. But a handful stayed. Real badasses, from what I hear. Cops hate them. But they stay off the radar, mostly. Stick to the shadows. Whatever this is, sounds like its big enough to look into."

* * *

Murph had them leave the car a block away, planning to sneak in on foot. She ordered Lyd to stay with the car, doors locked, monitoring the radio. She was about to direct Red, but Molly had already launched into the sky, the dark outfit making her all but invisible in the shadows of the night.

"It's still gonna take me a minute to get used to that." Murph pulled her .45 and kept it in the low ready position, sidewinding her way down the dim alley toward the old Market Street power station.

She scurried along, dodging what few lights there were. Just to the south side of the building, she caught a glimpse of movement above her. She motioned the go-ahead to take the roof of the plant. Murph raced along, eyes skinned for anything that might shoot at her. Or worse.

"Can you see anything up there?" She kept her voice to a whisper into her mic. Some garble came back, then a "Not really."

Murph snuck along until she was near the loading docks. She crouched on instinct. There was a light and voices. A batch of weirdos in black getups and spiked hair mulled around a couple of single-unit freight trucks. They loaded boxes onto each one, a few on lookout, but no guns she could see. That was maybe something she could use.

"Hey, kid, you read me?"

"Yeah."

"Look, hang loose for a second, but watch my back. I'm gonna try something." Murph clicked the safety on her pistol and tucked it away. She pulled her beanie off her head and let her hair out. She ran back a half a block where she'd passed a filthy, torn box of Mardi-Gras shirts (probably fell of a truck headed to or from the big warehouse up the river). She pulled the biggest one out, put it on. Rubbed some dirt on her face, grabbed an empty bottle from the gutter and wandered toward the trucks.

The gang moving the product—whatever it was—didn't seem too chatty. They moved almost like machines. They saw her bumbling her way up to the trucks, dangling the bottle and humming some song out of tune.

"Say, any you help me out I'm just trying to get on back to Metairie. I just need a dollar or two to get a cab." She sealed it with a hiccup at the end.

"Get lost, dog feed." One of them moved toward her, sniffing her.

"No, I need to get back. I could just ride along in the back or hold on or something. If you give me a ride or a dollar. Just two dollars be enough, I can get the rest." Murph pressed her luck and went for a closer look at the cargo. They got antsy, and one from the truck jumped down. Barely bent her knees when she landed and didn't make a sound. She had almost stark white hair cut in a mullet and spiked in the front. Black and leather all over her.

It was a good con, and one she'd run a hundred times before, and it would have worked if the blue lights hadn't ruined the party. The black coats scattered, most of them running into the building or making a break down the street. Murph froze for the moment, giving a subtle hand signal for Molly to do the same. She turned and smiled as uniformed officers approached her and the half-loaded rigs.

"Why hi, officers!" She grinned a toothy grin. "I was just about to dial up your number, you see, 'cause I think there's something funny going on here, you know some kind of funny business. I was just happening along, and I saw all this doing and whatnot down here and at this time of the night and you know, I figured I'd just—"

"Shut up." An officer pointed his gun at her face. He leaned over to his radio on his shoulder. "Yes sir. We've got movement in the building and out the back. Sending in units... No sir, no sign of... will do, sir."

The truck behind Murphy rumbled to life followed by the one next to it. The cops shouted, some shooting at the tires, others yelling into the radios and scrambling for their vehicles. Others ran into the building after the rest of the gang.

"Kid, if you can hear me, get inside and see what you can see." Murph didn't waste her shot. She sprinted for the moving truck, cargo doors still swinging. She leapt and snatched the locking handle of the door just as it swung wide and slammed her against the side of the rig. She knew she'd feel that in the morning. She tried to kick herself off the side and swing back around into the cargo hold, but they took a curve and she flew out again. She caught a glimpse of the driver through the side mirror, their eyes meeting. Now they actively tried to shake her off, aiming for the walls of the buildings as they barreled through the empty streets.

Murph managed to swing her door away from the oncoming walls and traffic. Any second now, she'd fling out again. She closed her eyes, took a deep breath, focused. Somewhere she could hear her father's voice. She *could* do this. She let out her breath, held the door with one hand, pulled her pistol with her other. In a fluid movement, she swung her door out and fired twice into the rear tires, blowing one out. The truck swerved, lost control and careened toward the buildings on the passenger side. Murph saw an opening and leapt for a low balcony, grabbing the railing as the truck slammed to a halt, smashing into a parked Volvo.

The driver bailed and didn't wait around for the blue lights to show up. He took off into the night before Murph got a solid look at him. She caught her breath and her bearings, dropped to the ground and headed for the wreck. She jumped into the open hold and tore into the boxes, not knowing what she'd find but never expected what she saw.

"Masks?" She held one up into the light from the street. Just cheap plastic Mardi Gras masks. She checked more boxes—all the same. It didn't make any sense. "Kid." She gripped the radio button from the receiver miraculously still stuck in her pocket. "Tell me you got something."

XI
"SAME OLD SITUATION"
—MÖTLEY CRÜE, 1989

MOLLY SWEPT THROUGH the old power plant, seasoned over the years with graffiti and trash. Someone had been using it recently. She smelled the electricity in the air. There was movement beneath her, goons walking the gangways on the upper level. More ran into the building, shutting the docking bay doors. In the brief distraction, Molly dropped behind one of them like a cat. Before he could turn, she thumped his head and sent him to sleep.

Murph's voice garbled in her ear. Something about masks. Molly didn't want to speak, lest she alert them to her presence. She ducked into a corner, reached down with her senses. These...*people...* They were different somehow. Their feelings were dim, lifeless. She'd never sensed anything quite like it.

* * *

Far to the opposite end of the plant, beneath Molly, in the sealed-off section used for their experiment, two women watched their monitors, switching between cameras. The police outside would break through any minute. Dr. Bianca Tesche gathered notes and materials, shoving what she could into a satchel. Evilyn Jareth watched the television monitors, then glanced around her as if she felt a chill in the air.

"Something is here." She looked off into nowhere. Then back at Bianca.

"Oh no." Bianca shook and looked around her, the coldness visible on her face. "Is it *him?*"

"No." Evilyn smiled. "I'd know if it was. He doesn't like to reveal himself. Lets his police dogs do his bidding now. This is...something new."

The crashing sounds from the entrance reported that the police—the night shift—had broken through. It was always just a matter of time. A few more days wouldn't have made much of a difference. Now was as good a time as any to try her golem.

"Wake the Axe-man." Evilyn whispered as she drew a chalk circle in on the wall and stepped through it into an abyss.

Seconds later, she walked out into the control room above the main floor. She cranked the generators, roaring the old facility back to life. They would need all the power this place could still produce. She yanked levers back, sending the amps surging through the cables, sparks and sizzles popping as the old infrastructure threatened to give way.

She saw her acolytes, those poor damned souls, they would give everything they had gained to serve her purpose—a necessary sacrifice. Then she felt it again. One of hers went down, moments later another—but not dead. Something—someone only knocked them out, tying them up. Surely it couldn't be...? No, that flame had long since burned out. Her minions or not, *D* would just kill them, like he did all the rest.

* * *

As the main doors gave in, an army of police burst through, their sound cacophoning through the charged facility. Shouts rang through the rusted corridors as Jareth's people scrambled. The cops formed a front line, shotguns and rifles at the ready. An officer with a bullhorn demanded everyone come out.

Molly continued dispatching goons quietly. She caught one off guard and looped a chain around his legs, ripping them from under him and popping him in the temple. She hadn't quite knocked him cold, though, as he began to shout, his voice ringing throughout the plant. These were tougher than the average goons she was used to.

As the rest of her foes either fled or fell before her, Molly leapt for the top of the building, aiming to make a quick and quiet exit from the plant, see what she could from up high, and touch base with her crew.

Then she felt it. Something crashed through a wall, wailing and booming with every stomp of its feet. Sparks and electricity shot all around it. Molly looked down as the police opened fire into... some kind of monster.

She sighed, took a breath. Murph would yell at her for this, but there wasn't exactly a choice. She thudded down onto the floor in front of it, catching a barrage of gunfire into her back as the cops didn't care to differentiate. The thing was an instant reminder of the undead creatures Blake had sent for her back home. This one was different, though. Electricity coursed through its veins. She smelled every volt, almost intoxicating her—or something not unlike that. It wore a goalie's mask that looked bolted onto its head. Its rotten flesh bulged with new muscle as its height easily reached eight feet or more. And it...sang?

"Oh when them saints!" it muttered as it hurled itself at her. Molly ran for it, but it swatted her with a massive axe, shooting her into the side wall of the power plant. The monster charged into the line of cops, slamming its axe down onto them, hewing one of them in two like he was made of butter. "Oh when them saints!" It pulled the weapon back, now dripping with the rapidly-blackening blood of the slain officer, its strangely bright, silvery blade gleaming in the flashing lights from the electric current coursing through its body and all about the plant.

The other police panicked at the sight of their fallen comrade. Shouts, screams rang as many of them retreated and ran for safety. From behind cover, they resumed firing their weapons at it.

Molly got to her feet, got her bearings. The rampaging creature tore through rusted metal railings like tin foil. It raked across the chest of another cop with its axe blade and the cop fell to the ground, his face rotting like a decomposed corpse in an instant. *What the hell was that blade?* Molly asked herself the question as she reached behind her for a set of her own. She slid the twins out of each other, the snake and the wolf she'd inherited from Blake.

She ran for the creature, slid under its swiping axe, sprang up and shoved one blade directly into its heart all the way to the hilt, which did—nothing.

"Oh when them saints!" The monster seized her with its other hand and smashed her against the floor repeatedly. That annoyed her. She gripped her remaining weapon, flicked the switch to lengthen the blade and sliced the arm holding her right off.

She leapt up, kicked it in the chest, hurling it away from her. She gripped the handle of her short sword, zeroing her eye on the other one that lay sunk in the thing's chest. Then she watched in amazement as arcs of electricity reached out of its stump of a severed arm and began to form a new arm.

"Oh, like hell you get to do that." Molly ran at the creature and it flung its excess voltage off its newly made arm and into her body. The arcs lit into her skin, coursed through her, giving her that tingling sensation she'd felt the time she fought her twin sister. Her mind flashed for a split second. Some woman, green-skinned, gold hair, holding a weapon, a spear. A memory? Molly came out of it. Then, as if by some forgotten instinct, she threw the electricity out of her body with her other hand, right back into the beast, knocking it backward.

So, this was new. She made a note of it for later—after she finished the job.

* * *

In the observation room, two women stared into the monitors as the scene played out. Dr. Tesche, having studied the arcane science of the other world for a decade, watched the culmination of her life's work dismantled with precision ease by the black clad form of what appeared to be a teenager. More to her dismay, she turned to her compatriot and benefactor and saw the hungry, toothy smile of Evilyn Jareth who seemed to revel in their failure.

The figure on the screen retrieved the dagger from the corpse's heart, doubled the length of its blade in an instant as she had the other before. Now, armed with two swords, she made quick work of what remained of their project, their great plan to unleash upon the city, *his* city. She spiraled and spun and sliced. Arms, legs, then she took its head.

"He—" Tesche shook her head, sighing. "He never stood a chance."

Jareth's smile grew wider, her eyes in lust at the sight of the dual-wielding swordswoman on their screen, now instinctively looking toward the camera.

"No." Jareth licked the front of her top teeth, lingering on her canines. "He didn't." She drew another circle on the wall.

XII
"POST MORTEM"
—SLAYER, 1986

BACK AT MURPH'S, Lydia slumped on the couch, both relieved to be back and aggravated at the other two sharing their exploits with one another—yet again. Being there in person for it this time had only made her feel all the more useless. And the way Murph bolted and leapt onto the moving truck, like some stuntwoman out of an action movie—*what even was that?* Molly was a horse of another color, she'd long accepted that. But Murph made her feel that much smaller, more pointless.

Maybe she should just go home. *Where Robo-Molly will still make me feel like nothing,* she considered. She couldn't win from losing.

As Molly finished her account of the events, Murph rolled it over in her head. Her eyes grew wider as Lydia could tell her sense of the world—and whatever lay beyond it—grew as well. *Welcome to my life,* Lydia felt in her mind. She clicked on the TV, lowering the sound, and turned to see if anything was on the news about what happened. Zilch. Just something about the new tower opening soon, Maggie Thatcher coming to town, and some science guy driving a rocket-truck through the desert.

* * *

Murph couldn't wrap her head around what Molly told her. The stupid masks in the truck still vexed her. Who would go to any length of trouble over a bunch of cheap plastic masks? What was the real contraband? What had she gotten herself into? Her father's maniacal superstitions crawled their way back into her brain. Murphy tried to shake out the spiders, but the super kid smiling at her as she wolfed down pizza and cereal was the real deal. And that monster. The Hēishǒu Móguǐ. All of it. And masks? She grabbed hold of the wrong truck was all she could think of to rationalize it. *Why all that, for stupid masks?*

EPISODE III

"MASTER AND SERVANT"
–DEPECHE MODE, 1984

THE PRINCE OF DARKNESS stared out over the starlit bog. He tried to remember why he'd first come here, *when* even. He reached back through his younger selves, half of them long forgotten, bound to this hurdling rock for an eternity—one he felt every waking moment of. How old was he now? He knew time was but an illusion, but he felt it the same as they did, those pitiful concoctions of the gods, to him nothing more than food—or the occasional plaything.

Perhaps it had been the music? He did enjoy that. A New World, they had called this place. He'd heard those words in one language or another at least a thousand times. And soon there would be another, and another. Would he be crushed under a mountain when the earth ruptured and tore itself apart? Drowned as the world flooded again, or trapped in another ice age, frozen immobile but his shattered mind ever awake? How he longed to cross to the next realm. His dark matriarch even now plotted to undo reality, as she did every few millennia. Perhaps this time, she might even succeed. But would waking the dreamer end his hated existence? Or would that still not lift his eternal curse? But he had long stopped praying for death. Who would *he* pray to? Certainly not the god who did this to him. Nor the others who looked away as he'd suffered so long.

Perhaps it was the gateway. The new conquerors had merely seen a hill to build their city upon, irrespective of any who'd been here before. He'd felt it the first time he set his foot on this soil. A myriad of dead souls, some still wandering this plane, some coming and going. Such places existed throughout this spinning rock—doorways where the veil between life and death grew thin, thinner at each turn of the season. Those with knowledge of it could pass through, come and go. But not him. He would never cross over. All because a drunken god demanded blood.

"My lord." Evilyn bowed before him. Her spiked boots hadn't made their usual sound marching into his throne room. *Or had they?* He ceased minding her comings and goings so much. She brought him food—as he commanded her, as she deserved. Her punishment for allying herself with that comical fool. A joke, it had all been, the very idea some mortal in a silly helmet could rival Him? Thus, his favorite name for his pet, a trophy of that sad little war.

"My Jester Queen." He licked his lips, his long black tongue finding his jagged, brutal teeth. His yellow, beastly eyes settled on her dim face from the candles burning around the room. "Tell me, my pet, what is it has come to *my* city? I sense something...different." It was true enough. Its presence had not escaped him. Indeed, it unnerved him. Something, *someone* powerful had arrived. He thought of his half-brother, the great wolf bound so long in that unnatural chain—the very chain that, according to the prophecy, a chosen one would wield against him. But he, Belial Qayin the Ever-Living, had defeated that prophecy when his Black Hands, his Hēishǒu Móguǐ, wiped out the ancient order that guarded that foul concoction of the Fae against his own kin. But even his brother had broken free of his bond—only to be cut down—by yet another petty god. How he hated gods, all of them—even She who bore him.

"Indeed, my lord. I have found something you will wish to possess." Evilyn stood, her head bowed before him. "I shall deliver her to you soon."

Evilyn turned and proceeded down the long hall, the candles licking her eyes as she walked away, a curling smile on her lips.

I
"HUNGRY TOWN"
—BIG PIG, 1986

MURPH DROPPED STACK after stack of the folded gray sheets of newsprint— having grabbed a copy of everything they had on hand in the lobby—slapping them on the glass coffee table. Molly removed her well-worn Converse as the papers slid and fell.

"*Picayune, Gazette, Daily News, Register.* Hell, even *The Advertiser.*" She folded out the front pages of all them, picking them up one at a time. "Nothing. Not so much as a word about what went down at the plant last night. Hell, kid, I saw electricity shooting into the night sky from eight blocks away. Half an army of cops saw that thing you fought—and *you* fighting it! And not one paper has the story? Or even a bad lie to cover for it?"

Murph slumped into the soft white chair at the head of the coffee table, wrinkling her left eye. Lydia zoned out, clicking the channels, settling as always on MTV. Salt & Pepa whispered in the background as Murph shook her head at her slipping grip on what she could still be sure was real. She'd seen a hundred textbook cover-ups in her career but never anything of this scale. It was as if every part of this town worked in unison toward maintaining the same great lie: city hall, the cops, big business, the media, even the gangs, all connected. She couldn't fathom the kind of iron hand it would take to hold something like that together, without so much as a crack of truth slipping through.

"I'm telling you, this town stinks to high heaven." Murph looked out the window at the dim sun, still new in the morning sky—the clouds that hung over this town rolling in. She let it calm her. Things here always seemed better, calmer in the light—what little there was. Like whatever awfulness that poisoned this place slept when the sun was out. "Walk me through it all again." Murph's hands shook as she poured her coffee.

Molly started on another recap of the fight with the big axe-man.

Lydia noticed the stress Murphy wore on her face. She'd taken to observing the two of them, as she'd long done Molly since the whole *super* thing started. Something bothered their newfound companion, and it went well beyond what happened last night. She could tell Molly's senses were off too. The Sledgehammer had her big mission, a new mystery, some grand darkness to dispel from the world. Again.

Lydia knew better than to question a word Molly said about it. If she said an eight-foot-tall axe-wielding maniac corpse shooting with electricity came alive and sang old jazz tunes, then those were the facts of it—god's pure gospel. She listened to Molly give Murph the greatest hits of their Blake ordeal—again. Lydia saw his face across the sky as it had been the night of prom. She shivered at the memory.

She walked to the windows, staring at the town as they talked. Somewhere down in her gut, Lydia knew she should cut her losses, write off the truck, and head home. She didn't belong here with the important people fixing the wrongs of the world. She didn't really belong back home either. Her brothers, her dad, they loved her, sure. But she never fit in with them. Since her mom took off, it was just a gang of guys and her, dressed in black, listening to Sabbath and Depeche Mode records. *This* city was supposed to be her escape. Dragging Molly along was an excuse to come to town. This place—what it had always been in her mind—it hadn't turned out like she thought. Nguyen feared this town, and he grew up here. Maybe he had a reason after all. *I should go home.* Lydia thought of that fortune teller their first night in town. She looked at her palm, then at the gray clouds swallowing the sky. It was going to be *another* dreary day. Another day without the sun.

II
"EDGE OF A BROKEN HEART"
—VIXEN, 1988

MURPH JOGGED A BLOCK or two before her racing mind slowed her legs to little more than a fast walk. The faces of the city blurred around her. Oblivious to whatever devils had rooted here—or worse yet, *not oblivious.* How deep did it all go? What did the dots connect to?

She trudged on another block before deciding the run wasn't happening today. She needed answers. She needed to think—somewhere by herself, without the bubblegum brigade up her ankles every second. She already knew where.

* * *

Fitting her ear protection, standing in the number four stall, Murph laid out her spare mags along the bench table. She hit the button to send the paper target downrange. She'd paid for an hour, already thinking she might make it two. This wasn't her first time at the Gretna Gun Works. She'd found the joint less than a week after arriving in town. It was always good to stay in practice, and she could pick up tips at the range. Gunners got chatty with her pretty quick. They didn't run across many like her at the range. And besides that, shooting calmed her nerves.

She slapped a mag into her Colt, sent the slide home, gripped, steadied herself, righted her aim, breathed, and squeezed off her first round. The report rang through the thinly attended range. Another stall down from her followed suit, a 9mil from the sound of it.

Murph fired again. She blinked her eyes at the sound and opened them on the sight of her old house. She was four, maybe five. Her mom stood in the kitchen watching her play on the ground with her father. She would climb up on the couch, raise her arms, and then fly off the couch and slam onto his belly, the two of them bellowing out laughter at each other each time she did, her mother's giggles echoing along behind them. Her father's eyes glowed at her, lighting up with each smile she sent him.

Murph sent another round downrange. The pop of her pistol, its slide slamming home again, priming for the next shot, sent her wandering brain to the sight of that goofy gas gun. She smirked at how silly it had been, and how badly she'd wanted one. She saw The Hornet, stiff and wooden now that she looked back from her current perspective. And there was Kato, flying in with a kick, a chop, and a body throw—always the real star of that series. She saw her younger self leaping off the couch, mirroring his movements: kick, chop, block. Her dad walked in the room, his eyes—more somber now—looking at her flailing motions.

"Not like that," Murph heard his stern voice in her head. He gripped her wrists and walked her through a set of basic motions, mostly blocks and defensive moves.

Her mother watched them again, this time without the smile on her lips—just a thin flat line.

She wiped the sweat off her head despite the cold chill running through her trembling body, everything but her arms and hands—those steady as rocks. She gripped the pistol and sent the last of her magazine into the paper. She dropped it into her free hand and popped in the next one. The guy over from her, breaking in a new Beretta from the looks of the shine on the piece, raised an eyebrow at her. She ignored his leer and pressed on with her shots.

She'd lied to the girls about quite a bit, but it wasn't her first time in the city. She was born not far away but left before she could remember anything from the place. Her mother used to tell her stories of the old New Orleans. She did remember Houston a little. L.A. had its moments. She remembered driving out to the beach, playing in the sand, getting it between every crevice of her child self, being hosed down in the yard before she was allowed to come in. But nothing would ever last. Next came Denver. Then Pitt. Always the looks, every new place, at the odd little family with the Asian man and his black wife and daughter. She had his eyes and nose. She could see him in the mirror, now more than before. As she grew older, more like him, he grew sadder. And each town, just as she got used to it—found something, someone in it to connect with—it would be time to move again. The black shirts, she began to see them, as her father did. And then it would be time to leave.

She finished her second mag and slammed in the third, one-handing the piece now, going against everything the academy taught her. She fired off in succession, rattling the reports through the range like a machine gun. She saw her cap soaring through the air along with all the others—a sea of pomp and circumstance. The girls and that one boy—*what was his name again?*—all planning to head into Motor City for a night of celebration. She ran into her house to change clothes from the formals of the ceremony. Hǔ Quán stood there in the den, stone-faced, crushing her elation at her achievement—she'd graduated with honors for crying out loud, and he'd tried to forbid her from attending ceremony. He had a letter in his hand—*her* letter. She'd been accepted into the academy upon completion of her diploma, starting the next week. She'd have a badge by August. She was so proud of herself, and all she'd wanted to do was tell him, but she hadn't. She hadn't because of exactly this.

"I forbid it!" He shouted into her, right into her bones. "The Devil that rots this world does not relent. The demon's black hands never rest." He tore the letter in front of her.

"You're crazy!" her 18-year old self screamed. She reared her arms back, her bell bottom pants nowhere near as wide as her nostrils in the moment. "You're nothing but a crazy old man, and I hate you! You can't stop me! I don't believe in any of your bullshit. It's not real! I never want to see you again! Never."

And she never did.

She ran upstairs, shoved clothes in a backpack, and climbed out her window, not even wanting to see his face. She put him out of her mind all that summer through the academy—focused on her tests and training. Graduated again top of her class. She swore in, got her uniform, her first assignment. She ignored their calls, never speaking to either of them. She hated to punish her mother, but Murph hadn't been ready to cross that bridge yet. Demons and black hands. Prophecies of doom. The ancient order of guardians. Magic weapons. The armor of god. It was all horse shit, and he might as well be raving with a bible in his hands just like all those others had at the sight of their mixed-race family. She hated all of it.

Murphy emptied her last magazine downrange as fast as her finger would go. Tears waterfalled down her face. The sight of a redheaded kid in a rainbow denim jacket leaping a five-story church like someone jumping a curb, crushing steel in her hand. Murph's lip quivered. She hadn't even gone to the funeral. One of the hundred unanswered calls during her first year on the force was to tell her he died. Another to tell her of the funeral. Already an older man when she was born, his heart finally just gave out, and he was gone. She only read about it in the paper.

Her last words to him stabbed into her head like a hot knife.

"I hate you." She hated the sound of that girl's voice, her shrill violence.

"You're crazy," the stupid little bitch said a thousand times a day in her memory.

"It's not real." Murph saw the image of Molly Slater—*The Sledgehammer*—burned now in her eyes. A resurrected axe-murderer. The ordeal from the beach town, easy enough to ignore along with the rest of the tabloid nonsense. Now it lived at her suite and ate *all* her food.

Then there were the gangs—more like cults. Domnii Morţii. Hēishǒu Móguǐ. Filles Purdues. Children of Night. And then the locals, Chante Toujours. All converging. Just as the kid arrived. The detective in her didn't believe in coincidences. Even when it meant she'd been the asshole and never said goodbye to a man who loved her—and maybe wasn't so crazy after all.

Murphy shoved her gear back in her carry bag, leaving her spent brass all around, her face wetter than if she had run twice her normal routine. She started out the door. This hadn't helped at all. If anything, she felt worse than when she walked in. The other man shooting saw her on the way out, looked at her face.

"Hey, miss, are you o—"

"Fuck off, asshole." She slammed her open palm into the door, both her hands trembling, tingling.

The man stood, shaking his head for a second after she'd gone. He looked downrange at the target she'd left behind. He hadn't counted her shots but knew it had been several mags worth. There was a fist-sized grouping of holes in the paper, all center skull.

LYDIA STUCK A CLASH tape in the player and cranked it. Molly rolled her eyes but smiled. She had the broom in her hands, twirling it like a baton, switching hands behind her back, thrusting it forward—another muscle memory from the life she couldn't remember. Lyd clicked through the TV but didn't find anything. Murphy had taken off that morning in a huff. Molly felt her emotions running all over the place. When she came back, she hadn't been any better.

"Y'all take a day," She'd said after a shower and donning her go-to outfit of jeans and letter jacket. Molly saw her slide extra mags into her pockets.

"You sure you don't want me to—"

"I just need to follow up some things by myself. Meeting your reporter friend later." Murph grabbed a soda from the fridge and went for the door. "I made it this far without a hammer. I'll make it another day. Y'all get a pizza, or something. Just, you know..." She looked at them both. She felt something Molly gleaned—guilt? No, that wasn't it. But something like it. "Just be cool."

An hour later, Lydia bounced off the walls of the apartment. There were only a few others like it, most of the building a traditional hotel. The upper-crusters liked to have a crash pad when they came through town. Such was this supposed "writer" Murph worked for or pretended to. Some of the more questionable liberties Murphy took made Molly uncomfortable. Her interrogation methods scratched at the line Molly wouldn't cross. It made her think twice about Murphy being out on her own. *What was she up to today?*

Molly closed her eyes, felt the broom handle in her hands, found her spots on its haft, gripped, spun it around her head, and stabbed the bristles out at her imaginary enemy. Somewhere that robot vacuum beeped.

"What's this little dance about?" Lydia looked at Molly then stared more at the image of Thatcher on the TV than her friend.

Something about that women irked Molly the more she looked at her. *The Iron Lady,* what a bullshit nickname. If anyone was an Iron Lady, Molly figured it should be her. She basically had iron skin. *Or green skin? Gold hair?*

"I think I had a memory." Molly one-handed the broom, spinning it in a whirlwind, alternating sides of her body.

"Wait, like from...before?" Lydia muted the TV and turned to her friend.

"I don't know. It was just a flash. A woman, she had green skin and gold hair. She was teaching me. I think—" Molly held the broom tight, seeing the image in her head—she could almost hear the woman's voice, just barely beyond her reach.

She desperately wanted to hear it. "I think she was my mother—like my real mother."

Lydia didn't say anything, but her eyes said enough. Molly put the broom down. She felt how alien she looked, how Lydia retreated from her, not wanting to, but doing so all the same. Molly went to her, hugged her, looked her in the eyes.

"It's still me." Molly touched Lydia on the shoulder, sending her peace. There was only goodness in Lydia. Fear, confusion, pain, as much as anyone, but all born of a place of innocence. "Just plain old Molly from the corner of Elm and E—not some green-skinned alien."

"Yet." Lydia laughed it off, hugged her friend back. "Let's bail." Lydia scooped her purse and walked to the bathroom to check her mascara.

"Where?" Molly didn't hate the idea of getting out, even if she knew Murph would throw a fit about it.

"Let's go shopping. Get a drink, or at least me a drink. You can eat ten Lucky Dogs or whatever."

* * *

The day couldn't even be called one—the purple sky never saw a single ray of the sun—just a perpetual dusk, a chill humidity lingering, smothering the city. Its brick, stone, and steel faces wore the weather like a shroud, covering its secrets old and new. The girls wandered up Gravier into a few shops on Canal. Two hot dogs and a hurricane later, they cruised through the front doors of Maison Blanche.

"Man, I've always wanted to come here." Lydia twirled as they entered the store. Molly grinned at her friend dancing and enjoying a moment of levity. They seemed to have so few of those since she became... *what she was.* Lydia deserved a better life than this. Molly felt that guilt again. She wanted her friend with her, but she hated putting her in danger all the time. It wasn't fair.

The store distracted Molly from her thoughts. It was massive—an entire mall unto itself. The first floor housed mostly accoutrements: handbags, leather, jewelry, hats, hosiery, handbags, accessories. It also had a snack bar and a sit-down café.

Moving up the escalator, the second floor boasted all the clothes they could imagine. Dresses for every occasion. A full-scale shoe salon. A lingerie section, complete with corsets and bodices on display. Lydia mocked all the bright colors and neons that were still en vogue, though she did find one skirt she liked—black of course.

Third floor housed housewares, gifts, sports, and toys. Molly joshed with a pair of extending boxing glove guns, bopping Lydia in the face over and over with her little plastic fists, the two of them laughing like they were fourteen again at the old Edgewater Mall back home. Lydia grabbed a light-up ray gun that made the most annoying sound and returned fire at her redheaded assailant from the planet

Bavmorda. The two of them giggled and horsed their way around the toys and games before heading further into the shopper's labyrinth.

The fourth floor was lame: bath shop, linens, curtains, rugs and furniture. They had a sewing machine center, fabrics and all that grandma stuff that could barf Lydia out. One glance around and they rode the stairway all the way up.

The fifth floor was music, electronics, instruments, a full service beauty salon and a Merrill Chase Studio. Lydia wanted to get their photo taken with a crazy outfit and one of those fake backgrounds behind them—maybe a creepy castle or outer space. Molly's eyes went right for the axes the two of them would never afford even working all summer at Germain's. They had Gibsons, Strats, even a Les Paul. She'd always wanted a Les Paul.

A thought dawned on Lydia. What if they just stayed? If they could shake this Murphy character—Lydia could tell she was hiding something from them—maybe they could move here. Étoile and the girls she'd met the other night were cool as hell. Molly would totally dig them, and she'd told them all about her—well, not *all* about. But still. Andi could finish out Molly's summer classes and none be the wiser... And what about Andi? The poor girl, or robot, or someone. Maybe she could come too. She needed to pick her own face though. The two Molly's thing was beyond weird at this point, and besides, Andi deserved her own life. Lydia felt bad about ditching her with Becky. She wondered what Nguyen was doing. He said this city was cursed. She could see that now. Maybe she should call him... Maybe later.

The girls meandered their way through the instruments, headed toward the records when they heard piano tones reverb through the store. The ground lit up and the tones changed with each step of their feet. They looked down and saw the yellow-lit keys they stood on next to the black and white ones. It was an FAO Schwarz giant floor piano stretching out another six feet on either side of them. The two girls laughed and stepped on another key, sending tones through the store.

Eyes darted to them, including a certain smoky pair framed by dusky locks and a billion-dollar smile. A sharp cut suit belied the even sharper cut man inside it, taking note of the pair as he finished speaking to the other suits and made his way to them. Lydia had long known that anytime anyone in a suit came toward them in a public place usually meant it was time to bail, but then Molly had to go and wave and... *blush* at him? To Lydia's absolute horror, the suit waved back.

Dude, she facecoded at Molly with a vengeance.

"That's Germain," Molly said through her teeth, continuing to smile and wave at the pair of carved shoulders headed their way. *Were those shoulder pads or was he just built like that?* Lydia waved while rendering a haphazard smile. Getting canned for clowning around would dampen her dreams of relocation.

"You work for me don't you?" The rake grinned as his eyes lingered on Molly, then Lydia. And Molly bought everything this guy sold with a stupid bashful smile. "Ms. Slater, assistant to the new VP of Development, correct? Or is it Miss?" He smiled again right into her eyeballs and Lydia could vomit.

"Uh yeah, uh..." Molly looked to Lydia, her face as red as her hair.

Get it together, Sledgehammer, Lydia shook her head.

"We... uh. We mostly work in the uh... the mail room. Mostly." Molly turned to Lydia for an assist. Lydia had only seen her friend lose her words like that once before. This was bad... *or, maybe it wasn't.* Lyd took a step away, watching her friend forget everything else but her own goosebumps in that moment.

"Sorry if we're making too much of a racket." Lydia jumped in.

"Nonsense." Germain tapped his canvas shoe—Vans, Lydia noted—onto the giant keyboard, the tone resounding through the room once more. "It's why I put it here—for people to play it!"

"You put it here?" Molly squinted her eyes.

"Oh yeah. I bought the store a while back, the whole building, in fact. Board makes most of those decisions—I mean what do I know about it, right? But this one, this one I just wanted." He put his foot on a key, then another, tapping out a quick tune. "Come on. Do it with me."

He did have a nice smile, Lydia admitted, as its charm snaked its way through even her.

IV
"CRY LITTLE SISTER"
—GERARD MCMAHON, 1987

THE THREE OF THEM DANCED out a bit from "Home Sweet Home" because Molly lived and breathed the Crüe. One day, Lydia would *Cure* her of that. They moved into some Joel and a little Elton. The dude was more old school than they were. Lydia couldn't quite peg his age. He could be thirty, maybe. His eyes seemed older than his skin suggested. But his movements proved he was built out of rock and sinew underneath that suit worth more than her stolen truck.

Lydia watched as her friend fell out of herself and lived in the moment. Her smile, her laugh, both as contagious as a virus. She peppered her feet across the twenty-foot floor piano, not a care in the world that their boss, a man who could buy half the world if he wanted to, danced alongside her—like they were two normal people. Lydia smirked at the irony. Two very different kinds of power, each oblivious to how the small people looked at them.

And suddenly Lydia felt precisely that: small. Then came a tinge of guilt at her own jealousy. Not that she dug the rich guy in the Armani—wasn't her type—but of the way Molly walked on air and sunshine. Like rainbows bloomed just for her—to transport her off to some magical kingdom in the sky.

But Molly deserved her moment. She deserved happiness. She'd earned this. And seeing her smile like that, a smile Lydia hadn't seen since... since prom, when it all went to shit. Somewhere into their second rendition of "Piano Man" Lydia wandered over to the records and poked through their selection. Mostly bubblegum pop, not that she was against that. She found the new Social Distortion she'd been wanting. She wanted to give the two of them distance, not be the third wheel she always was, always had been since Molly suddenly became Super Molly last fall. She knew Molly would say no to the mere mention of a date. Maybe this guy was too old for her, or maybe Molly was secretly some thousand-year-old green alien, so maybe it didn't matter.

Lydia glanced at them one more time, grins and laughs on their faces—Molly not even noticing she was gone yet—and very suddenly she needed some air.

* * *

Without meaning to, Lydia found herself outside. The night had crept in while they'd been in the store. The clouds that blotted the sun for the day had since rolled out to leave the bright moon shining down on the neon of the city—its own sights and sounds singing into the evening. Lydia tightened her jacket around her shoulders, stuck her hands in her pockets. A chill blew down Canal. Even this deep into summer, the winter cold reminded everyone of its long reach.

Lydia walked up the street, noting the characters out and about. She caught a familiar spiked haircut and slashed jacket sucking a cigarette near Bourbon. Lydia waved at Étoile and the girls. They leaned against a trio of ragged-out street bikes parked at the curb.

"Sup, kid?" Étoile killed her Kool on the ground, looked up at the bright moon and licked at her front teeth. "Want to take a ride?"

"Where?" Lydia looked back toward the store, to Molly. Had she missed her yet? She started to head back. Molly *would* worry. It was her way. *No. Have fun, Molly. For one night in your life, just do something for yourself.*

"There's somebody I want you to meet." Étoile's toothy smile flashed in the neon. "She's out of this fucking world!"

V
"TWILIGHT ZONE"
—GOLDEN EARRING, 1982

MURPH SCOPED THE SCENE at the address on Marais out in St. Roch the reporter had given her. An odd place for an art gallery, but Murph found little of this town that wasn't odd to her. The neighborhood was about like the rest of the city—lot of shotgun houses all around. A few turn-of-the-century brick jobs. A tenement building that had seen its better days. An empty lot next door. And the gallery itself, housed in a decaying old Catholic church: The Annunciation, according to the faded cornerstone that still bore its prior name. Nothing overly fancy like some of the bigger cathedrals in town. Just the usual red brick face, some nice windows, a few engravings, big cherry wood doors.

The weather grated Murph's nerves along with everything else. A few bag ladies and other indigents wandered about. Most of them stuck to outer areas of the city or wandered into the suburbs. From what she'd seen, the city police kept them under control. A few of these looked gaunt, sickly—close to death. Gave her chills and visions of the worst of old Detroit.

The Motor City had been going to hell long before Commie Ron sent it there with a bullet. Nixon hadn't been their friend by any measure, opening things up. Imports killed the auto market. Unions got badmouthed when it wasn't their fault. Then The Gipper opened the floodgates—his stuck-up English girlfriend coming right here to New Orleans soon, Murph had seen on the news. Ol' Ronny beating the peanut farmer in '76 hadn't surprised anyone. Changing the constitution to run a third time, only to lose out on the fourth to a cartoon like Hogan—that had been a laugh. But the damage was done, the English witch still exerting her influence over the handlebar mustache, stoking the fire of the Cold War. And the cold itself, that ever-creeping ice coming from some frozen hell had made her city unlivable. Less than half of Old Detroit remained, clinging to what, Murph still didn't understand.

"He rules this darkened city that stands on the gate." A voice shook her out of her head. Some old man in a tattered brown coat slapped at her window. She stuck out like an idiot in the bright red car out here. The reporter was late. "He turns day to dark. It's the only way. He can't walk in the light." The indigent bared his yellow teeth, pointed up at the purple sky.

A gray Chevy Citation rolled up, brakes squealing as it parked. Murph shook her head, but it looked more at home here than she did. Her reporter contact Alex stepped out and waved her over. Murph got out of the Mondial, clicked the alarm to make a point to the old bum. She noted his white collar on her walk over to the building and gave him a second look.

"They dug him up!" He shouted as he pointed at the old church. "We held him secret. Our cross to bear. But *She* found him. She knew. Somehow, she knew. She came for him. The Night is coming!" He started toward them then turned and stared at the others gathering on the street near him, some pawing at his clothing, not speaking, like wandering mutes. Or zombies.

"Dug who up?" Alex pulled the tape recorder from her jacket pocket and clicked it on.

"Some nut." Murph stared back at the threadbare clothes—the tattered remains of the priest collar sent ice up her back. She kept him in the corner of her eye as they walked the steps into the gallery.

Inside the building, the vibe was somewhere between art deco and gothic Byzantine. The colors and themes clashed: Neon pink triangles next to a bleeding Mary. A polka dot crucifix. Statues and carvings spray-painted with graffiti. Who would do that?

"An' may I help you?" A man walked from a back room, twirling and flitting about the pieces, giving each woman a wrinkled lip and a raised eyebrow.

"We came to look at the Sardo painting." Alex whipped out her press pass like a gun. "I made an appointment."

"Yes, and you did." He rolled his eyes at her outfit. It was a little drab, even Murph had to admit. "I am Sergei. I will direct you. Please..." He sneered at them both again. "Don't touch. Anything."

He walked them to the back room, through the former sanctuary turned display floor for the tacky artwork, not that Murph would know art if it bit her in the neck, but this didn't feel right.

Alex had called her that morning with a new lead. She'd dug through the archives again, this time up all night, she'd said, looking for anything on their vigilante. No luck there, she'd told Murph.

"I looked into this Count Sardo—the castle guy some more." Alex had said on the phone. "Apparently he's never been photographed. Refuses it. But he sits for paintings once a year. He's donating one to the charity auction gala at the Lili Tower's soft-opening."

"This is the guy?" Murph cocked her head to one side as she took in the image. The guy had a flair for the dramatic, but then he *was* a "count" after all. The painting was a life-sized full-body portrait. The man wore a long black cape, draping most of his body (a shortcut for the artist, Murph thought), a flash of red on the cape's underside as his bony right hand stretched out. A grim expression on his face. Slicked long midnight hair combed back, leaving enough forehead to project a movie onto. Behind him, a massive castle on a craggy hill. A rotten tree reached its limbs out like dead fingers. A blue haze covered a full moon. Beneath, prostrate and hovering at his knees, lay two ghostlike women, all in white, wrapping themselves around him like lapdogs.

"Are you fucking serious?" Murph's eyes couldn't blink from staring at the audacity of it.

"That's the castle." Alex pointed at the background of the painting.

"Do what?" Murph snapped out of her trance. She swore for a second the painting watched her, followed her eyes with its own. She shook her head to clear the spiders.

"The moving castle?" Alex raised both her eyes. "I told you about that. He's moving it brick by brick. Some piece of land way, way out in the freaking swamp. I haven't been out there yet. Hard to get to."

"I bet." Murph's eyes went back to the painting—squinting. There was *something* about it. About *him.* The place. The castle. Or *this* place? "You said there was something else? On the phone."

Alex looked behind her. Sergei lingered a few feet away, watching them like they'd steal something. As if Murph would be caught dead with any of this psycho trash.

"Do you have a ladies' room by chance?" Alex smirked at Sergei, shrugging her shoulders.

He wrinkled his mouth and nose again. "Down the hall, left side."

The lights dimmed into the back halls behind the old pulpit. They passed a stairwell that had flights going up *and* down. New Orleans wasn't big on basements. It gave Murph a chill like she'd never felt before in her life. Cold right down to her soul. Her father's fierce eyes on his wildest rant flashed into her mind. She wanted to leave this place. Now.

Alex turned on the faucets as soon as they walked through the door of the restroom. She cracked the door to make sure they weren't followed, then walked back to Murph by the sinks.

"So here's the deal." Alex whispered. "Before it was an art gallery, the church had already been shut down—basically abandoned sometime after the turn of the century. The diocese kept it up during that time but closed to the public. No mass. No nothing. A caretaker, a few groundspeople. That's all."

"Why?"

"That's what a professor from Loyola wanted to know. About ten years ago, the priest acting as caretaker of the property had a research team from the university out here. I found an old clipping about it." She handed a copy of the article to Murph. "The guy was a lecturer on metaphysics and the occult. Other worlds, interdimensional mumbo jumbo. He published one book. I tried to read it, but it was nonsense. Ancient gods. Giant monsters from other realms. They let anyone teach at these colleges, I guess."

"Okay, cut to it, typewriter." Murph's nerves tingled all over her body, concentrating in her hands, her fingers. She glanced down and hadn't realized she'd balled her right into a tight fist.

"That's just it. They never came out."

"What?"

"I know, right? I only found the one article. They went in on a Friday. Monday morning, the prof and a handful of grad students never showed back up. Poof. Gone. All but one, some grad student named Kobayashi."

"Can we find this Kobayashi?" Murph looked at the stained and leaking corners of the ceiling. This place had eyes. And ears. The whole city did.

"Finding him isn't hard. He was all over TV last week driving a rocket truck in the desert. Getting him to return a phone call?" Alex shrugged. "That's tough."

"Okay, well what about the priest?" Murph somehow already knew.

"I made some calls. The church was sold right after that."

"Let me guess." Murph thought of the godawful painting again.

"Bought this church right after the disappearance. Starts building a super tower in central city. And now he's moving a thousand-year-old Romanian castle into a swamp. Yes. Count Sardo Sandor."

Murph's shaking worsened. She shoved her palm into the door, making a dedicated march toward the front of the building, shivering again as she passed the stairwell. All she knew was she had to leave this place, and now.

"You will leave here now, Monsieur. We have done this dog and pony too many times." Sergei's voice went an octave higher as Murph entered the main showroom and could make out his wild gestures in some awkward attempt to ward off what appeared to be an indigent who'd wandered in. "Monsieur, I *will* phone the police if I must do so."

Murph caught the old man's eyes in a flash, his locking on hers in return. He shot his arm out like a gun, his finger a bullet pointed at her. She saw then he was blind.

"He's returned. He's claimed the city as his own. He was born of Darkness; she bore a thousand more by him. The Beast. The beast cursed to wander for eternity! He calls his acolytes to him, his black hands to do his evil work! She raised him from his tomb! Only the chosen one can bind him again, cast him into the lake of fire!"

Alex caught up with Murph to see the tail end of the spectacle. Murph looked away as the raving man said those words and pointed where she already looked.

His Black Hands echoed a thousand times through her head as she gazed at the painting, its eyes seeing into her—her hands tingling, her whole body radiating.

Murph ran to the car, jumped in, and cranked the stereo as she tried to breathe, steady herself. She did the thing again, the thing her maybe not-so-crazy father taught her. *Breathe in through nose. Breathe out through mouth.* She repeated his words in her head as she went through it, her palms pressed together in front of her, motioning them back and forward with her breathing.

"What is this?" Alex stood at her window, looking back and forth from the gallery to Murph in her car. "Some kind of prayer?"

"Something called Yoga I learned at the YMCA back home." Murph didn't know why she lied. But she'd always lied about her father. It came naturally.

"Oh, Yoga. I read about that. What the hell was that in there? You flipped out."

"His black hands." Murph said the words out loud again. "Hēishǒu Móguǐ."

"I've heard of them." Alex folded her arms, looking up at the steeple and then her watch. "They're cartel or something like that, right? Relic hunters, I heard. What the hell are they doing here?"

Murph slowed her breathing, trying to shake her father's face out of her mind, only to see it replaced by red hair and freckles. "I know what they want."

VI
"I'LL SHOW YOU SOMETHING SPECIAL"
–BALAAM & THE ANGEL, 1987

MOLLY LET HERSELF get distracted for all of five minutes before she turned and saw Lydia missing. She'd seen her head over to the records while she danced with Richie Rich. He lost all interest in her and their big piano when the little phone in his pocket took him wandering off, not so much as a "see you later." Molly had crushed massive steel monsters in her bare hands, but she still couldn't fathom what it must be like to have so much money that the world barely existed beneath you. She wondered at someone that could have that much power and not use it to help the world.

"Lydia?" Molly called her name several times as she wandered the aisles of the department store. She checked the usual suspects: bass guitars, punk & metal records. She went back down to the toys. "What the hell, Lyd?" She muttered on her way down the escalators toward Canal Street.

She let her mind quiet, stopped her fake breathing–she'd gotten good at maintaining a steady rhythm to keep from freaking people out. She made her eyes into slits, slowed her time to a standstill. She scanned everywhere, searching the massive crowds out that night. Nothing. She closed her eyes, reaching out with her feelings. She and Lydia had a unique connection. She could always find her if she focused herself and listened.

It was faint, fading, but enough. Molly moved up the street, sliding past the pedestrians, weaving through the throngs in a hurry, trying not to knock anyone down. A rat clawed at her gut, and she knew she needed to hurry. She wouldn't get far like this, and barely had enough for a cab–not that she had an address to give one anyway. *Hey, follow my gut feeling,* wouldn't exactly go over well with the driver.

Molly glanced down at her denim cut, hands in its pockets, and looked around her. She ducked down the next side street, quickened her pace, moving to the unlit sections of The Quarter. She found a deserted alley with plenty of bins and debris to hide her. She flipped her jacket inside out, zipped it up to her neck, her rainbow-framed hammer emblem catching the sliver of streetlight creeping at her. She pulled the wadded black balaclava Murph insisted she keep to "cover that flaming red hair."

"Yo, chick, you get lost?" A voice behind her snickered.

Molly turned with a laser glare as she slid on the mask, her face still uncovered, but the rest a shadow in the night. Some dipstick had followed her down the corridor while she had her mind locked on Lydia–him thinking this was his lucky night.

From high above The Quarter, a degenerate shot out from an alleyway into the brick wall of the nearest building, his spinal column cracking in one or two places. A denim-clad girl launched into the air, cresting and landing atop the building at 901 Canal, then bounding again to the top of the Royal St. Charles.

From her perch above everyone and everything, the hidden guardian found the direction of her friend and began her journey, leaping her way there—one building at a time.

* * *

Lydia had hopped on the back of the streetbike with Étoile and the other girls, feeling their hair dash in the wind behind them as they sped through Uptown, then into Irish, winding their way back toward the river. Images from her and Molly's first night in town flashed across her memory. This was supposed to be *their* trip. Was she being a bad friend? She felt guilt at her own guilt. Was she wrong for wanting to have some fun? For just wanting to drink, go to a club, meet a guy or two—it's not like she was going to marry Nguyen or anything—for just being a kid their last summer she got to be one? Did Molly always have to go fight all the battles and right all the wrongs of the world every time she found them? *Yes, Lydia, she actually kind of does, you dolt.* She shook her head. She knew what Molly was and had no right to ask her to be anything else.

But Lydia very much... wasn't. And maybe that was okay too.

She rode with Étoile and her crew all the way back to the J-Queen, that same bar Murph had brought them to their first night in town. Lydia wanted to try that singing machine. She'd read about those—along with a long piece about a supposed Japanese Space Fleet being built. If she wasn't best friends with a super person, Lydia may have marveled more at the crazy stuff happening in other parts of the world.

"What have you brought me?" the woman at the bar grinned as they walked in, the girls' studded leather gleaming in the neon lights of the old-meets-new bar decor. Lydia recognized her, the two-tone hair a dead giveaway. She had more eyeliner and longer lashes on one eye than the other, a split makeup pattern right down the center of her face.

"Show her your book." Étoile nodded at Evilyn Jareth, already mixing a round of shots, pulling liquids from unmarked bottles, flipping and catching them, making a whole show of it.

Lydia got a cold sweat, fidgeted. She looked around. The joint was empty—early in the evening for their regulars, and the tourists hadn't made their way down from The Quarter yet. Her gut told her to head back, find Molly. *She'll have noticed you're gone now, dude,* Lydia thought. *But what if she hasn't,* came another thought. Was that one even hers? Lydia shivered, looked at the almost-salivating faces of her new compatriots.

She reached in her bag and pulled out her grimoire, some dog-eared pages in it from where she'd thought she'd seen some cool stuff. This one drawing inside of a dark mistress surrounded by crows and casting some sort of spell over a battlefield intrigued her for some reason. She still couldn't make out any of the words.

"Some light summer reading, I see." Evilyn took the book without it being offered. She flipped through it, muttered some phrases to herself, Lydia honing in on her pronunciations, her reactions to them. The woman flinched when she got to the drawing of the Phantom Queen and flipped quickly through the rest of the book. "Not a bad buy, kid."

They all grabbed a shot and turned their elbows–Lydia last of all, glancing back at their faces, looking into her own head at the mistake of coming here. The shot was sweet, lingered on her tongue and lips–it was *really good.* She wanted another even as Evilyn poured it–but also knew that she didn't.

"Look, this was awesome and all, but I really need to get back to my friend." Lydia wanted to go for the door, but for whatever reason her legs didn't move.

"Yeah." Evilyn handed her another shot. "Tell me about your friend."

* * *

The Sledgehammer–wrapped in the moonlight dimmed by lingering clouds from the ungodly darkened day–sprinted across the rooftops of the city, moving into the residentials, following the river. She saw the smokestacks of the decrepit power plant where she'd battled some electrified, undead axe-monster. She looked down at her hand again, the one she'd fired his own electricity back at him with. She still needed to know more about that.

People on the streets noticed the figure dashing across their shingles, some pointing and shouting as she darted by. Bounding onto a rumbling freight train, she rode the top of it until she came to a long storage warehouse adjacent to the tracks and the riverside. She leapt onto the tin roof and went full throttle, cooking her superhuman legs as fast as she ever had. There was no radar gun or stopwatch to clock her, but Molly felt herself splitting the wind in her face. Her mind felt Lydia closer and closer with each thundering step across the metal roof.

* * *

Evilyn Jareth listened to every word fall from the kid's encouraged lips like drips of sweet red onto her thirsty mind. Her widened eyes danced to each of her underlings in their turn. The kid rambled on, flowing from one unfinished thought to another–the poor thing really just wanted a friend to listen and be with her. Such a pity how it had to be. This child had potential. She ranted about some woman police officer from out of town, of little use to Evilyn, but she noted the name. And so much about wrestlers and football.

"Yeah and then this guy–I forgot what I was saying." Lydia looked down at her arm, her watch. "Hey I got a question for you?"

"Shoot, kid, you've earned one on the house." Evilyn poured herself a drink—so much to process. "In fact, that's a deal, squirt. Ask me anything. I'll give you the straight answer."

She saw the kid slow herself down, put the little rat back on the wheel in her head. She grinned as Étoile and her girls sneered back.

"Okay, I got one." Lydia sat upright in the stool, shifting the black headband Étoile had given her higher on her brow. She looked out the front windows, then back to Evilyn. "Why don't any of the church bells here ring? Like, ever?"

Evilyn winced and cursed under her breath. She turned away from the child, squelching a wetness in one eye. She surprised herself that she could even still make tears, ever since—it was no matter. Her lip quivered, and she didn't know why she felt obliged to answer the child. Maybe she just wanted to.

"Because *He* won't allow it." Evilyn turned back to the kid, that simple, dumb innocence she held. Evilyn hated it. She missed it. Had she ever even had it?

"What? Who? Why?"

"Because." She poured herself another drink and fired it back. "They're made of copper."

The answer left the child knowing less than she already had, Evilyn saw that, as she looked away toward the door. As if her own nightmares—or were they fantasies?—made manifest before her, that door burst open. But no battle-armored foe had risen against her, weapons blazing, helmet gleaming. No. Just another kid in sneakers and a bad denim cut. Red hair flaming in the breeze off the dark water flowing ceaselessly into the vast gulf.

"Speak of the devil child." Evilyn raised a glass to her new arrival. "And she shall appear."

"What did you call me?" Molly glared at the two-tone smiling face—the one that masked a sadness deeper than any she'd felt before.

VII

"SHADOWS OF THE NIGHT"
—PAT BENATAR, 1982

MURPHY LONG PUT HER FOOT on the floor. She burnt blacktop on her way through the city, shooting across intersections, putting the Mondial through its paces. It didn't disappoint as she flew by shotgun houses and the old neighborhoods. As the clouds of the late afternoon gave way into night, she drove through Gretna and Timberlane. At one point she swore she'd picked up a tail. *Who could it be?* She figured it was paranoia when she hit the Belle Chasse tunnel and the following car turned just before she went under.

She cooked on into Belle Chasse, curled her lip in irritation at the whitebread suburbs, the affluence of it. She recalled the story of the old plantation mansion nearby, its sordid history—a history that flared her temper just imagining it. *That figures*, she thought as she shook her head at the brand-new school, then turned south, following the river.

She cruised through Live Oak, tried to turn inland. She found a dirt road—hell on the Ferrari—and headed away from the river until it dead-ended into nothing— just trees and boggy swamp. She cursed and turned back, stopped at the last gas station she'd seen—bought a Tab and popped the cap off with her thumb. She needed to calm her nerves. *Breathe, Murphy.* The caffeine in the soda wasn't going to help, she knew, as she gulped it down anyway.

"I'm looking for this castle they're putting together." She glanced at the lady at the counter, a couple of good ol' boys chiming through the door. They gave her the up-down, one of them still gawking out the front window at the fancy red car. "What road do I take?"

"Sure ain't no road." The woman spat a sunflower seed into a cup.

"What? How are they building it then?" She looked at the three guys staring at her, their mesh caps sitting on top of their heads. Coveralls. Skoal rings in the back pockets. Hands browner than hers from working outside in the sun and dirt all day. This usually meant it was time to go. Last thing she needed was the attention a fight with some yokels would get her.

* * *

Murph waved at Hegs at the front desk of the Windsor, sweet old guy, but English and always a bit fussy about her using Riz's car so much. It was a nice perk of the *job* she took. The number of jobs she was technically doing while she dug into the city sometimes threw her. Soon enough, the bill would come due on one or more of them. They still had no idea what was what at Germain Enterprises, and now that she'd finally met the guy, she could see why. Talk about a rudderless ship. She did want to know more about all this money they pumped into R&D projects, most of which they had locked up on the 40th or offsite.

She walked in the door of the penthouse, dropped her jacket on the counter and slumped into the chair next to the couch while two teenagers stared at MTV in weird silence.

"I would ask." Murph looked at Molly, then Lydia sulking, the two of them sitting together and looking away from each other. "But I'm too tired."

She felt that painting stare at her again. She didn't know why she couldn't shake it. The way her knuckles itched every time she thought of it—she could use an afternoon on a heavy bag. Times like this, she really missed her old precinct. Her partner, Baskin, had walked her through the first years with the detective shield like an old softy, despite how he otherwise looked and sounded—gravelly voice and mud-colored hair. They'd become friends as they got to know each other. He'd never made it weird between them, and she always wanted to thank him for that. It was one more thing on the tab she owed him. And she'd pay it out when she found these cult bastards that iced him. He deserved that. So did her father.

As if Red was in her head that very moment, she stuck her fancy knife right into Murph's deepest hidden corner. "Can I ask about your tattoo?" Her stupid, innocent child eyes held nothing but kindness. Murph fought a war to stop her eyes from dripping, and to her credit, she won that fight.

"What does it say?" Molly folded her legs and sat facing her. The dark one behind her on the couch folded more into herself, leaning her shoulder away but perking her ear up.

"It's okay, yeah." Murph sighed. She pulled the back of her shirt down to show the two characters: 最终. "My father, he—" She looked out the window—seeing his tired face, or was it disappointment? She still wondered. So much of the man remained a mystery to her, despite knowing him for eighteen years. "I think he wanted a boy. Zuìzhōng. It was a sort of nickname he called me sometimes, usually when he was into his wine or in one of his moods. It meant something to him, I think. I don't know."

Murph folded her legs up next to her chest, wrapped her arms around them. She shivered. Red offered her a blanket, but she waved it off.

"Since you brought it up, I guess I might as well say it." Murph got up, collected herself, went to the bar to pour a drink. "My father was a good man. No, he was a great man. I want to start with that. We were always close, best friends—he took me everywhere with him—I mean *every*where. But as I got older, we—he would talk about crazy shit sometimes. Really bugged my mom when he went off on a tear." She gulped her drink and poured another but only stared at it, running her finger around the rim of the glass.

"It's okay." Molly said, like she felt what Murph was feeling. Everything about the redheaded kid unnerved her, now more than before. She studied her face for a moment. So simple. Just any other kid. "You don't have to—"

"No, see. I think I do." Murph paced. "See he, uh, I guess a lot of people have their religious side. I had friends in school that got spanked at home for saying the f-word. Plenty of white kids got punished for playing with me at recess. Because the bible. That kind of shit. My father wasn't much different—least that's what I told myself. Talked about demons and black magic. Monsters in the dark. Ancient gods, that kind of crap. I mean, when you're 7 that stuff sounds awesome, you know?"

Murph fidgeted as she paced. She wanted to go outside, find some asshole perp to try her. Now she wished she had pushed those three hicks down in the boons. The dark-haired kid sat up, turned to face her, both ears wide open now.

"Hēishǒu Móguǐ. The Black Hands of the Devil. He talked about them, muttered their name at night in his sleep. When he did sleep. I thought he was crazy. He never talked about his life before America. I knew he was Chinese, Nepalese, somewhere in the middle of that. He was brown enough here, though. He got called all the usual names from—well, down here y'all know all about that."

She finished that second drink. Molly got up from the couch and came at her like she was about to hug her, like they were even friends like that. Murph flinched and waved her off.

"I don't need none of that." Murph picked up her bottle and put it back down again. She thought she would leak again any second. *You stupid old fool.* That's what she'd called him. But now she said it of herself. "In the end they killed him. It was his heart. But really it was them. Because he believed it so damn much, you see?"

She slumped in her chair—the girls staring at her like that boy on the bus that said she had squint eyes. Called her *Squint* all that schoolyear. Until she popped his jaw one good time, and he never said another word to her after that.

"Hēishǒu Móguǐ. I looked them up a few years into making detective. Had the resources. I always figured they were just any other gang, a cartel. They had fingers in shit all over the world. Cairo. Eastern Europe. Russia. You name it."

The redhead leaned forward, hanging on her every word. Like some kicked dog, half-starved and thinking it was about to get fed.

"See, they had this whole mission. Crazy shit just like dad talked about. An ancient prophecy, if you can believe it. Their master, an unkillable demon, bound here by some vengeful god before the fourth world was born—shit is wild, so bear with me—would never die, but only be defeated, bound by some legendary weapon. And—here it comes—only the sacred warrior, the one who wears *The Armor of God* can claim the weapon. Their sole mission, the root of everything they do, their entire cartel enterprise, is governed by one goal: find this *chosen one* and kill them."

She looked Molly dead in the eye.

"It's as crazy as it sounds, and until a week ago, I never thought there was a lick of truth in it. But it's been a hell of a week for me. And now they're here. And see, maybe my crazy pop wasn't so crazy. Because, I'm thinking here—" She looked away from Molly, out the window, down at her hands, shaking, tingling, radiating with heat—the painting still haunting her, those eyes staring back into her—*like a demon.* "Kid, I'm thinking that's you."

VIII
"DEVIL INSIDE"
—INXS, 1988

DR. BIANCA TESCHE STUDIED THE BOOK Evilyn had obtained from some dead Dökkn or rogue Fae. She'd found it easy enough, knowing what to look for, what spirits to talk to. When the news of the strange events of the nearby beach town reached the Crescent City, Evilyn needed to see it for herself.

And here it was in the flesh, its cover and binding formed from skin, its pages inked in blood. Alchemy. Sorcery. Incantations. Potions. Machinations. A trove of knowledge, some lost since the time of the ancients. A dozen years of study in the arcane, genetics, chemistry, all paled to what this one book—penned in the knobby hand of some mad creature—contained within its macabre covers.

But they never dreamed the warrior that defeated him would come here, right to them, as though she were drawn here, by whatever forces still governed this forsaken universe, if any did at all.

The sparks of the circle lit, the power flowing through it as the wall opened, Bianca seeing again the images that terrorized her dreams, that hateful world beyond, its endless gray, its many-tentacled monsters, the tormenting demons that grinned and mocked—for they awaited her, awaited all who'd ever taken the mark of this hateful beast. It was her unavoidable doom.

Evilyn Jareth crawled through the hole between the worlds, its mist and ice creeping in along with her. She collapsed, exhausted, weaker this time than she'd ever come back. Bianca reached for her benefactor, her partner and sister in this maniacal gambit. If they failed, she'd see the other side of the circle sooner than later.

"I'm fine." Evilyn waved Bianca's hand away. She climbed to her feet, her hands, her whole body, trembling, shaking.

"How long this time?" Bianca had clocked her gone at just under 36 hours, but the land of mists had its own time, abided by the laws of no god.

"Long enough." Evilyn rose to her feet, her eyes flashing in the light of the new lab after losing the one at the Market Street plant.

"You found it?"

"Yes." Evilyn licked her shiny new canine teeth. "Now, I must go to Him. I must set up the final piece. Soon, Bianca." Evilyn touched her friend on the chin. "Soon."

"BLACK ANGEL"
—THE CULT, 1985

THE GIRLS BARELY SPOKE to one another the past day or two, and Murph didn't have any time for whatever that was. Boy, did she not miss being their age. She knew she had been every inch as full of herself, and it was a miracle she made it through the academy.

Even weirder, Red hadn't made the least attempt to quiz on her any more on the news she'd hit her with. *Seems like if I was 'the chosen one' I'd want to know all about that,* she thought. *Damn kid acts like she hears shit like that every day.* Murph sat in her office at Germain's and took a breath—figured she knew about jack and squat about what that kid felt like and let it go. She had plenty to do already.

"They called him The Copperhead!" A dingy-haired scribe bowled into her office and slapped a stack of rotten newspapers on her desk. Murph glanced at them, then back at the reporter. "The vigilante."

"Do what now?" Murph picked through the papers. They looked like they'd been used to line a doghouse, or worse.

"I got a hunch after the gallery the other day and all that weirdness and you took off—I was worried about you by the way—anyway that crazy bum, right? The preacher collar? I tracked him down." Alex went into the whole thing. The guy had been the priest and caretaker of the old church before it sold. After the incident with the college people, he'd gone mad, wandered into the streets, been in and out of the hospital and the shelters. Always going back to the old place.

"But this—" Alex flipped through the filthy, brittle newsprint. "The priest had stacks of these in his, well, his hovel—Look, I bought him lunch and drove him to the big shelter next to the Tulane center."

Murph nodded her head. That was one of Germain's shelters. Had several through the city. Guy gave tons to charity. She thought about Victor, the sweet old man she saw on her morning runs—always there waiting on her with a smile.

"There." Alex folded out a page. The photo was old, darkened, mostly just a black shape of a man with some Greek-looking helmet on his head. "That's him."

Murph pulled up the paper, scanned through the print.

"Guy ran around town like that, only at night, roughing up the gangs, but also took down bankers, even fought bad cops. Far as I can tell, he was around for a few years back in the late 70's and then vanished. Except..." Alex trailed off, glancing around Murph's sparsely decorated office. "You just move in here or something?"

"Okay—but nothing about this guy says *bats* to me."

"Right. See. I don't think he did vanish. I think he just went dark. Got slicker with it. Changed his M.O. I hear things here. See something there. I've worked a few cities, seen some bad beats. This town's always had a rep. Then I come here, and for years now, this place is clean as a whistle, so to speak. I mean almost no gangs. The ones that were here? Ran off years ago. Fled to the 'burbs. They're scared shitless. Of what? The cops? Nah. They won't say his name. Nobody will talk about it. People shut up *that fast* and walk away from me? That always means it's something. This guy's out there. I'm sure of it. Or if not him, something even bigger."

"Anything in here on why? Who he was—or is?" Murph flipped through the stack.

"Yeah, no." Alex dropped into a chair in front of the desk and pulled out a pack of Strikes. "Cool if I smoke in here?" She lit it anyway. "Nothing about a name, identity, none of that. Cops barely looked into it. Hell, he did their job better'n they did—least until he went after *them*. But I got a thought on that."

"Yeah?" Murph wrinkled her lip at the smoke, waved it away from her face. She didn't know what use this angle was to her now, anyway. She still had to process what to do about Red and the Hēishŏu.

"Yeah look at this stuff." Alex flipped to another paper, another article with a photo, just as old and blurry. "Guy had all kinds of gadgets and wild weapons. Knockout guns and stun gas. Flamethrowers. Flying cars. Bulletproof suit of freaking armor."

"Armor?" Murph's mind flashed to the figure the dark-haired kid ran over, or through, or something that first night they'd come to town. That thing wore some kind of armor, like some gothic knight. She'd left it in the back of her head with a note, but it'd been lost in the chaos since.

"So he's rich." Alex popped her feet up on the desk. "You got an ashtray? But, yeah. Gotta be, right? I mean, it'd take gobs of money to create shit like that. Hell, you'd need access to major R&D. Resources out the wazoo. So yeah. We're looking for someone rich, stays out all night, sleeps in, isn't around much. Bit of a recluse, probably. Bet he's got a mansion with secret rooms full of all his weird stuff. Know anyone like that?" Alex shrugged her shoulders and widened her eyes.

"I might." Murph looked out her office door.

* * *

Molly stared out the window on the 71st floor of the Germain Enterprises building, looking over the city—another dreary afternoon with no sun—staring out over the world as far as her eye would see. She looked west, saw the curve take the horizon away, but she could just barely make out the tips of the state capitol building in Baton Rouge before she finally lost the horizon. At night, she sometimes looked at the moon, its various hills and craters, every detail of it— sometimes Mars when it was in the sky. She thought she saw a face one time, but it was just a hill. One of the many new things about herself she still hadn't gotten used to. Nor had she told Lydia that she could see all the way to other planets—could stare at other suns, or directly into their own for as long as she wanted without so much as a blink.

She'd finished her last cart for the day and already gone down and punched out, always dropping by Murph's *office* before she started each round so the dodgy detective could sift through for anything she thought looked interesting. It felt wrong, the way Murph had them operating.

Lydia had 60-64 today and would probably be done and waiting on her in the lobby by now. They hadn't talked a lot since she drug her out of that bar, drunk and rambling on and on. Molly had felt how Lydia's heart dropped into her gut at Murph's "chosen one" bomb. None of them mentioned it again—it was still too weird to process. Molly knew when Lyd was in the dumps, and she didn't know how to make it better. It's not like she asked to be some stupid *chosen one,* anyway. She missed them just playing rock and roll in the garage. She missed being *no one.*

"Yeah that's what I'm saying—yes, I want all of it moved to the new building ASAP." The voice behind her sounded familiar, Molly looked back and saw Jack Germain—tailor-cut suit built on top of his sharp-angled body—leading a troop of walk-behinds, some fumbling with folders, one of them giving her the stink-eye in return for her stare. "Yes, the artwork is already on site for the auction. No, the soft opening is tonight. The dandy will be there. Yes, *him.*" Germain put his hand over the receiver of his little pocket phone.

It still shocked Molly when she saw those things. Back home only the richest people had them, and they were huge as bricks or built into their cars. Some days she wondered if she would see a car blast off into the air. What was next? A robot cop? A TV in a refrigerator?

"You guys go on ahead and get everything set up. I'll be right behind you." Germain's troops hopped-to just as he told them, the same one dead-eyeing Molly all the way to the elevators. "Yeah, no, he's not my favorite either. But it's an all-hands-on-deck sort of thing. Look, let's talk later, I've got something real quick." Germain flipped his phone shut and tucked it away. He noted Molly's interest in it. "They're neat, huh?" He smiled at her.

He—she just liked looking at him for some reason. She always felt like she blushed when he came near.

"I've got a whole division working on them." He went on.

"Yeah they're cool, I guess." Molly wondered if a set would be useful for their little outings. Could they do three-way calls? Using radios wasn't exactly high tech.

"So, mail room, right?" Germain smiled again.

"Yeah, that's me." Molly curtsied in her uniform and then immediately wondered why she did that. *Who even was she?* "I'm done for the day. My friend and I are gonna grab a bite in a few minutes."

"Was that an invite?" Germain had pretty teeth when he smiled. Why did Molly notice that? Why did she care?

"I—uh..." Molly's eyes got wide.

"I'm kidding. Relax." He walked toward the elevator. "Want to walk with me a bit?" Molly nodded and found herself following him. "You know I should come down there more often—the mail room, I mean. It's hard keeping track of everything. We're working on this thing with the phones right now, trying to build a major network, let them all talk to each other."

"Talk to each other?" Molly felt edgy on the elevator, just the two of them. The way she was around this guy, it made her feel bad about Easton. Like she was doing something wrong. She rolled her eyes at her thoughts. *It's not like he's even interested,* she reminded herself.

"Yeah, that's kind of the simple version. I've got a big company, and I dabble in a lot of other ones too. We're in a lot of cities. I'd like to be in more. But keeping everything under foot, it can be hard, you know? Quick communication, that's the key. I want information at the press of a button. The tip of my fingers. Beamed directly into my brain if I could have it. You'd be amazed what good you can do for the world with technology. We're doing interesting things with the hematology research center at the hospital I'm funding—like you'd be surprised at the lives *that* saves. Plus, I've a few other irons in the fire. Keeping the city in order. Someone's got to, right?"

That grin again.

The elevator dinged. He got off and found his entourage. Molly saw Lydia waiting for her, already out of her uniform and back in black. She dropped her head when she noticed Molly walking with the big boss. They all walked toward the door, veering into their separate spheres. Worlds apart, Molly thought to herself as he and the suits walked to the street and got in a team of pristine black towncars, each with its own tuxedoed driver.

"Till next time, Mail Room." He started into his towncar, turned to look at her one last time. "I don't recall your name. I'll get it from HR. You guys enjoy the city tonight. Should be a calm one."

Molly started to wave or nod or something at him, she wasn't sure which, as she and Lydia wandered up the street toward some food. She botched the whole thing, not looking where she was going, and almost made Lydia run into some street tourists.

Like some sort of radar, Molly turned her head to the next corner up the street, a stone-faced stare pierced into her and snapped her out of—whatever she'd been in. She shook the haze from her head. There was The Sergeant from the VA—

from the bookstore. He looked back at Molly, then Lydia, then past her to Germain's car as it drove off toward some important rich people thing. Molly felt him—he didn't feel happy. He hadn't in a very long time.

* * *

Back at the Penthouse, Murphy greeted the two of them in a slick evening gown, this one black and glimmering in the lamplight from the den. She tossed another one at Molly, dropping a set of shoes at her too.

"So, you sing, right? How's your dancing?" Murph fixed her earrings in place, bright flashing danglers, her hair a picture of elegance.

"Um. okay, I guess." Molly glared down at the gown in her hands. "Why?"

Murph smiled at her perky redheaded sidekick. "We're going to look at some art, kid."

WALKING THROUGH THE MAIN entrance into the atrium of the Lili Tower, Molly felt a deep cold slither down her back, wrap around her waist, and crawl its way back up to her throat. She felt naked in the dress and heels—no Chucks, no swords—just some sequins and her increasingly angry partner. She felt Murph's unease these last days, worse now that she'd dropped the *chosen one* bomb on her. Molly tried to put that out of her mind, but it stuck in the center of her skull, right alongside the green-skinned woman, Blake's last words about some mother of demons, and what that hillbilly preacher had called her: *The Devil's Child.*

And into the Devil's lair they walked. If the *outside* of the Lili appeared gruesome, it was only to those who'd never been *inside.* Half the attendees wore black ballroom masks, many more taking them from baskets near the stairwells. A faux-candle, fur, and bone chandelier hung four stories down in the center atrium as they walked in, its crags and points culminating in a carving of a wolf's head biting a bright orb. Staircases moved in waves and semi-circles, making no sense to any human eye, nor even Molly's—whatever she was. Stone faces, carved into the walls and pillars, leered back at them, their lifeless eyes trained on her anywhere she stood in the room.

The opulence of it all felt drowned in its sense of doom, yet all other patrons appeared immune to its ambiance. Many familiar faces from the previous Germain soiree mulled about, some admiring the artwork on display, much of it for sale in the silent auction—the proceeds all to benefit the charity hospital and hematology center, another joint venture of the city's elite.

"What asshole at the zoning office approved this shit?" Murphy whispered as they both fake-smiled at the others. The center fountain, half the width of the sprawling room, underneath the wolf chandelier, featured a massive coiled snake around its rim, the head of it biting into its own tail. Molly's nose and eye twitched. She knew this imagery, and she hated the sight of it.

"This place is evil." She turned to Murph, her eyes feeling those around her, some staring, most unaware of anything but sating their own lusts; such was the dominant emotion of the evening—as if all they wanted to do was writhe their bodies against each other in the marching doom of the coming cold.

Murph shrugged at Molly's warning, scanning the room for whatever she hoped to find here. Molly steeled herself for the job they came to do.

"You don't leave my side tonight." Murph had insisted, authority in her voice as she'd said it back at the penthouse. Lydia had slumped against the couch, pouting that she was housebound again. Molly wanted to stay with her, wanted to bail on this whole stupid charity gala. Lydia had been weird since the night they went shopping. Molly didn't like that crew she'd found her with at that bar. That woman pouring the drinks held an aura Molly couldn't make sense of, not unlike Murph herself. Sometimes she wondered who the goodguys and badguys in this town really were. Nothing here made sense—as if the whole town messed with her instincts.

"It's fine." Lydia had said. "You two go save the world. I'll see what's on MTV and order a pizza. Or I'll call Étoile and them, see what they're into maybe. You know, normal human stuff."

"Lydia, it's not like that, you know I—"

"I do know, Molly. I do." Lydia had stared back at her. She wore that black headband again, the one from the other night. Her emotions had been—all wrong. Molly hadn't wanted to leave her behind.

"Kids, you can hug it out over some *Care Bears* later. We're on a clock, Red." Murph threw another magazine in her purse, racked the slide on her pistol, clicked the safety and put it inside too. Then she grabbed a small knife, slid it in a sheath tucked in the inside of her garter belt.

"We going to a dance or to war?" Molly had flashed back to her prom night. Sometimes they were one in the same.

Molly did as instructed, sticking to Murphy as they made the rounds, checking out the various *artwork*. There was a wide painting featuring a gang of pilgrims burning a witch at the stake. Molly felt the woman's cries in pain as the fire licked the empty eyes of the men presiding over her death. Various portraits of historical figures hung all around: Genghis Khan, Alexander the Great, Xerxes of Persia, Oliver Cromwell, Churchill, Robert E. Lee, and a host more like that.

"Bunch of shitasses." Murph shook her head at all the dead men.

"Yeah, they were all assholes." A voice behind them chimed in, but Molly knew it as soon as it warmed her brain. He sounded the way good coffee tasted. Murph turned to see that rakish smile and another suit that was more built than sewn. *Where does he get those wonderful clothes?* Molly caught herself wondering as she drank his body with her eyes. He totally busted her at it too, and she didn't even care. *Molly Slater, what the hell?* She scolded herself, coming out of it.

"Ms. Hammond, right? VP of Development, you mentioned." He took Murph's hand, looking at her eyes the way he had Molly before. Whatever charm he had didn't work on Murph. Molly felt her cold resolve, looking through the suit, down the staircase they'd walked up, and staring at the main entrance. Molly felt the hairs on Murph's arms and neck stand stiff as spikes. Her eyes flared, ignoring the man in front of her for the one walking through the door with two gangly servants on either side of him.

His long dark hair fell down either side of his face like black curtains, blending into the sharpened beard coming off his chin like a dagger. His black eyes pierced every direction in the atrium at once. The exaggerated collar of his cloak rose at its tips nearly to his eyes. *But really who wears a cloak?* Molly shook her head. The inside of his garment sang a blood red song into the room as he reached a pale hand out making a demand quickly met with a goblet of dark wine. His boots thudded as if he needed everyone knowing each step he took. He flashed a gnarly set of chompers as he cocked his head, taking in the various patrons. If Murph's eyes had been guns, he'd already be dead.

"Boy that guy sucks." Molly blurted out like she was back at Bay High. *Oh lord, Molly, you dufe. Where is your damn head tonight?* It was the stupid pretty man, Jack, and she knew it. Pretty men did bad things in her head.

"Yeah he kinda does." Germain smiled, not missing Murph's ire aimed at the new arrival. "But he's paying for the better half of the building, not to mention this whole gala is all him, too."

"Why's he dressed like that?" Molly asked the questions she thought Murph would, but Murph only stared more holes in the grim dude in the stupid cloak.

"It's a bit ostentatious, I agree. I like things more..." Germain pursed his lips. "Restrained. Less is more, right?" He smiled at Molly again, his stupid pretty smile. She smiled back like the idiot she was in that moment. "Excuse me," he said.

Germain walked down the staircase, cool and professional. He shook the man's hand, the two of them looking back up at the women. Widening Murph's eyes even more—Molly thought they'd fall out any minute now—Germain waved them down.

"What do we do?" Molly side-mouthed to Murph, waking her from her hate-stare.

"Just be cool, kid, and stick next to me. Don't take your eyes off this thing." Molly knew by *thing* she meant the reject from *Tales From The Darkside.*

They descended the stairs with their eyes on the two men who couldn't look more mismatched, Germain cool and collected, a drink of scotch in a suit, the other one bordering on a clown complete with a cane.

"Ms. Gina Hammond, Ms.—Molly isn't it?" Germain looked her in the eye. *Did this dude still not know her name?* "May I present this evening's benefactor, Count Sardo Sandor of Moldavia."

Molly hadn't a clue where that place was. It probably sucked too.

The silent-screaming hate coming out of Murph made Molly grip her arm, sending waves of calm into her to minimal avail—the sensation of Murph's emotions so intense it threatened to overtake Molly herself. Then she felt it, deep inside—Murph had every intention of killing this man. It was just as she'd been that night in the alley when she pulled the trigger on that goon. Had it not been for

Molly's indestructible hand, it would have been murder. A doubt grew in her mind. *Did she really know anything about this Murphy Long?*

If this so-called Count had unnerved Murph, the next arrivals did so in triplicate to Molly Slater, tearing her mind in half and scattering the pieces to either side of the great hall in which they stood.

A violet-gowned flamboyance strode into the massive atrium, the lights from every corner of the palatial tower danced across her two-tone face—one half of her hair a rich purple, the other a rich gold. Dark eyeshadow adorned only one eye just above a long line of blood-red lipstick reaching almost to her ear—the other half of her face elegant but earth-toned. She flashed a gleaming, metallic smile at all the faces in the room, mocking them with her audacity, her garishness at their formal affair.

"Evilyn?" Germain raised an eyebrow at the spectacle walking at them. "What are you doing here?"

"Can't I broaden my mind?" Evilyn ran her fingers underneath Jack's chin, a shiver of jealousy flinching Molly's shoulders. Jack's mouth straightened, eyes furrowed as the flamboyant woman gave a knowing wink at Sardo, his face a sneer at her, as if she were any more awfully attired than he was.

An equally gaudy entourage followed behind her, more punk than ballroom but somewhere between the two. Spiked hair, piercings, leather and lace, colors that didn't fit the occasion. On any other night, Molly would have laughed and called them radical—might have even had a drink with them. But these weren't her people. These weren't any people. She felt their hollow souls, as she had before.

"You can relax, my fine gentlemen." Evilyn took each man by his arm, sandwiching herself between them. Murphy lost focus on hating this Count and grew curious at the Jester making a show of herself in front of everyone. Jareth caught Murphy's eye, the two of them squinting at one another.

"What mockery is this, witch?" The Count boomed, his voice a growl that put Murphy right back on her target. Molly saw her hand reach in her purse. This was all going sideways faster than Molly could think their way out of it. Not a person in their group seemed to have any idea what was happening, save the garish woman now commanding the room.

"But, my lord," Evilyn smirked, leering back at the two women she deemed beneath her. Murph's eyes stayed on The Count while Molly's darted between the four of them. "I've quite the surprise in store for you tonight." Evilyn's teeth gleamed like polished steel in the light as she smiled again, nodding at her entourage.

The third arrival took the wind from Molly's gut despite her not even needing it. Through the arching doors, Lydia Stiles waltzed into the room as all eyes darted to her direction. Her eyes hid behind her own black mask, her hair jutted out in spikes as thick as blades, her eyeshadow darker than even *she* had ever worn before. Her black gown presented a gothic nightmare as she appeared dressed to match the grim count standing next to them.

"Lydia? What?" Molly blurted without caution. Germain's eye looked to her at the comment, then at the new arrival. All eyes left Jareth and locked to Lydia, *Molly's Lydia.* Murphy had The Count. Molly shifted between Jack and Jareth, Jack seeming more out of sorts than any of them.

Evilyn walked to Lydia flowing through the room as on a cloud, her feelings empty, a blank Molly couldn't read. As if *her* Lydia was somewhere far away, going through some pre-programmed motion. Evilyn took Lydia by the hand, Molly noting a small scratch near her thumb, a bead of blood peeking out of it.

"My dear Count, may I present Ms. Stiles." Evilyn led Lydia to The Count as though she were some servant girl being auctioned along with the art. And to Molly's chagrin, Lydia curtsied at the fool in the cape. Molly shook her head so fast it vibrated, trying to clear the image.

Molly started for her friend, ready to ditch Murphy's biffed plan and be gone from here already, this whole town in fact. The devil could have it for all she cared. Murphy grabbed Molly by the arm, begging with her eyes not to blow their cover. Molly almost spoke her mind, but Lydia beat her to it.

"Would you dance with me, Count?" She bowed her head at him again. Molly's ire flared. Her fist balled, a thing Germain caught as well.

The Count raised an eyebrow at Jareth, then took Lydia by the hand—the one with the scratch—and led her to where a few couples waltzed to the orchestra playing in the far end of the atrium.

"What's this about, Evilyn?" Germain's face grew grim, stern—showing another man underneath the exterior he presented. "You don't belong here."

"You know each other?" Molly looked at Germain, then to Evilyn, then Murphy, who had Lydia and Sardo in her crosshairs.

"We go back." Germain didn't take his eyes off Evilyn, hers mocking him and somehow flashing to Molly's at the same time.

"Look, I'm ending this. It's gone far enough." Murph turned toward the dance floor. She still held Molly by the arm, and Molly felt Murph's hand grow hot as she released and started toward Lydia.

"Ah yes, the detective." Evilyn widened her grin, aiming it at Murphy like a gun. "Murphy, right?" She glanced at Germain, then back to Murph. "Or is it Gina Hammond? Or something else entirely tonight? Vice President of Development? Mail Room Associate? Detroit Police?" Evilyn enjoyed herself. She liked to play. It was the one thing Molly felt from her.

"Bitch, I fucking know you?" Murph squared her shoulders at the purple-haired woman. Molly's mind cracked from sensory overload. Her eyes blinked, always going back to Lydia dancing with that creepy Count.

"Or how about Wayne County Inmate #55731?" Evilyn pulled a mugshot photo from behind her back—*where'd it come from?*—showed it to Molly before handing it to Germain. Molly's eyes shot to the photo, Germain studying it, shaking his head, staring back to The Count and Lydia, then to Murph. "Assault against an officer of the law. Three years, wasn't it, Ms. Long, or Hammond, or whoever you are today?"

"Wasn't a goddamn officer. It was a fucking robot, you bitch piece of shit. The fuck you get that? Who the hell are you?" Murphy squared up, ready to go off. Molly felt something burning inside her, something...

"I *was* an investigating attorney for this city before—" Evilyn's eyes flashed for a second, looking to Germain, feeling...*regret.* She slipped for only a second, but Molly caught her. There was some history here, but its nature stayed locked between the two of them.

"Ms. Hammond, I think you should go now." Germain looked at her, his face stern, all business.

"Look, I—" Murphy stared at him, then Evilyn, then Molly, her eyes lingering on Molly, offering their saddest apology at her, and that's when Molly knew it was true—all of it. She'd sensed Murph's lies from the start, always spiked with enough truth, their common enemies enough to keep them going along with each other...until now.

Molly looked away from her toward Lydia, the only thing that mattered now—getting her out of here and the two of them home.

"Look, Kid, I—" Murph started.

Germain nodded at some suits at the door who marched toward them. "You're leaving now. Go quiet and I won't involve the police. I don't like *attention.*" Germain squinted at Jareth who smirked back at him.

"Yeah, I bet you don't, Copper." Murph had the building security behind her now. She threw her hands up, looking one last time at Molly.

"What did you call me?" Germain's face flushed, unsteady—the only time Molly had ever seen him lose any amount of his practiced cool. Evilyn Jareth roiled a deep belly laugh. She enjoyed this too much for Molly's money. "Ms. Slater and her *friend* may remain. Do not come back into my building. Ever." His stern face messaged something unsaid to security, then fell into a grim suspicion at Evilyn Jareth.

They walked Murphy out the front door.

XI
"NIGHT SONGS"
—CINDERELLA, 1986

MOLLY CALMED HER MIND. She focused her thoughts. The cop was a crook. She made her peace with that. She kept her eye away from Germain but always one on Jareth. She put the other on Lydia. She had one job now.

"I have to get my friend." Molly looked at Germain and started for the dance floor. The mask. Lydia's mask. They all wore masks. There were masks that night at the plant. "We need to leave."

"No, let me." Germain took Molly's hand, a strange reassurance coming into her from his touch. She glanced at his eyes—soft, kind in that moment. "If I do it, he won't make a scene." Molly nodded at him to go, keeping her eyes on Lydia dancing, using moves she'd never seen her do before. Like she was some other person—under some spell. "I'll speak to you later, Evilyn." He flashed a stern warning with his eyes, then bent his head to Molly and went to the dance floor.

Molly watched the scene unfurl. The high and mighty count chatted briefly with Jack Germain, billionaire, industrialist, philanthropist. He nodded his head forward, taking Lydia's hand and placing it in Germain's, deferring to him entirely, moving out of their way as he turned to select another dance partner to finish the serenade.

Germain kissed Lydia's hand as he took it, then led her in the same waltz, the trance she'd been under still thick on her mind. But whatever oddness Molly had felt at the count holding her best friend hadn't yet abated—wouldn't until Lydia was in her arms, hurdling high above this wicked town, moving as fast as her incredible strength would take them.

"Truly something isn't he?" the voice behind her spoke like a sip of bourbon tasted the very first time—bitter, biting, but alluring all the same, making you already want more of it. "The way he glides in, everyone doing as he wishes. Like he bought the world and would make it his slave."

Molly glared at Jareth from the side of her eye but kept her focus on Lydia. Her gut told her to go to Lyd. Molly searched for The Count. There was still something here she didn't see. She searched all of them, looking for the answer she needed to find. Her mind raced back to the green-skinned woman with the spear. Who was she? What was really going on here?

"I just need you to know one thing." Jareth placed her hands on Molly's shoulders. The clown was about to catch a beating, spectacle or no spectacle.

"What?" Molly's shoulders tensed up, her fists ready to punch.

"It was never personal."

Evilyn wrenched Molly's neck with her hands—incredibly strong for a *human.* Before Molly could think, jerk herself free of it, Evilyn sank two metal fangs deep into Molly's neck, tearing into her, blood pouring out as she felt the witch *drinking her.*

Molly's scream burst every window in the building; ten thousand pounds of glass exploded in an instant. Thunder boomed from the sky, and a gale wind blew through the atrium from the now open airways. More screams followed suit as the giant wolf's head chandelier crashed down from the ceiling. Every light inside went out. Darkness took hold.

Molly turned on the witch, gripping her hand from her neck and throwing her off. Blood ran down her neck and chest, soaking her dress. She kicked Evilyn hard enough to send her through a brick wall—she knew she did—but Evilyn planted her feel and stopped herself. The witch closed her eyes, then opened them again, flashing white, the same way Molly's had the night she fought Blake at her prom.

"Yes!" Evilyn bellowed. "Yes! The power." She looked at her own hands, curling her sharp-nailed fingers into talons.

Molly felt sick in her stomach. Something...inside her. Something awful. Evil.

Then, in the dark and chaos and confusion of it all, descending from the emptiness left behind by the crashed chandelier, a thing darker than night itself fell upon them. A cape—or wings—or just more darkness flowed behind it, around it. It landed in front of her, a black-armored centurion. Every piece of armor formed and fitted perfect to its wearer, all of it, all of *him* moved in unison. Three sharp horns protruded from the grim helmet covering his face but for his lips and chin.

The knight looked at Molly, then turned his black gaze upon her enemy, the witch's fangs still dripping blood. The thing charged at Evilyn, the darkness flowing along with it. It seized her with its mighty arms, their faces almost touching—smelling each other.

"El Shaddai!" The grim knight turned to Molly again, then to Evilyn.

"Not today, I think, darling." Evilyn smiled, then kicked the warrior across the atrium, through the opposite wall, just like—just like Molly would have done. Evilyn turned to Molly, her tongue lapping up the last drops of blood on her chin. Her eyes became fiercer, her hands...transforming into claws. "I want more."

Molly screamed another roaring scream, the wind on her breath pushing the sorceress backward, deafening any human ears in the room, if any here even were human. One of them was. "Lydia!" Molly's scream boomed with the thunder outside.

In the darkness, the chaos, the scrambling and screams, Molly reached for Lydia—found only emptiness and the cries and prayers of dozen patrons. Double that number spat curses. Some evil worm crawled in Molly's belly, wriggling its way through her skin.

"Lydia!" she screamed again. Each time at a decibel that shook the earth. She dashed around, vomit welling in her throat. She spat out something in the night. Then the dark grew dimmer again. That grim knight returned. Someone— something snatched at her from behind. She turned, the blonde spiked hair of Lydia's *friend* Étoile, her own set of fangs reaching down from her gums, snarling at Molly.

Molly punched into Étoile's chest, grabbed a rib bone, broke it out and sank it into the bitch's head. More of her gang crawled out of the chaos. The knight and Evilyn locked up with each other in some old duel between them. None of it made sense. She grabbed at the wound on her neck, the blood already clotted—she felt her skin sealing itself.

Étoile's fanged companions growled at her, their bones snapping and bulging under their skin, hair growing out of them everywhere as they dropped to all fours, snarling at her—wolves. They were wolves. Big ones. They stood between her and the door.

So, Molly made a new one.

XII
"HOLDING OUT FOR A HERO"
—BONNIE TYLER, 1984

MOLLY FLED INTO THE NIGHT, the city looming down at her as thunder clapped above. A storm grew by the second, lightning turning the night to day every few moments.

"Lydia!" Her scream exploded the glass of every building on the block. She city ran into the streets. Half the town trembled as the sky lit up, and her screams boomed all the way to the river. She wretched again, holding her guts, as black sludge crawled from her mouth onto the ground at her feet. A howl raised her eyes to the Lili, to the hole she'd knocked in the wall to escape. The wolves had found her again.

She ran. The Sledgehammer, the Baytown Badass, the girl with iron skin, ran into the night. She ran slow—slow for her. Her writhing stomach stopped her every few blocks to wretch and vomit more black goo.

The howls stayed with her, her steps coming slower and slower. Her head stabbed her. She'd left Lydia. *I left her.* Tears flooded her face, washing some of her blood from her dress. It wasn't red anymore. It wasn't even blood. She felt it in her fingers. It felt like—metal.

Teeth grabbed her from behind. One of them caught up with her, snapping its wolfen jaws on her left arm, biting and gnashing its teeth to no purchase. She seized the wolf by the throat, ripped it off her and hurled it into a wall, its dog yelp echoing into the dark.

She ran on, the night following behind her. Howls. And more. Something worse followed her. She ran through parks, streets, alleyways, across the parking lot of the Dome. She didn't know the city. She tried to leap for high ground, but her legs failed her. Her strength came and went. Her screams woke the dead from their above-ground graves. The rain fell around her, soaking the city.

Molly found herself nearing the interstate, traffic on it slowing to a halt as the lights of the city failed. Lightning blew a transformer, wrapping everything in more dark. Molly was lost, and she knew it. They would be on her again any second. She made her way under the overpass, scanning, searching, everywhere.

Two homeless men crawled out from a pile of cardboard and dirty blankets. They pointed up, the lightning scattering itself across the sky. In its brief flash Molly saw her, those metal fangs gleaming in the electric light. And then she knew. Somehow that witch had found it, whatever her swords were made of: the metal that could cut her skin.

"Come on, little godling." The witch moved toward her, a host of her dire wolves gathering behind her like a small army, the click of her stiletto heels making

Molly hate her more with each step. "I will make it quick for you. As I said, it's nothing personal."

Molly's eyes lit, grew fierce. The witch had Molly's own strength to use against her now—plus those fangs. If she came for a fight, Molly would give her one to remember.

But the night had other plans. Bats flew in every direction. From all across the city, they flapped their wings in tune with the booming thunder above them all. They swarmed in. The grin on Evilyn's face shrank to a thin line under her flaring nostrils as she looked through Molly toward the opposite end of the overpass. The swarm gathered as the grim knight walked out of it, his horned helmet housing those dark eyes intent upon her.

"You will not have her." Evilyn's hands glowed with a purple fire, a ball of it forming in each of her talons.

Molly turned to the knight reaching his hand toward her.

"El Shaddai." Its—*his* face spoke with a commanding bass, but familiar. He held out his hand. A sparkling ball fired into his chest, knocking him back. Molly looked at him, gaining his footing again, the bats swarming in a circle above him as if he commanded him, which he clearly did. She looked to Evilyn, forming another ball of purple fire—then back to the knight.

He lifted his helmet, it retracting from his head on command, as though it too were made of some unearthly metal. His eyes bored into her. His face—that beautiful face she'd stared at so much in the last week—smiled kindly at her. Jack Germain—his smile warmed her as he held out his hand

"Come." He waved her on. "I will not hurt you."

Molly's mind ached. Then the night tore itself apart again with another scream. Not human, not wolf, not the screech of bats, but now of high-octane horses. More of them than Molly had ever heard tethered to one engine in her life. The awesome wail of Old Detroit muscle drowned even the booming thunder above.

Evilyn Jareth hissed, baring her gleaming fangs at this new arrival to their contest. Germain's eyes grew fierce, dark, angry. One of the homeless from the pile—too drunk or unmoved to have fled—stood up, his eyes awakening as the sound of the engine screaming into the night grew louder, closer.

"It's him." the man pointed his gaunt finger—a pair of headlights close enough to light up the scene. "He's back! Get up, boy." He kicked his companion cowering under cover beneath him. "You're about to get a hell of a show."

The whine of the engine came upon them. Screams and dog yelps burst into the air. The car—that's what it had once been from the looks of it—mowed down Jareth's wolves beneath its spiked wheels. Silver blades gleamed from everywhere on it. All black, bits of scrap iron and steel welded onto it. Like some hound of the apocalypse, it roared into its foes.

Evilyn turned one last time to grin at Germain opposite her, then burst into a cluster of owls, fleeing into the darkness.

The car braked into a 180-degree turn. Still coming to a stop, the driver's door flew open. A man—a very big man wearing a copper Spartan helmet and heavy armor of his own—stepped out of the car, held out two grenade guns aimed at either side of him, and fired.

The grenades exploded into a silvery mist, shrouding everything. Molly looked through it as best she could. The man in the copper helmet stomped away from his car. A heavy pauldron on one shoulder but not the other, he pulled another gun from a holster on his belt, firing into more wolves, creatures, whatever they were. Some charged at him, choking from the silvery gas. He sliced them across the face with more silver blades jutting from his arms, his shoulders, everywhere on him some gleaming, sharp piece of metal. He made his shots like a practiced expert, hitting everything he aimed at, moving in perfect form—*like a soldier.*

Molly turned to Germain, his face twisted. He looked back at her, his mouth wrinkling into some snarling, pale monster—his eyes red, hair black, like some...demon.

"El—" He choked as he tried to speak.

"Get in the car." Came a gravelly voice behind her. Molly turned to see the Copper helmet moving at her, pulling out another gun, a shotgun from a back holster.

"What?" Molly turned to Germain, then to Copper. "I don't—"

"I said get in the car." He reached his thick human arm down and threw her into the open door of his cobbled together war-car. He opened up his shotgun on Jack Germain, her boss, the owner of the biggest corporation in the city, a guy she'd played the big piano with, a monster, a demon. *A vampire.*

The big man, his armor as thrown together as his car, none of it matching any other part, like he made it up as he went along, fired blast after blast into the snarling Germain until he spent the gun. He sprinted back to the car, leaped into the driver's seat and stomped the gas.

The muscle car burnt its rubber on the New Orleans blacktop, its smoke adding to that already in the air. The copper knight floored it down the road, putting blocks between them and Germain within seconds. The inside of the cabin, lights and blinking everywhere, buttons and toggles and switches, it reminded her of Lydia's truck. *Lydia!*

"My friend." Molly tried to see out the windows—the city still black as pitch. "I have to go back for my friend."

"Your friend is dead." The man behind the helmet didn't turn to look at her or offer anything more, just kept the eye slit on the road ahead of them.

"That—" Molly gulped, her lip quivering at that hateful thought. "No." Tears poured from her face as she reached her feelings out, blanketing the city around her. She would find Lydia. Now that she had a moment to focus, concentrate, she could find her. She sent herself to every corner of downtown. Every alley, every building, every rooftop, every car, everywhere.

But there was nothing.

A crack of thunder boomed so loud it shook the earth beneath the speeding car. Buildings rattled from it. A bolt of lightning slammed into the Superdome as they sped by, the car braking into a 90 degree turn toward Canal. Bricks and dust rained along with the water down on them as the car sped under the falling debris.

"His damn weather machine's gone haywire." He braked into another turn.

Sirens wailed.

"The police." Molly looked out the window.

"They're *his* police. Half of them bloodsuckers same as him. And god damn Evilyn. God damn you, Evilyn." He turned his helmet at Molly and jerked her head to reveal the bite mark on her neck. "She bit you? You're fucking bit?"

He pulled his pistol from its holster and shoved it in her neck. She snatched it from his hand and crushed it.

"Don't ever do that again. I swear I—" Molly felt another wretch bubble up. She vomited it onto the floor at her feet.

"God damn it." The man shouted through his metal façade.

More cops pulled behind and alongside them. He flicked a switch and all his lights went out, some thick smoke gushing out of his exhaust. He slammed his fist on a button in the dash.

"Tell me we got a jump!"

"Jump in 15 seconds." A small screen next lit up as it spoke back in a computery voice.

"Your car talks?" Molly squinted at it. But. then, she had a computer that walked and talked and was the very spitting image of herself, so the shock wore off fast.

"What? That's just the radio."

Okay, that makes more sense.

The helmet-man dropped his foot to the floor, putting every horse under that hood to work. The blue lights trailed but stayed with them as the car hurtled toward the other end of Canal.

"Dude, what are you doing? The river!" Molly shoved her finger at the windshield, pointing at the giant Mississippi that surely no one could miss. "We're about to run out of road."

"We're about to not need one." He gave it every last bit the car had. A light on the dash kicked on, blinking bright. "Hold on." He slammed his armored fist into another switch and the car blasted itself into the air just before they hit the riverbank. The cop cars screeched behind them. Molly looked back and *down* at them.

The car launched itself into the sky, not unlike she had done herself a hundred times by now. But, unlike her, the car didn't fall. It flew.

Across the river, high and away from the unlit city, they flew. Molly's eyes welled again at the thought of Lydia. More lightning flashed like it was trying to grab them—like it wanted to strike her. Her head reeled, and some darkness flooded into her. Somewhere over the swamp outside the city, she passed out.

XIII
"PARTYMAN"
—PRINCE, 1989

High above the city, in the top floor senior office of the Cain Capital building, its CEO toiled away into the night. The lights had finally come back on only an hour ago. If he hurried, he could finish going through the reports before dawn.

The storm had been unusual. He'd need to inquire about that. The weather machine was still new technology, a test run here in the city. If it could be perfected, they could branch into other areas, solidify *His* network around the world.

"Sir." An assistant made his way into the office. "Dawn comes, sir."

"Yes, yes. Draw the curtains, then, Smythe." He had lost time to the outage. The master would expect this to be done. *He* didn't tolerate failure.

"Don't bother, Smythe." A giggle entered the room. The few lights around the large suite hinted at her face as she clicked her heels toward him.

"Evilyn." The CEO sneered. "You can't be here."

"I can't?" She brought her face into the light, smiling like a jackal at the simple pawn before her. "It was my family name on this building for three decades."

"That was before. Our master put—"

"*Our?*" Evilyn snarled. "No. Not *our* anything. This building, this city belongs to me now." She walked behind his desk, stood next to him as he rose to face her.

He reached his hand toward his drawer.

"I don't think so." She crushed his hand with her own, still getting used to all her wonderful new gifts.

"Smythe!" He winced as his hand bones began to reform themselves. "Call the—"

Evilyn gripped his throat with her one hand, then waved the finger on her other in a circle, opening a door behind poor Smythe and blew him through it. Into the Land of Mist.

"What have you done, witch?"

"I've only done what I always meant to do." She licked her shiny metal teeth, gazed out the window at the cresting hint of light on the horizon.

"Evilyn...the curtain—the sun!" He rasped, his throat gripped tight in her iron hand.

"Yes, the sun. Let's watch it rise together, shall we?" She smiled again.

"Evilyn, we can't—"

She gripped his throat tighter, cutting off his words. *So* beneath her now—they all were. How delicious it would be, what was yet to come. And now—yes now that her old friend had returned—oh how wonderful.

"There is no *we.*" She let the light of the sun pour onto her face, closing her eyes to its warmth. How long had it been? Eight years? Had it been eight years here on Earth? So many trips into The Land of Mist, she was older now than she could even know. The smoke flowed into her nostrils, filling the room with its stench. She looked over, the poor creature in her arms a flaming corpse, crinkling and popping as the sun burnt him to ash. "Oh, sweetie, you don't look well."

She dropped what little of him remained to the floor. She'd get a new assistant to clean it later. She'd be getting a whole new staff starting today. First order of business would be the sign on the building. Putting things right again. How they belonged.

She giggled at herself, spinning her chair, basking in the first light of dawn.

She spun back to the desk. Flipping through the files and folders she'd go through all in good time. She glanced at the newspaper laid at the corner, pulled it up to see what the fishwrap had to say about things.

"Alex Charlton." She curled her lip as she read the byline. "What Darkness Haunts the Crescent City?" Evilyn laughed a heavy, booming laugh to herself, looked up from the paper, kicked her legs up on the desk—*her* desk. "All hail the new queen in town."

EPISODE IV

0
"WITHOUT YOU"
— MÖTLEY CRÜE, 1989

MOLLY SAW HERSELF, all those years ago, eight years old—so they'd guessed when they'd found her wandering into town dressed in those ridiculous clothes—sitting at the lunchroom at Bay Elementary. She poked at the food in her tray. It wasn't good, but she ate it anyway. Those first days remained a fog to her. She hadn't gotten used to speaking, learning as she went. It was something she'd only told one other person in her life—the very one that sat down across from her that day.

"Hey, you're the new girl they found last month, right? Do you really not talk? Did your parents die? Here, you can have my roll—I don't like them." Her dark hair and raven eyes comforted Molly, as if they reminded her of someone she couldn't remember. "I'm Lydia, by the way. My dad always says I should tell people my name but sometimes I forget."

"I'm um..." She'd searched her empty head. Molly was the name they gave her, but there was some other one—one she couldn't find or say. Everything felt weird and wrong. But this kid across the table smiled as she gave away her food—to a stranger.

"Wh-what's th-that thing?" Molly pointed at the boxy device peeking through Lydia's bookbag.

"My Walkman?" Lydia pulled it out and set it on the table. "My daddy got it for me for Christmas even though they're kind of expensive, he said. We're not supposed to have them at school, so you can't tell anyone."

"Wh-at does it do?"

Lydia scoped around for a teacher, then handed Molly the headphones over the table.

"Do you know The Runaways?" Lydia pushed play and cranked it.

Little Molly's eyes grew three sizes that day.

* * *

Two men watched her scream into the night in the tent they set up for her—the rain pouring down onto the earth around it, the boom of thunder a constant. Twice a bolt struck the lightning rod at the far end of the compound.

"God damn weather machine's busted-ass." the older one with the bad leg looked up at the sky, shook his head, and got another beer from the chest under the covered porch.

They stood there, behind the salt line clear-coated in their own brand of sealant, watching her through the night. Somewhere just before dawn she finally cried herself to sleep.

I
"THE NUMBER OF THE BEAST"
—IRON MAIDEN, 1982

THE PRINCE OF DARKNESS stormed through his castle atop the murk. The stagnant waters of this hateful bog had taken their share of souls even before he'd arrived to command the night here. One of his own daughters, Meggoth, had taken up residence some millennia ago. He still heard the echoes of those dead souls that hadn't found their way across the veil. Some said there had been an uprising, a detachment of union soldiers and freed slaves lured into ambush, cut off from any way out, and succumbed to the silent sadness of the swamp.

It amused him, the thought of these fetid mortals wandering lost in search of what was denied him, would always be denied him. But today, even their cries on the summer wind could not abate his rage.

"What has she done?" The beast hurled his great table onto the floor, its settings flying about the hall. "She, this paltry witch, this human maggot, this clown I kept as a pet, *she* dares defy me? ME?" The beast stomped his hooves to his chair and slumped. He had to inter soon. He needed rest for the now inevitable fight. And to make it all the worse, the bronze-headed fool had crawled out of his eight-year hole—of all nights.

"I told you to kill the witch years—"

The dark lord silenced the gaudy-clad fop. "I do not invite critique, Sandor." The son of the Eldar demon queen waved his gnarled, clawed hand. The candlelight flickered across his horned head as he shifted his form, putting on the face called Germain.

It was as good an identity as any he'd taken, and one he'd used before in this city, over half a century earlier. It had been easy to walk back into, dormant accounts with decades of interest accrued—how he loved that word: *interest.* Of all the curses he'd wrought upon that petty god's pets, this might be his favorite—that the surplus of their labor, their hard spent days and hours away from everything that mattered and they loved, should all trickle upward—*to him.* It brought a grin to his lips, even in this audacious betrayal.

And Evilyn, what *had* she done? Who was the red child? The blood lingering on the witch's lips—that smell. It had been ten thousand years. Twenty? At least a full age before the flood when his serpentine brother had risen from the depths and challenged heaven itself—never to return. And his other brother—the one more akin to his own more brutal, lupine form—bound as he had been... That awful chain.

"Can it be?" His eyes showed fear for the first time since his mother had found him ten years ago sealed and buried beneath the mortals' little church. "This child who fed her lips. I must find this child...before she—" His eyes flashed—memories of the decades, centuries he'd been bound before. His mind flayed at the thought. As dull as his endless life had become, he still preferred to be above ground and mobile for it. A century interred was maddening enough—but infinity? He felt the plight of the Eldar—cursed with true eternity like himself—and his vile mother who bore him to a mortal man merely to mock some lesser god. He called Evilyn his Jester Queen, but it was *He*—his cursed life—that had been the joke of the ages.

"If she is the one, my lord." Sardo bowed low before his master—his long black cloak flapping from the draft of the dreary castle on the mire. "She will be found. And eliminated."

"No!" Germain boomed, standing again, shifting into a dire wolf's head—his gryphon's claw pointing forward. "I shall have her. If she is El Shaddai, The Destroyer, she could end this wretched curse. With her power and her at my side, I could challenge the fool himself, the one that did this to me. I could at last have my revenge." He slumped again, turning back into Germain, a half smile forming at his lips. "We must draw her here—to me."

"How, my lord?"

"My children." the beast licked at his fangs. "Call my children forth."

"But, sire..." Sardo trembled before the Prince of Darkness. "The Fae?"

"Once I have the power of that red child, I will crush the Fae."

II
"I'M COMING OUT"
—DIANA ROSS, 1980

Evilyn Jareth, the biggest smile on her face in years, twirled her way into the room housing the weather generator, already billowing out the morning's clouds for the *Master* to walk in the day. She danced into the room, her trailing teal gown with garish orange trim and cuffed sleeves flowing in waves around her.

Three lab techs tried to stop her. She hurled them away into the Mist Realm with a circle of her finger and a gust of her breath. That lovely little trick was *so* much easier to do now. No more drawing on walls with chalk. She need merely whisper the cast and twirl a finger. So pleasant. Simple. She was getting used to her newfound abilities and how they augmented her others. Yes, she was quite going to enjoy all this.

Jester Queen, he'd named her eight years ago when he made her his puppet, a pet, a joke against his bronze-helmed enemy—she nothing but an object between them.

"Oh, D, you sweet foolish man." She chuckled as she cast an energy bomb at the machine, its sparks and fizzles shooting in all directions. She tossed another bomb, and a third, each time picturing his face, both their faces. "Why did you have to come back now? Of all the times..." But she already knew. She felt it crawling in her own veins. The girl was more than just this raw power. She was something much...*more.*

A tear threatened to roll out her dry, dead eyes. It wasn't her doing. The little brat was inside her. Telling her things. Or was it? It couldn't be that—at moments since it began she'd almost thought she felt...*alive* again. She couldn't entertain such fantasies. She was who she was. And she would show them, this whole city, her city, the one *He* claimed as his own—she would show them a true Queen.

* * *

Dr. Bianca Tesche looked into the microscope in the control room at the plastics plant on Poydras. The bits of the ground stone Evilyn had enchanted interacted with the micro-neuro-transmitter in fascinating ways. The earlier prototypes had shown utility, but this next batch was on another level. Outside, the production assembly churned out the masks by the dozen, ready to be sent to paint and design and then delivery.

"Have you finished any of the new units yet?" her benefactor's voice called out from the opening portal as she stepped from it. Evilyn stood—a new woman, taller than before—smiling bigger than her usual grin.

"Not yet. They're just coming off now."

"Shut them down." Evilyn dropped a sack of ground stone on the lab table. "I've got a whole new plan!" She giggled and walked through her still-open gateway and vanished.

* * *

Upper Magazine Street burst with life that morning. The last of the clouds drifted out of the sky, sending more than a few of the *elites* indoors, all muttering as they shuttered their windows. The sun grew bright in the sky. Families, children, young couples littered the storied district, ready to enjoy the rare bright day—though it would not be rare anymore.

Unknown to them as the reason for it all, Evilyn Jareth, still loudly dressed in her orange and teal with a matching top hat cocked to one side, strode down this hallowed stretch of the old Crescent City, *her* city. She would make this town sing again.

Eyes gazed at her, the light dancing off her shining face—how warm and comforting the sun felt after all these years. Children pointed, some smiling, some concerned. Mothers pulled them away as couples separated their arms to give her wide berth as she walked among them.

"Fear not, lovelies." She circled her arm and bowed to a cluster of young things—so sweet, innocent. She flipped her hat off her head and pulled flowers from it—handing them to the children. Then she reached in again, grabbed a handful of petals and flung them into the air, all becoming birds before their eyes and fluttering off into the sky. "Enjoy this. Dance in it. Sing in the sun!"

She took a young girl from a cafe chair outside The Sea Witch Cafe—such a lovely name for a tea house—her paramour left dumb as the garish woman danced into the road, halting oncoming cars and bikes with a wave of her hands. "The day is yours, darlings. I give it back—I give it all back to you! Go out. Eat. Drink. Make love to all that is. Live. Breathe. Dance."

She studied their confused faces, some giggling at her ostentations. The new day had just begun. But there would come more, and more, and yet more beyond that. She had much to do to see it all finished. She marched toward midtown, dancing and twirling in the brightening sun, singing to herself—hurling her magic into the blue sky.

III
"COPPERHEAD ROAD"
—STEVE EARLE, 1988

Boscaux Maximilien St. Michel Chevalier DeBrousse—or just D to those who knew him—rattled down the road in his big block Dodge Ram. He had Jerry Lee sitting up next to him in the cab eyeing those biscuits from Granny's shack out on 90. Jerry-Lee was a good boy, but he hated to be away from his brother Hooch. One of them always had to stay behind to watch the yard, so D took turns with them when he drove in for biscuits.

Al had the coffee going when D got into the kitchen and handed him a cup. The dogs ran at each other. D broke a biscuit in two and threw a bit to each one. They snapped them out of the air, snarled at each other like they hadn't just been hugging and playing, and then both hauled off to different parts of the yard.

D eyed the pop-up tent outside, quiet as church in there.

"She ain't budged yet." Al leaned more than sat against the rusty steel milk can he used for a stool in their 'mess' as the two men called it. Old habits faded slow.

"Hmm." D sipped his coffee, pinched a bite of his biscuit. He glared at the pop-up, then down at his hands, still trembling after they'd done their work last night. He grabbed the Colt Python he kept on the side table, checked the hollows for silver salts, and clipped the holster to his belt.

"They don't change that fast anyhow. You done knowed that." Al folded out the paper and flipped through it. "Ain't a word about you in this damn thing."

"Ain't never is." D sucked his coffee. "*He* don't like the attention." He took the sports section from Al and thought again to the night before. He swore he'd seen Evilyn's eyes flash at him just before he broke through the dogs. Probably some of them were her crew. Then the gods-damned monster Cain himself— slobbering his gnarly teeth all over that redheaded girl from down the way. He'd looked her up after she left the hospital that night. Wasn't hard to find tell of some fire-hair in a pink dress smashing cars and some kind of steel beast across the Bay. Why in the cold hell did she have to come here of all the places on the gods' cursed earth? He swore about it two or three more times. Somewhere at the top of his second cup he dozed—just for a second.

"Excuse me, but where am I?" Her voice jolted him awake, his hand going straight for the Colt and had it cocked and trained on her in a second.

Al hopped on his good leg, trying to get his other in gear but the batteries had gone off again. They still needed to work on that.

"Boy, she done cruised right over that salt line like it ain't even there." Al slapped his knee brace a time or two and got the leg buzzing.

"Is that a robot leg? That's cool." Molly watched him move the leg with a TV remote.

"Just a brace, and it ain't that cool, girlie. Still aches me something powerful."

"Here, I can help that." She reached her palm for his head, and he leapt back like she was snake would bite him. "I'm not gonna hurt you."

"Ain't been seen yet." Al fidgeted.

The kid looked around, taking in where she was. She peered through the back window onto the yard itself—heaps of old cars, rusted out junk from ages past. The crane that still needed hydraulic fluid. The two Dobermans running and playing out amongst the scrap. The wind blowing steel against rusted steel.

"Is this a junkyard?"

"This here's Hat Creek Iron and Scrap, little girl. Name of Al Davenport, owner-proprietor. You done met Sgt. D, time or two he been said."

"I thought—"

"What was you expecting? The Ritz? Some big mansion on a cliff?" Al laughed, sat on the couch and grinned at her.

"You, sit." D pointed her at the chair with his pistol. He could tell from her squint she didn't care for his posture. "I got questions."

Molly glared back at him, then at the chair, then at the biscuits. She dropped into the seat, looked at them again, then at the food. And the coffee. She looked tired.

"That won't do anything." She noted the pistol then reached for a biscuit and a knife of butter from the tray. "Can I have this?" She didn't wait for a yes before she bit into it. D studied her neckline. Those shocks of red covered half of it. He reached over to flick it out of the way, but she gripped his fingers like a damn vise.

"I gotta see your bite." D's eyes said more than his words had because she let him go and brushed her hair away There wasn't a mark on her. Like fresh baby skin. "I don't—I saw it last night. You were bit, bad too."

"Yep." She tore into a second biscuit, got up and ran through his fridge, pulling out the milk and a slab of ham on the bone they'd smoked a few nights ago. She went at it like she was sure enough gone feral. "Some witch named Jareth."

Evilyn. He knew he'd seen her. *God damn. Just god damn it to misty hell and back.*

"But I told you I'm different. I'm not—I'm not human. Least I don't think." The kid went through the ham and the rest of their milk in short order and was in the fridge again. "She had metal teeth. There's only one thing I know that can cut me. Some kind of alien metal. I have some. Not here, though."

"I need to know everything. Everything you can do. Where you came from. How you—work, I reckon." D sat down and carved a slice of what ham was left after she'd been at it.

"I go first." She glared, drinking the last of his damn coffee. "I need to know what those things were, what *he* is, who you are, that witch, and most of all...I need to know what happened to my friend."

D sighed. The kid's face in the morning light, if he caught it right it almost reminded him of—no, he wouldn't go there. He hated this part. Every time.

"They ate her. *That's* what they are. What they do." He watched the kid's eyes quiver up, her balled fists shaking, vibrating. He needed to calm her, placate her somehow. If she went turbo in nothing but a two-room clapboard shack, they'd be bathed in splinters in a second.

"Here comes the rain again." Al stood up and managed to kick D in the back with his 'bot leg. "Go hug the damn kid, man. She ain't gonna bite nobody."

D, six foot seven and pushing three hundred last he'd checked, put his huge arms around the strange kid that he'd seen could hurl him into the sky if she'd wanted. Something happened when they touched. Some part of him went into her and her into him and it made him wince and want to jump back, but he held on. He saw *Soleil* flash across his brain again. He thought he'd lose his own grip and go to tears. *What the hell was this girl?*

"I can't believe it." She shoved her face into his sleeve. The pups ran back in from the yard, and both coiled at her feet, whimpering for her. It's like if she cried, the world cried with her. Even the sun outside slipped behind a cloud again. "I can't believe she's gone. She's my—she was my best friend—and I—"

"I know, kid." D saw Evilyn again. How she'd been before. When she—when they... "I know. They're the damn demons straight from hell itself. And *He's* the goddamn devil."

"He called me something." She looked up. "A name, I think. El Shaddai."

Al Davenport's eyes widened and went for D's, a whole face-code of their own passing unsaid in an instant.

"He said that?" D put his hands on her shoulders—looked in her eyes. "He called you El Shaddai?"

"Yeah." She raked wetness from her face with her arm. "What does it mean?"

IV
"METAL GODS"
–JUDAS PRIEST, 1980

MOLLY SLATER SLUMPED back in the dog-bitten old recliner, the stuffing coming out of it in four places, duct tape and prayer holding it together at this point as she stared at the laid-out, leather, table-length collage of glued-on drawings, scribbled words, and foreign script all over it. The old man rattled on as The Sergeant, or D as he said to call him, dropped a handful of books into her lap. She held her head with her hand. *Was this another hangover?* She felt like she could use one of those drinks that produced her first one.

It's all my fault, she told herself over and over. *Never should have come in the first place. Never should have left her alone. Stupid, stupid, Molly.* Her eyes watered again, her mind reaching for her friend, across the distance. She tried reaching all the way back home, pushing herself to new limits. She felt her mom— her foster mom—Clair. Hurl. In the garage Becky laughed with *Andi?* She'd never felt Andi before. Andi wasn't like *people. Was she?* It all confused her even more. And through it all: No Lydia. Nowhere.

She was truly gone.

"God? You're telling me there's gods. Like Big G god?"

"Well, Big G is saying a lot. I ain't met a one of you yet's worth a capital letter." D folded his arms while Al chuckled and cracked an Old Milwaukee. "No offense."

"Yeah sure." Molly blinked. She'd told them the whole story, all about what she could do, what she had done. She even told them about sensing people's feelings and how that worked.

"Prayer. More or less." D told her. "It's why you're stronger the more they like you. That's how gods work, way we've figured it. Ain't never met one of you before that didn't know you was one though. Usually it's the first and only damn thing y'all ever talk about. Can't shut up about it. Bunch of shitasses. Again, no offense."

"And *Him?*" Molly took one of Al's beers even though it wouldn't do anything. "Germain?"

"We just call him Cain. He's half god. Was half man. Now? Well, he's what you seen. Goddamn monster's what he is. The beast that stalks the night. Cursed. Can't be in broad sunlight or he'll burn, rot. Eats people, drinks their blood like wine."

Molly thought of that first night she met him, the cup he'd held in his hand. She shivered that she'd been so close. *Gods, you danced on the big piano with him, you twit! Gross. He's literally WORSE than Blake, Molly, you absolute dip.*

"Who is he? You said he's half god?"

D dropped a James bible in her lap. Then a book on Egypt. Another one with strange symbols on the cover.

"Hebrew. Babylon. Sumeria. Canaan. Hell, even Egypt and Rome. Dozen others. All got some ancient story of one brother kills another. Some of them gods. Some men. All damn similar, you ask me. Well, whatever truth there ever was to it—he's the brother-killer. Along come a pissed off god to play cop after it too. Lays this whole curse on him. Can't walk in the daylight. Has to drink blood to live—what kind of asshole god adds that line item? Takes on the form of anything he eats or drinks. Can't cross the salt line. Can't abide silver. Worst part of all? Can't die. Ever. From nothing. Not a damn thing."

"But I thought the sun?" Molly sat up, trying to make sense of it.

"Hurts him. Slows him down. But won't kill him. Never will. That's his real curse—to never die. Walk the earth for eternity. Can't even imagine how old the damn thing is. How old are you by the way?"

"I'm 18." Molly shrugged. "Or, I think. I don't really know. But, the other ones—like him. You killed them though."

"Them, sure. His offshoots. Byproducts of his curse. He figured out how make himself some *friends* long time ago. Vamps. Werewolves. Striga. Ghouls. What have you. He's the daddy of them all. You've heard tell of Beelzebub, the beast, Baphomet, or whoever? Way we figure is that's all rooted to him. If there's such a thing as the goddamn Devil, *He's* it. And he's been at it a long damn time."

"Why here? Of all the places in the world?" Molly's mind kept crying out for Lydia. The thought of that pack of dog-monsters ripping into Lydia haunted her mind, tore it apart. She couldn't shake it. She wanted her fist through their necks, their bleeding throats in her hands. *He* couldn't die? She'd put that to the test.

"Search me, kid. Why's anything for that matter? Why's the damn Earth fucking spin on a tilt? Y'all the ones made all this shit." D shook his head, folded his arms and walked off into the yard. "Fuckass gods."

Al patted her on the shoulder. He gave her a short version of the tour, the crib notes of their own story. Both ex-soldiers, Al from the older wars. D had come home from Vietnam—studied chemistry and engineering in college. Molly examined the car again, the one from last night.

"Started as a '73 Ford Falcon, yes'm she did. Fine car, too. 429 Cobra Jet V8. Damn fine. Detroit steel for you. Yes sir. See D yonder?" He pointed at his friend tossing the stick to the dogs. Molly felt he wanted to be alone. He still held some deep sadness, some old awful guilt, away from her, locked in his soul. But she was used to people guarding their secret shames. It was theirs to hold, not hers. "He's a actual damn genius, he is. See here?" Al knocked on the metal of the car. "You try it. Do it hard, like you do."

"No, I don't want to break it." She cocked her head to the side. The car was something else. It had been souped-up, turbo-charged, lifted in the back. Ramrods on the front end. Dual exhaust.

"How 'bout you just try it anyhow?" Al grinned, hopping with excitement.

"Okay." Molly knocked her knuckles against the steel hood.

"No, you go on and knock it a good one. Like you mean it."

Molly shook her head. She gave the hood a decent pound, enough to put a dent in it.

Nothing.

"Uh huh!" Al's eyes lit up. "See, I done told you. That's D. He made up this formula. Spray it on just right. Make anything like that. He done his helmet that way. Whole suit, too. Yes'm. D's the real deal."

Al talked more like D's biggest fan than a partner or caretaker or whatever they were to each other. Told her about the first few times *The Copperhead* had gone out. Well before Germain had showed up. "Back then we liked to beat up bad cops. D even got him a hold of a couple shady bankers. They was running a scam foreclosin' houses and buying 'em up themselves cheap. Selling 'em to these dang ol' snowbirders and northerners moving down. Driving up the price. D run through their own houses in the Falcon. Dropped files on 'em with three newspapers." He laughed as he told it.

Molly laughed to herself. She saw it then, who they were to each other. She started to reach for Lydia again but gave up.

"So now what?" She folded her arms, staring at D as he walked toward them followed by the dogs. "Where do we start?"

"We? Start?" D cocked one eye, the eyebrow lifting nearly off his face.

"These *things*. Vampwolves. Creatures. Whatever. How do we fight them?"

"*We* don't do squat, kid. You go home. I go back to being retired." D threw the stick one more time, sent the dogs hauling after it. "Tried waging that war for a couple years. There's no winning it. Only one defeat after another. Cost me more than one dear friend. And now you one too. Cut your loss and quit now. Believe me, it only gets worse."

"I'm not much for quitting." Molly walked out into the yard, found an old steel drum to spar with. She took a few shots, dented it up good, but drew back after one hit. She rang her hand on that last one. She was weak again. Not weak as before when she'd, well, made an ass of herself, and Andi had first shown up. But she wasn't at her top speed.

"Looks like you ain't all that." D noted her wring her hand out.

"I need to be out there. I need them to see me, see me fighting for them. They'll root for me. I'll get stronger."

"Now you sound like a god." D turned to go inside the house.

"You will too." Molly called to him, stopping him in his tracks. She felt her words hit his spine and ice up his neck. He turned. "You'll believe in me."

"Don't hang your hat on that, kid. I got no love for gods, big or little G's."

"I know." She smiled. She felt him starting to crack. "But you will. I promise."

She went back to knocking the drum around. She needed to gather her thoughts, put it all together. She needed to know more, see more. She put the god thing out of her head for the time. She'd deal with that later. It felt too big for her. All that mattered was getting these people out from under this shadow. Destroy this beast, or Cain, or whatever demon he was. And the witch—the one who caused all this, took Lydia from her—she would die first. Molly pounded the metal again.

"You said silver will kill all of them but him?" She looked at them, then down at the ground. She found a long piece of pipe, kicked it into her hand with her foot, spun it with one hand, then gripped it with two, going through motions of some long forgotten martial ritual. She saw the green-faced woman again. "Maybe a spike at each tip. Or one big blade."

"Or guns." D shook his head at her playing kata on the scrapyard with the trash metal. "Guns work great. Least until you had to go and make one of them goddamn bulletproof."

"I what?" Molly's eyes fixed on him as he spun the cylinder of his pistol and placed it on the table.

"I told you. Anything they drink, they absorb, they become. Now that includes you, you stupid asshole." D swore again under his breath and spat. She saw him mouth the name *Evilyn*. She felt their history with each other, more than he wanted to tell her. For now. "So, unless you got any of this magic metal you say can cut you..."

V

"HEY PAPA LEGBA"
–ELTON JOHN, 1982

EVILYN BOUNCED HER FINGERS across the ivory keys of her grand piano, careful not to damage the antique with her newly acquired strength. Moving the two-ton piece of art—once played by Professor Longhair himself—around the room with naught but the nudge of a finger made Bianca uneasy, she could tell. She'd always sensed how others felt around her—or at least since she'd chosen her path all those years ago—how long had it been? By the Earth's count only some eight years and a little to spare. But so many times she had walked the Land of Mists, seeking, searching, finding, there was no number that could describe her past. Time didn't make sense there, as so little did. A day here could feel like hundreds there. She grinned at her own millennia of memories as she laid out a riff from Stevie Wonder's last single.

"Tell me, Bianca," She got up and flowed to the wet bar in her massive office suite —her lavish silver evening gown (it amused her to wear it now) flowing in the breeze from open windows. The bar had always been for entertaining business *clients* she now courted to herself from Germain's other companies. Strong as she was, she still needed her own army. The old Cain Capital letters came down from the top of *her* building and JarethCo installed. "What does one do when one becomes a god?"

Dr. Bianca Tesche sat at her desk to one side of the room. A brand-new Apple computer array, a full megabyte of RAM, dot matrix printer, all sat at her fingertips. She looked to her mistress, pushing her glasses onto her face with one hand, seeking a pencil for some notes with her other. Bianca tilted her head. "Well, to be quite perfectly honest, your—"

"Evilyn shall do just fine. Titles and honorarium are for silly little man-beasts with inferiority complexes. *That* I shall not devolve to—and you may hold me to it."

"Well, right, Ms. Jareth." Bianca stood, straightened her papers. "But I wouldn't know, is the thing. I never quite knew what *you were*, nor I'm sure I should like to. But now, from what I've seen—I would say you can do most anything you want, have ever wanted. But—"

"But? But what?" Evilyn glided to her compatriot, lifting the woman's chin as she whispered into the fingers of her other hand, conjuring energy from the *other* world. In a shock to herself as much as Bianca, where normally a few purple sparks would appear at her fingertips, now a full bolt of energy appeared, a veritable javelin of dark power—ready to be stabbed into her enemies. "Aha!" Evilyn laughed at her own strength, admiring the rod of raw power in her hand.

She stood away from Bianca who backed further from it. She peered out her tall open windows onto the sunny city across the CBD and found her target—that hideous six-post shrine to *his* demon mother atop that awful building that bore her name—*one* of her names. Evilyn flung the bolt at that monstrous tower that cut into the skyline of the city.

It fired across the sky, slamming itself into the concrete and marble, exploding bits of stone, steel, and dust into the air, raining onto the street below.

"Ha!" Evilyn retracted her hand, coiling her fingers, staring at her appendage as if it were brand new. "Ah, Bianca, but I love this! That sweet, red child! Oh, D, but do you even know what you have?" She stopped as she said his name. *Maybe if he saw her now, what she'd become, what she could do? Maybe—No.* She put that thought out of her mind. There was no going back.

"A god, indeed." Bianca walked to the window, peered through a small telescope to study the impact of the hit. "You could change things here, fix things now, surely?"

"Yes." Evilyn made a fist—her smile melting into a thin line. "Surely."She called her matching silver top hat from her chair, along with a sceptre she'd had forged for herself in the other realm by the same master who'd made her new teeth.

"Where are you going?"

"I'm off to see a god about a horse." She put her hat on her head, tilted it to one side, nodded at her only friend in this world, and stepped through the circle she drew with her finger.

* * *

The figure in the wide-brimmed straw hat, worn overalls, and red longjohn undershirt lit his corncob pipe, pulled an apple from his pocket and fed it to the horse hitched to the wagon outside Jackson Square. He smiled as he spoke its own language back to the fine animal; it certainly was, too—a very fine animal, one of the best he'd seen pulling these carts.

"Yes, that's a fine boy right there. Yes sir."

He closed his eyes onto this moment, opened them onto another—one long before, when all this same square fluttered about with such carts, quite a coming and going. Horses and dogs and carrying on. The zydeco filled the streets. Sweet smells of pots cooking the food of a hundred other places, all boiled together here.

He blinked again and watched the blue-clad soldiers forming their ranks, guarding their newly captured city from a re-invasion—more coming in every day to sign their name and take their blue jacket, their smoking steel pipe that spat metal and death. He had blessed their cause, patting the heads of the ones who wavered, giving them enough courage to go on, do what they felt must be done.

With another blink, he looked into the hollow eye of a metal horse, all cables and circuits, its aluminum chassis and steel-shoed hooves an anachronism of everything before—but so much that always was—always would be. The low hum of electricity filled the air around him, the hovering bikes and cars zipping by, the neon lights flickering everywhere, the towers of the now ancient city rising higher and higher into the sky, machines flying above him, as a mighty train roared across the old super-highway at half the speed an ear can hear. The lifeless metal horse brought him no comfort, but at least then, in that yet to be, the bells of the old cathedral rang with the hour. The bells would soon ring again.

"When are you now, old timer?" Evilyn Jareth's voice called to him across the moments. So many moments—all of them, all that ever had been or would yet be, collapsing into one they called *now.*

"I am here—always here, then, tomorrow, it is all the same."

"You'll have to show me that trick one day." She walked up, offering her hand to the horse's nostrils, letting him test her. He found her wanting and lifted his head away.

"They always know. They can smell death."

"Ah, but I've changed, Leg. I'm a new woman, don't you see?" Evilyn curtsied to the Loa leaning into his old sugarcane walking stick—one she had no desire to test against her new staff...*yet.* He gazed upon her with one eye, the other watching another young lady elsewhere, crying over a lost loved one, feeling her shame, guilt, and regret strangling her. She would come out of that soon. Her time had arrived. The Cainslayer had come at last.

Evilyn gestured at herself, her loud ensemble, then raised her arms to cradle the noon sun.

"I see you walk in the day. You've pulled a veil over yourself. But you are still the same. Nothing has changed. Nothing will change. All that is, was, will have been—all the same."

"No, Leg, this is different. *I* am different. We can beat *Him* now. *I* can beat him." Evilyn's confidence slipped. He saw her, for the first time. Young then, vibrant—so full of life. She found him—all on her own. None did that. To reveal himself to them was his prerogative and no other's. But *she* found him. Determined, tenacious, dedicated. He cried for her, staring at the young woman, seeing her moments, who she'd been, would be.

"You should go now." He told her in both times. "You should not be here. I cannot help you." He hung his head, patting the horse's neck one last time before its driver left on another tour. He liked the tours. He would sometimes show some of the outsiders a thing or two, send them home with a tale to tell. Keeping the *old* magic alive in this city.

"You don't get it." Evilyn raised her voice at him, as if that mattered. "I'm different. I'm like you now. I have power. We can fight him together—all of us." He felt her as she said it. She still wanted her old friend—beneath all her guilt—her murder, her betrayal, feeding the beast as she had, her sins a thousand-fold—was some half-forgotten allegiance. To an aging hero.

"The Loa do not interfere in mortal matters."

"Since when is *He* a mortal? It's no wonder D hates you all. You never do a damn thing when you're needed most. Even the Fae don't seem to care."

"You should say what you have to say—to *those* you have to say it. The sands fall. The glass is flipped. The sand is always falling." He turned, opening his white eyes to her face. "You are nothing like us. Nor ever shall you be." The horse gone now, he walked up Decatur. Music wafted from further down. Smiles and laughter spoke to him.

"Legba!" Evilyn shouted. "I will destroy *Him.*"

"That is not your path to walk." Legba faced her again. "The one who was chosen has come now. She is here even this moment."

"Where do you think I got this?" Evilyn clinched her fist, slammed her god-strong foot against the pavement. "I'm as much the chosen one now as she is. I *choose* to fight him. While you all—with all your power and *wisdom*—choose to wait out some stupid prophecy, another silly riddle. Gods, you're all the same. Some half-wit girl wandering the city like a buffoon. That's your great hero?"

"She is lost now." Leg leaned on his stick with both hands, looking away into elsewhere—smiling to himself. "She doesn't know yet who she is, cannot see it. But she will. She's weakened, defeated." He smiled at the image of her at her full power, wrapped in glowing light, flinging her mighty weapon toward death incarnate. "But she will find her strength. She builds allies for herself now. Coming to their aid as they also hers. She is on her path, one denied for too long, but no longer. A goodness burns bright in her heart. One you gave up. Always, you did, would do, have done. She is the one. Not you."

Evilyn's jaw tightened. Her face grew stern. He felt the power tingle in her fingertips as she considered conjuring a weapon against him. But she knew better—he felt that too. He cried for Evilyn. Now. Then. Tomorrow. They were each the same for him.

"Maybe I'll go and see Mama, ask her instead." Evilyn found her smile once more.

"If you go see Mama, Mama will kill you." Legba continued on his way to laughter and life. When was he now? A party. All Saints Day. The city had just bought its football team. A second line walked through the streets. He liked the tuba.

"Why don't *you* kill me?" Evilyn flipped her staff under her arm, its silver, spiked hilt pointing at the sky.

"You have your own path to walk. Dead you'll be plenty enough for me."

"Guess Mama better not kill me either, then." She smiled, but the pain of knowing that he already knew, would know, had known, bled through her face.

"Mama don't care." He nodded to her one last time. That fiery girl that day in the square—such tenacity and energy, but all focused on vanity, on her own ambitions. That determined mortal who'd found him on her own. Papa Legba shed one tear for poor Evilyn Jareth.

VI
"TOUGH LOVE"
—SHANDI, 1984

MURPHY POURED THE LAST of the 151 into her glass along with a shot of her Pepsi Free and a few more chunks of ice. She took one cube and held it to her throbbing head. A pair of nice-suited goons had walked her out of the charity gala after Jareth outed her, and right in front of the kid too. Murph had waited for her opportunity to slip away but hadn't expected it to come in the form of every window in the building exploding at once. That scream still rang in her ears.

In the chaos, she'd looked for the girls, but the screams—so many—drowned one another, everyone fleeing in every direction. Somewhere in that mess, she'd heard wolves growling. The lights of three city blocks had shattered along with the glass—like some angry god roaring in the darkness that swallowed this city.

She sat alone in the suite, nursing her bruised head, bruised ego, and drowning her vast chasm of failure and regret in the river of rum that ran through this southern metro. He'd been there, right in her grasp, and she'd blown it. She tightened her fingers into a fist, a hot tingle in her knuckles as they went white from her pain and rage. That garish bitch with the two-tone hair—the goddamn bartender from the Jester Queen, some ten-cent dive off the river. The hell did she think she was?

"Should have told them the whole of it from the start, Murph." She glared at her reflection mocking her from the blank screen of the TV. Her image melted in her mind into that of the barking machine, its chicken-legs stomping through the streets in the snow-covered city in the north, her city—the one *she'd* sworn an oath to protect. What oath did a machine swear? What prime directive did it follow? It served and protected one thing and one alone: the company that built it, that bought it—that bought every damn thing: Allcorp, a Division of Volund-Yöndemoni Interglobal.

And this place was no better—the whole city bought and owned by a bunch of rich bloodsuckers, soulless monsters that couldn't give an iota about the lives they trampled underneath them. The cops here were as faceless and heartless as the steel monsters that patrolled Old Detroit. Every bit as inhuman. They made her regret she'd ever worn a badge.

Another face glared at her from the empty screen. Not unlike her own. Older. Sterner. More lines. A hardness to its edges. A sorrow as it looked in her eyes and called her that name again.

"Zuìzhōng." Her father's voice echoed in her head.

"I'm sorry, Daddy. I had him. Or I thought I did." It all clicked together. The kid. Her power. The Black Hands. Murph was a fool. She'd led them right to

Molly. It was all her fault. And now the kid was god knows where. Maybe dead already. If she could die. *Where are you, Red? Raven?* She'd let them both down.

Her head pounded. She reached for her glass to kill what thought remained and maybe herself along with it. She felt the pounding again as she gripped it. Everything swam around her. The lights blurred. How much was too much? She decided to try and see—lifted the glass to say goodnight to it all—but the pounding knocked it from her hands; the brown liquid ran across the glass table in front of her.

The front door burst off its hinges as a red streak flowed into the room. Some tattered clothes, too big by a size or more, wrapped around the frame she thought she knew.

"Mother of the beast, Murphy, I knocked for ten minutes." Red said.

Is she here? Or is this more rum reverie? Murph laughed as she tried raking the spilt liquor back into her glass. She could order up another bottle, put it on Riz's tab. Damn writer was loaded to the gills—probably no better than the vipers Murphy worked for—*had* worked for. So much for play-acting the VP at Germain's. She'd been so close to everything too: inside the belly of the beast.

"Stop." Red took her hand, put the glass and bottle away, and cleaned the mess with a towel. "Look, I just came for my things."

Molly went to the spare room—came back out with her bag of clothes, that silly rainbow jacket of hers, and the twin sword-cane thing. She watched the kid watch her. Murph knew she was a mess, and she didn't know why this kid's opinion mattered to her so much, but it did.

"Where's your friend?" Murph closed her eyes because she already knew as soon as she saw Red alone, those hangdog eyes—she knew that look. She'd watched it every morning in the mirror since she'd heard about her partner Baskin. "I'm sorry, kid. I'm so sorry. For all of it. It's my fault. I should've never—"

"Murphy." The kid's voice echoed in her head like voices bouncing off a cathedral ceiling. "Pull yourself together. I can't stay. I just came for my stuff. I'm glad you're alive." Molly pulled her off the couch, hugged her with those iron arms.

Murph slumped back to the couch as the kid geared to go.

"The chosen one." Murph gave a half salute. "You gotta stay here. I gotta watch over you. Murph started off the couch but slipped, caught herself with her hand on the floor. Those reflexes still worked, even drunk as a skunk. "I gotta protect you from the Hands. Hands of the Demon. *His* Black Hands. They want you. They want the weapon."

"Yeah, I don't know about all that or this god shit. I just need this." She gripped the cane tighter.

"What god shit?" Murph sat upright, started her breathing. Just like dear old dad taught her.

"Apparently I'm a god. Or something. Maybe. I don't know." Molly looked into her eyes. Murph felt her crawling around in her sadness, like she was trying to take it away. *The hell does she want with it? Let her have it if she wants it, then.*

"Yeah, well, fuck gods." Murph looked away, not sure what to make of that last thing she'd heard. She closed her eyes, managed her breathing—felt some of the haze wash out of her head. A lot of rum still swilled around in there.

"That's fair." Molly dropped her bag, walked to the counter and scribbled something on the pad by the phone, then walked over to Murph, crouched beside her. "Look, I have to go. I've found something—someone that knows what's going on. You should..." Molly looked into Murph's sad eyes.

Stupid god kid. What is she doing? "Yeah, what? Get out of town while I still can? Leave all this to you, *the chosen one?* So stupid. Can't believe that shit is actually real."

"I don't know, Murphy. I don't know what to tell you to do." Molly stood up, grabbed her gear again, then turned back to Murph, staring into her. "You do whatever you have to do. You be who you have to be. It's not mine to decide for you. When you sober up, you can come find me at the junkyard out on 90 past Avondale. Place called Hat Creek. You can't miss it. I wrote down the number. Just—just get it together, Murphy." Molly turned to leave.

"Wait, kid." Murph stood up, wobbling at first but found her feet. "I'm sorry. Please, you have to—"

"I forgive you, Murphy. For everything." Molly's eyes burned into her own. Murphy felt hot and cold and like she was drowning all at once. "But you have to forgive yourself too. I can't do that for you. Be safe, Murphy. And come find me. Or not. Up to you."

Molly was gone. Out the door she'd knocked off its frame. Another in a stack of things for Murph to deal with. How would she explain that, and to who? Hegs at the front desk? She sank into the couch. Thoughts swirled in her head. Voices. The past talking at her. Mocking at her. Washing away from her. She felt some old familiar pain drain out of her. This feeling she'd held for so long. Like it just got up and walked out of her life. A weight so long crushing down on top of her, heavy on her shoulders—gone.

"Get up, Murphy." The voice commanded her off the couch. *Stupid kid.* Or was it her father's voice. That hardness he had in him. Pushing her like he did. All those years. Teaching her. Molding her. Training her. And for what? "Get up, Murphy." It told her again. Her own voice. The same as his had been. She'd become him, hadn't she?

Murphy stood up, her head clearing. The alcohol ran out of her, into her bladder—that train was never late. She blinked, walked to her bedroom. She took her shoes off, the dress she'd never changed out of. She slid on a pair of sweatpants and a tank. She stared into the floor-to-ceiling mirror on the closet doors. Some woman stared back at her. Some girl.

"Zhī yī!" She yelled at the mirror as she threw her first punch, watching her form, pulling her hand back, opening her palm outward, breathing, holding her pose. "Èr!" She shouted as she thrust out her other palm and continued. Breathing and counting with her movements, thrusting, pulling, shouting, shoving. She heard him correct her as she flipped into a kick. She felt his hands move her leg where it was supposed to go.

She kept it up, an hour became another. Her face grew tight, grim. She had seen this city now, seen its true face. Now she would make it afraid of her.

VII
"EYE OF THE TIGER"
SURVIVOR, 1982

MOLLY SLICED THROUGH a truck axle she'd stood upright just for that purpose. She alternated strokes with the twin blades, the snake and the wolf, the crystals they once held in their mouths now safely in the keeping of her twin sister back home. Molly hadn't called her to check in—she couldn't bear to tell them the news about Lydia. She still couldn't accept it herself.

Each slice, Molly pictured the face of that witch that bit her, stole her power, set Lydia up as *bait* for that monster, that demon Germain. How had he fooled her? He'd seemed so charming, so alluring. She kicked and cussed herself for falling for his routine.

"It's part of him, how he works." D and Al had tried to explain him to her a few times. "It's like a kind of hypnosis. Anyone close to him falls in. It's what happened to... A friend of mine. Long time ago." D always got sad when this certain friend came up. She felt the years of loss built up in his heart—including one so awful and devastating he could no longer go to it. He kept it locked away in the deepest part of him.

Molly spun, sliced, making ribbons of the steel cylinder. She focused her anger, her hate, her rage at those who did this. An unkillable demon? A curse transmitted to an army of his acolytes? Monstrous offspring? Her eyes flashed in the fading light of the evening, the orange-purple of the horizon heralding the coming of his night creatures.

"It won't matter if those pigstickers can cut through god himself—"

"*Her*self." Molly corrected him, though she still held her doubts about that. She couldn't *actually* be a god. Like...that wasn't a thing.

"Yeah. Whatever." D rolled his eyes. "You can't cut what you can't see."

Molly looked at her weapons. She held one out, sighted down its edge, aiming it at some imaginary foe. He was right. She slid the blades into each other—each the other's scabbard. She still hated the idea of it—two skinny blades with oblong handles. *Some ForgeMaster*, she told herself. This was a bad weapon. She put it on the rickety fold-out table where D and AL sat, a cooler of beer beside them as they watched her. She found the piece of steel pipe she'd played with before, spun it around her a few times, then shot it forward, its shaft sliding through her clasped hand like a bullet—then she jerked it back again. How did she know these things?

D shook his head. "Forget it, kid. You're out of your league in this. You should go back home."

"That's not happening." Molly fired her pretend spear again, knocking an old paint can out of her path. "I'm staying till it's finished."

D walked to her, took the pipe from her hands, gripped her by the shoulders, stared right in her face.

"You can't kill him. He can't *be killed.* Believe me, I've tried. I've shot him, stabbed him, gassed him, burnt him, blown him to hell, and even drowned him. Every damn time he comes right back. I've seen him grow back from nothing but a head and some torso. The thing is a demon, a fiend left on earth by some asshole god to torture us. The only thing to do is stay out of its way, help as many other people to do the same as we can."

"That what you do?" Molly stood back from D, formed her hands into wedges, poking and jabbing at him. "Stay out of his way?" Molly stuck her hand in his side, just a tap. He flinched, flared one nostril.

"We help who we can. We get people out of the city. I'm done fighting a losing war."

Molly jabbed him again. And again. He flinched and lurched back each time, his nose wrinkled, his eyes zeroing on her.

"Yeah well that was then. You didn't have *me* then. I'm the game-changer." Molly faded, twirled, and stuck him again, playing. Like a kid teasing her da... like a kid would do. D shook something out of his head. Molly twisted and stuck him again, over and over, just a tickle each time. She'd learned how to not hurt people. She had control. She'd felt some of her strength return. Every time Al smiled at her. Her visit to Murph. Each had boosted her—given her energy. But D was the one she wanted, needed to believe in her.

She laughed and smiled as she got him again, this time a goose right under the ribs. D had enough. He seized her wrist, lurched backward with her thrust, and hurled her headlong into a pile of trash. Molly leapt to her feet, laughing. She ran back at him, hands in wedges ready to go again. He dodged and sent her sprawling, Molly laughing all the way. She bounded back to him, squaring off, striking and slapping at him as he blocked and parried her every move.

"See, you like it." She smiled into him. "You're made for this, same as I am."

"God damn it." D slapped her arm out of the way as it came in for a strike, blocked her other one, and then front kicked her dead to the chest, putting her on her ass again. "Fine. You want to ride with me? See this city for what it really is? Okay, kid. But I've got rules. You follow my orders to the letter, you get me? Waver one bit, disobey me in the slightest, it's over. You're fired, you hear me?"

"Loud and clear." Molly's smile lit the night. "You're the boss, boss! Whatever you say."

D shook his head while Al laughed, tearing into a bag of Rice's potato chips. D slumped back in his chair, closing his eyes, breathing for a second, calming himself as he looked at the beer Al offered, then waved it away and sighed.

"Go get some rest." D sighed at her. "Your training starts tomorrow."

* * *

Molly lurched awake, one fist balled, one reaching for her swords, her mind ready for the fight. Some ice-fiend woke her from her dream of the green-skinned woman and back into the old Air Stream they'd given her for a bunk. D stood in the doorway, short-shorts and tube socks all the way to his knees, a tank top t-shirt cut off above his navel. Still had the silver bits around his neck and wrists—and an empty bucket in his hands. Molly realized what had woken her as she saw the ice cubes in her bed.

"Up and at 'em. Long day." D left for her to change.

He started her with a run, getting one in himself. He told her it was a half a mile all the way around the yard. He'd even made himself a track for it, years ago, back when he kept up his training. Molly ran. D jogged. She lapped him. And again. He wheezed and coughed, stopping more than once to recover. Molly paused to pat him on his back, smiling at him.

"Come on, you got this. You're strong. Stronger than you think." She jogged in place, watching her words wash over him like cold water, filling his lungs with new air. She felt him feel better, stronger.

"What the hell are you, kid?" D got his feet moving again, Molly leaving him in her dust, coming back around on him. She'd lost some speed, but it was coming back. "Who's training who here?" D got his nerve up and took off into a sprint, trying to match her. It was cute, so she dropped her pace to let him, for a minute.

After a few miles, they stopped. He sat, laughing, sweating buckets. Now the sun shined bright every day, some of the old heat of the South flowed back in. D told her about Cain's machine to make the clouds, to block the sun. "She must have turned it off," D spoke of Evilyn. Molly recalled the way the witch and Cain fought over her. A war for hell's throne.

After running, D put her on the tires. She tried not to laugh at herself as she tripped and fell the first three times. D blew a whistle, meaning she'd earned herself five laps around the yard. She thought of Bay High, how she and Lyd had sometimes watched the boys practice football after school from the windows of the band hall, when they'd snuck in to practice their *devil music*. Something told her this Germain-Cain character wasn't a Crüe fan.

After tires came dips, then bear crawls, then some dodgeball. She had him on that one. Try as he might, her strange muscle memories always kicked in, slapped that ball right back at him, twice in the face.

"Okay, so your reflexes are good." He tossed the rubber ball to one side, nursing his red face with his other hand. "Damn good. But let's try something else." D pulled a rag from his pocket, wrapped it around her eyes. "You're fine at dodging anything you can see, but what if you can't?"

"I don't understand." Molly's world went black around her.

"They live in the night. They can change into anything, anyone they've ever bit. They blend into the shadows as they please. They *are* the night. The powerful ones, Him, Evilyn, his generals, they can burst into smaller creatures. Bats, owls, birds, what have you." D slapped her on the right temple. She heard him pick up a handful of scrap from the yard. Rocks, bits of metal slapped at her. She twisted, turned, each time catching something to the face or her chest. "That's a bite," he'd say each time. "That's another."

"They can't bite me. Only she can."

"Far as we know. But she's enough. We don't want her coming back at you, trying to finish the job. And if she can figure it out, others might."

Another rock struck her head. She grew irritated, grasping and slapping wildly as he pelted her.

"See, it doesn't matter how hard you can hit, how sharp your little swords are. Silver's what hurts 'em. And even then, it still has to be a lethal shot. A cut to the leg or shoulder may put 'em out of the fight, but they'll heal. You want 'em done? Gotta be a killshot." He nailed her head one more time, then took the blindfold off, nodding with heart in his eyes. She'd never had a teacher like this—at least not in this life. She liked this. She liked D. "We'll work on that."

After dodge practice, they hit the weights—or rather he did. He had a bench and some dumbbells set up in one part of the yard. He put himself 350 on the rack, managed to get it up five times before he lost the sixth. Molly pulled it off him with one hand.

"God damn, I'm out of shape." He sighed.

"You'll get there." Molly touched his shoulder. "We both will."

* * *

Each day repeated the same. Running. Tires—now he ran them along with her. Dodging. Lifting. Al watched them with his cold beer from the back porch, D struggling to get a few hundred pounds off his chest. Behind him, an old rail car lifted off the ground as Molly pressed it over her head, over and over, then dropped it behind her with a thundering clang. Al's eyes grew wider at her by the day.

She grew stronger. She felt it. Day by day, watching him watch her, seeing her for who she was, who she was *going to be.* For him. He needed this. He deserved this. He'd stood alone too long in this war, fighting this evil so far beyond him, fighting for this city, *his* city. She loved watching him fight, train, teach her, remind himself. He grew as she did, her touch, her words helping him grow stronger even than he had been.

She would make him believe. In her. In himself.

El Shaddai, she thought. *We'll see about that.*

VIII
"HELL ON WHEELS"
—CINDERELLA, 1986

MOLLY WAS UP with the bright shining sun of what summer remained in her ever-cooling world. "I bet it's the Russians," Lydia had always told her when they discussed the shifting weather, each winter worse than the last. The South hadn't known winters like they'd seen these few years. And the North, poor Murphy—it'd been a while since they'd last spoke—had told them of the frozen wasteland of Old Detroit, some awful company buying the power and gas from the city, charging everyone double. People had cut down the trees from the parks, burning them as firewood to stay warm in the winter. Most, those who could, packed up and made the trek south. Hence the booming Metropolis of this once sleepy Southern city, its own unique charms fading, giving way to the blandness, the ubiquity of One-America, one of Commie Ron's old sayings—yet another thing he'd copied off his big sister Maggie and her One-England idea she hawked. According to the news, she was still coming to town—later in the year.

"Try that on." D hurled a black long-sleeve unitard at her.

"What's this?" Molly stretched out the fabric. She hated the all-black look. Like, she got it and all. But it just wasn't her thing.

"Field trip tonight. If it fits, we'll spray it. I know you're already invincible and all that shit, but your pants ain't. Leastways, you'll have something that won't come apart on you in a fight.

"Wait." Molly jumped up, dug through her pack and grabbed the last of the old blue and pink striped suits she'd snatched from Tracey's shop. "This one."

"Look, kid. I get you like bright lights and pretty rainbows, but we're going into the world of Hel's own kin. They'll see you a mile away in that."

"Yeah, well, maybe they should."

D pulled his head back for a second. She could see him thinking about it, grinding it around in that gravelly head of his.

"Hmm." He grunted as she tossed it to him.

* * *

Al had the hood up on D's tank of a car. He checked over every hose and connection, topped the fluids, the oil, anything that needed any care, like it was his own baby. Molly watched him go over it all twice. She liked seeing people do things they were good at. D stood beyond them, her new suit hung from a line as he sprayed it with his chemical formula.

"Bonds to damn near anything." Al dropped the hood on the old car. So much of it had been bolted or welded on, it was hard to tell what it had once been. All black, but for the silver-tipped blades and spikes jutting out everywhere. "Those were a later addition." Al noted her inspecting the vehicle. Like a race-car had been converted to a war machine. "Yeah, she's an ol' dog, but she's still got some bite."

Molly gave the fender a good kick—not even a dent. All this stuff impressed her even if she couldn't understand it. She barely got out of 11th grade Chemistry with a C.

"Why doesn't he sell it?" Molly looked to D finishing her suit, leaving it to dry. "The stuff, I mean. He could be rich from this. Wouldn't the army want this?"

Al laughed, a sadness behind it. "Yeah, I'm sure they would. Whether they'd pay or not, well..." Al wandered off as D walked up.

"Soon as the sun's down, we ride."

Molly pulled a long sleeve flannel shirt from her pack and tossed it to him.

"The hell's this?" D held it up to his face, staring at it like more nonsense.

"Those suits are so tight." Molly shrugged at him. "I don't like showing my ass."

"Well that's fair." D walked it back down to spray it with the other.

* * *

Molly had on her SledgeHammer outfit, almost as indestructible now as she was, the flannel tied on at her waist flapped in the wind along with her unzipped denim cut, her trademark rainbow hammer emblem on her back. Her hair moussed into a mohawk for the outing acted like a sail every time she turned her head, but she didn't care. Riding on top of The Copperhead's Battle-Falcon, as she'd already decided to call it, felt more like home than anything ever had.

"Don't call it that." D had said over the radio in her ear as they rolled out of the junkyard toward the city.

"Too late, I already am." Molly felt his irritation from inside the car, and she giggled the more at it.

"Remember what I said, kid. Follow my orders to the T. Deviate even the slightest—"

"And I'm fired. I know. I got it, boss." Molly liked calling him boss, mostly because she knew it bugged him. She didn't know why she liked teasing the old man so much—but she did.

They rode stealth—as stealth as they could with a blazing neon god perched on the hood of a screaming steel rhinoceros—to the edge of town. Molly launched herself into the sky, landing atop the nearest building. She zeroed the car, kept one eye on it at all times as she bounded the rooftops, headed into Carrollton.

"They like them young." D had said, girding himself for the night. His suit held both plate armor and leather pads, few of which matched—like he'd added bits and pieces over the years. "They need to feed at least once a month, each of them. One college kid, healthy enough, will feed a handful of them. Some get greedy, might go for two. But he keeps a tight rein. Too many murders—disappearances rather—and he can't stay under the radar. Attention is his enemy as much as the sun or silver, or anything else."

They'd run her through the crib notes on his history. Cain had been around since the dawn of civilization, glomming on to any major society as it built itself up—some legends said he'd built the first cities. But it always ended with him being discovered sooner or later, exiled, chained, imprisoned, or otherwise dealt with.

Now he owned *this* city, buying influence in more than a dozen others. A blood research hospital had been genius. Masquerading as the philanthropist, Cain had a steady supply of *food* donated directly to him for free. No murder required.

"His foot soldiers don't always follow orders." D told her. Sometimes they spawned more of themselves than they could feed. Left the dregs to fend for themselves. Apparently being bit wasn't enough. There was something of a ritual to it. Without the ritual, the bite-victim would begin to rot and waste away into a walking corpse, like a ghoul or *draugr, as* Al and D called it. They had all kinds of words for this stuff. Molly had a lot of homework to catch up on.

She dropped into an alley, made her way to Oak Street, toward a bar called The Maple Leaf, another juke joint popular with college kids and the odd tourist that discovered this part of town. Her outfit got the looks it was designed to, her mohawked hair making her popular with the crowded streets. Soon, she had a tail. She didn't have to look behind her. D had been wrong about one thing. The bloodsuckers may have stuck to the shadows, all but invisible to any naked eye, but she didn't need to see them. She closed her eyes, sensing around her—the laughter, the energy of the kids out for a good time, the desperation of struggling musicians hoping to make some rent money, each of them full of life and emotion. But the ones that followed her—a void, a hole in the crowds that stood out as much as she did. She didn't need to *see* them. She sensed the darkness in them a mile away. She was learning.

Molly led a trio of black-clad *suckers* into the side streets, toward the Mater Dolorosa, just as she was told. She veered into the alleyway between the brick buildings, the twin cupola belfries looming at them. She felt them licking their teeth behind her, and she grinned at that. In the pitch dark of that empty alley, she turned, facing them for a half second. They stopped short, her smiling face shocking their confidence. Molly flipped backward, cascading herself through the air as she landed with a thud onto the reinforced steel of the Battle-Falcon. Its lights flared—ultraviolet beams blinding into them as its V8 roared to life.

Screams—closer to shrieks—silenced into the night as he rode into them, the jagged silver blades jutting from his crash-guard doing their work. Molly felt a smile curl onto D's lips. He'd missed this—she sensed it. A smile grew across her face, her eyes narrowing. These demons would pay for Lydia. Every god-damned one of them. And they were; Molly damned them herself.

* * *

Making a night of it, they roared through town, she always going ahead, making a scene. She honed her sense of them, the suckers. She learned to smell their rotten souls and found two more in Uptown, already following a set of sorority sisters. Molly's nostrils flared. Soon that would be Becky, would have been Lydia, her friends. Just out being normal, being human, alive. These beasts got what they had coming to them. She walked between them, stared at the suckers, then backflipped into the night.

Taking the bait as if they hadn't a fear of anything, they followed her. Right into D's knives. Molly walked up to them as he gutted the first one from behind, and then he slit the second's throat. She watched their bodies rot instantly as their blood ran black out of their fetid corpses.

"Why do they do that?"

"Their looks are an illusion. When they die, their body shows its true age. Some just burst to dust. Others—the young ones, you might not could even tell. If they just got turned a year ago, two? They'd be the same corpse as you or me, or, well, just me I guess." D shrugged at Molly, cleaned his knives on the suckers' clothes, and headed back to his car.

He hadn't meant to, but he made her feel weird again. Alone. A freak. She hated the thought that she held more in common with these rotting monsters than her own friends—than humans. What even was a god? It was too big for her head.

* * *

Another few rounds, and D finally got what he came out for: blue lights.

"There's his true soldiers." He said over the radio. They'd told Molly about it, how he put his own kind on the force. Murphy had been right all along. The night cops *were* weird—they weren't even alive. They kept *His* peace, making the city quiet, calm, unremarkable. *He*, they, all of it. They had been the reason the gangs left the city years ago—why her friend Nguyen had moved to the coast, nothing left for him after his parents died, him an orphan at fifteen.

"Look alive, kid. They're coming after you." D squawked in her ear as she bolted from the police car. It sped along behind her, followed soon by another, then a third. "That's it, you blood-drinking bastards. Come to Big D."

Molly grinned at the fourth pair of lights behind her—the Falcon had found its prey. She sprinted forward, leapt into the air, and flipped herself backward. She landed fist-first into the hood of the first car, crushing the metal, flipping the whole thing over her head. She jump-kicked it, hurling it down the street, bashing its steel chassis.

D lit up the one in front of his Falcon, setting his mounted machine guns to work. They spat lead, ate rubber, and ripped through sheet metal as the car spun out of control, slamming into a post. He hauled after the last car fleeing from the fate of the other two.

Molly stayed behind to finish off the drivers in the wrecks. She took the silver knife from her belt and dead-eyed the first driver climbing from his wrecked car. She marched to the second, the sound of spitting gunfire and screeching metal signaling the third wasn't long for the world.

The last creature pulled himself from the smoking ruin of his car, his fangs flaring in the moonlight, his arms growing, claws forming at his fingertips. He snarled and gnashed at her as he crawled from the wreckage.

Molly seized him by the hair growing longer on his head. She gripped his collarbone with her other hand and tore his head from his body, his spine dripping black liquid down onto his sputtering corpse. His eyes glared at her as she thought about what they'd told her—that these things could grow back even from this.

"He will come for you, Shaddai. He will make you his own. He is eternal. He is the night. He—"

Molly sank her knife into its temple. She didn't need to hear anymore.

"That's for Lydia."

She dropped the rotting head and walked into the darkness. The Battle-Falcon's engine sang its song on its way to her. They had more work to do. A lot more.

IX
"LUCRETIA MY REFLECTION"
—THE SISTERS OF MERCY, 1985

THE NEWSROOM WAS A FLURRY of paper and ringing phones. Editors shouted at copy. Copy shouted at printing. No one could move from everyone bustling about. Murph faded, ducked, and dodged her way through the chaos.

"I don't care what they say they saw!" the chief shouted so loud from his office the world heard him pop an artery. "I'm not running that. I have *orders!*"

"The hell's got this place so wound up?" Murphy plopped herself at Alex's desk, Alex already a machine gun on her typewriter.

"Hold up, I'm almost done with this draft." She banged away at the keys, her face stern but alight.

Murphy wished she could find that energy again. Her heart panged every time she thought of the raven-haired kid. Lydia. Her name was Lydia Stiles. She always treated them like kids, and they were, but she'd listened to them more than she let them know. Why was she always like this? Why did she push everyone away? Even Baskin. A hundred times he'd asked her by the house for dinner with his wife, his daughter. A hundred times she'd said no. "A hot date," she'd lie to make him feel better. The truth is she'd be out jogging, or in the dojo, or just beating the hell out of her practice dummy in her apartment.

"There." Alex ripped the page from the machine and handed it to Murph.

"The New Orleans Guardian Returns." Murph read the title aloud, skimmed the copy. "Wow. He's back. Just like that, huh?"

"You don't see?" Alex waved all around them, the frenzy still at its peak. "He's got the whole world upside down." She stood up, grabbed her coat and hat. "Come with me if you want to talk. I've got a presser in five."

"What? now?" Murph tailed along behind the only friend she had left in town.

* * *

Two dozen reporters, twice as many mics, cameras, and a handful of *concerned citizens* crowded the front steps leading up to the Germain Enterprises building. One of the senior VP's Murph had worked with just weeks ago stood along an entourage of other stern-faced suits. Murph pulled the ballcap she'd borrowed from Alex lower on her head to keep from being recognized.

"...And so Mr. Germain, in his absence, has appointed me and the board of trustees to handle the affairs of the corporation until further notice." The VP said into the mics at his podium, some nods of agreement from his crew beside him.

"And why don't we hear any of this from him?" Alex jumped right in. Always the reporter. Always with that fire. Murph saw how the rest of them sneered at her.

Like they were all happy enough to take the company line and run the standard story.

"Mr. Germain has been taken away on other, urgent business."

"He didn't give any hint at when he'd return? What about his stockholders?" Alex pressed her luck. A few *yeahs* and *what about that's* rippled through the crowd as Murph could tell she'd touched a nerve. A guy like Germain couldn't have his hand in virtually every part of the city's business—including damn near relocating Wall Street to Canal—and expect to just go AWOL without so much as a how you do.

"Mr. Germain has appointed me to lead the company in his absence. I have no further—"

"Of course *He* did." A voice sang out of the crowd. A silver dress, covering barely enough to call it one, flowed up the steps toward the mighty commercial building. Two-tone purple and gold hair flowed in the breeze of the crisp, sunny day. Murph noticed there'd recently been a lot of these. "I have no doubt he's— indisposed, what with this *terrible* weather and whatnot?"

Evilyn Jareth grinned ear to ear at the frowning suits at the podium.

"We have no further comm—"

"Why, it's easy to see why most anyone might not be feeling their full self these days. In fact, I hear there's something going around, some kind of *bug.*" Evilyn laughed as Murph saw her making some motion with her fingers, mouthing some words under her breath.

"I can't—I—" The VP stopped, scratching at his arms and neck. His compatriots did likewise. From the distance, Murph caught something crawl up his neck out of his suit—like a cockroach or a spider.

"Ms. Jareth." Alex didn't miss a trick. "Is it true, you've taken back over your family's old company?"

"You see the letters on the building from here, don't you?" Evilyn gestured at her tower rivaling Germain's. "And you are?"

"Alex Charlton, *Register.*" She folded over a new slip of paper on her pad. "Can you give the readers a comment on what your next steps will be? How'd you come by the capital for such a takeover? And what of your rumored past working with the vigilante? What's your connection to Germain, to The Copperhead?"

"Alex Charlton, *Register.*" Evilyn licked the words off her lips. Murph could knock the grin off her face. She hadn't forgotten this bitch outed her in the middle of the gala, sent her packing just as she'd broke the case wide open. "This town needs a shot in the arm!" Jareth smiled wide again, the suits behind her frantically scratching and swatting at themselves, one almost crying in shock at whatever beset them. "And I think I can give it to them. I plan to sponsor the city's Midsummer Music Festival. And the Fourth of July party. Bastille. The Feast of the Assumption. I say we bring back what made this city La Nouvelle Orleans! Laissez les bon temps rouler!" She whipped the crowd into a furor. Claps and shouts. "I'll be in touch with you, Alex from *The Register*." Evilyn's teeth showed with her smile. Murph's eyes narrowed. "I may have use for you."

Evilyn waltzed down Canal, the bustling center of everything. The other reporters packed up for their next move, their crews rolling up cable. The men on the steps recovered from what had *bugged* them before. Murph shook her head at all of it. Something didn't smell right.

"Hey, all right, an exclusive." Alex smirked. Murph glared at the strangest person she'd ever seen, Evilyn Jareth, dancing down the street.

X
"FALLEN ANGEL"
POISON, 1988

THE COPPERHEAD—SHE LOVED THAT NAME; it was so badass, him in his Spartan helmet and all that gear—took Molly out for a few more *field trips*. He always had her hold back and let him do the heavy lifting. "You're getting slicker, but you're still learning the ropes. These are just pawns we're taking down. His generals are a lot tougher." He kept a leash on her, said it was so she could learn. She could tell there was something else to it—the way his heart hurt so much when he looked at her sometimes. Like he was looking at someone else.

The days stayed the same, training at dawn—him working himself to the edge, her pushing her own strength into him through her words, her touch on his shoulder, the kind smile of a girl just happy to have him there. They ate together. They ran together. They lifted together. They fought together.

Her blindfold instincts improved. She blocked everything he threw at her. He'd even let her upgrade to her swords. One day he tossed an apple and she sliced it down the middle. The next day they did the same, only she caught one of the halves and took a bite of it, smiling under her mask. She felt him smiling back—he *totally* did.

One morning she rode alongside him coming back from the Granny Shack with a bag of biscuits and a tub of gravy. She fiddled with the radio to get the rock station on. He tousled her hair with his right hand, his left at noon on the wheel of the big Dodge truck. She beamed up at him. Lydia flashed across her mind, how Molly'd sat with her and Lydia's daddy just like this when they were kids, watching that man stare at his little girl out the corner of one eye the whole time he drove. Lydia often complained how she felt like the odd one out of her dad and brothers, but Molly knew that man would probably fight hell itself for his little girl.

Lydia. Molly shuddered at the image of the two of them arguing before the gala, when it all...when she lost her. She started to push her tears back but let them fall instead. There was no shame in feeling two things, so she did.

D put his meaty hand on her far shoulder and scooted her next to him, hugging her tight.

"I know, kid." He patted her shoulder. "I know."

* * *

Pulling back into Hat Creek Scrapyard, Molly lit up when she saw a burnt-orange Manta Montage parked at the entrance to what served as Al's front office, even though she'd never seen them have a single customer in the weeks she'd been there. Molly piled out of the truck, already forgetting the fresh hot biscuits she'd been excited about seconds before. She fawned over the car, its slick angles, its cockpit seat, the oversize radial tires with big white lettering on each one.

"I've never seen one of these in my life. I didn't think they were even real."

"That one right there's a one of a kind, darlin'," The thickest, drawling accent west of The Muddy she'd ever heard said on its way out the screen door of the office. "But you look all you want, 'cause lookin's free." The voice came closer, accompanied now by a set of jet black, cobra-skinned boots, black slacks bell-cut for the boots and tapering to the knee where they went tight from there north to the waist. A burgundy shirt sat flat against a flatter stomach, both wrapped in a cowboy-cut blazer. A set of pearls so white they reflected the sun ran around his neck and beamed back at her. A shock of black hair, cut in a mop and moussed back underneath a black Stetson ten-gallon. The wrinkles by the bourbon eyes belied a man north of forty, maybe closing fifty, but a very different fifty than what D wore, muscles or no muscles.

"Ah shit." D sighed on his way to the door.

"Well, Sergeant Dee-Brousse." The man drew D's name out like that on purpose, like he knew it bugged him. Molly couldn't fault him; she'd found at least ten things just like that she did to him—because he secretly always loved it. She knew. "As I live and breathe, I declare you have taken up a sidekick. You could bowl me over right here. I never thought I'd see the day!"

D shook his head and tossed the bag to Al hobbling his way out the door for his breakfast.

"God damn it, Buck. The hell are you doing here?" D sat on the fold-out chair under the awning, dipping a biscuit in his bucket of gravy.

"Well, you're in every damn paper west of Baton Rouge. Copper helmet vigilante prowls the night. Leads police chase through the city. Officers still missing. Sound familiar?" The man smiled at D as he propped his shiny boot on the chair next to him.

"I'm sorry, who is this?" Molly looked to D for the answer as she felt the man with all the teeth might be the next day getting to it.

"My apologies, ma'am, I have done gone and left my manners along with my senses, both befuddled at this fine, bright, shiny, freckled face and shock of fire red hair." Molly was right, he was taking forever to get to a name. "I am none other than Buck Kobayashi, Lieutenant Buck Kobayashi at one time or another, if you believe that from seeing me." He smiled ten miles wide and stuck his hand at her like he was about to try to sell her a used car.

"Buck?" Molly gripped his hand tight, just to make her own point in all this. "Kobayashi?"

"That's right, little miss. I'm half Japanese, half American, and darlin'," He smiled even bigger now, "I'm all Texas!"

"He's all bullshit." Al fidgeted with this mechanical brace on the fritz again.

Molly let Buck go, and he pulled his hand back, wringing it a little.

"So it's true then." Buck aimed his grin at D. "She's the real deal. The little girl from the Bay ain't made up. You were next on my list, you know." He looked to Molly as she shook her head and reached for her biscuit. "Thanks for saving me a trip to the boons—not that this ain't the boons. D, when you gone grow some sense and move into town if you gone be running your ass around in that tin can again?"

"Buck, I'm just about worn out on you already, and you ain't been here ten minutes."

"Then I'll get right to it. See, I been busy—not lounging around hocking scrap like some worn-out old-timers. Reckon you seen me on the TV last month?"

"Didn't." D put his feet in the spare chair to keep Buck from sitting.

"I drove through one world into another, son. Damn. Well, I'll get to that part directly." Buck pulled the chair from under his feet anyway. "See, I went looking for it, you know. Searched all across the white-top mountains. Nepal. Tibet. Hell, I flew every inch of them peaks."

"Looking for what?" Molly asked.

"He ain't told you squat yet, has he, little darling?" Buck held his hands up by his chest, cradling some invisible trophy. "Xanadu. Shangri-La. Shambala." He smiled. "The Order of the Dragon. I found 'em, D."

"You what?" D sat up, chagrin replaced with wonder now.

"Well, I say I did. I found what was left. Burnt-out old temple. Couple sets of bones. Place been abandoned what looks like 30-40 years now. Reckon the Hands got to 'em long before I did. But, there it was all the same. So that part was real at least—so I reckon a fair bit of the rest of it is too. Now lo and behold, here you are in the proverbial flesh, and a redhead to boot. Imagine my surprise." Buck took one of the extra biscuits Molly'd gotten for herself. She wrinkled her nose at this guy. He sure liked to hear his own voice. "I say 'flesh' are you flesh? Forgive my assumption." He pinched at her arm. She seized his hand tight to let him know his boundaries.

"Don't touch. Will somebody here translate his Texas into something that makes any sense."

D gave her the short version, speaking as little as possible which she'd now developed an appreciation for. He told her of some ancient Order of the Dragon, formed centuries ago when the world had rediscovered Cain. They'd fought him, drove him out of eastern Europe back then. They pushed into the Himalayas. It was there they found *the weapon,* according to the legends Buck talked about. A length of chain that fell from heaven in the last war of the gods, "The Great One" as Buck put it.

"And only the chosen one can pass the trials, walk the path through the white mountain, face the burning staff, and return with it to bind him once and for all. Have you taken her to see Mama yet?"

D walked away from the table, leaned one arm against the house, facing the wall. "No, I ain't taken to her Mama's."

"What's Mama's?" Molly's face lit up. "Is it a food place? I want to go to a food place!"

* * *

Molly went through the paces of her morning routine, leaving the two old men to catch up. She liked that Buck made D laugh a time or two despite himself. She gathered they'd been part of a team back in the old days. They knew each other from the army and then worked together again when D had first put on the helmet.

"I helped him with his formula," Buck had told her. Buck was even more the scientist than D had been, though he focused "mainly on the metaphysics and quantum mechanics these days" as he put it. It was all ancient Mesopotamian to Molly.

She turned on the automatic pitcher and loaded it full of steel ball bearings. She took her twin swords, pulled on her blindfold and went to work, slicing every ball out of the air without any of them touching or getting by her. When the machine ran out, she spun her blades in a kata, twisting and jabbing with them until she finished with a soaring backflip high into the sky, still blindfolded, landing in a perfect perch high atop the crane in the center of the scrapyard. She felt like showing off to the show-off.

"Now those look mighty curious." Buck studied her blades as she walked back toward them. "I'd love to get a gander at them under a scope—if'n you'd allow."

Molly took one blade and used it to slice a splinter off the hilt of the other one and gingerly handed it to the "scientist" though she still managed to prick her finger with it. She sucked on her metallic blood, but the wound was gone as quick as she'd made it.

"Don't spend it all in one place." She slid the blades back into each other and laid the cane on the table.

"I won't, darlin." Buck nodded his thanks. "Now tell me why in the hell she's not in the wingsuit," Buck turned his eyebrows to D.

"That thing is stupid." D frowned.

"The what?" Molly looked to each of them.

"Buck here thought it would be a fine idea to drop me into the air wearing a damn kite on my back."

"Yeah, for you, I allow that wasn't my finest idea. But Molly Indestructible here, well she's a horse of another color now ain't she?"

* * *

Molly fitted the contraption on her back. The "wings" were a set of hardened, sprayed fins that folded out by grabbing a set of handles and extending her arms to each side. D said it for sure; it was basically a big kite on her back.

Molly went for broke and fired herself upward, stretching her *wings* as she crested. The kite caught the air, gliding her across the sky—for about a second. One sideways gust sent her spiraling, flipping out of control and slamming into a heap of rusted metal and trash.

"And now I'd be fucking dead, you asshole." D shook his head as he and Buck ran to help pull Molly out of the rubble. "I told you it was stupid."

"Yeah well—" Buck ran out of words as Molly came up laughing, bursting with more energy.

"That was awesome!" She beamed at them, hugged D tight and then stood back, giving herself room. "I'm going again."

"Kid, wait!" D held an arm out, but she was already in the stratosphere.

Ten crashes turned to twenty. Molly put her sprayed-suit, the wings, and herself through a batch of punishment that had D and Buck cringing more by the minute. The sound she made every time, slamming into steel, pavement, all of it. Every time she popped right up and went again—a smile on her face and eager to get it right. Like a girl showing her daddy "no hands" on her bicycle.

And then she had it.

"Gliding through the sky like an angel on high." Buck clicked his bottle against D's. D grew a smile on his face watching the kid soar above them. Something washed over him, a thing he'd never felt before—or at least hadn't since... He watched the kid come in hot, drop the wings, and thud her feet onto the ground with a stomp that rocked their seats underneath them.

She'd done good—he had to admit it. She was a good soldier.

"I don't get it, though." Molly folded her fings behind her like a stiffened cape. She sat next to them, Al coming off the grill with a slew of burgers and andouille to feed half an army—or just three men and a Molly. "Why would you need something like this if your car can already fly?" She looked at D, then Buck. Buck looked back with as much confusion at her as she at him. D sighed. "And how does that even work, by the way? It seems kind like a regular car, I mean... you know."

Buck bellowed, holding his gut with laughter. "You ain't showed her the best damn part, D?" He fell out of his chair. "Oh man, I'm so glad I'm here for this."

"Buck, I swear." D folded his arms.

"Where's the damn clicker. He saw a remote on the table and grabbed it.

"Hey that's for my leg." Al snatched it from him. He pulled another one from his front overalls pocket. "Here."

"Buck, don't. It's still broad daylight."

"D, they ain't a soul for a mile any side of you and this damn dump. It's fine." Buck held up the remote in his hand, his smile the widest he'd worn yet. "Hey kid, I'm about to rock your whole world upside down."

Molly rolled her eyes and shook her head. *Did he really?*

"Bet you ten dollars I do."

"Deal." Molly folded her arms. This guy was so full of it.

Buck pressed a button on the remote.

Molly's eyes exploded out of her skull. Beyond them in the yard materialized a massive floating machine, twice again the size of the house, hovering perfectly still as if frozen in the air just above the ground. The thing was pear-shaped with a bulbous front bridge at the fore-end jutting down like a beard against the rest of it. It was smooth—no hard lines. She blinked her eyes a dozen times before her brain found words to process it. She reached into her pocket, folded out a crumpled up ten-dollar bill and handed it to Buck without a word as she stood and walked toward it.

"Is it—is this..." She held her hand out, walking out to touch it. "A spaceship?" She turned back to the three men.

"We still don't rightly know." Buck clicked the button, disappearing the craft again underneath its cloak.

"Where'd you get it?" Molly had seen a lot of things in the last year of her life that made her world bigger, but this one took the cake.

"It's kind of a long story," D said. "See the Colonel told us the Military had it and—"

"We stole it from the dumb bastards!" Buck bowled himself over laughing, holding his belly, bellowing like a clown out of control.

"Yeah that's basically it." D sighed.

XI
"SHE SELLS SANCTUARY"
—THE CULT, 1985

MOLLY WALKED THROUGH the bridge of the ship—touching everything despite D instructing her to touch none of it. Nothing about it looked human. There were no labels in any discernable language. There were lights all around it, but no sense to them. At times it almost felt alive—as if the whole thing were organic, a lifeform of its own.

Buck showed her around, the captain's seat-as he called it, and the four bucket-seats right behind it along the sides. It was clear he didn't know all that much about it either. D explained the tractor beam function they'd figured out long ago.

"Honest to Betsy, darlin' there's still a host we don't know about this sucker. We just figured, why let the damn government have it? Figured they owed D a big one, anyhow."

"Owed him?"

"Damn assholes stole his formula. Done runnoft with it without paying him a red dime." Buck spat sunflower seeds in a white coffee cup while they climbed out of the ship. "Hell, them assholes owe a lot more debt after—"

"That's enough, Buck." D glared at his buddy and finally shut him up.

Molly sensed D's gut turn over, his heart sink from some distant memory. She didn't know what awful thing he held back, but she knew the kind of hurt he had inside him. She felt it every second of every day. And the guilt too. D blamed himself for something terrible—just as Molly blamed herself for Lydia. Her poor Lydia. No—her *great* Lydia. She closed her eyes and felt them leak as she walked off to let it out again. D had come to accept her moments like these and let her have her pain without spoiling it with talk. She appreciated him for that.

She reached back again and found one of her old favorites. Eighth grade—Ms. Garlon's math class—they got afternoon detention for laughing at her giant beehive haircut and winged glasses. The vice principal had them out cleaning up trash around the building when Lydia's brother came to pick them up. He drove up in that great big Silverado dually—the very same one Lydia inherited when he went upstate. He'd just gotten a pocket full of money—they hadn't known where he got it back then—and took them both out for snow cones and then to the movie store. They got to watch three rated-R slasher movies together and crashed somewhere after midnight, two empty pizza boxes and popcorn all over Lydia's room. That had been a good night.

Molly wiped the water from her face with her arm, but more kept coming.

"What's eating at the kid?" She heard Buck aim his question at D and Al. D let it lie there a moment.

"Vamps got her friend." Al said. D brought Molly a coke from the cooler. She took it but didn't let him go. She leaned against his chest instead. He patted her on the head.

"Well hell. How's about a little payback, then?" Buck sprang up. "I'm itching to see this little queen fight as it is. I say we bring him some pain."

"Hadn't planned on hitting the streets tonight. Falcon needs tuning."

"Yeah, when don't it?" Buck shook his head and spat seed on the ground. "I ain't talking about no nickel and dime bloodsucker. I say we take one of his *kids*." Buck grinned.

"His kids?" Molly cocked her head.

"You done killed one of 'em," Al said. "That big ol' gator swum out of Pontchartrain. Been laying down there a century or more, according to some old folks. See, when he messes around, he can't have no normal kids. It's how come he turns people like him, just so's he has something normal to look at, talk to. His kids always come out ugly-assed monsters. Another part of the curse. Ol' Yhwh did a damn number on him, he did."

"Yep. And there's a hell of a lot more where that gator came from. You know what I'm thinking, don't you?" Buck looked at D, tilted his head to the side, smiled. "I say we go for the Rougarou, boys."

D breathed for a minute, then smiled. Molly's eyebrows rose.

* * *

The plan was to track the giant wolf-monster out in the woods near Lake Charles. Apparently, Cain had children all over the world, always had. He spread his seed far and wide, but always kept a cluster of them handy wherever he set up shop. The Rougarou was an old legend—even Molly had heard of it down in the Bay once or twice—always from her brother Hurl and his friends. When they found it, Molly would drop from the cloaked ship with her spanking new wingsuit and her super swords and go to work, just like she had the croc—she insisted to them it was more croc than gator, but they agreed to disagree.

"Y'all gon' need a pilot for that dang thing." Al waved his arms at the whole affair. "I done come bailed y'out one time in an emergency, but that's it. That thing put snakes in my head."

They'd explained it to Molly. The ship used a cerebral interface, a kind of hat the pilot wore, mentally connecting him into the ship's controls. You had to think of what you wanted it to do, and it would do it, they said. Mostly.

"Problem is it talks back to you." Al's eyes bugged out of his head. "Makes you crazy. I still have nightmares and that was just the one time."

"It's no big deal," Buck said. "So, we go get The Colonel. He loves the damn thing anyway."

"Damn thing's why he's in the hospital to begin with." Al crossed himself looking at the ship and shivered.

* * *

"Here's the plan, I'm thinking." Buck put his foot on the dash as he poured him some more seeds to spit out the window. "By the way when'd you get this beat up old shitbox?"

"Al buys these seizures from impound every other week. We fix 'em and sell 'em. Gotta make money somehow. Ain't nobody calling me to drive rocket trucks in the desert."

"Wait, that was really you?" Molly's eyebrows raised. She'd watched that test drive on TV with Lydia just before...all this.

"Told you I'm basically famous, darlin'. Now like I was saying—we go in, I throw on a little charm while Red here causes a distraction. Do that wind-breath thing—that's fun. D, you grab the Colonel and slip out the back exit."

"Won't work. They got alarms on all the doors now." D turned onto the ramp headed into downtown and started explaining his own drawn-out idea.

Molly saw the dome, the overpass where Cain and Evilyn had fought over who got to *eat* her. She saw the scaffolding and construction crews hard at work putting new glass in the Lili tower—named for *His* mother. Just who the hell was his mother? The boys kept arguing over who's bad plan was worse.

"We don't have to do any of that." Molly spoke up from the back seat. "I'll get him." The two men stared blank-faced at her, waiting for her elaborate scheme to get The Colonel out of the VA. "Trust me."

Molly walked right up to the lady at the front desk, the two ex-green berets behind her, hands in their pockets, shaking their heads.

"Hey, you probably don't remember me, but that's okay." Molly looked directly into her eyes. "I need you to do a discharge for Colonel Carthage, if you would please? And I love your hair today, by the way. And you shouldn't worry so much about you know what. It's time to move on and let that go."

The woman stared at Molly, their eyes locking on each other. She blinked, shook her head out of her daze.

"Yeah, sure. Of course." She pulled up her phone receiver. "Can I get an orderly to Carthage, room 221? Yeah, bring him up for discharge." She put the phone down. "And thank you. I been worried about that for weeks. That's a load off. You sure are a sweetheart."

* * *

Colonel John Carthage sat next to Molly in the van headed back to the scrapyard, D chuckling from the driver's seat at Buck who'd finally been rendered speechless. The Colonel kept asking for cheese whiz the whole ride home until finally D stopped at the store and bought him a tub and some pretzels to dip in it.

"No, it's for my hair." The Colonel's eyes insisted on his point.

"Don't you dare put that in your hair, Colonel."

"Yeah don't." Molly glared into him. She had some work to do with The Colonel.

* * *

The team suited up—D's helmet by his side even though this was a Molly mission. They sat in the red-eyes as The Colonel pulled on the pilot's headgear. Molly felt the energy flow into his brain as the ship lit up all around them.

"I missed you too, sweet baby." The Colonel smiled as he gripped two round knobs by his armrests. "No, they never let me stay up for the late show. I always miss it. We'll watch it together tonight, though."

"Is he?" Molly looked to D and Buck, shaking their heads.

"You got yourself a date, girl!" The Colonel rocked the ship forward, the boys getting butterflies in their guts as the ship gained speed and altitude, headed west—for the wolf.

Tall as a house and near as big, they'd said. It roamed the woods and swamps southwest of the city for decades, maybe more. Cain had made this one of his favorite haunts—long before even The French had.

"He's tried to cross over, many times." D had told her. "There's places on the earth where the veil between worlds is thin. Places where the dead are gathered, or anywhere a cataclysm occurred. With the right words, a bit of sorcery, you could open a door."

"But he can't go through. The curse bars him, no matter what he tries." Buck added.

"How do you know all this?" Molly felt them getting close...to something.

The boys looked at each other, then to Molly.

"Evilyn." D hung his head in his hands. "She wasn't always what she is."

A tenacious prosecutor, he told her, she'd always been a gifted investigator. She'd found D out at the junkyard. The cops and half the city had been convinced The Copperhead had to be some rich guy with an ax to grind. They had files open on everyone with a net worth over a million. But Evilyn followed the evidence, looked at the facts in their face. The Copperhead took down bankers, politicians on the take, fistfought bad cops in the streets—broke them and left them bloody with the evidence to convict. "'A rich prick would be out there clubbing muggers and junkies for the fun of it. They don't know real pain, real struggle. I grew up around them all my life. All they do is hate the poor and buy things that aren't for sale—or shouldn't be.'" D quoted Evilyn's words back to Molly. He spoke of her with panged affection.

"When Cain showed up, she became obsessed. She read everything in every library in three states. She flew herself to Egypt, Istanbul, Wallachia, anywhere she could go that had a part of his legend, his myth. She taught herself spellcasting. She was determined to beat him. It's what made it all the worse when he—"

D stopped himself, Buck nodding to his old friend. Molly didn't have to hear the rest. It was written across his face. Evilyn was only one more loss in a life of loss lived by this man who'd fought The Devil himself and lived to tell it.

"Going to infrared." The Colonel called out. The glass all around the bridge switched color, showing a pitch-black landscape beneath them. Little dots of warmth peppered across the ground before them. All the gods' creatures flitted about, the little ones hiding away in their holes from the night hunters.

Molly felt it before they saw its deep orange glow. Big as a house was right. The ship clocked its speed at 30 miles an hour as it tore through the woods, racing after its chosen prey for the night—a pack of wild hogs it gained on with each step, already gobbling up a straggler. She reached down, felt the same dark emotion she had when she fought the big croc.

The Colonel opened the bomb-bay doors as they called them. She'd asked if the thing had any weapons when they'd geared up for the fight. "None that I've yet found," The Colonel had told her. "And believe me I've gone looking."

Molly liked The Colonel. He was sweet. And he wasn't half as crazy as he made out to be. He just liked pretending.

"If there's any on here, you'll find them." Molly had kissed his forehead and took her seat.

Now she was up and ready to test her flying skills. She tucked the twin swords into the rig D made to secure it to her back while she flew. She steadied, seeing the galloping wolf with her enhanced eyes as they flew past, giving her a lead on it.

"Bombs away." She saluted the soldiers and dropped.

Molly gripped her handles, extended her wings and caught the air. She aimed dead at the monster. She felt its murderous rage at its prey, at the world, at its own self, at its father, and the mother that bore it. She couldn't imagine that life. His children came into this world with just enough sentience to know what they were— and what they weren't. She pitied the poor beast, as she had the massive crocodile. But they were also born with their father's thirst for blood and flesh—his hate for mankind and their gods that did this to him.

Molly slit her eyes, pulled her wings back, and fired like a missile into the beast. She tackled it around the neck, gripping hunks of its hair in her fists, wrenching it to the ground like a bulldogger at a rodeo show.

Its mind screamed out. It gnashed at her with its slobbering jaws, growling, howling as it shook her in its bite. Molly kicked out of its mouth, slammed a fist into a fang, bursting the tooth to bits. Blood ran down its jowls as she dropped to the ground.

Molly gripped her swords, focused her mind. She closed her eyes as it ran at her. She dodged its bite, feinted left, and sliced off its front paw, then spun and took off an entire hind leg. The beast fell to the ground, its blood flowing back into the earth.

It cried out to its father as Molly ended its cruel life. She watched its spirit pour out of its body, already losing itself to the void, moving through the veil into the next realm. For a moment, Molly thought she glimpsed a doorway open.

She felt the invisible ship hover toward her. The Copperhead strolled down the gangway to survey her kill as Molly wiped the creature's blood off her blades with its own fur. She looked at the swords again, wishing she could remake them into something more suited to her style.

A creeping image emerged from the boggy woods, a presence. Molly's eyes shot toward it, her arm extending the blade it already held, aiming it at the dark green figure shrouded by forest and darkness.

"Hold." Copperhead pressed his hand on her arm, calming her. "That's Durok. He's on our side."

Molly watched the green man slide back into the night, gone as mysteriously as he'd come.

"Load up." The Copperhead moved back to the ship. "Time to go see Mama."

XII
"SKELETONS"
—STEVIE WONDER, 1987

MURPHY SLID ON her heavy-grip sock-shoes—she'd used them a time or two back in Detroit on some of her other *extrajudicial* work. She wore them to run sometimes, or just around the apartment—they were awfully comfortable. And those soles could grip oiled linoleum in the rain if they wanted.

She zipped her black jacket, pulled her black hat over her hair. She slung her gear bag on her back, put her nylon rope on her shoulder. One Shell Square, formerly the Cain Capital building now with JarethCo written across the top, was locked tighter than a maximum-security stockade. But the Place St. Charles across and half a block down was cake. A quick smile and some casual chatter with the front door guys got her in the building. Slipping away from them and into the service elevator was easy enough.

She tossed her decoy outfit to the side and popped open the briefcase, pressed the panel to lift the false bottom. She pulled out the pieces of her grappling rifle and screwed them together. She fitted the barb onto the end of the barrel, aimed across the way at the taller tower with Jareth's name on it—and fired.

Murph anchored her end of the line to the roof, ratcheted it tight with her clamp. She put her full weight on, standing on it with her grippy sock-shoes to test it. She checked her Colt in the shoulder holster inside her jacket and zipped back up.

"Here goes some crazy shit." She climbed onto her high-wire, wrapping her body around underneath it as she came off the building into open air. She felt every inch of the height. The lights and sounds of the city called up to her. There'd been plenty of action of late. News of a rainbow princess soaring above the city—knocking over cop cars. Murph would have to find Red soon, see what that was all about. She felt awful about the whole thing. She blamed herself for Lydia. From the beginning she'd used them as bait, then pawns—all in her private quest for revenge. But this was bigger now. This city was sick, eating itself. And this Jareth character was somehow at the center of it. Whatever she was up to, Murph would find it buried somewhere in those offices. Her time at Germain Enterprises had taught her where and how to look. She'd have to do more in one night than she had in two months at GE.

Thankfully, Alex gave her the window. She got Jareth to agree to an exclusive interview—under Jareth's condition that it be televised live over the local news. Murph tried to talk her out of it. Whatever else Jareth was up to, Murph already considered her a murderer—the only real question was her death toll. But Alex was ever the newswoman.

"A scoop is a scoop," she'd said as she worked up her interview questions. "How's my hair? I've never done TV before."

"They'll do that for you," Murph had said, though she had no idea.

She crawled her way across the rope, feet and hands gripping for dear life, her safety harness clamped to the line with a carabiner. Maybe after this was all over, she'd retire. Get a normal people job. Maybe substitute teach or drive a cab. Anything but more of this crazy shit.

She got to the end of the rope, let herself dangle as she pulled the glass cutter from her bag and made a hole big enough to crawl inside. She pulled building plans from her bag, clicked on her light and got her bearings.

"Okay, you two-faced witch, let's see what you're really up to." Murph traced a line on the plans and decided to move to the higher floors. She pulled a paintgun from her bag to gum up the security cams, knowing that would only buy her a few minutes before they sent someone up to check them. She had to work fast.

Moving up the stairs, she got to the top floor, splatted the cams and went to work on the lock to the executive suite—Jareth's central command. She got in with a quick pick and slid to the files. She flipped through all the usual minutiae, reports, and revenue sheets. She pulled drawer after drawer, looking at R&D, acquisitions, anything to give her a hint as to where this all went.

Jareth had a set of security-feed monitors in the office. Murph saw the whole building from her spot. She saw guards headed her way to check the gummed cams. She hit the switch to review the other floors. There were more people in the building besides her and security. Several bootlickers burned the oil in their offices, typing away or poring through their papers. *What was with this town and its night owls?* A whole team on the 33rd was going over a project together. And then there was what looked like a party in the bullpen on 20. A full array of yuppies blowing whistles and wearing cone hats, pouring champagne—someone's birthday, a big sale closed, or just any other day in this town that loved to party for any reason it could find.

Murph shook her head, flipped back to the guards moving her way. She had about three minutes to find a place to hide before they'd be on her. She spied the room, noting a liquor cabinet that might house her, an executive bathroom—all places any decent guard would check immediately if they suspected an intruder.

Her conundrum went turbo when the guard moving toward her collapsed, the black and white monitor showing dark liquid pour from his head. *Oh shit,* Murph mouthed, her eyes agape at the footage. Black shapes appeared, moving fast down the halls. Not just her floor now, but more of them. At least three dozen—all armed with sub-machine guns, dressed in black—toggle buttons on their shirts, black headbands. Murph heard the chaos in her head as she watched them— spraying the air with their guns to corral the others in the building, the party, the night workers, all of them.

Murph closed her eyes, breathed slow, opened them again. Hēishǒu Móguǐ. The Black Hands of the Devil. They were here. What the hell did they want here, and what were the odds? Murph slit her eyes, saw her father's grim face.

"Welcome to the party, pals." She cracked her knuckles, her hands already warm and tingling.

MOLLY DIDN'T WANT to stare at anything or anyone, but there was so much to see, she couldn't look at any one thing long enough to call it a stare. Still, she felt nervous, like an intruder in a sacred place. The power surrounded her as D led her through the gate, over the salt line, into the courtyard of the old clapboard house. Decor and gris-gris abounded as the energy fed into this place.

Voices whispered into her brain as they approached the front porch. The most electric sounds in the world filled her with song. No—it *was* a song. "Street Parade" wafted across the air from the back of the old house.

"Look, just be cool here, and follow my—"

"Is that Earle King?" Molly brushed D to the side. "That's Earle King!" She moved past Buck and The Colonel on a mission to get to the back and see whoever made that sound on the Gibson—she could already hear it was a Gibson.

It wasn't just Earle. She saw Snooks and The Doctor. The Professor worked the keys beside them. And even John Lee sat picking along, all having a jam session right there in the backyard of Mama B's. Molly couldn't believe her eyes as she stood gawking at the gods of guitar right there in front of her.

"I can't believe I'm seeing this." Molly's eyes bugged out of her head. "I swear when I tell Lydia, she'll—" Molly collapsed onto the creaking wood of the back porch, the weight of a dozen worlds shoving down onto her at once. It had come in waves since the night it happened, some of it seeming real but most of it like some evil dream. This was the moment it slammed home. This was when it screamed through her whole body like a flame blazing out of control.

Her face poured water onto the salted, hallowed ground. She was gone. Lydia was truly gone, and Molly couldn't take it. She felt like she would burst, lose all control of herself and smash the planet in half. And in that moment, she somehow knew that she could—maybe that she even had before. An ancient feeling crawled out of her buried and forgotten history. Someone she loved had died, and she'd murdered a world because of it. She trembled, terrified at the thought. Her body shook, vibrated there on the boards as the music flowed into her, unable to soothe from where her soul had taken her.

"Why does she cry like that?" Mama leered down at the fire-haired godling wailing on her porch. "What have you brought to my house, Chevalier?"

Molly looked up at Mama B's fierce eyes, finding a comfort in the stern gaze. Mama wore a bowler hat, feathers and ornaments strung around it dangling from the back. Her dark hair crawling from underneath had a rusty tint. Her face had dark and light splotches like someone with vitiligo. She wore a brown feathered long coat. She was phenomenal and beautiful and powerful in a way Molly felt and knew instantly. This person felt good to be around, familiar, like someone she knew she should be around but didn't know why.

"She lost a good friend." D bent his head to Mama, almost like a bow. "To *Him.*"

"*Him* is why you've come to me." Mama turned away, having seen what she cared to of the crying girl on her steps. "Him is not the concern of The Loa."

"Not him." D followed along behind Mama, Buck and The Colonel giving Molly a hand to her feet, The Colonel offering a shoulder to wipe the last of her sobs onto. "Her." D pointed to Molly.

"Me?" She eked the words from her mussed face. She'd tried to look strong, competent as they came in. She'd wanted to wear her best face, both nervous and excited at the same time.

They're basically gods too is what D had told her. The nods and shrugs of agreement from the rest of the guys had driven the idea of it home to her. *El Shaddai* kept ringing through her head. The God of the Mountain, D had told her. She read all about the ancient gods in the old books they'd given her. It felt like homework at first, but then she got hooked. She thought Zeus and Diana felt familiar. But the older stuff fascinated her more. The Sumerians. The Babylonians. The Orishi. D had a lot of books about a lot of gods.

Mama took them inside. Molly recognized the man in the straw hat sitting in a chair, his eyes staring into her, through her, into some other place, some other time.

"Leg." D nodded his head in another half bow. Buck and The Colonel did the same. Molly wasn't sure if she should or not, but what threw her the most was when Leg did it *to her.*

"Chevalier." Legba touched the brim of his worn hat. "Baron wants to see you."

D hung his head away. "Baron always does."

Mama B's house swam with ornaments and old hand-carvings of saints and spirits—some far older than any human in this room—and not everyone in the room *was* human, something Molly knew, felt. Now that she understood more of them, this place, herself, she recognized kin and kind. Leg had power she couldn't fully fathom, but she felt it all the same.

"Who is this godling?" Mama took Molly's face in her hand, studying her features. "She's awful little. A scrawny thing. But this ain't your skin, is it, child? You wear a mask, don't you?" She smiled, her teeth showed the colors of different metals, gold, silver, copper, iron.

"I um–" Molly didn't have words. She had a thousand questions and now couldn't add the words together the right way to make any sentences.

"We came to talk about the prophecy, about the weapon." D hugged Molly to his side, like she was his own—a pride in his face like that of a father she had once known and long forgotten. It was almost a memory—a whisper on the rain now falling outside them, sending the musicians in from the yard.

"The one who is chosen? She who will go through the white mountain? She shall put on the armor of the gods. She will survive the burning staff. Reclaim the chain that bound the brother of the beast, defeat him, cast him into the lake of fire for all eternity?" Mama smiled her beautiful metal smile.

"She has come. Her time is now." Legba's somber voice echoed through the room. Molly turned to face him, remembering something he told her before. *The power of the father restores the daughter. The power of the sons destroy the mother.*

"Who is my mother?" Molly blurted, losing the plot for the moment. The green-skinned woman was all she could think of. Mama's remark about wearing the wrong skin—it all made sense but also didn't.

"I cannot say to you, child." Mama held her chin in her hand again, softer this time—kinder now. "A dark magic hides you—even from me. This is powerful evil. Only one has this much power." She looked at D when she said it, the rest of that conversation happening unspoken between them.

"*He* called her El Shaddai." D stared at Mama. Mama stared at Molly, building fear and awe together in Molly's mind.

"The line of Oya?" Mama curled her lip. "El Shaddai?" She studied Molly, looking over every inch of her, looking for some hint of the truth beyond the veil of whatever darkness hid Molly not only from herself, but also from literal gods— a terror washing through the both of them. Molly knew that Mama was like her in that way, the two of them feeling, sensing one another. And the thing Mama feared poured into Molly and curdled her mind to ice.

"The Night comes." Legba leaned back in his chair. "She brings the cold from the world beyond. She brings her children. The destroyer will be remade."

"I don't know what that means. I don't know what any of this means?" Molly whipped her head from one god to the next, then to the humans. "Why can't you— you're gods, or whatever, right?" Molly gestured her hands in confusion. "Why don't you go kill this thing?"

"It is not our fight. We stand watch at this gate until the horn blows." Mama wrinkled one eye at Molly. D scolded her even worse with a look. He had warned her not to overstep with them, and she hadn't meant to. But she needed something to make sense and soon.

"Look, it's not coincidence." D deferred to Mama again with a nod but still pressing his issue. "She's here, like Leg said. She's got this power, like none—" D bowed his head lower this time. "I mean no disrespect—like none of you I've ever seen. She's—" D smiled at Molly, like she'd just broke four tackles and ran the game-winning score into the end zone. "She's amazing. She's the one we've been waiting for."

Molly smiled at D. She'd never wanted to hug him as much as now, and oh boy was she going to as soon as they left—she didn't want to embarrass him in front of his god friends, but it was *so* happening. Plus, she wanted to get food. She really thought there would be food here.

"Yeah, so what am I supposed to do?" Molly perked her shoulders up, ready to get on with this *chosen one* stuff and bring some heat down on these godless monsters that took her Lydia. '*Godless,' was that even a thing she should think or say now? It was so weird, being a god. Like, really?* "Where's this mountain?" Where do I go get this chain or weapon or thing, whatever?"

Mama B shook her head at the blusterous, chipper young god. Legba chuckled his low rumbling laugh. D looked at Buck, then at Mama. The Colonel looked off into space.

"Baby darlin," Mama laughed. "But you ain't the chosen one." Her metal smile brightened the dim, candle-lit room a little more.

"What the—" D shook his head, swore in three languages under his breath and turned around. Molly shook herself out of the moment of it. She had been all set to climb this white mountain and go get some cool-sounding wolf chain and beat Dracula's ass with it—D hated it when she called him Dracula, though she still did it in her head anyway. But it was all the same to Molly. Chain or no chain, old Cain and his witch Evilyn had a fight coming.

"If *this*—"D held both his arms out at Molly. "If *She*'s not the one, then who in this goddamn world is?"

XIV

"STRAIGHT OUTTA COMPTON"
—NWA, 1988

MURPHY PUT HER PISTOL in her hands, dancing her nearly barefoot feet down the naked hallways of the top floor, moving away from the executive offices. She'd clocked The Hands on three separate floors before she left Jareth's suite. It occurred to her that in any other city, she would just pull the fire alarm and get some backup. But this town and her own had taught her not to trust other cops.

Two moved up the building toward her. Whatever they came for, thought they'd find, she intended to beat them to it. Plus the people in the building—she had to figure a way to get them out of harm's way. She ducked into a supply closet, no time to pick the lock, so she shoved all her weight into a front kick and knocked it open.

She crawled into a ventilation shaft from there and made her way toward the faint sounds of her targets. She got above them as they walked through the unlocked door of the head office where she'd just been.

"Someone's already been in here." Came an English accent with hints of Eastern Europe thrown in. The Hands were all over the globe, though had always been most concentrated in the mountains of East Asia. "He wants to know what she's planning. Can you get into her files?"

"Depends on what she's put on this thing. It may take some time."

"I wouldn't mind knowing that myself," Murph whispered to no one. She crawled back down the shaft, moving through the top floor to get near the stairwell. The top floor crew had the ringleader, it appeared. If she could pick off a few downstairs, maybe she could get them chasing a ghost.

She slid out a vent and into the stairwell, hugging the walls on her way down. Her seven *very loud* shots in her Colt weren't much comfort considering she'd counted at least a dozen or more, all with SMG's—all Black Hands with years of training even without the guns.

Murphy got to the 20th, to the party where the Hands had moved all the strays they—just like she—hadn't counted on. Three stayed to guard the crowd while the rest swept the building for more.

Murphy got into the vents again, moving through the rafters toward the back of the bullpen. She clocked the guards watching the exits. Through the grates, Murph saw the hostages, all ziptied, most leaking from their eyes and scared out of their minds. *That's what you get for being at work at night, you dipsticks,* Murph thought, shaking her head at them. But, then here she was breaking into a building, investigating a cultist conspiracy, solving a rash of murders, and she hadn't been a cop in over two years.

She dropped into a supply closet and crept out the door, well away from the eyes of the three guards. She slinked through the room, staying behind cover, until she got near a hostage at the back of the group. He spotted her, and she gave him the shush finger on her lips. She got to him, slit his bond with her pocket knife.

"Stay cool, I'll get you out of this." She slit the ties of the two closest to them, then handed off the knife to keep it moving through the group. "Stay still until the shooting starts, then move like hell to the back stairs and haul ass down to the emergency exits."

"With them shooting at us?" One whispered.

"They'll only be shooting at me." Murphy smiled through her screaming panic.

"Are you a cop?" One of them whispered.

She paused, closed her eyes, breathed. The question stuck in her gut. "No. No I'm not."

Murphy leapt to her feet and ran across the tops of the cubicles like a trained acrobat, blasting her Colt into the chest of the closest guards. The third got a bead on her, spraying bullets. Murphy side-flipped off the edge of the cubicle, ran sideways for several steps across the wall, kicked herself off, her whole body spinning into a flip that became a leglock around the last guard's head before he got his submachine gun to bear.

Murphy brought her enemy down, sprang back to her feet, flung the gun upward into her own hand and dropped her heel onto the goon's temple, leaving a nice sized dent.

"Who's got a machine gun now, ho?" Murphy checked the mag and dug out the two spares he had on him, along with his radio and earpiece.

Murphy charged into the hallway from the bullpen, racing toward the detachment of backup headed her way. The hostages did as she told them and booked straight for the back stairwell as Murphy ran at the next batch of guards, emptying her mag into them then leaping into the wall, kicking off, flipping her body sideways over their heads, landing in the center of the ones still standing. Then she went to work. Fists and feet flew from her center mass faster than their guns could move. She socked guts, kicked balls, broke necks, a tornado of fury none of them had ever seen.

Murphy dropped the last of the second group when the third dinged from the elevator, bullets already blazing. She swooped a gun into her hands and tore off down the next hallway, the bullets closing behind her. She sprinted for the window at the end of the hallway, snatched the emergency fire hose on her way, sprayed the glass with gunfire and took a flying leap out the 20th story.

Wind rushed into her face as Murphy Long soared high above the gothic city. The firehose caught tight, sending her careening back toward the building. Her rubber-soled socks hit the glass at a run. She blasted her way into the lower floor just as someone above sliced her hose from the wall. She pulled it in behind her, wrapped it across her chest and shoulders, leaving the brass nozzle dangling from her left hand. She ran till she hit the back stairwell, heard the sounds of the hostages moving fast as they could beneath her. She went up, ready to go to war with any who came after them, making herself the target in their stead.

Why, you dumb bitch? Why do you do this shit? She asked over and over. But how could she not do it? She checked the radio she took from the guard, heard the frantic chatter, the English/European guy shouting orders to find her, to kill her at all costs.

"It's *her!*" came the angry voice over the short-wave. "She's here—in the building! She doesn't leave here alive!"

Murphy needed a plan. Her gun was spent from shooting her way back into the building. A gang of four headed her way. She got into the halls again, slipping into an office, moving in the darkness until she could maneuver behind them. She popped out just as they made the stairwell, flung the heavy nozzle of the firehouse like a missile, smashing it into the back of one's skull. He dropped to the floor. The other three turned but not before Murphy snapped the hose back to her, flipped and whirled it around her body like a tentacle appendage she'd been born with. Murphy Long became a maelstrom of swirling punishment. Each swift move of her body and arms flung the hose into another foe, its brass fixture thunking into their chests, their heads. The wet pops of their bones inside their bodies sang to her as they dropped one after another.

She picked up a fresh gun and kept moving. Something cooked inside her, a rage bubbling up from inside her. She breathed, focused it, felt it course through her, another weapon she could use, control. The next floor, she took out five in a flash. She didn't even feel it now. Her body moved like it was supposed to, like she'd trained it to do. Like *her father* trained her to do.

Every day after school. Hours of her forms. Then hand to hand. Blocks. Fists. Kicks. Flips. Parry. Return. Then the sticks. Batoning at each other back and forth until the bruises ran up and down her like polka dots. Bo staff. Boken. Morning star. Sometimes just anything in reach.

"*You* are the weapon," he'd always tell her. Her father. "Never forget that."

The weapon rained down on the Hēishǒu Mógui. The next group, she decided to show off, slapping the weapons out of their hands with her firehose, spinning kicks and hurling the brass nozzle into their faces for her own joy. The last one ran for it, and she sent that firehose like a bullet to his back. She knocked him to his feet, walked up and kicked his head, crunching his face into the floor.

She made her way to the top floor, the last three, including the ringleader, saw her bolt out of the stairs, and they didn't even bother to try. They ran for the opposite end of the hall, headed up the next stairs to the roof access. Murphy booked after them, making it onto the roof just as they boarded a chopper. They sprayed at her with machine guns as she dropped and rolled for cover. The chopper lifted and turned to make its escape. Murphy jumped back and pulled her Colt, one shot left in the pipe. She fired and put a hole right through the glass into the pilot's skull as they got airborne. The copter fell sideways, rotors spinning, ripping into the concrete roof, splintering a hundred shards in every direction. The engine flared, and flames erupted into the fuselage.

"Gonna need some more Black Hands, I guess." Murphy released a heavy breath from her chest. She let herself relax, calmed her mind like her teacher taught her—a damn good teacher. She looked at the destruction, a burnt body crawled out of the wreckage only to die three feet away. She stared at their charred remains and shook her head. She still had no idea what they'd come for.

ALEX CHARLTON FIDGETED with the lavalier mic clipped to her blouse while the makeup girl brushed at her face. She felt the goosebumps running up and down her body grow a size larger as the hard lights of the studio fired up.

"Oh wow, this is all... so much. I've never done TV before." She glanced at herself in the mirror. She felt like a different person stared back at her. "I hope I don't stutter or look like an idiot."

"This'll help you relax." Evilyn handed her a drink, her liquor-smooth voice washing over Alex's turbulent mind, as it had the night before, when she'd agreed to be interviewed...if it was televised live. Evilyn insisted. "When I'm done with you tonight, you'll be the talk of the town." Evilyn smirked, checking her image in the mirror. She did her own makeup.

"We're on in 5, ladies." A grip tapped on his clipboard as the makeup lady finished with Alex. It was go-time.

* * *

Lights from every direction bored into her brain as the cameras stared into her like hungry animals. She closed her eyes for a moment to put liquid in them. She glanced down at her questions.

"We have a special guest here with us today." The main anchor looked into the camera as he read the cues. "And by request, a guest interviewer as well, Ms. Alex Charlton from *The New Orleans Register.* Alex, what does it feel like to be in front of the camera rather than behind the typewriter?" His teeth reflected the thousand lights of the studio as they pivoted to her.

"Feels great, Todd." His name was Todd, because of course it was. "I'm here with New Orleans' own native daughter, a face and a name known well to many, and one that's been back in the headlines of recent. Ms. Evilyn Jareth, glad to have you here with us tonight."

"Happy to be here, Alex." Evilyn's face felt brighter than the studio lights. The crew, anchors, all stared at her with eager attention.

"You've had a whirlwind few weeks—a hostile takeover of your former corporation. Your own board had voted you out some eight years ago, I believe. Would you care to talk about that?"

"It's true, there were setbacks, but always I bided my time, waited for the right moment to stage a comeback. When you see your opportunity, you bite right into it." Evilyn smiled, her teeth flashing the light from the studio into Alex's eyes. "But I'm not here to talk about business and corporations. I have something far more urgent and dire to bring to the attention of the people of this city."

"Yes, you mentioned that when you offered me this interview. So, what is it, Ms. Jareth? What do you have to tell us?"

"This city is held captive." Evilyn folded one leg over the other, her outfit pushing the boundary of what the network could legally allow on the air. "By a sinister force. One Jack Germain, as he currently calls himself. He commands his own private army. Owns or holds significant shares in nearly every major company operating in the city, and a dozen more on a global scale. Many won't believe it when I say this, but dark forces control this city, his monstrous, beastly acolytes hold positions of power at every level, and they feed on the ignorant, unknowing innocents. It's a secret half known, unspoken for a decade now. And I've come out tonight to expose it, to say its name, to warn the people, open their eyes to see what cannot be unseen."

"Wow." Alex tried not to roll her eyes. The guys at the bullpen would never let her hear the end of this one. "That's a big claim." Up in the studio, she already saw the producers bug out, looking to switch to commercial if it got any weirder. "I suppose you have some more details, proof, of these 'beastly acolytes' as you called them?" Alex pushed her eyes into Jareth's. If she could rope this back into a story, she'd pat herself on the back.

"Of course I have proof." Evilyn smiled, the crook of one side of her mouth raising higher than the other, the twang in her voice confident, cold as she said it. "Because you're one of them."

"I'm sorry, I'm what?" Alex shook her head, losing her cool on the camera, just like she feared she would.

Evilyn muttered something under her breath Alex couldn't make out, her fingers moving in some odd pattern.

"Ms. Jareth, if you could elaborate further on this—" Alex choked on her last words, her mouth quitting on her at the end. Something crawled into her guts and gripped her. She almost doubled over. She gasped for breath, her face hurting all over, her muscles spasming.

"You see?" Jareth stood from her chair, the cameras staying with her and whatever was happening with Alex.

Alex fell out of her chair, her hands, her fingers aching, bursting, like the meat on her bones would rip out of her skin. Her mouth protruded from her face, her ears growing longer, her hair—hair everywhere.

"He takes his *favorites* and turns them into what *He* is. Together, they feast on the flesh and blood of innocents, children even—they prefer the blood of the young. It keeps them fresher, allowing them unnatural lifespans, youthful faces for decades, centuries. And they are here. Look at her, look at *it.*"

Alex's bones broke, rebuilt themselves inside her body, growing bigger, longer. Her fingers grew claws, her hands paws. Her hairy flesh tore from her clothes, shredding them off her body to reveal her changing form. The last of her audible words struggled out of her labored breath.

"Wha-wha- is happening 'oo me?"

Her face was no longer human—her body a gangly, ferocious monster.

Screams tore from the booth. Camera operators ran from their posts. Todd, the anchor, had long since bolted for the door. Evilyn walked over to the camera to widen the shot, making sure to get the whole of what had been Alex Charlton, career veteran reporter—now a hideous thing crawling around, slobbering on the studio floor.

Like an animal.

Evilyn leaned down to Alex's sobbing, beastly face, her mind tearing itself in half with madness as she lost all sense of reality in an instant.

"Sorry." Jareth whispered. "Nothing personal. But you were getting in my way."

EPISODE V

"STRANGERS' THOUGHTS"
—CAMOUFLAGE, 1988

CAIN STOOD ON THE HIGH balcony overlooking the wetlands. In the distance, he heard his dear daughter devouring some pitiful lost souls—poachers, maybe. They sometimes wandered into this area not realizing who controlled it, nor what a wondrous creation that daughter had become—truly one of his favorites of his myriad children sired over a dozen millennia now.

Or was it more?

He had so long forgotten the beginnings of it all. Watching even the gods themselves change over the centuries as their worshippers' tongues twisted their names—altered their natures, their attributes, their origins, even splitting them in two or fusing two into one and then thrice over. Their ability to remake themselves into whatever they need be, or just wanted to be in some fleeting moment, amused him—his own mother's current form the most amusing of all as she moved the mortals further toward destruction at their own hands. She was always so bent on undoing reality. But now the fates had gifted him with a means to stave her madness.

Ever thus it had been with him—a series of their fleeting moments. How his mother slithered her way into that hidden garden—his birth the product of a petty feud. She cast him off, having given him the form of his father, raised alongside his half-brother. How they doted on that *pure* son. Untainted. Another fleeting whim, the anger of the petulant shepherd god, demanding only blood, the blood of beasts. Cain lamented his whim in cleaving the poor idiot's skull with his silver knife.

"There be your blood offering," he had said when the little god asked after the boy. His father and stepmother—weaklings, mortals, cowards—too groveling to argue with their "maker" after he'd cast them out of his pretty arboretum.

But their age came to a twilight—followed by another. The bronze gods faded, wandered into memory, then myth. Most died in the first war. Then came the iron gods, their golden one slain, their champion storming against the tireless march of Mother Night and her dark terrors. How he had raged, year upon year upon year, driving back those who would swallow all light and wake the sleeper from this endless, banal dream.

Would even that fail to end his forever curse? Or could the waking dreamer end this eternal prison?

The one called they called Cain—among so many other long forgotten names— stared at his whispering marsh, thinking these thoughts. As he had so often before.

I

"FIRE WOMAN"
–THE CULT, 1989

IT WAS A GOOD PLAN—or it had been—perfectly executed. She had even impressed herself, a thing so rare she could count on one hand the times she had. The two-story rock monster called forth from the aether—that faraway realm of lost souls and terror—bore down on the bustling streets of the city in the broad light of day. Evilyn adored exploiting Cain's weakness she no longer shared. It curled the tips of her mouth upward. Her good doctor friend watched in awe as the behemoth crushed car and asphalt under its stone fists.

Evilyn admired the chaos she wrought—not without its purpose—upon the town she loved despite how they'd so quickly abandoned her. She drank the fear and confusion that flowed from the torn minds of the people fleeing the maelstrom. Her mighty golem raged, mindless, a bloodless automaton entirely under her control—a perfect weapon to sow the terror needed to rouse these simpletons from the beast's evil illusion. With their minds awake to his darkness, she could draw him out, weaken him, and imprison him in a mirror box. At the very least, the spectacle would draw the Fae, not that they were any friend to her.

Formed of a cabal of iron-hard stones held together only by the whisper of her voice and the right words spoken in an ancient tongue, it stood tall. The booms rang out for a mile in any direction. She directed him with motions of her fingers from the distance, watching him through the arcanery of her wall of television monitors.

The break-in to her office, the commotion in the building hadn't surprised her. Germain, or rather Belial Cain, had sent his Black Hands to snoop on her. Their centuries-old mission to assassinate *the chosen one* had brought them to the city. She expected them. For who now was "the chosen one" but her? Having tasted the blood of so sweet a victim—such power. Soon, Cain would unleash worse—his own blood-born children of darkness. Today was merely a test drive of what she would unleash to break his hold—and establish *Her* as the true demagogue of this city.

It was such a beautiful day, the sun warming her long dead skin. Was she alive again? Could that be? Had the godling's few gulps of blood restored her life? So many interesting new questions. But then it all came to crashing ruin...again.

Like a rainbow bullet from the stratosphere, the fire-haired god slammed into the golem's chest. Boulders crumbled and fell as the gorgeous monster lost its balance. Evilyn muttered her words, strained her fingers and brought it back to its feet, slamming its mighty stone fist down onto the interloper.

The little meddler sprang to her feet, gravel dust flinging from her undamaged costume—an upgrade Evilyn knew all too well. *Why, D? Why now? Why can't you just let me end this?* Evilyn swore at the battle happening at midtown. She wrinkled her eyes as the kid produced two flashing swords, reflecting light back onto Evilyn's monitors.

She sliced with her Eldritch blades, taking chunks of rock from the golem. Evilyn summoned them back into the creature with her words, but the do-gooder moved too fast. Then the worst of it began. The shouts. The cheers. The claps. They clapped for her—her rainbow wings flowing behind her as she slammed her godstrong fists into the monster, pulverizing it to naught but new pavement for the city's roads.

"You stupid little bitch." Evilyn wrinkled her face, pouring herself a glass of heavily enchanted wine—the only thing that could half intoxicate her now that she'd *improved* herself. "This is the opposite of what we need. She gives them hope, good doctor." She gulped her drink and poured another, looking at her trusted confidant and accomplice, gesturing at the carafe as an offering.

"I'm pretty sure that would kill me, boss, but thanks." Dr. Tesche waved her hand at it, shaking her head. *In frustration or admiration?* Evilyn began to wonder, furrowing her brow at her familiar.

Evilyn watched the peppy child making shadow-dance moves with a group of children as they laughed and hugged one another. A black-armored muscle car roared onto the street near the commotion. A bronze-age helmet appeared from the turbo-tank. The people of the city swarmed the one they knew as their hero of the hour. Not a single drop of fear echoed from such a perfectly-wrought scenario, only pure elation.

"Yes, Doctor, I have cause for my newfound dread." She downed another swig of elder wine. "And it is the little girl who rides with The Copperhead."

She flung an energy bolt into her screens, exploding them into the executive suite around them, the doctor ducking for cover.

Evilyn poured.

II
"FLIP CITY"
—GLENN FREY, 1989

THE OLD MAN READ his paper on the bus bench outside the hardware store, checking his watch every few seconds—always a stickler for his time; he timed everything, knew the duration of his movements, the time of sunset and sunrise. Down the long, visible stretch of street, the bus lumbered along. As it got within six blocks, the man checked his watch again, noted the time, and stood up. He walked to the storefront and inspected a hickory handle from a bin by the door along with a few lawn chairs, shovel and rake racks, and other odds and ends to entice passersby to come in the store. He stared down the haft of the ax handle, deciding it suited him well enough.

Buck Kobayashi watched, out of sight, from his vantage as the bus pulled to the stop, its doors creaking open. A mousy woman stepped off, looking to either side as she clutched her bag in front of her. She looked maybe forty, but tired, cat-eyed. She kept her purse tight to her chest as she hurried down the street. A group of young men stepped around the corner from an alleyway by the storefront.

They bore no kind of visible insignia and were probably just local strays. Things this far north didn't fall under the influence of a certain totalitarian night creature, and Red Stick still had its share of run-of-the-mill street problems.

The old man moved quietly behind the gang as they called at the lady hurrying her steps. They shouted and made vulgar gestures at her. She glanced back enough to increase her trepidation as she stepped along the path. The old man moved well for his age, though Buck knew there was barely half a decade between them, a fact his back reminded him harshly of on the daily. The man's silver hair wrapped around his thin, white, well-kept beard, framing his square jaw. If Buck had been any less confident in himself, he might even be jealous.

The man walked like someone three inches taller than he was. The boys got more aggressive, tailing closer behind the lady, and one tugged on her shoulder as they catcalled—that was the mistake the old man had been ready for.

The broad head of that ax handle slapped the handsy idiot's head with a nice pop Buck heard it a block away. He walked closer, tempted to join the fray, but always liked watching his old captain work. The rest of the crew turned on the geezer. With well-timed precision, the old man stepped back, slung the ax handle in an uppercut to the chin, sending that one to bed. The last two squared-up and charged, and the old man whirled the hickory stick, slapping each of them a good two or three times, jarring their heads. One managed to pull a switchblade only to have it knocked to the ground from his now-broken hand, Buck figured. The last man standing set himself to running.

"Nothing like a good piece of hickory." The old man spun the stick in his hand, handing it over to the lady to keep. "You hang on to that. I 'spect they won't bother you again."

The woman stared for a moment and then went on her way.

"By god, Boudreaux, you always throw quite a party, ain't you?" Buck licked his grin as he closed the last of the gap between him and his old army buddy. Callum Boudreaux, army ranger turned government agent turned anti-government saboteur and thief, shook his head, not even turning to the sound of Buck's voice. "Now did she take an ad in the paper or was this one just a happy accident?"

"I come this way time or two." Boudreaux popped his neck. "Seen 'em behaving atta way before. You know I don't tolerate rude behavior."

"I know you don't, partner." Buck propped his shiny snakeskin boot up on the hydrant next to where they stood, glared off at the sun creeping low in the sky. "Reckon you seen the news. We're putting the band back together."

"I figured that's why you come. Who's the girl?"

"Oh, she's a pistol, Cap'n." Buck grinned. "I just can't for y'all two to meet. She's an absolute pistol!"

* * *

The Pistol aimed herself at the massive bear-like golem whose bones jutted out all over its body like grisly spikes. Ten feet tall, it towered over the spitting engine of The Copperhead's heavily-armored Ford Falcon. Scratching at the impenetrable chassis, the beast roared as Molly slammed into its chest from high above the city. She'd taken to her glider wings as though she'd always had them.

Sirens wailed in the distance as blue lights grew closer to the grim scene. The Copperhead spun a 180 degree turn in the tank-like car, preparing himself to fire into the bloodsucking cops.

As the lights flickered, so did the snarling beast, its form growing intangible as Molly sliced her otherworldly blade through a wisp of air where it had been. The Copperhead jumped from the car toward Molly as her eyes focused through the haze of the darkening alleyway. A purple energy lingered as the last remnants of the monster whispered out of the air. A flowing, dark violet gown appeared before them, housing the pale skin and two-tone hair of Evilyn Jareth, her smile wider than the alley itself.

"Hello, darlings." She looked like she tasted a strawberry as she spoke.

"You!" Molly braced for a launch. "You took my friend from me. You used her as bait."

"Indeed I did, and such a small price for our delicious kiss. I am so enjoying being..." Evilyn sneered. "You."

"You'll never be me!" Molly charged at the grinning witch before The Copperhead could grip her shoulder.

"Kid, No!" He shouted as she thrust through the air.

Evilyn raced her left arm in a circle as her right sucked the pistol from Copperhead's hand. Molly shot through the opening, and Evilyn circled her arm again, closing the portal.

"All too easy." Her face grew solemn as she stared at the lonely visage of that bronze helmet. His shoulders slumped, and she felt something catch in her throat—but the feeling passed.

"What did you do?" The Copperhead's voice reverberated through his helmet. He pulled another pistol, but The Jester Queen hurled it to the other side of the alley with a wave. She flowed forward, pushing all sound away from them as she embraced her old comrade, her former...whatever they'd been to one another.

"I did only what I had to. You must believe me." She closed her eyes a moment as she lifted the helmet from his head, him not even fighting the intrusion. She turned her head as she saw the water leak from his tired *old* eyes. How he'd aged since... She studied the lines in his face. She'd been older than him when they first met. She was hundreds of years old now—more than she could count as time in the other realm could be *difficult* to track, a sunless void of lost souls, wandering eternity in the mist.

"Bring her back. Now." D squeezed his eyes, trying to dry them.

"I may do that." She kissed her words into his ear, her tongue flicking against her shiny metal teeth. "For you." The blood in The Copperhead's neck pulsed, hot and thick, his heart racing, raging. How she wanted him then, so much she almost felt her heart beat again. Almost. "But not until I'm done. Not until *I* beat him. You could join me, you know?" Evilyn closed her eyes, smelling his skin, sensing his anger, his hate, his loss. "You could finally put aside this silly nonsense and give yourself to me. You could have *real* power."

"Never, Evilyn." He turned his head to bore his eyes into her. "You gave up. You quit on us. Sold yourself—seduced by—" He wrinkled his lip at her. "This."

"No." Evilyn glared back at him, losing what rekindled interest she'd fleetingly held. "I did what had to be done. As I do now."

"Why, Evilyn? Why her? She was special. She—" D composed himself, held back that last bit. Evilyn felt him gulp it into his throat. Her soul, whatever of it remained, flinched for him. She saw it now—what the child had been for D. Her eyes didn't produce tears to belie her weakness. She thanked *Cain* for that.

"She was in the way. You and your little friend were ruining my very good plan. You don't get it, D. This city needs to despair. They need horror. They need their minds flayed and peeled back to see the evil that he is. Only when they dwell in abject terror will his whole mirage fall apart. He can't hide in plain sight if they know to look for him, what he is, what he commands. I will expose him. Their screams will chase him from *our* city. You should trust me." Her eyes pleaded with him to understand or at least go back to not being in the way. It was the least he could do—the least he owed her.

"No. They need hope. They need to see a hero fighting in the street for them. Remind them of what's good and right. No one knows that more than I do." Copperhead steeled his eyes to her, that beautiful face nothing but a lie covering a rotten corpse.

"Hope?" She sneered. "When was the last time you heard those bells ring? They don't even remember you."

"She—" he muttered, pulling his helmet from her hands, putting it back on his head. "She was hope."

He got in his car and drove off, as he had all those years ago—the first time she'd offered him this chance, this power. Evilyn Jareth stood alone, wrapped in her blanket of night, its Eldar god somewhere out there in the universe, working her will, raging always toward the dying of the light.

Evilyn would end it. She would destroy the Prince of Darkness. She didn't need anyone anymore.

III
"CRUEL SUMMER"
—BANANARAMA, 1984

MURPHY STILL HADN'T come to grips with it, the thing she saw on the news. Poor Alex. It didn't feel real. She'd somehow compartmentalized everything with the super kid. Seeing Alex on the television as had half the city—it was front page the next day, and the next—slammed the shock of everything home. Then the rock monster got pulverized by The Hammer and some big guy in a metal mask. The Copperhead. *It all had to be joke, right?* Like some evil clown playing tricks on the whole city.

Or a Jester Queen.

Murphy's eyes turned to slits. She kicked herself. She'd been right from the beginning. She'd been there, in the lion's mouth and missed it, distracted by the redhead and all she was. Now the kid had tagged up with some dinosaur from the city's past, out there chasing monsters. And the cops? The rumors floating the dregs said The Copperhead took down cops more than he did crooks, but nothing about that ever hit the news. Why would he target the cops? And why would the city cover it up if he did?

She had to ditch the car. Her free ride at the writer's pad was burned. All of it gone down the tube. Germain, Jareth, the Black Hands, somehow all connected. She still didn't have the missing piece—the weapon. The Hands had been at Jareth's looking for either the weapon or its wielder, she'd made out from their radio chatter. But the kid was with the tinhead. Murphy should have joined them days, no, weeks ago. She'd wanted to stick to her own script, and now it had cost her everything.

A deep sigh crawled out her mouth as she ditched the car under the I-10 overpass not far from the dome. She'd be hard-pressed to drive something that fine ever again. She put distance between her and the bright red Mondial. She looked at the bleakness of the city, darker tonight than usual. Faces followed her. Whispers in the dark. Some silent name on their lips. She recalled the street urchins outside the old church-turned-art gallery. That painting. The man from the gala.

She checked the cash in her wallet. She would have to come up with a new funding source soon or start boosting wallets off the suited yups. That gave her an idea. Half those greedy bastards worked late shift hours all through downtown. If she could catch one of those Brantleys, she could work him for information *and* get some folding money. It was about the only lead she had left.

She darted and hugged the shadows, pulling a hood over her head. From a distance came a scream. Had she heard it or only sensed it? She followed it, came to a set of kids, not more than pre-teens. A pack of maniacs chased them through the back alleys. Murph thought she recognized them—the faces of this city's goons all bled together in her mind. A guy and a girl, they wore ragged-out clothes, cut leather jackets, spiked hair, piercings everywhere, their eyes bloodshot, and their teeth—fangs. *They had fangs.*

"Hey!" she shouted and then couldn't tell herself why. The fanged punks aimed their piercing eyes at her, licking their teeth. The kids seized their chance and booked, and Murph was thankful for that at least. The goons narrowed their eyes at her, skulking in her direction. She took her Colt from its back perch and showed them her iron.

They weren't impressed. One laughed. The girl stretched out her fingers, her long neon nails lengthening, growing into jagged claws. Her teeth grew longer. The dude followed suit, his face twisting in the moonlight. Both chuckled at her and her pistol.

"Right." She had a gut feeling it was no use, but she went ahead and dropped each one with two in the chest. They went down but not for long. The sound of bones twisting, breaking, reforming as they rose back up from the ground, their faces like nothing human anymore. "Big nope." Murph tucked the gun and ran down the alley.

Murph didn't wait to see any more of the sideshow. She sped, leaping and dodging trash cans and debris along her path, bounding fences and short walls like they were barely there, sometimes not sure she'd even touched the ground when she stepped, but that couldn't be right. She never looked behind her but heard the snarls and frothing growls growing closer by the second. She cut a ninety degree turn and fled up the next street, then a hard left. She found herself moving into The Quarter. Her next sharp turn ran her right into two blue uniforms.

They looked less friendly than the damn dogs chasing her. Her eyes popped at them and theirs at her. A split second and they went for their guns.

"Someone's looking for you." One cop grinned as they put a bead on her. A growl from around the corner gave Murphy just enough of an opening. She wrenched one's gun away from him, wrapped her legs tight around the other's arm and flipped him onto the ground. She brought the cop's gun to bear just as the punk-dogs came around the corner and put a set of rounds in each, only slowing them down. She flipped herself over the cop, then kicked him at the incoming beasts. She flip-kicked the second dog square in its snarling jaw as it leapt at her, then palm-punched the first cop she'd put on the ground, hurling him away.

The cops recovered and roared into the beasts, their own faces twisting, bones cracking, fingernails growing. And then it all clicked. The kid. The man in the metal hat. The cults. The Black Hands. Murphy ran it through her mind for all of one half a second. Then she put her Converse to work again.

She burned up the streets, baking the soles of those flat-bottomed sneakers on her way to—where could she go? She ran down Peters, then found Canal, still busy as ever. More blue uniforms found her, their eyes zeroing like the animals she now knew them to be. Detroit had its robots. New Orleans had dogs right out of hell.

She moved onto Bourbon, hoping the crowd could blend her, shield her long enough to come up with an idea, some sort of plan. She started her breathing again, seeing her father's face, that quiet voice telling her everything would be okay. "You can do this," she heard her memory whispering to her. "You have the power inside you. Always." *Yeah, well, could use some of that right about now, Pops.* She moved further down the street. They found her again. A team of blues went into a sprint, already pulling their pistols. She ran through the 400's into the 500 block. She saw the old man, Victor, at the curb where he always sat during her morning runs.

The dog-cops closed on her, the clicking metal of their pistols telling her it was about to be over. Then came the bang. The flash. The light shut her eyes. A quietness filled her. She almost saw her father again for one brief instant.

Murphy opened her eyes. Victor stood there, his open palm facing out toward the doom and death that had terrorized and chased her here, to him, to this moment and place in time. She looked behind her. The dog-cops lay across the ground, cast in all directions, their faces smoking, smoldering from whatever that flash of light had been.

Victor. It had been Victor, the old man who sold trinkets on the street corner.

"I told you, Murphy," he flickered in the darkness. "If you need help, I told you where to go." He faded out of her vision. Like he'd never been there.

"Yeah." She looked back at the unreality behind her. "And something tells me they're at a junkyard outside of town."

IV
"FAST CAR"
—TRACY CHAPMAN, 1988

BUCK ROLLED UP to the compound with Captain Boudreaux. The two aging veterans pulled themselves from the low-lying sports car, ambling up to the main house. Boudreaux stared at all of it. It had been some years since he'd last seen the place, not that it had ever been a sight to behold, but it had really gone to pot. He shook his head as they walked through the ill-kept home and out to the scrapyard. The sound of metal beating against metal clanged out along with the haunting sound of a man's screams—a very big man.

Boscaux Maximilien St. Michel Chevalier DeBrousse slammed a four-foot pry-bar against the hood of his armored car. The metal rang out into the wee hours of the morning, the light not yet above the horizon for the day. He wailed on the turbo-charged Ford Falcon, some of the best steel ever to come off the line—and that was before he had added his formula to it. None of his blows left so much as a dent nor even a scratch, his own ingenuity getting the better of him as his mind spiraled out of control, splintered into the wind, feeling all of it, all that loss, all over again.

"What in the Sam Hell?" Boudreaux stared into the raging man as he slammed the bar against the unbreakable.

"It's the kid." Al limped past them to grab them each a beer. "He lost the little girl."

Buck's eyes sprang a leak.

"I swear." Boudreaux shook as he stared at the mountain of a man burn energy into beating an indestructible horse.

*

D had been so proud of it when he rolled it off the showroom floor. The 1973 model, a true piece of history. Slick black and paint so shiny it practically glowed in the dark, beaming the moonlight off its mirror finish. He'd used part of his army pay he'd saved up the whole time he did his two tours—he and the boys never sure if they'd make it out of their next mission. And then one fine day he was on a plane headed stateside, discharge papers in his hand. He took a taxi from the base straight to the dealership and bought the only one they had. That V8 growled like a demon all the way home. He had a new car, a GI Bill paying his tuition to LSU's chemical engineering school, and a whole new life.

*

D finally hit the car so hard he bent the pry rod. He flung it from his arms and scanned the scrapyard for something bigger, heavier, knowing it would do him fuck-all of good. The other men watched, each knowing from experience not to get near the tornado while it raged. D blinked over and over, closing his eyes, opening them back each time like she'd be there again. Like it had all been some evil dream.

*

He only thought he'd never seen a more beautiful face than Letia's—those cheekbones, her eyes that lit up from the beginning when they walked into their first lab together. She'd bump hips with him on purpose, always locking her eyes on his through their safety goggles. It took a good dozen such exchanges for a medal of valor decorated Green Beret to muster the courage to ask a woman to dinner. It took well over thirty such dinners and outings to ask her another question, even though the answer had always been yes.

But hers wasn't the most beautiful face in the world, as he'd believed. Another one came along directly, stealing everything else away, none of it or anyone else ever mattering again. Those brown eyes like the river that poured all life into the world opened and looked at him, and he belonged entirely and evermore to her—her tiny hands barely clasping around his smallest finger, the two of them touching, each knowing who the other was to them. D had never felt anything so vast, so uncontainable. *Soleil.* The sun shone through her face at him.

Her eyes erased his war.

*

His eyes flooded as he dragged the jackhammer from the yard, fired it up and went to work on the wretched metal beast he hated so much. He powered into the chassis. He'd done all this before—and worse.

*

"I did it!" He'd hugged Letia around the shoulders then picked up a beaming toddler and twirled her around the room. " *We* did it." He corrected himself.

"We did what?" Letia had smiled at him, so lit up, so excited. He wanted to put all his energy into her, into both of them. This was going to be it—their ticket to the big house, the big show, the big time. He'd cracked the formula—a spray-on compound that would bond with any surface, making it virtually unbreakable.

He tested everything he could throw at it. Blunt force. Bullets. Fire. Cold. Water. Acid. Everything under the sun. He rolled a semi-truck over it. Dropped it from high altitude. Nothing. Never so much as a hint of damage. It would be a revolution.

No soldier would ever need to die in the field again.

Letia had celebrated with him, smiling through that awful cough she couldn't shake.

There were phone calls and meetings and meetings and phone calls. Colonels and Majors and Generals with all sorts of names. Civilian contractors got involved. Hands were shaken. Pitches made. Offers spoken, rescinded, amended, each three or four times over. D grew antsy, weary, frustrated with the bureaucracy of it.

What would it cost to mass produce? How durable is it really? There were tests again, this time on their own terms, on their own equipment. Some officer wanted a full demo on a convoy truck. They'd sprayed it all down—hit it with tank fire and hellfire missiles, fed belts of ammunition through the miniguns.

"Impressive." They'd shaken his hand. "We'll be in touch."

*

D cranked up the crane, moving the heavy ball hook into position, getting a good pendulum swing going, and rammed the steel ball into the side of the Falcon. Still nothing. Always nothing. Buck winced at it. D boiled hotter than he ever had before—like he might spill over this time and burn himself down to nothing. It's what he wanted to do. He wanted to not even have been born.

*

Letia got worse. Then Soleil started. He'd worked every weekday at the chemical plant—waiting on that phone call that never came. Letters stopped arriving. A hole in his gut grew. Letia worked on a master's degree, wanting more than once to drop out and get a job to help with the bills. D hated himself for the stupid loan he took on the car, doubly so the mortgage—too eager and excited to have looked closer, thought better of it all.

He had everything on *his* body covered by the VA, but he remained a picture of health. That only stabbed him harder in the gut. Watching the two of them get worse with the knowledge his own government had taken his formula from him without a dime. He was double stupid. Spraying their truck like he did—he practically gave it to them. Of course, they took it and reverse-engineered it. After he'd watched them send thousands of boys into the meat grinder to chew up other boys in black pajamas fighting for nothing more than their own right to live, to live without lack, to live a life of basic decency. Even the communists let everyone see the doctors. The god damn commies.

"I'm afraid without insurance, I just can't treat them." came the excuse of one doctor or might have been another. They were all the same. "There's no way to guarantee payment. This is a serious condition."

Clerks. Administrators. Doctors. Bankers. Crooks. Thieves. Evil.

D had been downtown at the mortgage office half the day, waiting his turn in line most of that, watching men in better suits with lighter skin go ahead of him as he sat, getting hotter, meaner. And after all those hours only to be told "there's nothing we can do. We'll need full payment by the end of the month." He slammed his big fist into the glass door on the way out, all those beady eyes looking back at him. The whole front of the bank was glass doors. Ground level. He didn't know why he noted that when he did.

He trembled as he walked through the door, trying to shake off the hate and shame of his whole life. How had it come to this? Down to the last dollar in their account. Barely a jar of change in the house. He looked at Soleil lying there in her bed, the sweetest being that had ever lived in any world ever known. Her eyes closed. So quiet. So still. Not even moving. He looked away from her.

He walked to the bedroom, Letia lying down. Half a glass of water next to her pills. She'd left the lid off. He went to put it back but saw she'd taken the last of them. They had nothing left to get more—why did they have to be so expensive? He shook his head and kicked himself for not going into pharmaceuticals. Could have made a mint. Millions to be had in treating. Little profit in curing. Zero in protecting lives in the first place, it turned out. She lay there motionless. There was a chill on the air. It had been getting colder the last several years, he'd noticed.

The phone at the bedside rang. He picked it up from habit. The bank again, this one the account on the Ford. He'd only had another six payments to make. But they'd missed the last three. They'd be coming to pick it up tomorrow, they said. That's fine, D told them.

He laid a blanket over his wife, kissed his still daughter on the way outside—to stare at that stupid car. He stared at it until he hated it—hated the very sight and thought of it. All he wanted to do now was hate, and destroy, and kill. He wanted to murder the whole world.

"The hell with tomorrow," he muttered at the car. "I'll drive you over to them today."

He sprayed the whole thing down, every square inch of the body, the windshield, windows, even the tires. His eyes grew hollow, empty as he'd worked. When he was done with the car, he took off his coveralls and the welder's mask he used working with the chemicals and sprayed those too. The face mask was so old, the metal had rusted into a dingy brown or *copper* color. Within seconds the agent bonded and dried. Ugly as it looked, it would stop any munition in production anywhere in the world.

He put his service Colt in a holster on his waist, every spare mag he had. He suited up in his homemade armor, got in his now-indestructible car, prepared to make war on the world that took everything from him. First, he would plow through those front glass doors of the bank, smash into the tellers' desks. He'd drag the managers out as he tossed all the cash into a pile in the center and burn it. He'd make them watch their beloved burn into nothing but air. But it wasn't just them that owed. He'd go to the hospitals. Drag the doctors into the streets and tie them to the hood of the screaming Falcon and let them feel the terror, the agony that everyone else had to feel every time they got sick. These shitfucks could end people's suffering any time they wanted. They just didn't want to.

He damned every one of them to the hell he knew waited for him as his foot glued itself to the floorboard of the steel monster he'd made. His crying face hid its weakness behind the rusted metal mask. Two cold eyes stared into the blurring white lines of highway. Somewhere in all that hate and haze—the formless shroud of mist that had fallen over him that afternoon—there had been motorcycles. He didn't recall them—swore he never saw them. They only told him of it after the fact. A slew of them, they'd said. Some bad gang of thieves and outlaws that had come in from further north. The Drednecks, they'd called themselves. Gearheads who modded their bikes with weapons and blades, terrorizing outer neighborhoods. Flashing white-pride signs. Some even wore hoods.

But D didn't remember any of that. He didn't remember riding into their formation at full speed, scattering and shattering their machines, grinding over their metal bits like gravel under his invincible tires. He didn't remember they'd been tearing up the diner just outside the city—a little place he'd taken Letia and Soleil sometimes for pancakes some ancient lifetime ago. He didn't remember getting out of the car, pulling his pistol out—as their guns pinged uselessly against his bulky coveralls and helmet. He didn't remember putting holes in their legs, knees, shoulders. He didn't remember the screams. The faces. The confusion. The shouts of praise and thanks.

He didn't remember any of it, his head in his hands, tears flowing out of his face. Back at the house, the car pulled under the carport, still in his coveralls, helmet at his side, shaking. He couldn't even remember driving back home.

"I figured it had to been you." Al Davenport had sat down next to his friend and nearest neighbor. "Ain't anybody else I know has the last of the Falcons. It's a hell of a car." Al held his friend in his arms as they both wept together. "They saying you're a hero on the news."

D knew he was no hero.

He hadn't been then. Not when the guys from his old unit showed up for the funerals. Not when they came on with him in those first days, setting everything up at Al's scrapyard. Rebuilding the Falcon's engine top-to-bottom. Reinforcing every part of it. Spraying every piece he'd skipped the first time round. Adding tools and gadgets—how Buck loved to fool with gadgets and toys. Flamethrowers, smokescreens, and machine guns. The captain called out strategies. Knew where the gangs would likely go next. D insisted they go for the white-shirt crooks. He wanted dirty bankers and lawyers. Then came The Colonel. And the space-bird. A thirsty prosecutor who thought she could help. All of it blended into some strange past he still didn't see as his own.

Then Cain had come and ended it all—too big for any of them. Even Evilyn— poor Evilyn.

But D was no hero.

Not then. Not now.

*

He slumped down next to the worthless heap of metal he could never kill—this evil thing that started it all, led down a road to utter ruin and pain. *Was there never an end to the awfulness? Why them? Why her? Why couldn't it be me? Just take me.* He yelled in his mind at all the gods he knew to be real. That's what made it the worst. He could take it if they were all made-up bullshit. But they were real. He'd seen them. Talked with them. Ate with them. Where were the goddamn sons of bitches when it mattered? Bastards, the lot of them. He'd never pray to them. He'd never call their dirty names.

Buck went to his friend, as did Callum, then The Colonel. They wrapped their arms around the biggest one of them, all their heads leaned-in, touching one another. They held him, held each other. Four men who'd seen the worst that humans would do to each other, had stared into the sheer abyss together without blinking—four men who'd seen the god-damned prince of Hell itself—held each other as tight as they could hold. And they cried together.

*

"Hey, um, I'm really sorry, uh... I think I'm walking in on something here, I just..." A voice pierced into the quiet of the morning. The men turned and observed the woman in the Detroit letter jacket, still catching her breath from whatever kind of night she'd had. She looked frazzled, worn, and scared out of her wits. They'd seen the look a thousand times. She'd just learned the truth about this town.

"Look, I'll just get right to it," She said, her eyes still bugged. "My name's Murph, and I've got a huge problem. And I think you're the only ones that can help me."

V
"PLUTO DRIVE"
—THE CREATURES, 1989

MIST HUNG THICK in the air. It bellowed from everywhere so much Molly could barely make out her hand in front of her. She wandered in it, feet clinging to the ground lest she trip or drop off a ledge. She walked into the nothing for hours, then more. It felt like a day had passed, or maybe two. There was no sun, no direct source of light, nor was it dark here either—some place that existed between them.

Chirps and creaks gnawed at her ears—squawks, crunching rocks, leaves, debris as other things moved and skulked about. She wasn't alone. Wherever she was— this place—it had its own creatures. She tempted herself more than once to launch into the sky and look down from above, gain some bearings. But what if it was just as hazy there? And how would she see where to land?

Where the hell was she?

Her mind flashed images of everything she knew, the world she'd left behind. People. Places. Her life. Was any of it real? Was this place real? Was she dead? She felt cold, which was odd. She never felt the weather back on Earth. She wrapped her arms around herself as she walked on, stopping sometimes, wanting to call out but not trusting it was safe to make any more sound than she already did.

Her hands found the bark of trees. After what seemed like days—*had it been days? Could that be right?*—the mists grew thinner. Shapes appeared before her. *Have the mists grown thinner, or am I just used to it now?* Her thoughts raced constantly, haunted her. Something boiled deep inside her, telling her this was wrong, that she didn't belong here.

The thinness in the air revealed trees, clusters of them, craggy and old and cruel as they crawled their gnarled fingers toward the rocky, cold ground. At times, she swore she felt them move when she touched them.

She could make out hills and cliffs beyond her. She found her way to higher ground, to gain a vantage and see as far as she could. When she got to the base of a rocky plateau, she tried to bound atop it only to slam her face into the rock wall not three feet above her.

"What the hell, man?" She brushed the rocks off her face and clothes. She punched into the stone, drew her hand back with bruised knuckles. "You gotta be kidding me." This stupid powers thing just turned off and on when it wanted. But she knew that wasn't true. *You need people to believe,* she reminded herself. *Seen any people around here, Sledgehammer?* That thought struck her as odd. She'd always thought of herself as Molly. But her self-appointed codename came first to her mind. She didn't know what to make of that as she moved on.

She decided to take the old-fashioned route up the rocks. Moving slow, careful, she got high enough to look out onto the horizon. She saw running water not far away, higher mountains beyond that. Deep in the distance, fire spat in the sky—a volcano? Something roared beyond that, some deep, piercing, *evil* roar.

Something very big.

She climbed down and walked toward the flowing water, some brook or stream. If she followed it long enough, it might lead her *somewhere,* she thought. To some*one.* If there even was someone in this strange nowhere place.

* * *

More days she marched, staying along the banks of the running stream. She'd seen some of the smaller creatures of this world, most of them familiar, only minor differences with some analog back home. Squirrels with longer tails. Birds with wider wingspans, louder calls. Dogs, or wolves, howled in the mists. Little flying things darted and sparkled through the air. Whispers. Moans. Cries. Magic ran through the veins of this place. Molly felt it.

She came upon a deep pool amid the stream. Something like mule deer, but bigger, more antlers, lapped at the water's edge. And then more creatures came— *horses?* No, they were bigger, also leaner. They had big bushy humps on their backs running down to their tails. And—horns. They each had a single horn jutting forward from their foreheads.

"Unicorns?" Molly gawked at them. She never ceased to be amazed at any new fantasy in her life. She crept toward them, still as her toes could take her. She wanted to get close—just touch one, feel that it was, in fact, real.

She got within feet of one of them as it gulped from the pool, its glassy eyes focused on its task but not unaware of her proximity. She watched her reflection in its eye, moving closer, almost touching its face. She felt its breath.

The creature reared at her, its eyes flashing hot orange and yellow. Its compatriots followed suit, all rearing upward, their forward hooves slapping at the air. Their nostrils flared and blew fire at Molly. She sprang back, crawling out of range of the heat emanating from their flaming faces. Fire scorched from their eyes, noses, and mouths as they stamped at her, nodding their heads forward, showing their aggression, their dominance. Deep inside, Molly felt it. They were about to charge her, stampede her, she weakened and vulnerable in this strange land of mists.

A battle-scream rang out, some high-pitched squeal. A blast of violet energy slammed into the ground in front of the stamping beasts, reeling them back. Two warriors hurled themselves into the scene. A man and woman, neither a day older-looking than Molly. The girl, ebony-hued and muscular, pulled back the string on a bow—two ghostly arrows appearing from thin air—and fired at the creatures, the arrows shattering into light as they struck the unicorns. The boy charged them with a war-club and a shield. A piercing shriek hung on the air as more magic energy frightened the things. They whinnied, turned, and the bushy humps on their backs shot out to either side as—wings. They flapped and neighed and ran upwards into the gray sky, disappearing into the shrouded air of this world.

"Don't you know better than to get this close to firecorns?" The boy offered her a hand up. The girl tucked the bow behind her and pulled a short stick from her belt, whirling it in her hands, extending it to a full staff as she spun it. She darted her eyes everywhere, as though she expected worse than the flaming, flying horses to leap out any second.

"Firecorns?" Molly brushed off her embarrassment for the second time in this hellish world.

"Yes, very dangerous, and vicious. Like most things here." A third voice called out, one cruelly familiar. A veil lifted off her head, and she appeared in the half-light. Some cloak had masked her form through the ordeal, rendering her entirely invisible.

"Lydia?" Molly's jaw dropped to the ground.

She looked at Molly without a drop of recognition. Her arms showed themselves from beneath her dark, flowing clothing. Odd tattoos of some other language covered her wrists and forearms. Some violet energy flowed underneath her eyes.

"Lydia, it's really you? How? Where?" Molly looked at the other two, then back to Lydia.

"I'm called Caster. I don't know you."

Molly saw in her eyes. She didn't.

* * *

Molly fell in with the ragtag trio. The boy introduced himself as Cav and the other girl Grace, though Molly somehow knew those weren't the names they'd arrived with. She walked with them what felt like another day and a half, learning what she could about this world from them. She tried to talk to Lydia, or Caster as she insisted, but it was useless. She looked at Molly like a stranger, and Molly saw this was not the Lydia she remembered. Her face hadn't aged a day, but her eyes told a bleaker story, like they'd seen a lifetime of this dim world.

They led her into a village of sorts. People—*humans?*—mulled about doing chores. Others, smaller, much smaller, but still human-looking wandered about. Huts and brick buildings from some time long forgotten housed the people. Many wandered as if lost or misplaced, muttering to themselves. One small, older man approached Molly as they walked into the village.

"It's you, isn't it?" He walked to her, grabbed her hand. "You're one of them, aren't you? I'm sorry. I'm so sorry. Please." His eyes watered and pleaded to her.

"Please forgive me. I didn't know. I didn't. I've suffered so long. Please forgive me." He pawed and glommed at her hands, all over her arm.

"Okay, whatever, dude, I forgive you, just let me go." Molly pulled him off her arms, but then he dissipated before her, his whole body shooting upward in flashing green light. He was gone. Erased. "What just happened?" She asked anyone with an answer for her, about anything.

"How did you do that?" Lydia, or rather Caster, stared at her like she was an alien. At least *that* part felt familiar.

"I don't—" Molly looked around, the dull faces, the shame, the regret, the fear, the guilt in all of them. She felt it, felt them, all of it hitting her at once—the dread of it gulped in her throat. She couldn't be where she thought she was. This couldn't be right—couldn't be real. "Back on Ea—where we're from, *Lydia,* I—I have this power, these abilities. But I don't, or didn't, have them here—I don't really know or understand it. I'm not—I'm not like everyone else. I had this strength, and—I don't know. It's gone now—here. I don't have it."

"Here you have only what you bring with you." Lydia marched on through the village, intent on arriving wherever they were going.

Molly gazed at the faces moving on like nothing strange had happened. Some stared at her, moving closer, like they might start pawing at her soon. She moved with the others, leaving the guilt-ridden faces behind her.

They made their way to the far edge of the village, to a house of beam and mortar. Dogs, or doglike things scurried around, tearing at bits of food. Voices carried on the wind. A hiss whispered nearby. Molly saw it, a gruesome, slithering viper crawling at them across the muddy ground. She reached for her cane swords tucked behind her, but Grace was faster. She struck the serpent with the end of her staff, extending its length in a flash before Molly got her blades out.

"That's pretty neat how it does that." She looked down at her twin swords, how each hid inside the other's handle, extending their own length with the flick of a button. She still thought it was a dumb weapon. The girl's staff and especially that bow—those were cool. "Where did you get it?"

"From the ForgeMaster." She shrunk it and tucked it in her belt. "He made all our weapons." She indicated Cav, holding his shield in one hand and his club over the other shoulder.

"I'm sorry." Molly blinked, her eyes flashing, the hair on the back of her neck standing. It couldn't be... "The who?"

VI
"IT'S A SIN"
—PET SHOP BOYS, 1987

EVILYN HOVERED DOWN from the walkway to the ground level of the warehouse where her crew assembled the lavish floats for her upcoming event. She needed to correct the decorations on her mainstage float that would carry her and her entourage through the city during her showcase. She tingled at the thought of how spectacular it was going to be. She no longer cared for any pretense of normalcy as she flaunted her godlike power over those beneath her.

Many of the late shift workers were former acolytes of Cain like herself, all converts to her cause, committed to ending his dominance over them, even if it meant oblivion. Evilyn caught Bianca observing her from above, a terse line across the doctor's lips. She moved to the crates of repurposed masks, all be-glittered now in star-spangled excess. They'd be in every shop and on every street corner by the morning of the parade. And the light show would be truly out of this world.

Evilyn squinted at Tesche's chagrin. She knew she'd lost the doctor's confidence. It was no matter. But she regretted the loss of her last friend. This endeavor, finally coming to fruition, her singular life's goal, had cost her everything.

She smiled at herself in the mirrors across the warehouse, no longer shunning them, not even the ones backed by silver. Somewhere across the years, that same smile had donned the face of a young lawyer, finishing top of her class. A clerkship with the parish court had fast-tracked her into the D.A.'s office. "The most gifted investigator I've ever seen," her first boss had told her. Across a thousand years of memories in the Land of Mists, she still held on to that one.

Drug dealers, pimps, prostitutes, negligent parents, deadbeat dads, corporate fraud, embezzlement schemes, misappropriation—she'd worked it all in those early years. She jumped from Red Stick to the Big Easy on her way to the top. As the cold north drove the big players south, Evilyn wanted to go after the heavy hitters. She soon found the same old story written since the dawn of time: power protects itself. The worst ones wore white collars and were off limits. Even by her own family, the JarethCo Board of Trustees. Her lineage was as much a curse as a blessing. She was told in no uncertain terms who she couldn't touch—no matter how many bodies floated out of the Pontchartrain.

She examined the wiring on the mainstage float, whispering a spell to ensure it worked perfectly. There could be no mistakes for her main event. She'd come this far. She'd earned this. She'd eaten so much shit. From the beginning, watching known crooks and traffickers walk up and down Canal with smiles on their faces, shaking hands with mayors, aldermen, even the DA—her boss.

Then came The Copperhead. A whisper at first. The street gangs, used as muscle and buffer for their corporate masters—Commie Ron's "War on Drugs" plan to flood the streets with rock and powder—they had spread his legend. A demon on wheels. A Spartan warrior wielding weapons they'd never seen. They said he couldn't be killed. Some said he drank blood—what a cruel joke that turned out to be.

The suits began to suspect each other—surely only one of their own had the liquidity, the access to produce the things he had. But Evilyn always smiled. She'd been around the rich her whole life, worked alongside them, born into their luxury. They'd never once in all of history donned a costume and roamed the streets doling out justice—they weren't about to start now.

And besides, Evilyn knew a soldier when she saw one.

"You're a big guy." She'd winked her thirstiest smile the first time she saw him at the V.A. Muscles bulged from his scrub sleeves. His thin beard back then framed his warm face just right. But his hollow, sad eyes were what really gave him away. She got his name from the front desk girl. The rest was what she did best—paperwork.

Of course, it wasn't just one man. She laughed at herself, almost having believed the myth. A team, they'd been—The Colonel going back the longest. Between the four of them, they held more decorations than she'd ever seen on a whole platoon. Bravery, Valor, Purple hearts plural for each. Their dossiers wrote the story every would-be Metal Jack told their kids at night.

"Ma'am, you dropped this." His hand gripped the file she'd pulled from her briefcase during her feigned visit to some veteran she'd never heard of.

"No, I don't think I did." She remembered her smile as she'd walked out that day, so proud, so sure of herself. A corporate boardmember high up the pecking order had made sure his pretty little son wouldn't see a cell despite what he'd done to the sorority girl. Halfway through her case, the girl had dropped the charges, barely audible on the phone from stammering out her words. Three days after Evilyn's visit to the VA, the shit-lord walked in her office and confessed. Well, he didn't walk. He was pushed. He'd never walk again.

"A couple ground rules." His stern eyes had glared at her, making her heartbeat quicken—back when it *could* still beat—the next time she paid him a visit, another file in tow. "I won't go after the poor, not if all they did is steal."

"I can live with that." She moved closer, letting her words spill over her lips, making sure he noticed those.

* * *

Back at her executive office, she whispered into her brandy to strengthen it—maybe this time chase these evil memories out of her head. She hadn't gone over any of this in ages. *Why now? Why, D?* She gulped and then poured another. She flowed across the room to her piano as the camera crew finished setting up.

"All set, boss." The guy gave a thumbs up. "But we're not patched into the network. How're we gonna go live?"

"I'll take care of that part, darling."

She placed her cold fingers on the ivory keys, played out a piece of a lonely jazz song, the one she'd played for D at her old apartment in The Quarter. She'd convinced him to meet her there. He wasn't stupid. He knew what he would walk into, and he showed up all the same.

Those were their salad days. She still liked to tell herself that she gave him something, some small piece of what it felt to be alive again. He never told her his story—didn't have to. She was *the* investigator. She went wherever she had to go, where no one else would. She never told him she'd cried when she learned of his poor daughter.

Then Cain and his darkness drowned the city. There'd always been murders. The Mob. Gangs. Corporate greed. But not this. Throats torn apart. Bodies mangled. And the stories... Giant wolf. A beast with horns. A winged demon. An army of screeching bats.

And poor D, bless his heart—he didn't hesitate a moment. All of them—the four of them, five if she counted old Alfred Davenport who at least made sure D had a bed to sleep in and food to eat—they put everything they had into finding him. Buck brought the missing piece—some old church where he'd studied with some grad students. Some ancient evil long buried—woken by some far darker terror.

But the power... Soon, he multiplied—his acolytes coming from across the globe, many of them old money from centuries on end. They brought their empires here, centered around *Him*, their paternus, the original. She learned the tell-tale signs, how they marked their familiars, their daywalkers who kept their affairs in order—all under the promise of some future immortality. His Black Hands scoured the earth for some ancient prophecy—a chosen one that would bind him forever. She licked her metal teeth at that. Evilyn was about to make her own destiny.

"Ready to go in 5...4...3..." The camera kid held up his fingers for the last few numbers. Dr. Tesche tuned the array to the local six o'clock news, the anchors discussing the city cancelling the 4th of the July celebration in light of the recent *events*.

"Hello, New Orleans!" Evilyn turned her wicked grin on like a light switch. Her dress shimmered in the stage lights as she stood from her piano bench and glided toward the camera like a sultry apparition. "You all know my name—a name that helped build this city. You've now seen a taste of what evil lurks here, but know this too—this city, *our city,* has its protectors. I will stand against this evil. I will fight this darkness. And we will not cower in the night. We will come out. We will frolic, make merry, show we're unafraid. We will fight back against the tide. So, in spite of what tepidness the mayor might project, I will be putting on our festival all the same—a parade down Canal, a party in The Quarter! And free festival masks are everywhere to be had in the city. Look for the JarethCo brand. Pick yours up and bring the family. We will sing. We will dance. And we will show this evil we do not fear it, nay we strike back. And if evil should appear, then I will show it what *real* power looks like. Come one, come all. Commence au festival!"

Tesche saw the spill go live across the feed, Evilyn's dark power superceding the broadcast waves across the city. When the news anchors returned to the screen—their expressions white, befuddled—they had no words. They mouthed at the camera, but no sound came out.

Evilyn winked at her compatriot, then returned to her piano to strike her chords. Knowledge was its own curse. Seeing Cain's grim, godlike nature, she had known other such powers must exist. She did what she always had—she learned. Words, symbols, simple spells at first. But always, that allure, the real power: immortality.

"We can use it against him, D!" Her eyes had flared into the mirrored finish of The Copperhead's newest helmet. She saw herself then as she knew he did—wild, reckless, ambitious. But she had determined to show him it was the way. "We can destroy him, the whole system, from the inside. Come with me." She pleaded, knowing before she'd ever said the first word what his answer would be. She hadn't told him the full truth of it. But she wore it around her neck—a black lace choker. He stared at it, through that darkened, impenetrable glass visor, and he knew. He never took the helmet off that night, but she felt his eyes. He pulled his pistol from his belt, its magazine loaded with his special rounds—she'd taught him and the boys so much—why couldn't they just trust her?

That was the last they'd seen of each other as allies.

* * *

Evilyn drank herself numb in her office, the darkness rising out her windows. Cain would come for her now. As he had then. His hold over her, over all his changed ones, finally broken, but its hateful memory tormented her, rent her mind apart. Her first feeding still tattooed her soul. *He* made her do it. Calling her to him as she turned, finishing the ritual—lest she rot into the walking dead, a mindless biter—a draugr.

"You mocked me, you and your silly knight." Cain's somber, beastly treble echoed in her memory. "Mortal fools, to think you would make war against me? I have laid waste to armies, empires of your pallid kind. You are nothing but fodder to me. A joke, that's all you are. My Jester Queen."

So, he'd made sport of her. He locked her in a room with a child. Evilyn begged and cried and screamed. Cain grinned and watched as she finally grew so hungry, so ravenous, unable to control herself, that she tore apart the little girl—not even three years old. Ripped her bones from her flesh and drank every drop. And then she did it again. And again. He made her eat her cousins. An ex-boyfriend. But mostly children.

"They do taste the best, do they not?" Cain's fangs smirked at her as innocent blood dripped from her own.

"You're a monster." She had glared back at him, her master.

"So are you."

Hate bubbled where blood once had in her dead heart. Evilyn Jareth vowed to destroy him, to tear down everything he had and stand above him, her boot on *his* neck in the end. Going where he could not, his curse binding him to this single plane, she would learn, collect, conspire, bide her time until she found a way. And she had. *She* would be the one to wield his power, to command his army. But she would use it for good. D might hate her for what she'd done—what she took from him, knowing all he'd already lost. She looked away from her memory, that godling's face as she'd been deceived—crossing to the other side. Sacrifices had to be made. But it would all be worth it. She would show D she was right, that she'd been right all along.

"Tomorrow we end his wretched reign, good doctor," Evilyn slurred out, D's empty, mirrored helmet still burned into her memory. She reached for her glass, tipped it onto the floor, shattering it, then summoned its pieces back into a whole with her whispers. "Doctor?" She called again.

But her friend had gone.

VII

"ON OUR OWN"
—BOBBY BROWN, 1989

BUCK, BOUDREAUX, AND AL sat around the folding table playing rummy and cackling like geese at their stale jokes. Buck and Boudreaux went at each other like a married couple past their expiry date. The Colonel sat to himself having a heated debate with not less than three fictional beings, one of whom he referred to as "Oberon."

"So, like, from the bible?" Murphy's eyebrows threatened to wrinkle all the way off her head. "Like the actual guy?"

"Not—" D paced around the living room floor trying to explain it again to their newest newcomer. "That book's mostly bullshit. Same as any other old myths. They all take big leaps and push their shitty agendas. Bastards, the lot of 'em, really. But you lay 'em all atop one another and some things start to overlap. Patterns, you know."

Rain misted at the windows as the dusk rolled in. A knock rapped at the door, and the fiercest twelve eyes snapped to the sound of it. Murphy felt the hair on her neck stiffen, and both her fists got hot. She glanced to her side and saw a compensated Beretta already in The Copperhead's hand. It blew her mind, what she'd heard, and just—him. He reminded her of...someone she used to know.

Buck popped a Colt Mustang from his pocket, even smaller than Murph's Commander model, and cracked the door. A woman known to none of them moused her way inside, hands high and surrendering.

"You have to stop her." she said. "I'm Bianca Tesche. I've been working with Evilyn. She's gone over the edge."

D pulled the hammer back on his nine. His eyes zeroed for the kill.

Murphy softed her hand on his wrist. "Wait. She's inside already." She nodded at the doctor, the others looking back and forth between them. "She wasn't invited in."

The men shrugged, acknowledging the point. They gave her a chair, The Colonel offering her a beer which she took, gulping it down as if it was the last one she'd ever have. They'd all seen Evilyn's stunt on the news—whole town had. Tesche filled in the gaps, going on about Evilyn wanting to draw out Cain, force him into an open battle in the middle of the city.

"It's pointless." D shook his head. "She knows that. We tried 100 different—"

"She thinks she can contain him, trap him in a mirror box, she said. She found this—little contraption. A cube thing. Somewhere on the other side."

"Other side?" Murph gained a new perspective on reality about every five minutes now.

"The Land of Mists. She's been going there—I don't know. It may have driven her mad. Or *He* did. She's drunk on her own power. She'll tear the city apart trying to destroy him."

"What are the masks about?" Boudreaux folded his arms across his chest. D nodded to him for the question.

"That's the worst of it. I don't know. She's been casting over them as they come off the line. She can command anyone who wears one. It's how we—" the doctor winced at herself. "It's how we controlled the re-animated dead. But now she has golems. She can make them do anything. Fight. Kill. She thinks if the city becomes terrible enough, with enough sorcery and phantasm, it will drive him out—leave him no shadows to hide behind anymore."

"What are you saying?" D asked.

"I—I think she's going to make the people tear each other apart until he shows up." the doctor finished her beer, trembling at her own words, her body shaking so badly they thought she'd collapse.

The men sat trying to process it all, Murphy with them. Her mind flashed to her father, all his wild tales paled compared to what unfolded before her eyes.

"Now, I told you. You'll do what you can. I have to try to find the one that can help you stop her." They all knew who she meant, and where poor Molly was— Murph still a bit hazy on that last bit.

"How? You can get in?" Buck's eyes widened—ever the student of the odd.

"In? Sure." She gulped, then pulled a gleaming knife from her purse. "Out? Not so much. But it's no more than I deserve."

They all reached to stop her. Dr. Bianca Tesche shoved the blade into her neck and bled out on the floor.

* * *

Sadly, not a soul among them lacked experience in getting rid of a body. The Colonel and Captain Boudreaux cleaned the blood and the gore. Al and Buck put the corpse in the trunk of an old Delta 88 and dropped it in the compactor. Those blocks would be sent to the foundry at the end of the month.

"Well, the meter's running, boss." Buck dropped a heavy hand on D's shoulder as they reconvened on the back porch. "You call it."

"Call what?" D twisted the top off a Coors and sank into the creaking lawn chair. "What the hell can be done? Couldn't stop 'em back then and hung up the helmet and that's *before* Evilyn drank the blood of a—" he swallowed hard, hesitating to say what they all knew was next. "They're both half-gods now, and ours fell down a hole into nowhere. And I ain't nothing but a broke-down old worn-out soldier."

"No." Buck took D by the hand and pulled him up to face each other, the others falling in around them, all laying a hand down on top of theirs. "No, buddy, we're *a team* of broke-down old worn-out soldiers."

"An' I reckon we got one more fight left in us." Boudreaux nodded a salute to his Sergeant.

"Shit, might as well make it five." Al hobbled over, his metal knee clicking. They'd need to oil it soon. "Y'all gon' need help building some'n big enough to tote you all to the shit. I'll work something up."

"You got six." Murphy folded her arms at the motley crew of oldheads. "Only I ain't worn out nothing. What about it, Colonel?"

Colonel John Carthage, eyes pulling out of space and into the world in front of him, looked at his team. "Sounds like a plan."

* * *

The plan split three ways. Al would ride out at first light and find a big enough rig to get everyone into the center of town, spray it with enough of D's bonding agent to drive them through hellfire and World War Three both—which was what they were counting on.

Buck pulled a video cassette from his briefcase and popped it in the VCR, showing a tricked-out black pickup full of enough space-tech and bolted-on rockets and fins, it was hard to tell any of it had ever rolled out of Detroit. In the footage, he climbed into the rig, fired off the rockets down the salt flats, shot some kind of laser out the front of it and disappeared before hitting the rock base of a cliff, only to re-appear right where he'd started from—the truck nearly frozen solid, chunks of ice falling off.

"I did it, boys. I told y'all I done did it." He re-wound the tape to run it again. "We fired concentrated negative particles at a distorted frequency, modulating for speed and air temperature. And by the damned gods, I split through the veil into some froze-ass hell-world. We borrowed the notes from the U.S.S. Eldridge test. They'd been so close and never knowed it."

"I don't understand anything you just said." Murphy's eyes bugged as she watched the video for the third time. This was all Greek to her, and she'd seen cops turn to dogs.

"Well, here's my thought. We know from Evilyn's early days playing with that shit, before—well, before she got herself bit—she draws her power from the other side. She can open and close the doors. But it's all negative energy—antimatter electrons. More or less—maybe. That's what the particle accelerator replicates. My thought?" Buck's eyes opened all the way up in his head. "We reverse the polarity. Fire destabilized protons right into the damn witch with all we got. She's negative, so we go positive. We neutralize her."

"What'n the hell makes you think she'll stand still long enough to give us a shot? She can fly if she wants." Boudreaux folded his arms at Buck, like he always did.

"Well, that's the other half. D's formula bonds to just about anything, hardening in seconds. Unbreakable. We've seen it. What if we lace it with spray-foam? Hit her with some sticky from a grease-gun. Trap her in a shell. Shit, if it works on her, I say we turn it on old granddaddy fangs himself. Tomb the undying son of a bitch and bury him somewhere can't nothing ever get to him again."

"Then what?" D shook his head. He hated this plan so far. "We got her still for—what? A minute, tops? She's strong as a god now. Eggshell won't hold her."

"Then this." Buck pulled a .38 hollow-point bullet from his shirt pocket. It had a shard of metal—the one Molly had sliced from the hilt of her sword—encased in wax in the hollow depression of the bullet. Buck winced at the sight of it, timid in its presence. He'd hoped to run more tests. But triage rules dictated otherwise now. "This will pierce her skin. The silver and garlic salt in the round will do the rest once it's inside. Least that's the idea."

"I'll do it." D took the bullet from his friend, steeling himself for what had to be done.

"I'm still a little lost." Murph's expression reiterated her comment. "You said this was a top-secret test, all that gear locked away out in Utah somewhere. We got less than 24 hours. How the hell we getting it, period, much less by tomorrow night?"

"We have a spaceship." The Colonel grinned and clicked the button to reveal Ol' Millie.

"Course you do." Murph's mind flinched there just for the moment as the hovering ship revealed itself from thin air. She wanted to close her eyes and wake up back at prison rather than see one more tear in the fabric of the world. But then she shrugged and rolled with it.

* * *

D and Buck stayed behind at the compound to work on the foam. They ran two or three different ratios until they found the right amount of stick and flow. Buck started building a backpack delivery system. Al rumbled in with a broken siren wailing on an '83 GMC Vandura meatwagon.

"Did you really just bring me a damn ambulance?" D blinked three times to be sure it was true.

"Ain't she a beaut? Got her for nothing at the impound. Got a V8—which I can turbocharge by this afternoon. Must have come down from the mountains somewhere 'cause she's lifted four inches off the factory and got these big mudders on her. She'll cook through anything ol' purple-hair pulls out the zone at you. Just you wait, boys."

Buck spat out another batch of foam, this group coming out white and fluffy. "Looks kinda like marshmallows, don't it?" he said.

"Don't eat it, Buck." D sighed at the plan.

* * *

Murph sighed at the plan. Soaring high above the world at a speed she didn't know just five minutes ago was physically possible, she watched Boudreaux cross himself for the umpteenth time. He'd lit a joint and slowed his breathing.

"Didn't peg you for a reefer man, Captain." Murph squinted at the smell, then accepted a hit when he offered.

"I don't care for flying on a good day, much less with a certified maniac at the stick, and add to that this flying goose ain't even human-made."

The Colonel wore a metal helmet that he talked to as he hurtled them across the world. He smiled—happy as could be—right at home where he belonged.

"I don't get it. Why don't we just blast those sons of hellfire with this thing? What kind of heat this baby got?"

"Ain't found the guns yet." the Colonel chuckled. "But I will. God told me I would."

"Good. Good." Murph hated the plan.

* * *

At the facility, Boudreaux zipped up his jumpsuit and stretched his knee. He'd given her his crib notes on the short flight over. Ex-ranger—like the others. Spook for the Feds. Wetwork. Then he ghosted them to go work with D. When Cain got too heavy, they'd all gone quiet. He stuck to getting people clear of the nightmonsters on the sly. He winced at his stiff leg more than once, preparing to go inside the building to get the particle blaster. In that moment, the old man that he was, she saw her dad again—wincing at that same leg.

"What happened?" Her younger self had asked her father. He'd always walked stiff since she could remember.

"Old sparring partner. Long time ago. Best I ever fought. She was the one," he'd say, then pat her on the head and smile. "She's the best there ever was."

Murphy's eyes welled full of old, unresolved emotions.

"Look, old man," She put her hand on the Captain's shoulder. "I'll take this one. Y'all just keep talking on the radio. Walk me through it. Can you do that?"

The Colonel pulled up a scan of the building on the cockpit's array. This iron eagle really was far out. He handed her a box about like a pager and pressed a button. A blinking light appeared on the array just outside the building.

"Reckon that's me, huh?" She fitted the radio in her ear.

Down the ramp of the invisible ship, she sprinted at the fence and cleared it in two steps, flipping herself over the top and landing like a cat. She never missed a beat and made the rear maintenance door. She pulled the strip of tape Captain

Boudreaux gave her and stuck it at the latch. The heat burnt through the lock in seconds, and she was in.

"Down the hall, stairs on the right," came over her radio. She followed to the letter as they directed her. Two security guards made their rounds, and she put them to bed soft and sweet. She got to the sub-basement and saw the apparatus— couldn't miss it. It was big, but not impossible to carry. She used the harness Buck had rigged for the job and strapped the whole thing to her back and hauled ass back the way she'd come.

"She's pretty good," Boudreaux said back on the ship. The Colonel shrugged in agreement, then laughed at something the ship said.

VIII
"THE ANVIL OF CROM"
—BASIL POULEDORIS, 1982

ICE CRACKED BENEATH their feet as the party traversed the frozen world. The trio of yet-livings marched their new companion to visit this ForgeMaster. Molly was stone-faced but eager to meet this person, a rat gnawing in her gut to be ready for anything here—including the worst creature she could name: Blake Elvis. She squinted her eyes imagining the rat-faced halfman that stabbed through the heart of her Easton and tore her city apart. Even if this place *were* Hell and him long dead in it—she'd kill him again. This wretched forever tundra was still too good a place for him.

"Why do you call yourselves 'yet-livings?'" Molly asked Cav and Grace. They moved like veterans of this place, ready for every awful thing it might throw at them—as though they'd lived here through two eternities already.

"Because we are. This realm is for those who can't be reborn. They have what they bring with them—their guilt. Their shame. They carry it until it either consumes them, or they break free. Most fall under." Grace used her magic staff as a walking stick, the bow strapped on her back. Cav walked point, his shield at the ready, providing an unseen barrier for all behind it.

They reached the edge of some water, a vast sea of pale green luminescence. Molly crouched at the edge to study the liquid.

"Don't touch it. It's the Sea of Souls. They'll take hold, draw you in, sucking your will away until you become as they are." Cav shoved a boat into the water, their destination an island that lay just visible on the horizon. "A week's rations of rowing." He checked their pouches, making sure they were full up.

Molly had come to understand meals were the only way to mark the time in this awful, gray place—a place where trees groaned and reached for you with gnarled fingers, some getting up and walking through the forests of wailing torment—a place where the wind howled like wolves, clouds forming in the shape of snapping jowls, frothing at the mouth, as though they'd swallowed the sun and moon of this world long ago—a place where souls wandered mumbling, naming their past regrets, their shortcomings, their failures, like broken records replaying the worst moments of their lives over and over.

And the giants—great old ones, Grace called them. Off in the distance, thundering steps as she could make out their silhouettes in the haze and fog, booming and dooming as they lumbered about their work—whatever it was. Every manner of awful creature existed here. Teeth from more than one of them hung from the necklace around The Hammer's neck. The longer she stayed here, the less like the girl from the bay she felt. *Is this what happened to Lydia?* she wondered.

The one called Caster always walked behind the rest with a kind of confidence Molly had never seen Lydia project in their old life. She insisted she was also a "yet-living" but couldn't remember how she came to be here, nor the others—only that there had once been more of them. They gave Molly the invisibility cloak, Lydia—Caster—saying she'd manage without it. Her spells were formidable. Molly watched her best friend, a bassist to behold once upon a lifetime ago, as she brought down a fireball onto a cave troll that had tracked them for nine meals. The fireball brought it to the ground, its chest and shoulders smoldering. Grace sent a ghost arrow into its gut. Cav clubbed it behind the knee, crippling it. Then a blade from nowhere took its gangly head from its body, red hair appearing from beneath a hood as Molly made herself visible when the feat was finished.

* * *

The ForgeMaster dug a cutting tool into the hilt of a broad axe, slicing away slivers into some shape yet to materialize to anyone else. His big, bulbous hands held callouses that seemed old as time. His face bore scars hardened by aeons of soot and smoke and cinder. Molly breathed a long sigh, despite the black cloud drifting off his cooking forge. This was definitely *not* Blake.

"Who are you?" She looked around his workshop. Its heat filled her, filled them all with a warmth they so missed in this place. His tools, an array of them, numbered more than she could count.

"I am just ForgeMaster. All other things slip away here, oh high one." His eyes didn't look at her, his voice a somber sigh.

"You know who I am?" Molly brightened at the prospect. It had occurred to her more than once that this grim place could be her home—but her gut told her it wasn't. Why didn't she have her powers here?

"We both know *what* you are. But the *who* is shrouded in Eldar magic. You have a powerful enemy." He hobbled to his fire and stoked it, breathing life into the flames he pulled from deep within the core of this evil realm.

"If I am...*that*—" Molly kicked a rock across the dirt, sending it maybe ten yards, no great feat. "Then why don't I have any power? How does all this work?" She had her doubts about all this *god* business. But everything was turbo-weird now, so what did she know?

"Here you have only what you bring with you."

"So I've heard." She had no idea what that meant. The only things she had with her were her clothes and Blake's dumb swords, which is why she'd wanted to meet this *ForgeMaster* in the first place.

Molly cut to it. She pulled out the twin swords, the wolf and the snake. She laid them before the ForgeMaster. He examined them, noting the fine work of the handles, the fit of the blades into each other, the mechanism to lengthen each blade. He slammed one down on a piece of ancient metal from his scrap pile and sliced through it like Jello.

"This is Eldritch steel." He marveled at the blade, holding it up to the lantern to see it in better light. "Where did you get this?"

"Long story." Molly's eyes flashed back to her battle with the hobgoblin Blake, the other "ForgeMaster" she'd known, his licking lips. She smoldered with hate at the memory, then again at the thought of the two-faced witch who sent her here, who she knew had sent Lydia here too—Lydia who now called herself Caster, a witch in her own right. Molly's godblood boiled with hate. "Can you rework it?" She looked back to the smithy. "I want to change it into something else, something that can kill an unkillable witch." She motioned to Grace, who handed her the staff. "And this. I want something like this for the handle." She flipped the staff in her hand, making it shorter and longer by her thought, by pure will alone. It was a wonder.

The ForgeMaster studied the blades again, looking down at Grace's staff.

"The handle is easy enough—the right elmwood, the right runics—I made that one, after all. But this?" He grimaced at the blades. "It's an odd design, I'd even say the work of a fool. But Eldritch steel is hard. Even if I get the metal hot enough to forge it—and I'll have to weld the pieces, fold them over again and again to make it hold—I don't know that I have the strength to hammer it out." His eyes told her he wanted to do it, needed to help her any way he could—that somehow he owed it to her.

"I can get it hot enough." Lydia—Molly refused to think of her as anyone else—moved toward them, holding her wrists out, reading from the garbled writing she'd tattooed across her arms until she found what she wanted. "I have the runic. I can magnify your fire."

"If I do this—" He looked Molly in the eye finally. "I ask one thing in return." He shivered at his own thoughts. Molly's mind tingled—his feelings revealing themselves to her, the first time in this place. Was she regaining herself?

"What do you ask?" she squinted at him.

"Forgiveness."

"Forgiveness for what?" Molly had gleaned enough from her first incident to know it was no simple thing to be granted.

"If I tell you that," he turned to his forge, then looked back at her, "you won't do it."

Molly looked to Lydia, then to the others. She would find a way—she would get them out of this evil world. She would get them home, all of them.

"Deal." She took his arm in hers, forming a compact—an oath. And as soon as she did, she bound herself to it—she felt it deep in her spirit. She could never break her word. Never. *It's why Blake insisted you give it,* she recalled. "And you needn't worry about the strength to work the metal," she added. "I'll do it myself."

He threw the blades into the fire. Lydia murmured archaic words in some half-familiar language. The fire burned the colors of the rainbow one by one, red to orange to yellow, white then blue, and on and on. The hot iron glowed with the light of a star across the night sky as the ForgeMaster removed the pieces with his tongs.

Molly picked up the cross-peen hammer, its short, worn handle comfortable and familiar in her hand. She felt—something. Almost a memory.

"You've done this before?" He noted her correct grip around the handle.

"Maybe." She slammed it home against the hot metal. Again. And again. She worked the blades against each other, folding them over. They put it back to the fire, Lydia raising the heat again. Molly folded it over and over. They worked through a day, then two. Twelve meals passed as she folded the metal again and again, hammering down like falling rain upon a thirsting earth. She pounded with a fierceness, a warlike intent. The hammer belonged to her and she to it. She doomed down onto the white-hot ingot, molding it, shaping it, remaking it. She had the picture of it in her head. She wanted an exact shape. During a break for mana, she drew out a sketch on a leather scrap for the ForgeMaster.

"This is the pommel for the handle I want. Exactly this."

"I've never seen this shape before." He gazed at the drawing.

"I have." Lydia took it from him. "I've seen this."

"Yeah you have." Molly smiled. Her heart leaped. Her friend wasn't all the way gone yet.

She went back to work. Bending. Shaping. Grinding. Hammering. She put three deep fullers nearly the full length of the fatter, shortened blade. She ground down the edges day and night. What seemed like weeks or even months passed. The others foraged for provisions. The dead needn't eat but the yetlivings did. If they died here, they stayed here, they'd been quick to inform her of that.

"Now for the silver bullet." Molly pulled the knife from her belt, the one The Copperhead gave her for the vampires back on Earth. "Melt this down and pour it in the fullers."

She had it pictured in her head. The Eldritch blade would pierce the witch's skin, just as it could her own. The silver in the fullers would do the rest once it got inside.

"This is paltry, cheap metal." He glared at the gleaming silver—probably a thousand dollars' worth. "It's good for nothing. It will just flake off once it hardens." He shook his head.

"I'm counting on it." Molly nodded.

They poured the molten silver, its liquid form running down the grooves of each fuller, both sides. Six grooves of poison for the undead. She'd send them all to this place where they belonged.

She finished the weapon with her own etching, writing down a pair of lyrics from "Red Hot" across the blade. The master fitted it to the handle, uttering the final words to bind them together. Molly took the weapon from him, gripping the handle. The broadhead blade curved in at the middle then out again at the bottom on each side, rounding into barbs. She thrust it out, doubling, then tripling the length of the handle with her thoughts. The hilt was perfectly shaped. The blade—just long enough to slice a head, and short enough to hurl through the air like a bullet—was perfect. It was perfect.

"I have seen this before." Lydia observed the weapon in its shortened form. "Why do I know this shape? What is it?"

"A name." The ForgeMaster spoke up, proud of his latest, and perhaps his last great work. "A weapon this fine deserves a name."

"I call it the Strat-axe." She moved beyond the reach of any of her compatriots, whirled it around her, spinning it, lengthening and shortening the handle as she willed it to do, a flurry of flashing, gleaming death. She hurled the guitar-shaped spear into the trunk of a craggy oak crawling out of the cold mists, sinking the blade through the other side. She ran to pull it out, wrapped it in a leather scabbard he'd made for it. "And you have seen it before, *Lydia Styles*. You played one every day for the last eight years back on Earth—which is where we're going. All of us."

"And me?" The ForgeMaster's eyes betrayed his guilt. "Our accord?"

"I cannot break my oath to you." Molly strapped the beautiful weapon to her back, took his arm again in hers, and looked him in the eyes, right into him. She felt him. Some good grew in his heart. "You have my forgiveness—just as soon as you forgive yourself."

His eyes sank into despair. He laughed. "Clever god."

IX
"FOR WHOM THE BELL TOLLS"
—METALLICA, 1984

THE MAYOR OF NEW ORLEANS walked so fast it approached a jog down Decatur Street, looking over both shoulders every few seconds. Sweat rained off his face despite the crisp air as the sun moved behind the buildings. He wiped his face with a rag and kept his pace, making an eager clip toward Jackson Square. Those who recognized him moving through the evening crowds wore their curiosity. Eyes followed as he passed the shops and bars. A policeman atop a horse tailed him, keeping a fair distance but staying on him. Mayor Mainotte wiped his brow again and watched the sun's last light fade into the west.

* * *

In another part of the city, high atop JarethCo tower, Evilyn readied herself for her big night, a night that would go down in history, become a legend in due course.

"Perhaps they will even write myths about me in some future scriptures," she said to no one as she slid inside tonight's attire. She fitted her silver gauntlets around her wrists—just another deliciously ironic touch it amused her to include in her dress. "I could even inspire my own religion, I suppose. Have them worship me. After all—" She smiled at herself in the mirror, admiring the fine work of her bone structure, her features, perfected over the years. "I am a god now."

She laughed at her reflection, flitting her eyelashes. How she did delight herself.

* * *

Murphy couldn't sleep—the old guard deciding to catch what little they could, having been up through the night and top of the day preparing for—she didn't even know what. She left the scrapyard, borrowing Buck's Manta—maybe she hadn't told him, but the keys were on the table. She ran down the road to the nearest cafe, got a donut and coffee, then sat and looked at them. Couples came in and out, holding hands, pecking on each other's cheeks. A family walked in, two kids in tow, grabbing some quick dinner. So much life just went on, as if any other day. As if they hadn't seen a human woman transform into some beast on television—a good woman, one who'd been something like a friend to Murphy. As if the city dwelling in artificial gray weather for years was perfectly normal. As if the whole town wasn't run by a cabal of blood-sucking hellcreatures all the way down to—and especially including—the cops themselves. And all spearheaded by basically the devil incarnate. As true a Lucifer as maybe there'd ever been.

"Oh, Daddy." She sighed out the cafe window at the car—even faster than the Mondial had been—a car so fast she could blast out of this town, out of this state, out of this whole damn country full of sleeping idiots and run by a sideshow acrobat on steroids. She could just leave.

* * *

Mayor Mainotte got to the square, stared at the gorgeous St. Louis Cathedral, the heart of the city. Its spires stabbed the purple sky pointing toward the long gone sun that seemed to have abandoned them for a decade, maybe longer with this ever-crawling cold each year. He shivered in July as he pulled his coat tighter and proceeded inside.

He twitched and watched over his shoulder. Pushing past the younger priest that met him at the door, the mayor marched toward the staircase up the belfry. An older priest stopped him at the door.

"What are you doing, your honor?" He looked into the mayor's eyes, saw the intent.

"Move aside. It's time." He brushed the priest to one side. "It's gone too far."

"But, Mayor, he—" The priest's eyes quivered, seeing the mayor wouldn't be swayed.

"Get your people out. I'll take it all on me."

The priest bowed his head at the mayor, stepping aside as he stomped up the long spiraling stairs of the belltower. The mayor heard the priests calling for everyone to leave the building, that the cathedral was closing—everyone had to go. *He* would come. There was no more time—the sun had set. The mayor picked up his pace, breathing heavy.

He got to the mighty brass bell, the biggest in the city—still tied down with heavy rope, as it had been those centuries ago when the city first burned. Had it not been tied, they might have saved the original settlement—the whole place built atop an ancient burial mound in the first place—a gateway to the otherworld. The French saw only high ground and built on it, no regard for the sacred land they stomped all over.

He pulled the knife he'd brought for the job and sawed into the hemp rope, making quick work of it. He'd nearly sliced all the way through when the squeak of the bat alerted him. The night grew dimmer as the shadows poured into the windows, forming into the shape of a man—but it was no *man.*

"What are you doing?" His fangs flared at the mayor, his face a snarl but also something else—flustered. The great and mighty Prince of Darkness was afraid. "We had an accord."

"Yeah, we did." The mayor kept slicing the rope. "We *had* a deal—one I never should have made, and now I'll burn for it, and that's on me. I sold my soul to you, damned myself. For the mayor's seat. For the city. You said you'd keep us safe, keep things quiet. Bring money and prosperity."

"Have I not?" *He* licked his foul teeth.

"You said It would all go smooth. Does any of this look smooth? No. No more. I'm calling the one who always looked out for this city—I'm calling our true hero." The mayor's face flushed with hot blood.

Cain winced, smelling it through the man's skin. "You'll die if you try to ring that bell." Cain's eyes flashed at the sniveling human meatsack.

"I knew that as soon as I walked through door." The mayor finished cutting the rope, wrapped it around his own neck and jumped through the window. The rope caught, snapping his neck with a pop as he fell from the tower. His weight hurled the big bell to one side, sending the clapper slamming home against the bowl.

The sound rang out, booming across the night sky. The Beast roared in the tower as the bell gonged, vibrating through him, echoing its way down the cathedral.

He closed his eyes—snarling, pulling back his ire. And within moments, it came again. Just blocks away, he heard the bells of St. Mary's. Our Lady. Immaculate Conception. All of them boomed—a cacophony of fools calling their would-be savior, most of whom had only heard his name whispered as legend.

Cain roared into the sound of clanging *copper.*

* * *

Well outside the city, inside the rundown shack next to a half-forgotten scrapyard, Captain Callum Boudreaux checked his watch, always a stickler for his time. The Colonel walked down the gangway of the invisible ship toward the house. Buck Kobayashi dozed on the couch. Boscaux Maximilien St. Michel Chevalier DeBrousse sat dead quiet in the chair at the far corner of the room, the light dim, shrouding most of his heavy, muscled frame.

A motor coming into the drive and shutting off roused Buck from his nap, the rest still shaking the cobwebs from their aging bodies. Murphy walked through the door with a brown sack in one hand and a coffee carafe in the other. All the eyes shot to her, and hers back to them. She handed the sack to The Colonel, reached in her pocket and tossed the keys to Buck.

"I brought coffee."

The moment passed as some distant metallic clanging rang in the distance, whispering louder each few seconds. The eyes of every soldier in the room moved to the dark chair in the far corner, its occupant sitting, fingers touching in front of his face as the bells grew louder—a Jesuit church just down the road joining the chorus now.

The Copperhead picked up his helmet from the table next to him and put it on. "It's time to go to work."

X
"THRILLER"
—MICHAEL JACKSON, 1982

THE NIGHT TEEMED with throngs of revelers as the lights down Canal Street and across The Quarter flooded the darkness with color. The bright full moon gazed upon them as they gathered in clusters on every street—the parade path well-known in this city. Many had come out upon hearing the bells, most too new to town to have any idea what they portended. But others remembered—from somewhere buried in the past, old forgotten legends grew in their minds. *Could it be true? Was he real?*

The sounds of Prince, Madonna, George Clinton, The Pointer Sisters, and more grew louder as the floats crept onto the main drag. Vendors walked about selling hodge-podge, trinkets, and handing out a free JarethCo mask with every purchase—or no purchase. There'd been at least a million of them flooded into the city in the last week.

The floats boasted largesse the likes of which had never been seen—even in this city known for extravagance. Mechanical busts moved their massive arms as giant mouths lip-synced to the music blasting in unison from all the floats at once.

A piercing screech rang out over the city as all eyes turned upward to see the massive owl, its wingspan stretched over seven meters, blocking the moonlight as it hovered above the city—then dove headfirst into the central float, transforming into the blinding, silver-clad Evilyn Jareth. She twirled in her shimmering cape, threw it off her shoulders, scattering it into the crowds as glittering confetti. They awed at her incandescence as she belted into song with her stage dancers. The queen commanded her court.

Many had come from all over—eager to join her rebellion against the master they'd grown to loathe in their immortal indenture. Evilyn offered them the promise of a better deal, a just society. For millennia, Cain had built a system around the world—he commanded nation leaders, owned parts of the largest companies and manufacturers on the planet. He had minions in every military and police force in the industrial world. Such a system was the wonder of the ages—why would she ever dream of tearing it down? No, the good doctor and her former ally in the metal mask were wrong. The system worked fine, ideal, in fact. All it needed was a benevolent commander—*Her.* Evilyn Jareth. Queen. God.

She smiled at herself. She would be a benevolent god. And the people would love her for it. Just as they did now—singing along with her—*to* her. She drank their praise and bestowed her blessing upon them with more song.

* * *

Burning down Tchoupitoulas Street, a growling black Falcon charged its 429 cubic inch, seven liter V8 into the city at full scream. 370 horses galloped into the maelstrom of the night. The police—*Cain's* police—ready and waiting for their old enemy, met the car before it made Market Street. An army called out for no other purpose than to put an end to the fly that he'd let buzz far too long—a game the Prince of Darkness finally grew tired of playing and would end tonight.

The battle-armored car slammed into police cruisers, spun, reversed, and fired flaming exhaust into them, peeling off into side streets and back avenues. The cop cars followed, giving chase away from the main area of the garish parade. More squad cars convened, corralling the black Falcon so it couldn't get downtown. But, then, it was never supposed to.

"I tell you what, sumbitch," Al Davenport shouted into the radio on the dash. "I can't believe I ain't ever done this with you before, D. This sucker's a hoot and a holler! Damn this is fun!" Al banked the car into a hard right, battering a police car into the opposite wall.

"Just keep as many busy as you can." D's gravelly voice came staticky over the com. "Then get clear and back to the river. The Colonel will pick you up directly."

"All the damn gods in heaven, hell and biscuits. He better!" Al shivered his head and hit the gas.

* * *

The upgraded Vandura ambulance cooked its own V8 into town, the old siren wailing to make its way through traffic. Cars moved out of their path, ushering them through uninterrupted.

Murphy fiddled with her helmet, trying to get it right. Looking through the clear plastic visor sprayed along with the welded aluminum around it, she could barely make out her hand in front of her. Big D's had more visibility from the looks of it, but not much. She hated how it and the heavy coveralls limited her, and the fight hadn't even started.

What the hell are you thinking, Murphy? Vampire wolf cops? Prince of Darkness? Creatures of Hell? A war among the damned? They didn't teach this at the academy, that was for sure. Not even the now not-so-mad ravings of her disturbed father could have prepared her for this. She closed her eyes and saw his stern face.

"You can do this." He'd held his arm against hers, teaching her a cross-block, about to spar again for the thousandth time—every time putting her on the ground. *Strike hard. No mercy. Your enemy is darkness incarnate. It will show you none.* "You hold the power inside you. Find it."

She breathed slow like she knew to do. The others psyched themselves up with their own rituals. High above the city, an invisible spaceship soared, calling out what lay ahead of them. She looked to D, nodded to Buck and Callum—each in metal masks and armored suits. Hers was heavy, clunky. She didn't know how they could stand it—even D, tree-trunk of a man that he was. It was a lot of weight.

"It's a mess in there, boys," said the Colonel over the radio.

Buck strapped on the pack with the particle blaster. Callum buckled on the foam sprayer. D tucked the revolver with their one and only shot at ending this into his belt holster. He pulled his twin compensated Berettas, each stacked with a stendo of silver-tips, and shoved them into his shoulder rigs. He tightened his silver-bladed bracers—each of the others sporting a pair too. Along with knives, spiked knuckles, and anything else they had with a pointy end.

"Are we ready for this?" Buck's voice cracked through his helmet.

"We ain't never been ready," Callum said.

* * *

On the mainstage float, Evilyn spun herself in the air, hovering to show her adoring worshippers she could. She swallowed their awe, sweeter than any fresh red blood she'd ever tasted. The crowds sang with her, catching at the beads and trinkets. She lowered herself back to the platform.

"I'm so glad you all came out tonight, you, my fearless friends and New Orleanians! Tonight is not just any celebration, no simple parade in our city of festivals. No, tonight is special. Tonight, we call out to the darkness, we command it back into oblivion. Tonight, I will show you your true enemy—and your true savior. I will show you what rots the core of this city, what evil drinks the blood of your own children. Feasts on their flesh and lords over you. But no more!" She grinned, seeing their curious faces staring back at her. The night grew ill around her. A grim quiet settled. Distant, the shrieks of winged rats called. "Tonight, I set you free of his chains. Tonight, you will be free! Vive la Nouvelle Orléans!"

Then she muttered away from her microphone, calling out the dreadest of incantations ever yet uttered over this ancient burial ground—a gateway between worlds. She called forth the restless, those who'd never crossed over, and then she twirled her fingers, pointed in the air above her, drawing her sparkling circles—the crowd enjoying the light show. She showed them holes in the rift, opening the veil.

She heard a new sound, a whining from a broken siren. She saw the van, her keen nostrils smelling the fresh chemical residue. The boys were back in town. She lowered her eyebrows and glared.

Evilyn threw her hands forward, hurling the raging spirits from the Land of Mists onto the bustling city streets. Howls and shrieks rang out as angry ghosts flew across the sky. The crowd ate it up at first, seeing only more spectacle, more illusion.

Then *He* landed. A thousand bats formed before her into the pitch-black knight damned since the dawn of humankind. His gruesome armor held the brutal beast contained within.

"Hello, lover." Evilyn stabbed him with her eyes.

"End it now, Witch." The bleak knight bellowed.

"I haven't even started yet." Evilyn hurled her chaos into her former lord. She relished the power she had—more than a match for him. She would see him bow before her. *He will kneel to me.* Her face twisted, darkened. She was the master now.

* * *

The Copperhead barreled out the side door of the van, dog-cops already inbound to meet him. This time they came prepared—body armor all the way up the neck, riot gear and ballistic helmets—an army come for battle.

"Save your ammo for killshots only. We ain't swimming in silver." He ignored his own order and blew out the knee of the first one that came at him, pulling his silver knife and shanking the night creature's neck as it fell forward. The others pulled their weapons and fired back. The team fell in behind Copperhead sawing his way through the fiends with blood gushing and streaking across the night from his gleaming blade. The team's armor and helmets did their jobs deflecting bullets from the cops' guns.

Giving up on the artillery, Cain's badged army charged into D's team. D crunched back at them, Murphy catching the strays with a long dagger they'd made for her. Watching them rot as she sank the weapon into their vitals was a thing to see. What a world she lived in.

Callum tested the spray foam and mired a band of the blue into the street. Immobilized, struggling to free themselves from the foam harder than any concrete on earth, D ambled to each one, took their helmets off—fangs snapping—and blew their brains out.

Giving up on the pretense of the uniform, two morphed into dire wolves and came frothing and snarling at them. Murph felt her hands go hot and steeled herself for the brawl, but it never came. Both dogs sprang into the air and then vaporized into blazing kaleidoscopic light—erased from the world.

The team turned back to see Buck gripping the nozzle of the particle blaster.

"Guess this works." They all felt his smirk through his helmet.

Ahead of them, the clash of demigods with enough hate for each other to flood the big river raged on. The crowds realized it wasn't part of the show. Panic crept through—sending them into disarray.

"We've gotta get to Evilyn."

"Do we, though?" Buck pointed at her—a warhawk clawing at the enemy of all humankind since the first written word. Evilyn Jareth fought the Prince of Darkness with a power and energy even *He* couldn't match. "I think she's winning."

"And then what? A kinder, gentler queen of the damned?" Murphy, a cop no more and never again, kicked a badge fallen from a demon into the gutter. D nodded to his new ally and she back at him.

Evilyn's army met Cain's in the street. D punched, shoved, and shivved his way through the turmoil, carving a path for the others behind him. Buck and Callum stayed in the middle, using their machines when needed, but keeping a mind to their ammo reserves. Buck had a little too much fun with his energy weapon. Murph held the rear, her mind keen, focused, doing her job—her arms boiling hot as they did their work.

Arriving at the main float, they gazed at the battle. Evilyn hurled a dark energy spike into Cain's chest, throwing him backward but still not piercing his dark armor. Forged a thousand years ago in the heart of the first crusade, when the Order of the Dragon had formed, discovering him in the chaos of that fool's war—vowing to fight him for eternity if need be. Now, long dead, the last of them slaughtered decades ago by his Black Hands, he remained—the unkillable monster.

"Throw it!" D called out to Buck. Buck fired an energy blast at the knight. He vanished in smoke just as it shot through where he'd been, blowing a hole in the building behind him instead.

Evilyn flung her head toward them, hissed and shot her arms forward. "Stay out of it." Her eyes flashed at D as she shouted at him. "I don't want to destroy you."

"You gotta stop, Ev." D pulled the revolver with the magic bullet, knowing he wouldn't hit her now if he fired it. But all he needed was her eye on him instead of Boudreaux. Callum let loose a stream of goop at her as Buck hit her full blast with the particle beam.

Evilyn ripped an arm loose, her legs sticking in the white, pillowy foam. She spat and cursed. "Don't you see them, D," she waved her free hand at the crowds, most of them in *Her* masks. "I have to show them. Then they'll see. The city will wake. And he'll flee. He must hide from *all* light, the truth most of all."

"I can't let you hurt these people, Evilyn. You know that." D cocked the hammer of the revolver, moving closer to take his one shot.

Evilyn threw a wave at him, knocking him backward and the pistol from his hands. Murphy cussed him for hesitating. Evilyn shouted a spell in the elder tongue. The portals she'd opened above her lit up. The people on the streets shouted bloodcurdling screams. Their faces coursed with terror. D jumped up and began ripping the masks from everyone he could grab, thinking he would save as many as he could. But they weren't dying. They weren't turning on each other like the doctor had said.

Buck, Murph, and Callum looked around. The people ran, shouted, screamed, and pointed, but they didn't die. D pulled the mask in his hand up to his face, stared at it, then looked through. All around them, he saw what they saw—a hundred thousand spirits, screeching ghosts flowing in from the other side. Re-constituting himself across from the Jester Queen—having performed her greatest joke on them yet—Cain landed again, his true form visible now to all wearing Jareth's eyes. Cain, the police, half the businessmen and politicians in the city, store-owners, bosses, landlords, the lot of them—all shone now in the light of the moon for the bloodsucking, rotten monsters they were, that they'd always been. Even the familiars appeared as dead-eyed ghouls. For no one took the mark of Cain but of their own free will. All of them made their choice, earning their fates.

Even Evilyn, once beautiful and full of fight and passion for justice, now stood before him a pallid, gangly witch. Behind the tinted visor of his helmet, a small drop of water ran down D's face for an old friend.

"Now they see," her timid, sorrowful voice haunted him. "Now, I finish it."

Evilyn ripped herself free of her white foam prison. With one hand she hurled the team across the street, sending them reeling in different directions. With her other hand, she summoned all the dark magic she could draw from the land beyond and sent it flowing into Cain the Cursed. He trudged toward her, his gnarled fingers stretching into talons reaching for her neck.

The Copperhead watched helpless from the ground. Jareth's army of beasts snarled and slashed at their counterparts, the whole city a demonic choir breaking loose, fire and brimstone, wrath of Hell raining from the sky, the souls of the dead careening through the world, shrieking their haunting cries across the air.

Murph struggled to catch her breath. D rolled to his feet. The dogs caught sight of them, lying there on the ground, beaten, weakened, meat for the slaughter. Buck and Callum struggled under the weight of their heavy packs. D pulled his guns, ready to end it in a blaze of fury.

THE BASILISK SHRIEKED from the gray sky as it dove at its fleeing prey. Grace and Cav raced across the wet tundra amidst the moaning elms of the otherworld. They'd come to the Plains of Despair, hearing tales of the creature that further tormented the souls huddled here. The winged devourer bore down on the runners, ready to snatch at them with its gruesome talons. Grace turned, fired a ghost arrow at its chest as Cav held his shield high, guarding them with its energy field. Another blinding flash blasted behind them as Lydia the Caster floated from her tree perch—a new trick she'd mastered in the years here in the gray nowhere. Lastly, as the beast writhed, distracted with its eyes closed shut, a spear shoved upward through its throat, ripping through its diamond-hard hide out the other side of its neck. The beast leaned and fell to one side, dead as the souls of the village beyond them.

Molly took the hood off her head, revealing herself—the trap they'd laid for the monster proving effective yet again. It was the twelfth such hunt they'd been on in months.

It had been long enough, the lure to stop counting gnawed at her. This place, its sadness, its deep anguish, wore down even the heartiest of spirits—as she knew Lydia's had once been. The first few months had been exhausting, Molly insisting on calling her by her Earthly name, she rejecting it every time, insisting now she was only Caster. The others shrugged, showing her the ways of this forsaken world, the traps and pitfalls of it as they went.

Later that day, or night—neither held any meaning here—as the flesh of the basilisk roasted over the fire for their last meal before they took shifts for rest, Molly sank her teeth into the meat, ravenous for it, for everything they could forage. If the others ate a standard portion, Molly ate ten times that much, hence their many hunts. She took fistfuls of the monster's carcass and absorbed them into herself. She felt the mass growing within her. *Only what you bring with you.* The words echoed through her mind. She'd long since had to slice the sleeves off her suit The Copperhead sprayed for her, having outgrown what the material could hold. It may be able to withstand anything on Earth, but her Strat-axe sliced through it like paper. The pants she'd shredded and remade into tassets over a skirt made of a fiend's hide. Her red hair had grown long and full, two thick braids of it hanging down either side of her face, the rest blazing behind her like the fire that burned in her eyes. A fire that burned to go home.

Some sad wanderer had come upon them days, almost a month back. She sang a melancholy song, wore a long lab coat, and muttered the words "Jester Queen.

My Jester Queen" over and over. She'd pawed at Molly, grasping at her hair, pointing to her, as though she had some desperate message this world had erased from her tormented mind. But somehow Molly understood it. Enough of it, at least.

She washed her hands in the basin, wiping her face from the meal still lingering on her lips. The others watched as she applied salve to her calloused hands, nursing the small cuts and sore spots. She'd grown used to such injuries, her memory of invincibility fading but not gone. Her skills with the blade had improved every day since its forging. She flung it with the precision of a sniper in a war movie—she did remember movies. She missed them. Some nights, she sat at the fire regaling the others with a tale she ripped straight from a midnight movie with whats-her-name, the goofy horror host.

She sat next to Lydia and dropped a hand on her shoulder as she stared into the tattooed words all over her arms. Molly wondered at the life she'd had to suffer to be who she was now—a person Molly both admired and sometimes feared. The Caster had called down acid rain on a camp of trolls once, burning their faces into mush as they fled for their caves.

The humans here may be only wandering spirits, but the monsters that tormented them were flesh and bone. The human souls languished here because their guilt wouldn't allow them to cross back through the veil, to be reborn. Some, they said, fought their way through it, and went back through the light to another womb, to try again—to live again. Others wandered on. But the worst, the ones who couldn't withstand their pain, their own self-hatred, eventually sank into the Sea of Souls, a grim pool of despair so terrible, it would pull any who deigned to touch it down with them. Molly had stared into it as close as any dared—felt its awful, sad power, and even she retreated from it.

"You never told me where you learned all those." Molly pointed to Lydia's tattoos, the spells she'd mastered as Caster.

"Here you have only what you bring with you." She didn't look at Molly as she said it, only focused on her needle and ink as she tapped a new one into what little "white space" she had left.

"Everyone always says that." Molly hated hearing it, another mocking riddle in the vast ocean of nonsense that had become her life since that day so long ago in a rundown shack full of dumb goons with guns, firing into her bulletproof body. It annoyed her not just because she didn't understand it, but more now because she had finally begun to—and she wasn't ready to accept it yet. *El Shaddai.* She knew that if she took on that role, there would be no going back—ever.

"I had a book." Caster looked at Molly, a timid sliver of the girl from Bay High still buried deep in that lost soul. "When I first came here. A book of spells, magic. All in another language. I learned it. Taught myself. It was that or die and dwell here forever. I felt I had to get back, somehow. Then they found me." She pointed her head at Cav and Grace. They loaned me the cloak as I learned, same as you. Their other friend who used it had died. They couldn't even remember her name anymore. The book grew so old, it started to fall apart, the pages withering. So, I had to save what I knew worked, what I knew I could use. I was afraid to forget. Like I forgot everything else."

Molly shed a tear onto the cold ground under her. She looked off into the haze of the horizon, across the Sea of Souls, into the towering mountain that lay beyond, the low murmuring roar of the great old one behind that, a terror, they said. The Bone-Cruncher, they called it—a monster so vast it couldn't be fully beheld by their eyes. Only its occasional movements betrayed its existence—its many serpent heads snaking themselves in all directions, charged with devouring the worst souls who ever lived—those cast upon its corpse shore.

Molly hated it. Her eyes sometimes pierced through the haze as the others slept, seeing its thousand heads, its central monstrous face, looking back, as if it saw her too. When it did, she would stand and point her Strat-axe at it, calling her shot as it were.

She hated this place.

"It's time to go." She stood up, wrapped the spear in its sheath and slung it across her back, grabbing her gear.

"Go where?" Cav stood with her, looking around as though she sensed danger. They knew she had a sense of it that they didn't. "We've just made camp. The village?"

"No. We're going home. To Earth." Her eyes steeled themselves. She'd let this go on far too long. "The towering mountain. The ForgeMaster told us there's a door at the top. A door we can pass through."

"We've been through this, Red." Grace shook her head, standing up. "It's beyond the Sea of Souls. Then the labyrinth, a maze none has ever solved. They wander its walls even now, a thousand upon a thousand years of walking nowhere. And then the climb." She pointed at the towering mountain.

"We don't sail the Sea of Souls." Molly sliced meat from what remained of their meal to make rations for the trip. "We don't wander the maze. We go over them. Straight to the mountain."

"How do we do that?" Cav asked.

Molly's eyes flashed with her plan, but it was Lydia, her friend, who said it out loud.

"Firecorns." Lydia's smile—not Caster's—shined back at Molly the Hammer.

* * *

They grazed in an open field, Cav and Grace watching them from cover—a full herd. A wisp on the air, a shadowy, flowing form eased toward them, calling out her song, a tune recalled from an age long gone—someone named Jett, which the spellcaster somehow knew. Lydia held out her hand, steadying them, calming them with her magic. She lulled them into a daze, whispering a spell of submission. Cloaked and out of sight, Molly climbed atop the first one. It reeled, trying to throw her from its back. Spitting fire from its nostrils, it bucked, but the unseen Molly held her grip. Lydia got it under control. Molly lifted her hood, motioning the others to come softly.

Before long, they'd all mounted a flaming, winged unicorn of their own, gripping tight to the thick flowing manes, Molly looked to her dark-haired best friend in all the worlds, and they winked to each other—some distant language they had coming to their minds.

And they were off. The firecorns flung out their wings and lurched into the sky alight with purple flashes of lightning somewhere far away. The Bone-Cruncher's distant grumble shook them to their cores, but they flew on, reaching the Sea of Souls. They pushed their heads low, gripping their hair-reigns tight, no going back now.

They flew. On and on, the screams of the damned behind and before them. The lightning flashes got closer but didn't bother the quartet. Molly's face grew grim with intent. The nearer they got to the maze, the mountain, the more she felt her resolve strengthen, her mission, her whole reason for being became clear. And the monster, she saw its face sharper now. Taller than any building on earth by more than double, a creature out of the darkness of space and time. The spawn of some ancient and evil god who hated creation itself.

Across the maze, they soared, seeing its terrors from above. The other kids— *could they still be called that?*—smiled as they passed over it. To the base of the mountain, they glided, then pushing the horses upward, flapping their wings until they could push no higher. The Firecorns spat flame and whinnied. The towering mountain still stretched high above the limits of the beasts. Molly led them in a circle around the tower, seeing a small plateau. She landed hers and hopped off its back, slapping it off into the wild again. The others flew to her, she helping them off one by one. The Bone-Cruncher's silhouette grew bigger on the horizon. It had sensed them, knew their intent, and moved to stop them. Molly sensed its evil intent as if it were some ancient enemy of hers, her immortal foe, their destinies bound to one another.

She started them up the mountain, beginning the climb the rest of the way to the top. The creature loomed. They had to be careful, but they had to be fast. Lydia's words made their hands coarse, rough, and sticky. Their feet slapped tight onto the rocky edge, finding grips. Foot by foot, they climbed higher. The air became thin, a howling on the wind, voices carrying, passing through from the other world, or worlds. *How many were there?* Molly wondered to herself.

The piercing, nuclear scream of the Bone-Cruncher shivered down their spines. Molly called out to the others, telling them not to be afraid, that they were close, that they would make it. She felt it, too. The closer they got to the top, to the doorway to Earth, the center of it all, she felt her strength return. She slammed her fingers into the rock, sinking them into it like brittle clay. She was The Hammer again. Each inch closer, the stronger she got.

But not Lydia. Beside her, the Caster's face paled, her eyes bloodshot. She weakened.

"What's wrong?" Molly shouted across the thin air.

"Molly?" Lydia cried out. "Molly? Is it you? It's really you." Tears streamed down her face. "Molly, I'm sorry. I—it's been so long. I couldn't remember. But I do now. I—I'm sick. I can't go back."

"Yes, you can, Lydia. I'm right here with you."

"No, Molly. I can't. I—" Lydia's grip slipped, one arm dropping, the other barely hanging on.

"Hold on, Lydia, I'm coming." Molly moved toward her friend, determined to help her all the way up the mountain if she had to.

"Molly, no." Lydia's voice rang hollow, sad. A sad so deep it stabbed Molly in the heart. She flinched at the pain of it. "You don't understand. I can't. You have to leave me."

"I'll never leave you."

Lydia's other hand slipped. She fell. Molly's soul dropped from her stomach, and she didn't think. She leapt. All her recovered strength fled her body again as she plummeted down the miles of the towering mountain, all the height from their climb *and* the firecorns lost to the fall. Molly's face quivered, a fear surging through her, but she reached her arm out to grasp Lydia, cradling her body in her arms. She let out a cry as the ground came into sight, them speeding toward oblivion. All her doubt, her weakness, her refusal to say what she knew was true and didn't want to be. She cried and cried at the speeding rocks that would damn her friend here for eternity. *Here you have only what you bring with you.* It echoed through her mind. She had to let it go. All of it. The nights playing music until daybreak in the garage. The trips to the mall to laugh at bad horror movies and tease boys in the back of the theater. Sunny days on the beach as water licked at their toes in the sand. Riding bikes down Elm and E Streets. Sleepovers. Road trips with the band. All the wonderful, amazing, beautiful parts of being human, of being one of them. They had to go now. Even her name, the one they gave her, it wasn't hers. It wasn't who she was. She knew now *what* she was. And she had to let the rest go.

"I—" Her eyes grew cold, hardening. "Am—" Her face steeled, her neck tightening, her shoulders tensing, her chest and stomach flexing, bracing for the impact, her legs and knees growing denser than any metal, even the one strapped to her back. "El Shaddai!"

God's feet slammed into the ground underneath her, Lydia's body cushioned in her almighty arms, the aftershock of her landing boomed through this terrible world, sending tremors for a thousand miles in every direction. The Bone-Cruncher's slow march toward them halted, sensing the wake she'd made—sensing *what* she was. But then it marched on all the same.

The god stared up at the towering mountain, the top of which no mortal eye could see from this distance—but hers could. She saw it clear as day. She bent her knees, gripped her friend tight, holding her life in her hands, and she leapt. She rocketed up the mountain, all the way to the top. Another plateau jutted out at its peak, a cave there at the cliff wall.

Grace and Cav lurched back as Molly landed herself and Lydia on the rock in front of them.

"How did you—" they stared. "We thought—"

"Let's go. I'm not done yet." Molly's glowing eyes told them to obey and they did. They had good souls, all of them.

Lydia hung at her side, growing sick again, pleading to be left behind. Molly marched into the cave, a cloaked figure standing guard over a swirling circle of lights in the center of the room.

"To open the door and cross over, you must answer this—"

"Fuck out of the way and open the god-damned door." Molly's fist pointed her spear right at the dude's face. He stared into her eyes and then blinked in shock. He dropped to his knee and bowed.

"Just tell me where you wish to go." His voice cracked, not looking back at her.

"Take me to the witch who sent my friend to this shithole."

XII
"STRONG AS I AM"
—PRIME MOVERS, 1986

THE WAR AMONG THE IMMORTALS raged at Baronne Street. Murphy dragged an injured Callum Boudreaux down to Magazine where they'd left the van. It was fortified with D's formula and would hopefully shield the old timer against whatever fresh hells came at them next.

Above the city, windows to another world poured in a slew of screaming souls, some bearing the image of alien creatures—gargantuan demonic apparitions with piercing shrieks. Some of the ghosts flew into the bodies of those on the ground, sending them into fits and convulsions. Others paired with Evilyn's army, bolstering them into even more powerful beasts—monsters to give the sanest men nightmares enough for asylums.

Across the street and up the block, Murph saw Buck struggling to his feet with the heavy backpack. He fired its laser into a charging rhino—a glowing rhino. Murphy shook it out of her head and ran to him, the heavy coveralls impeding her speed and reflexes. She took a glancing slash across her shoulder from a wolfcop and ran through it, the armor doing its job despite how slow it made her. She got to Buck and helped him to his feet. She had her pistol, loaded with silver tips, in one hand and held her dagger in the other in a cross-stance. She covered Buck all the way to the van, their stronghold amidst the chaos.

"Where's D?" Buck backed against the van and aimed his blaster at the nearest target and erased it from Earth.

"I didn't see him up there." Murphy strained her eyes, looking for a figure that any other time would stand out like a—a bronze knight. But with every bloodthirsty, flesh-rending demon in seven hells running and tearing at each other, he was a little hard to find at the moment.

"He's gonna go for her." Callum steadied himself, stood despite his leg wobbling. "He's gonna finish the job."

"She'll kill him." Murphy peered through the turmoil. The Jester Queen drew an elaborate glowing box around Cain, trapping him inside it, him tearing, clawing at the walls of it with giant talons. His face morphed into a fusion of predators, snarling and dripping from gnashing fangs. The dark spikes on his armor sparked as he raked them across his ethereal cage.

Callum sprayed the last of the foam in front of them, forming a wall with the van at their backs. Buck blasted into the sky at the winged demons floating at them.

"What do we do? We can't hold this position long." Buck looked to his captain for an order. Captain Boudreaux pulled a Colt M4 Carbine from the van, racked the charging handle and flicked the switch to fire, but he gave no order.

Murph unzipped the stupid heavy coveralls and pulled them off her shoulders. They hadn't had any boots on hand that fit her, so they'd just sprayed her sneakers. They slid through the leg holes. She tossed her helmet to the side, down now to her Detroit Mandley 82 Jersey shirt and her drainpipe jeans. "Shoot your laser thingy at that." She pointed at the portal in the air. "And you—" She turned to Callum. "Cover his ass. And mine."

"What are you doing?" Buck did as told and pointed the particle beam dead center at the vortex and cut loose. "You can't go out there without a suit."

Murphy slowed her breathing, closed her eyes, watched her father's proud but sorrowful smile somewhere back in her mind. She opened her eyes, breathing steady, grabbed her dagger in one hand and pulled Callum's knife from his belt with her other—and took off.

Murphy ran through Hell on Earth. She bounded over wrecked cars, sometimes not feeling her foot touch the tops of them as she floated higher, dodging shrieking demons. A gangly wolf leapt and snapped at her throat. Murphy lurched into a forward airborne roundhouse and slammed its body into the wall beside them. She moved through the wind, slipping and ducking away from the swarming spirits, dropping onto her knees, her body arching back as she slid under the apparitions, evading their search for hosts. She sank a silver blade into a fanged cop, then hurled Callum's knife through the air, bulls-eyeing another dog in the throat. She kept up her pace, snatching the spare knife from the rotting vampire carcass as she jumped over it. She slashed and carved her way through the fray. She palm-punched a man-bear with every drop of her essence—something building, bubbling inside her—hurling it back as she flipped over its fallen body. She jumped atop the parked cars, leaping from one to another with a speed the men she left behind blinked to be sure they saw it right.

"Who the hell is that woman again?" Callum asked Buck as he slammed another mag into his rifle. Buck shook his head wide-eyed as he poured particle beam into the hole to Hell.

Murphy ran, knifed, criss-crossing her blades. She kicked and punched monsters away from her like they were nothing. Her breathing steady, her focus perfect. She sprang through the air, slapping her feet on the heads of enemies and kicking off them to stay airborne. She never saw D on her way to the float housing Cain and Evilyn. She hurled one blade at Evilyn while the other she sliced through the energy cage into Cain's face. His skin smoked and rent itself, his eyes bleeding pus and gore. His roar became a scream.

The blade she threw at Evilyn bounced off her invincible face but distracted her enough for Murphy to double-kick her in the chest, knocking her off balance and losing the spell. Cain gasped, pulled the knife from his smoldering face. He spat and snarled and vanished into bats, retreating from the war.

"You idiot bitch." Evilyn raged, hurling dark matter energy at her new enemy.

Murphy backflipped, dodging every dart thrown her way by the garish sorceress. She shouted new words in some old-world language, bolts and darkness hurled and slashed at Murphy. Her body followed her every command at the fraction of a second. She moved like her father taught her, using the setting to her advantage. She gripped the debris beneath her with the tips of her feet, kicking it at the witch to throw her aim off, moving backward, looking for an out. *What the hell are you doing, Murphy? What is your plan here?* She focused on her breathing, letting the rest fade into noise, remembering what she knew. She felt her hands getting hot again, itching.

"I had him. I *HAD* him—after aeons, a thousand ages, the scourge of the world—*I* had him. You fool. Mortal idiot dimwit." Evilyn's rage poured out of her, pulling her force into chaotic waves of energy flung off her arms. Her shots grew wild, diffused. Murphy flipped off the float, slapping her Converse onto the street, and quickly moving backward again.

Evilyn descended, floating to the ground. She flew at Murphy, growing her fingernails into wicked bone blades, slashing with a madness. Murphy evaded every attack. Evilyn took both arms and cross-slashed her claws at Murphy's face, leaving her own chest exposed—for a single instant.

Murphy saw her opening, summoned her focus, and fired her fist into the witch's chest. Light burst between them, hurtling them both backward like speeding trains.

Murphy's back slammed into the side of a pickup some thirty feet behind her. Sore now and aching, she blinked, looked for her attacker but couldn't find her. The hole in the sky evaporated. Another blast from behind her disintegrated a spirit in the sky. The beasts brawling in the street saw the door close, Evilyn nowhere to be found. Each side retreated, neither seeing their commanders on the field anymore.

Murphy gasped, dropping her hands to her knees, pulling in her breath, trying to make sense of herself, get her bearings back.

"How the hell did you do that?" Buck's voice came from behind her. Callum lumbered along behind him, craning his neck looking for The Copperhead.

"Do what?" Murphy stood, popping her neck, shaking her nerves out. She still didn't see the witch—nor D.

"Your hand, your whole arm—" Buck's eyes gazed into her like she just grew a beard. "It's like they were on fire—they glowed red and blue."

Murphy swallowed hard, breathing fast and short. She couldn't process what he told her. Her mind fell out of the moment—focused on the figure approaching her through the smoke and scrambling people. Tall, framed by the bright moon and swirling lights of the lingering ghosts, he wore a wide-brimmed straw hat. His skin, darker than hers, opened to show a pleasant smile, warm inviting eyes.

"You're right on time." Legba said, and it seemed no one else saw him but her.

* * *

Far up Canal, past Roosevelt and Burgundy, the wheezing, panting body of Evilyn Jareth struggled to push herself into the wall behind her, hoping to use it brace her, to see if she could still stand. She winced, tried to find her voice. All that came were cracks and groans. She cried at the pain still coursing through every fiber of whatever she was—what she'd made herself. She coughed black blood onto her silver attire. She laughed, the pain stabbing her again with every chuckle. *The best laid plans of mice and men,* she mused to herself. She looked down at her chest, a black, smoldering depression in the shape of a fist. Her arms limp at her sides, black lines drawing from her chest wound through the old pathways left behind from when she used to pump her own living blood.

"You're a fool, Evilyn." She laughed at herself. "A silly clown to the bitter end. You drank the wrong one." She laughed again, even as the pistol pointed at her face cocked its hammer back—its metallic click sending an odd warmth into her cold corpse. *Isn't that all you are? What you let him make you?* "I'm sorry, D. I know it isn't worth much, but I am." She looked through his helmet, into his eyes.

The Copperhead stood above her, his muscled, aged shoulders blocking much of the light from her face. He held the pistol point-blank at her forehead. One shot—one squeeze—and it would all be over for her. She knew where she'd go—no mystery there. Only this time, there'd be no return trip.

"I think I'm dying—I think the bitch really killed me. So stupid. Always the forest for the trees. Stupid." She blinked as she struggled to speak. She wanted to see his face one more time. She wanted to ask but was too afraid. She deserved nothing from him, not even a single act of final kindness. But, as if he sensed her last wish, he reached up and peeled the helmet off. There was his gorgeous face, wrinkles and all, the warm life that remained in his eyes. The loss of so much, everything ever dear, and still he lived. She'd wielded power undreamed in the palm of her hands, commanded armies of spirits with her words—but D had always been stronger. She saw that now.

D held the muzzle of the gun steady, his finger ready to do the job. He gave her a sad smile, shaking his head. She knew him too well. Buck or Boudreaux would've shot her by now. She smelled the bullet in the cylinder, ready to pierce her skin. She smelled it every day from her new teeth she'd used to cause all this destruction. The city—*Her* city—its famous Canal Street in chaos. That part she'd at least given him as a final parting gift. Cain would never be able to hide here again—his empire weakened if not destroyed. And the woman, the ex-cop she'd run out of the gala—maybe *she'd* finish the job. Like she was supposed to do.

"I did love you," Evilyn whispered, still wheezing and unable to stand. "I did this for you. For all of us."

"You only ever did anything for yourself, Ev." D de-cocked the pistol, lowering it to his side, sighing.

"You can't do it. You never could. You let me live all these years, same as he let you and me both. I was nothing but his prize to mock you with. A joke. His Jester Queen. Just go ahead and do it, D. I'm done fighting."

"I'm not gonna shoot you. Evilyn." D put the pistol back in its holster. "Like you said. You're probably dead already. God'll be your judge." He turned his back to her to walk away—shaking his head at all the loss, all the wasted years. "And maybe you can still—"

A sonic boom deafened above the city. A spear fired from heaven stabbed through Evilyn Jareth's dead heart. Her black blood burst from her chest and mouth. The last of her energy fled her fading eyes. Her head sank. D's face went white, cold.

Two leather-wrapped, sandaled feet slammed into the pavement, sinking into it. The shockwave of their impact knocked all 280 pounds of the armored Copperhead to the ground. Thick, muscled legs ran into a tasseted waistguard draped over a leather skirt. Familiar, faded neon colors ran up the chest-piece, draped on either side by thick red braided hair. Tattered rainbow wings hung behind her back. Green lights glowed faintly in her eyes as the god's thick arms pulled her weapon from his old friend's chest. She stood taller than before, nearly D's height as he regained his feet.

"You sent my friend to Hell, bitch." Molly wiped the blood onto Evilyn's silver bodice. "Now it's your turn."

XIII
"SAVE OUR SOULS"
—MÖTLEY CRÜE, 1985

BELIAL, BAPHOMET, BE'ELZEBUB—all names he'd been called in this era of man and gods. There'd been others before. He'd seen the birth and death of empires and would see the dawn of a new age. It was a thing he knew that even his own dark mother did not—would not accept. As she raged endlessly against her fate, so too did he. He would never die—never cross over as his now departed Evilyn had many times, this time her last. He'd never taste of the redemption such penance might offer—a chance to be reborn. A chance to live, truly live, his heart beating, pumping, feeling, tasting, again. He could have new children, born fair and of proper form—not accursed monsters as they were here, bulbous and hideous—swamp hags and grindils.

For a time, they'd amused him, his abominable offspring. He'd made such awful things over the millennia—mating in his animal forms with other beasts—just to see what he could sire. Even with humans, they came out botchlings and succubi—incapable of honor, empathy, affection. He had never and would never know the love of his own child, made in his once true image.

But he accepted it. He'd accepted it before the dawn of writing. He would endure.

"What is your command, Lord." Count Sardo bowed low behind The Beast who gazed out over the dark swamp beyond his rising castle. "The people know of you, know of us. She gave them eyes to see. The Fae will come—their Phantom Queen—"

"Yes. It will be time to go soon." Cain turned to his prostrate acolyte, joined now by Chélicère, a fledgling caster. Many had come forward, eager to fill the role Evilyn once had. He lowered his eyelids at them. All would betray him if they thought they could gain the edge. Only Evilyn had ever come close. But she had given him one final gift in her betrayal. The blood. The El Shaddai reborn. *She* was the key.

"Prepare the great arcade. There's to be a wedding." He smiled as he heard the calls of his winged children, the first of his Horde arriving from afar. "I go now to my bride. Prepare the ritual."

"But, my Lord, she's allied with—"

"It's all right, Count." Cain smiled. "I've been invited."

EPISODE VI

"BAD OMEN"
—MEGADETH, 1986

D WATCHED HER POLISH the blade of that wicked spear like it were a precious pet. Specks of Evilyn's blood—and from the looks of it, countless others—adorned her tattered clothing. She *had* grown bigger, taller, almost gruesome in the pale moonlight of the waning dark.

The city had quieted after the ordeal. Spirits still howled in the distance. Something would have to be done about those. But Buck's device had proved useful in the end. Inside the house, Al wrapped Callum's leg with a hot pad and doped him with enough painkillers to send him to sleep.

The dark-haired kid Molly brought back with her slept in fits, sweating, mumbling. D had checked the girl's neck for bites first thing, but it he couldn't take his eyes off Red. She barely looked human now—nothing but wrought-iron muscle and the war that grew in her heart. D knew that war. He'd been fighting one or another as long as he could remember.

"Tell me again what happened." D unzipped his armored jacket and let out a long breath. But his mind knew no calm. Buck had told him twice already, wild-eyed at it still. The fighting, the flipping, the glowing arm that knocked a god-powered Evilyn into the wall. He'd seen the outcome of that with his own eyes.

"And you're sure it was Legba." D held his head in his hands.

"Ain't no mistaking Leg. You know that." Buck shook and shivered from the fight. "And then, just—poof—gone."

D knew it meant they'd finally found their *chosen one*. Where they'd gone and when they'd return was something only for them to know. *Gods...* D hated the gods. Every last one of them. The only one he'd ever cared about now faded in front of him into another soulless inhuman brute with naught but its own ends to accomplish. And since she *wasn't* their chosen one, then...

"'When I saw her, I was greatly amazed.'" Buck's whispered voice cut into D like a blade sharp as the one the god held in her hand. "'But the angel said to me, Why are you so amazed? I will tell you the mystery of the woman, and of the beast with seven heads and ten horns that carries her. The beast that you saw was, and is not, and is about to ascend from the bottomless pit and go to destruction.'"

Molly's grim eyes peered up at them as Buck quoted the scripture. D flinched.

The Destroyer had come.

I
"DEVIL'S CHILD"
—JUDAS PRIEST, 1982

THE MEN HAD GONE to sleep, all but D. Molly the SledgeHammer slung her guitar-shaped weapon across her back, her fierce eyes seeing everything in the house, the yard, taking it all in again as if for the first time. Everything seemed smaller than before—the world simpler to her now. She'd been so long in the otherworld, she had to remind herself how this one worked. Poor Lydia had been down there for *too* long. Molly's heart burned at the thought of it. She'd kill the witch again if she could.

Lydia's sickness grew worse by the hour. The others, Cav and Grace had come through the doorway with her. They'd grown ill at first, disoriented as their old lives, their memories came back to them.

"There was a rollercoaster," they'd said.

But they were mostly fine now, like a bad case of jetlag, nothing else. Grace even remembered her name—which had been Grace all along—and her phone number. Parents came to retrieve both her and Kevin. His name was Kevin. Lydia knew her name, could call out every Cure album by heart—Molly tested her. But her fever rose, her heart erratic.

Molly sat next to her best friend's sweating body on the couch, asleep but murmuring, fits and nightmares. Molly laid her hand on Lydia's head. She tried to push calm into her, to fix whatever was wrong.

A chill wind blew through the house from the open window, colder than the night outside. A howl. D tensed, pulling a pistol from his shoulder—he'd never fully unsuited from the fight. The hairs on both his and Molly's necks stood straight.

"He's here." Molly's eyes hardened. She stood up from Lydia, unsheathing her Strat-axe.

D walked to the window, racking the slide on his Beretta. Molly stood beside him. They saw the grim shadow fading into the outer reach of the porchlight. His dark armor covered him but for his head. Slick dark hair hanging halfway down his torso framed Jack Germain's deceptive face. His smile flashed his needle-sharp fangs. His forehead bore the mark, the ancient sign of who and what he was—laid there by some fool of a god Molly would have words with when all this was done. The others like her who roamed this world, seeding chaos in it with their meddling and interference, she'd set them right.

But first Cain.

"I come with an offer of peace, noble knight." His smile bore a lie that mocked them both. Molly gripped her spear tighter, hungry for its blade against the devil's throat. "A truce, a cessation of our sad little war." He squinted his eyes at Molly. "My offer is to *you*, their lives as a gift if you would but hear my proposal. With your consent, I ask you to be my final bride."

Molly's godblood boiled. It was Blake all over again. She wanted his head on her stick, held high for all his beastly acolytes to see.

"You'll get nothing but another bullet if you stay here longer." Copperhead aimed his gun at the beast's face. "You know you have no power here. You're *unwelcome*."

Cain's image vanished into smoke. Then he burst into the house, standing next to D. He snatched D's throat and held him to the ceiling, tightening his grip as he licked his evil grin.

"But I *am* welcome, Copperhead." He laughed, squeezing, his fangs growing longer, wanting to drink the blood of this foe.

He lost that arm for his trespass. It dropped to the floor and turned to rats and bugs scattering across the linoleum. Molly stabbed the tip of the spear at his chest, but he was gone into vapor, bats screeching into the night.

Buck ran out of the back bedroom with a rifle in his hands. Al was behind him with a scattergun. Callum and The Colonel clocked in for work.

"What's happening?" Buck stared all around. "How the hell did he get past the salt?"

D's eyes glared at Molly, then to Lydia on the couch. He pulled her coughing body up and scanned her neck again—he'd inspected it twice before he ever let her inside the first time. Lydia's eyes cracked open, staring back at Molly's, full of apology and hurt.

"I'm sorry, Molly. I tried to stay behind. I tried. I can't—" She fell limp, her arm dangling—her tattoos had begun to fade since being back, but they weren't gone. Her wrist hung at her side, wrapped in a leather bracelet. D tore it off, and there they were. Two puncture marks, scabbed over with her dried blood.

"Gods damn it to hell." D turned to Molly with vengeance on his heart. "You brought her here. You brought *Him* here." D aimed his pistol at Lydia's face and Molly crushed it.

A shriek pierced above them as the ceiling tore away from the house. Winged creatures soared above, one swooping in with its two gangly talons reaching for a victim. It lost them both for getting in range of Molly's blade as she extended the handle and sliced.

"You will not hurt her." Molly's eyes gave D's an order. His mind struggled, resisted, but there was far too much good in him. He obeyed. He had faith. "Can your friends fix her? Mama B? Can she be saved?"

More winged adversaries swooped in as bats squealed across the night. Buck and the others fired into their foes. Another set of talons approached—a wyvern. Molly'd killed plenty of them in the otherworld.

"There's a way. But it's risky. And it depends on how far gone she is." D looked at the sickly girl, her eyes sunk. She would become a ghoul if left to her own.

"Just get her there. Do what you have to do." Molly shrank her spear to a short sword and gripped her glider wings hanging from her back. "I'll cover your exit."

"Wait, you—" D started, but Molly burst into the sky.

They heard the screams of the dying monsters even if they could barely see the work of their ally. The Colonel helped Callum to the warbird as Buck and Al fired at the strays. More wolves howled out the front door—a pack of cops, lights and sirens blaring. The Beast still had his friends in blue. They fired their guns into the house. D grabbed the kid and ducked behind the couch, sending cover fire back at his enemy.

"Get to the ship now," he yelled to his team. They covered each other as they made their way out the back.

"D, come on!" Buck shouted back.

A drake got between him and the door. A laugh on the wind told him the bastard Cain was still here, watching the chaos. D and Lydia were pinned down, and he knew it.

"Just get to the bird and take off." He emptied the mag and popped in his last one. He looked down at the kid, remembering his promise. "I'll have to get her out in the Falcon." He jumped up, slung Lydia over one shoulder, making every shot count as he spent them.

Far above, the faint colors of a rainbow flew into winged serpents, gutting them in midair, dropping them like slithering sacks of meat to the ground. D blasted a pair of dogs leaping at him as he made the left side of the scrapyard—the Falcon tarped-over and just ahead of them.

"Just a bit more and we—"

Another wyvern—twice the size of the last one—slammed onto his Ford and flipped it over, leaving it sitting upside down in a pile of scrap.

"Fuck." D fired at the Wyvern but only grazed it. Another sonic boom reported just as the blade tore the throat away from it. God slammed for a landing and fired back into the sky. It still didn't solve his wheels problem. A whirring sound told him an invisible ship was off into the night. The boys were safe.

"Now what do you do, D?" He looked around. The old Dodge truck in the front yard wouldn't get him a quarter mile before they ripped it apart. "Shit. Shit. Shitty Shit."

The kid pointed her limp arm toward the far side of the yard—at one of the pickups Al had bought at the police auction the day before last.

"That's—" her voice squeaked, barely anything to it, "my truck."

* * *

D got her into the cab of a tricked-out Silverado that made his iron-clad Ford look quaint. She hit a button with her thumb on the dash and the thing roared to life with a growl so loud D thought it was another demon under the hood.

"The hell was that?" He watched the truck's array light up.

"6.66 on the Richter scale." The sick kid managed a chuckle from her pale face. She reached under the dash looking for something, then swore. "What the f—where's the radio?"

"First thing Al does is strip the radios." D put it in gear and floored it, ripping through wolves as he tore out of the yard. "What does it matter?"

"I was trying to call backup."

"What backup?"

"Molly's sister." Lydia's voice cracked. She faded. D gunned it for Mama's.

"She's got a sister?" That thought fumbled around in his brain giving him a goosebump.

"Yeah, sorta."

* * *

The red gliding god flew into the last of her winged enemies. She sliced its gut and dropped it along with herself to the ground. She scanned the yard for strays. Wolfcops backed away from her, but one got a spear in his chest just because Molly wanted to.

Cain materialized in front of her.

"There's a million more where that one came from." He smiled at her, like he had back at the department store when they played the big piano together. His face lightened. He waved his hand and his minions dispersed into the night, the lights of the cars flicking off as they drove into the dark.

She flung her blade at his throat, extending the handle to its full length. His face turned to smoke, and he appeared behind her.

"Must we dance this number? It always ends the same way." He stood behind her, she as tall as him. He put his hands on her shoulders. "We're the same, you and I."

"I'm nothing like you." She turned and glared at him, gripping her weapon, her eyes flashing with flickering light from thunder off in the night sky. "I'm a god. You're a demon."

"I am half-god. Did you even know that?" Cain tilted his head, his eyes softening to her. "And you are El Shaddai—The Destroyer. You are my destiny. I ask you only this: grant me an audience. Come to my keep, and see what wonders I can show you. Do this, and I spare your comrades."

Molly shook her head. She hated him and everything he said. He was the father of lies. The Prince of Darkness. The Old Nick. Mephistopheles. Here again to offer another Faustian bargain—Molly'd actually paid attention that day in Senior Lit. And she hated him for all that he was, and all that she now knew she was too. She closed her eyes, letting go of the last piece of her past. Molly Slater was gone now. There was only the Hammer. She would be the destroyer.

"I'll do it." She glared into his black eyes. "I'll come to you before dawn. I just have to say goodbye first. You'll grant me that." She pointed the spear at his face.

The Beast's face nodded with consent. "We have an accord."

II

"THE HEALER"
–JOHN LEE HOOKER, FEAT. CARLOS SANTANA, 1989

THE KID LAY ON THE TABLE, candles lit around her. Mama chanted in the old tongue, and D felt the energy in the room change. The rest of the boys hung about the foyer of the house chatting with some musicians—so many from all over came here to pay their respects.

"Can you pull it out of her?"

Mama's eyebrows furrowed as she twisted her head, whispering at Lydia's convulsing body, sweat pouring out of her as she mumbled deliriously. She spoke of robots and goblins and fighting trolls and cyclopes. Molly said she'd been through Hell itself, and D knew enough about the otherworld from Evilyn's first trip to believe it. It certainly wasn't a place he looked forward to going, not that he held any hopes for any other destination.

"You're a better man than you think of yourself, mon fils." Mama's eyes dimmed as she spoke again over the girl's shivering body. "You should speak to the Baron. He waits for you outside."

"I know what he wants. What about her? She may be the only chance we—"

"The only chance to stop The Destroyer?" Mama's eyes flashed at D, sending an icepick down his back. "The Beast shall summon his dark brood. He shall court the destroyer of heaven as his bride. Her likeness deceives, she shares her blood with Belial. Then shall she rise from the depths, an army of the dead at her command, and lay waste to all that stand against her. She is the cataclysm."

D trembled at the thought of it. Red couldn't be the second half of the prophecy—not that sweet, bubble-gum-popping kid who teased him and poked him, rode next to him in his truck on their morning rounds—woke him from a place so deep and dark he'd never thought he could come out of it. How could she be—she couldn't. She just couldn't.

"Tell me this one can be saved. Tell me *one* good thing."

Mama studied Lydia's face, noting the faded markings on her arms. "This one is strong. She fights him even now. She's gone too far. She's already at the thirst. She *will* change. But she may yet walk in the light. She doesn't have to share his curse."

"A dhampyr?" D looked at Lydia, her face full of sweat and tears. He didn't know if she could hear them where her mind was.

"She needs blood now." Mama hovered her hands over Lydia's shaking body, driving out the darkness and cursing it from her sanctuary. D took his jacket off, rolling up the sleeve on his shirt to expose his forearm—even pulling his silver knife from his belt sheath. "No!" Mama's eyes doomed at him. "She must never taste the blood of the innocent, never human flesh. She will live with what she's become, but only if she stays true. Do you hear me, child?"

Lydia's eyes blinked three times, some light coming into them now. She sat up slow, breathing, shaking, terrified. She *had* heard everything. "I'll do what I have to do." She looked at Mama, then to D.

"She must complete the ritual. She must call out the name. She must kneel and serve a master." Mama tossed water she'd blessed in Lydia's face.

"What name?" Lydia asked, her voice cracking.

"You must call the name of the god you will serve. Only the gods can keep your body in the way of the light. Call the name of your god, and *if* they accept you, you will replace Belial's hold with theirs. But you will belong to them, forevermore. You must choose."

"That's easy. I choose Molly. You said she's a god, right? I choose Molly."

"That is not her name." Mama's face grew grim at Lydia. "You must call the name of your god."

Lydia closed her eyes, started to cry. D shook his head. He'd seen it once already, gone through these same motions—all for nothing. Cain had taken Evilyn in the end—his allure, his dark charm, the offer of his power too much to resist. But D had hope for this kid. He didn't know why he had a single drop left after all he'd seen, but he did. Red gave him that, for better or worse. She made him hope again.

"That one. Her." Lydia pointed at the stained-glass images around the room in Mama's sanctuary—gods, saints, the Loa, the Fae. Spirits abounded in the room. Even D felt their presence. He'd never called the name of any god in his life, and he wasn't about to start now.

"That one?" Mama studied the image of a gruesome figure, her black feather-gown flowing into darkness beneath her, the shroud covering her face, her deep black hair flowing from underneath, the murder of crows surrounding her as she stood above the corpses of battle-slain warriors. "The Phantom Queen? You are sure?"

D flinched at the choice, looking to Mama B's face for some reassurance. None came.

"Yes. I saw her in my book. I remember her. I don't know why, but—she's the one. I'm sure."

"Then say the name, child."

* * *

D couldn't stay for the rest of it. They brought in a nutria rat for Lydia to drink—it was all too much. He'd seen more than enough to dispel any doubt of the veracity of them all—gods, demons, angels, spirits, Fae, the lot of them. It wasn't that he didn't believe in them—it was that *they* were the cause of so much of the awful in the world. *They* were the reason Cain existed in the first place.

"Wasn't *we* that made him." D felt the coarse voice waft over his shoulders—a feeling of anxiety and calm wrapped together in a blanket of contradiction. "And you know that."

"Get out of my head, Saturday." D turned to face the Baron—his stovepipe hat adorned his sugar-painted face. He pulled the cigar from his mouth and placed a hand on D's shoulder.

"You don't have to fight alone. I will come if you call me." The Baron nodded to D with respect. "But you have to call my name."

"Why?" D pulled away from the Loa. "Why can't you just help on your own? Why *must* I bow?"

"Yhwh says to bow. I never do. Just say my name."

D looked back to the house. The kid better be okay in there.

Both kids better be.

III
"NOCTURNAL ME"
–ECHO & THE BUNNYMEN, 1984

THE SLEDGEHAMMER SOARED above the murky, moonlit bogs sprawling across the horizon beyond the lights of the Crescent City. She felt the night wrap around her as she left the world of humans behind, gliding on the wind into the dark world of Belial Cain. Sounds of the night creatures crept up to her keen ears. Frogs, cicadas, the sluicing of gators, the hooting of owls—and *others*. She sensed, somewhere deep in the swamps, restless souls—angry, forgotten, abandoned. They called to her, dragging her mind down, weakening her resolve. It—they, this place— all reminded her of the otherworld, that icy hell.

Her sandaled feet slammed down upon the earthen path, shaking the roots of the cypress trees under the muddy waters. A twisting array of rocks, roots, crags, and stumps formed what amounted to the path toward Cain's grim, towering castle. If the wicked king wanted his stronghold hard to find and even harder to get to, he'd succeeded.

She studied the towers rising out of the mire. Heavy builders—a team of cyclopes from the look of them—carried titanic amounts of stone, handing them off to some darker, tentacled creature even Molly's eyes couldn't fully see. They sang as they plodded along in their labors, a grisly cacophony wafting up into the waning night sky. Dawn drew near, though she knew that only affected Cain and his converts. His blood-born children were immune to that.

A shrieking cackle pierced Molly's ears. She winced from the sound but already had the laser-sharp tip of her spear pointed dead center at the creature's face slithering at her from the shadows of the night—a great, bulbous head, angled, pointy features. A nose that hooked downward like a drooping spike. Black hair slick with swamp mud and slime. A pallid, greenish, translucent skin, overwrought with warts, knots, pustules, and tumorous growths. Jagged teeth formed a sinister smile as long spindly arms, coming out all over her elongated torso, dangled in the air like tree limbs waving in the wind. As her abdomen disappeared back into the waters, Molly saw the swishing, wiggling tentacles waving up in arcs all around her and understood they were all part of the same whole of this creature.

"Someone's come to my peat bog." Her shrill voice broke the sounds of the lesser beasts. "What succulent treat is this?" She gestured her cragging, bony fingers at Molly's face.

Molly slit her eyes, eager to slice this hag into chum for her own vipers. But the voices, their sad cries, pleading, *praying*—they clung to her mind, pulling her down, weighing her soul, crushing her spirit, her will to fight. *What is this place?* She thought, shaking her head out of the stupor.

"You hear them, don't you?" the swamp hag stretched two of her many arms outward. "What sweet somber they sing. Forgotten, all. They wander here, my little pets now. Will you join them?"

"MEGGOTH!" A booming voice deafened across the night. Molly turned her blade in its direction, knowing it the truer threat. Cain formed before her, his grim armor avoiding the moon's glow—a being darker than dark itself doomed his way toward them. Only his head, his face—the face of Germain—was uncovered. "This is our guest, daughter. She is to be treated with the utmost respect. Be gone with you now."

Meggoth, *his daughter,* of course—she sneered her hag face at Molly and withdrew her spindly limbs, skulking back from whence she came—but leering back at Molly through the rising fog.

"You honored your word." Cain curtsied to the god. There was no deceit in him now, his malice subdued beneath the sincere contentment on his lips which neither smiled nor grimaced.

"I am bound to it." Molly accepted the offer of his hand as he guided her across the crags toward the looming keep. "But you already knew that."

"I did."

"And yet you only asked for an audience, not more?" Molly lowered her eyes at his back as he walked, her spear never less than a whisper from his neck—though now wasn't her moment.

"You wouldn't have agreed to more." He walked on, leading her softly to the gates of the castle.

"You're right." She glanced back into the marshlands, their searing sounds rising again. She held her blade at his throat, which merely amused him. "I wouldn't."

"You will." His fangs poked down from his smile. "You'll see."

IV
"IF I COULD TURN BACK TIME"
—CHER, 1989

MURPHY BLINKED ONCE as the man in the straw hat took her by the shoulder. She opened her eyes to flashes of energy all around her, the shape of some long winding tube pulling her through a formless void, every color of the rainbow flowed past her eyes as she blinked again.

Then she stood, surrounded by old wooden houses, people scurrying about their day, carrying loads on their backs or behind them in small carts. A team of goats ran past her, herded along by a pair of girls no older than ten. Cool wind blew her twists away from her face as she saw above her the snow-capped mountains on all sides of the horizon.

"What the—" She stared at the people again, the place, some village. "Where am I?" She turned to the solemn figure in the straw hat.

"Less important where as when." His deep voice echoed as he placed his hand on her shoulder again. "Look for who you already know. They will guide you on your path."

"Who I already—What the f—Dude, I've never been here. I don't know where here is, I was—" Murphy shook her head in mind-bending confusion. She'd just been standing on Canal Street. Then the rainbow tunnel. Now she stood in some Asian alpine village without any power lines—a detail she'd quickly noted to the further sinking of her gut. "Look you gotta—"

"I'll see you again." He took his hand off her shoulder. His eyes went white. "At the end."

And he was gone.

Murphy shook again, blinking a dozen times to be sure she was awake. She checked her watch over and over as if it would jar her from this awful dream. *Was that it? That damn witch spelled me under some illusion? Fuckass Jareth.* Murphy flinched at the image of her reporter friend Alex turning into some beast.

Her second hand ticked by, the wind getting to her as she still wore only her street clothes from before. She put a foot in front of the other, picked a direction and moved. She watched the faces around her for some kind of clue. They wore drab outfits, though some color hung here and about. Paper lanterns adorned lines strung across the narrow streets. Merchants sold wares and food outside their storefronts. A blacksmith beat his hammer not far ahead.

"Look for who you already know?" Murphy muttered as she rolled the sleeves of her jersey shirt down over her arms. "The fuck am I supposed to know in this place?"

The clinking of ivory on ivory tinkled from down the adjacent alleyway. Voices cursed in some other language, and some teens carried off their defeat as they drudged past her toward some other part of their lives.

Murphy wandered down the path, seeing an older man shaking a cup and pouring out something like dominoes or dice, she couldn't tell.

"Excuse me, um—I'm sorry, I don't speak Chinese." Murphy didn't know why she even spoke out loud.

"That's fine. We're not in China." He looked up, holding the cup toward her, his bright smiling face a little scruffier than before, but still very much the same man. "Pour the bones?"

"Victor?" She balked, spinning her mind in a circle. The little man that waited for her every morning outside Lee's Laundry off Bourbon the last few months.

"Victor? I've never been called that before." He shook his cup again and poured out his pieces, apparently intrigued by what they told him.

"That's... your name, is it not?"

"I have been called many names, for many years. I've been called Mahakaya, others say the great Kong. Some even call me Monkey—can you believe that?" He laughed and shook his *bones* again. "You name us into existence, tell our tales—wilder all the time, I might add. Then you go and change our names as it suits you. Now I suppose I am called Victor—as good a name as any. What does it mean?" He looked in her eyes. She felt him searching in her—digging into her soul.

"I uh... I don't know what it—" Murphy curled one lip at the nonsense of all this, trying to keep her brain from turning to goop and falling out her ears. "Something like winner, I think, maybe."

"Ha." He rattled his cup. "That's true, then. I never lose this game."

"Look, this is all weird, and I don't know where I am or why I'm here. Some guy in a hat brought me here, and there were all these vampires and a witch and Cain or some guy and—"

"It's you?" Victor put his bones and cup away. He stood up and looked her over. She started to kind of see the whole monkey thing as she studied him, his stance, his movements, the way he crouched as he walked around her—as if he'd never seen her before.

"It's me who?"

" *You* are the one who is chosen?" He asked himself more than he did her.

"I? What?" Murphy blinked—hoping this time would be the blink home. "I, the chosen what?"

* * *

She wrapped the long coat tighter around her, cinching the rope belt at her waist lest it blow open from the wind howling as loud as those creatures from Canal Street—those cops. She kept reminding herself they were the cops. A whole city—

its entire system—so far gone it had been corrupted at every level by pure evil. And the Copperhead had told her they weren't the only one. She thought of that governor from Germain's big party. How high did it all go? Hogan? Higher? She shivered more at the thought than the cold, but both bit into her face as she marched up the long stairs.

"Climb the path up the white mountains; they wait for you there," Victor had told her as he'd pointed above the village into the misty mountains north of them.

"Who?" she had asked him.

"The Order of the Dragon." Then he wisped away into nothing and nowhere, just like straw-hat guy that ditched her here—wherever *here* was. Not China was the only clue she had. That didn't narrow it much.

Motherfucking hat guy could at least let me get my Sony from the scrapyard on the way, she thought somewhere into the second hour of the long climb. The stone steps of the path sometimes crumbled under her feet. She had to move, else the stones would steal the warmth through the thin soles of her Converse.

Two hours—maybe three—into the climb, the temple came into her view. It looked like something out of a dream—some long-forgotten primordial memory. The green-tiled canopies hung in layers off the rising red-stone tower from all sides. Soon she heard their voices carrying across the air from the courtyard, sounds she recalled from her childhood. She could almost hear Hǔ Quán—her father's voice echoing through the years at her as they counted out their movements. She eased herself through the gates and stood watching them for a moment, all lined up, their robes identical to each other's. Fists flung themselves forward, then retracted. They moved to horse stance, then true to their name, went to dragon. Their master watched over them, his robe white to their red. He had a shaved head. He wasn't particularly tall or muscular, but then, none of them were.

"Stop!" he shouted, and they bowed, standing with arms to their sides. The Master turned to Murphy looking on at their training, as though she'd broken some ancient rule. *You probably did, Murphy,* she cursed herself. "Announce yourself, intruder!" He made a fist and pointed it at her. The other monks turned to face her.

"I'm uh—" She was more confused that she understood them and wasn't sure what to say.

"I told her to come, Makoto." Victor walked out from behind the Master.

Murphy closed her eyes and wanted to kick the old man. *Could have just magicked me up those damn stairs, you wizard god asshole, or whatever you're supposed to be.*

"She has come to claim the Open One, to fulfill the prophecy." Victor winked at Murphy.

"This?" Makoto sneered, waving her to approach him. Murphy shrugged and moved through the group of monks, most of them gawking at her, her outfit, her hair. There wasn't much about her that didn't look as alien as Alf to them. "This is the one who is chosen?" He poked at her hair, fingered the cloth of her Detroit jersey.

"Look, old dude or whoever—" Murphy cocked her head at the shot-caller. "I don't—"

"Silence!" His voice boomed.

Victor laughed. "You believe I jest?" Victor pulled an apple from his pouch and bit it.

"You are known for it, Sun Wukong." Makoto wrinkled his lip at the old man, then again more so at Murphy. Whispers from behind her told of their fascination with the idea. "She cannot possibly face the guardian, much less the everliving beast. This—" Makoto walked around her like she was spoiled cheese. "This is to be our champion, our greatest and *final* warrior? She will face the son of the demon? *Her?*" He said it like she was nothing. She wanted to box the man's face so bad—put him on the ground.

"Look, dude, I—"

"Silence!" He spat as he shouted at her. "And look how old she is."

Who you calling old, old timer? I will knock you sideways, you punkass punk.

"No. She cannot be the one. Too old. She is too old to begin the training."

"Begin nothing." Murphy dropped to forward stance, presenting her fist to him. She really wanted him to give her an excuse. She'd show him who was old.

Makoto and Victor both laughed, big belly laughs.

"She has spirit, you must agree." Victor chuckled, patting Makoto on the shoulder.

"I will not train her." Makoto folded his arms. "We have other work to be about. The Hēishǒu Móguǐ have come to the near valleys. We must stand against them."

"And you see this as coincidence?" Victor walked around Makoto and nodded to the other monks. "But perhaps you are right. It need not be you who trains her." He looked at Murph, nodding kindness at her.

"To them, then." Makoto called out to the courtyard, the dozens of monks coming to attention again. "Who among you would take on the task of training this *outsider?*" He glared at Murphy as he said it. She wanted to pop him *one good time.*

"I will." The voice shattered her mind, pouring ice colder than these mountains down her back and punching her harder in the gut than even the bastard in front of her deserved. She didn't want to face him, but she knew she had to. The tears already flowed from her eyes before she saw his face—his much younger face, no more than twenty here, in this place, this time. Her jaw quivered as his moved again. "I will train with her," Hǔ Quán, her father, said as he bowed to her.

V

"SYMPATHY"
–JANE'S ADDICTION, 1987

CAIN'S CASTLE HALLS went in any number of directions, some slanting up or down, even curving. None of it made sense as he led her up a spiraled staircase to her "waiting chamber" where he said she may respite before the evening's ceremony—should she decide to acquiesce to his proposal of their union.

"We've a few moments before the dawn." He stood at her doorway, unable to enter uninvited upon assigning it to her. Molly managed a weak smirk, seeing his feet at the edge of the threshold. "Would you permit me to show you more of the grounds?"

"It's your funeral, chief." Molly gripped her shortened spear in her hand and gestured for him to lead on.

"I think you could leave that behind now, yes?" He raised his eyebrows at her. "Nah."

* * *

He took her first to the great open-space room he called his "grand arcade" where she was told their ceremony would be held. It felt like being inside some gothic cathedral—interlaced great arches stretched high above, the nexus of them forming a dome, like being trapped in a cereal-bowl turned upside down. Molly shrugged at it. The Mall of Louisiana was cooler, but she didn't tell him that.

After the arcade, they wandered the halls again, him showing off his vast collection of artwork through all of history, including times long forgotten. For someone who'd been around a few dozen millennia, Molly wondered if he'd ever been on an actual date. Like, for real all he did was brag about himself. *He might be worse than Blake. Ew, no. At least he's handsome—or appears to be. Blake was a dork.*

He brought her to a giant tapestry hanging from the massive vaulted ceiling. She saw a man, naked, sitting in an orchard while the torso of a woman, also naked, offered him an apple. Her waist morphed into the long coiling tail of a serpent.

"Good old Mom and Dad," Cain glared at the painting like he hated it, or them—probably them, Molly figured. "Do you know the story?"

"I mean something about the apple." Molly rolled her eyes knowing she was in for another lecture. "I never really read much of that bible stuff."

"Just as well. Mostly fiction." Cain moved them along, eager to get them away from the image of his parents, and she wondered which of them he hated more. "It was my mother who seduced the man you call Adam. She hated the *lesser* gods, and Yhwh's little vanity garden vexed her to her core. His perfect place, proof that creatures could exist together without malice, so long as none knew of their true nature—of what horrors lay beyond. Mother meddled. And so, *I* was born. That was my first curse."

He took Molly into the lower levels. She heard grunts, growls, a booming roar. He walked them through a heavy arching doorway into a vast green lawn stretching for acres, an atrium covered by a skylight showing the waning moon. He hadn't long now.

"My bestiary." He waved across the swathes of vegetation as an armadillo the size of a Volkswagen came out of the brush at her. Molly tightened her fist on the Strat-axe, ready to work. "Stay your hand, Shaddai. He's my pet. My Glyptodon. Isn't he fun? His mate is around here somewhere. They've littered recently. Their species survives now for another generation."

A reverberating thud moved closer as Molly's eyes beheld a woolly mammoth above her chewing the branches of a tree. She shook her head twice at it. Cain walked her through the thick brush, patting and speaking to his creatures as they approached him. He touched his head to theirs, scratching their necks or manes. A short-faced bear, as he called it, walked to them and Molly couldn't believe when it hugged Cain. It looked as if it would swallow him whole if it wanted to.

"See, I continued my father's work. Naming them, collecting them. Who do you think told the boatmen of the coming flood? You gods and your wars, never a care of what is lost in the wake. But I—I *loved* them. I always have. That's why, you know."

"Know what?" Molly studied the animals. Some of them she'd read about or seen their bones in the museum when Hoyt took her and her brother Hurl one year.

"My half-brother, Yhwh's favorite. He's always had his favorites, as you know." He wrinkled his face, but Molly definitely didn't know. "For dear daddy's *sin* we had to bring our offerings."

Cain told her the story. How he learned to till the ground, built himself tools from the finest of metals. He'd preferred silver to all the others, even fashioning an ornament from it. A gift, a tribute to the god who ever rejected him. "It's the purest," he told Molly. "It truly is. But the gods of gold and bronze didn't wish to hear that." He learned to manage roots and plants, to grow fruit from the dirt, to bring life where there'd been none. He learned to speak the language of the beasts of the earth and the fowl of the air. He befriended them—something gained from his dark mother, whose name he was never allowed to utter. Father's new wife spat each time she came near him, so he secluded himself further and further away. He knew he was not like his sibling, but he sought approval all the same, both from his father and their *creator.*

"He created nothing. He merely chose two of their kind to raise in his garden. He was always jealous of—well, the rest of you. You, most of all."

"Me?" Molly blinked.

"Your forebears, I should say. The line of El Shaddai, passed from mother to daughter. Always envious of your strength, your power. When the line ended, after the waters subsided, he took the moniker himself, along with others, claiming himself the 'one true god.'" Cain laughed a heavy laugh. "He thought you'd finally all killed yourselves, and he was the only one left. How sad was he when some returned from the fabled Twilight."

"Do you know who I am, who I really am?" Molly's tone softened. She felt in him a deep, eternal sadness—a void he could never fill and had tried more years than she cared to imagine.

"I know your bloodline. They said it died out, but I smell its power in you even now. I do not know your name, but I know whose magic binds you to this false skin and form." He sighed, sitting on a log in his bestiary. "The only one whose power exceeds yours. The last of the Eldar race. My mother."

Molly stared at him for so long she was sure the sun had both come and gone. He kept talking, sharing his story. How his brother slaughtered the beasts of the field, Cain's beloved friends—some the very ones he'd taught to help him in his farming. And then how they all mocked him, father, stepmother, half-brother, even Yhwh, drunk off his own wine.

"He laughed at me while I wept for my friends as they ate them. They tore their flesh from their bones, ripping them into bits, feasting. *He* dribbled wine from his lips as he pointed and laughed—my father, the coward, bowing to him and laughing at me." Cain's fists shook with rage at his memories. Molly wondered how much he'd lost to time. If she could forget every part of her past, how could he recall what happened 10,000 or 20,000 years ago? For that matter, how did anyone remember anything at all? What was time?

"And so, I killed the bastard." Cain stood up, moving further into the atrium. He laughed. "No, I guess I'm the bastard, aren't I?"

And he spoke of the curse he received. Yhwh's rage, drunken, rash, and ill-conceived—he spat his curse at the firstborn son of his pet mortal. *You shall wander the Earth forever in exile. May none give you shelter, nor may you enter where you're not invited. Your precious tools—you Qayin who loves silver, may it be as poison to you. Never again shall you walk in the sun that feeds your grains and fruits, lest it burn your skin to ash, but neither shall you die. May you never die. You will never cross over. You will never be born again. May you suffer forever, your only comfort, your only pleasure shall be drinking the blood from the very beasts you love. And...* He grimaced as he spoke of Yhwh's seething laughter...*may you take on their form as well. May you become what feeds you. Marked for all time as what you are: a beast.*

"And so it was, the sun a cancer to me." He walked Molly to flat grass, heavy stones forming a den wherein a long white tail swished. "I wandered as he said, taking on the form of whatever beast I last drank. But..." He turned and smiled, summoning the creature from its den with clicks from his mouth. "He was not specific as to which creatures I must devour. Any blood will do, and what is sweeter than human blood?" The animal from the den—a great white lion bigger than any horse Molly'd ever seen—joined them, her head hung low, sad-eyed, as she walked to her master. Then, seeing Molly, chose her instead. "She takes to you. That's good."

"She's suffering. What's wrong with her?" Molly let the beast sniff her hand. It licked her and curled at her feet.

"The American Cave Lion, long said extinct, but now she truly will be. Alas, her mate died before they could litter. She is truly the last. She's lost her will without him. Such it is. She will starve herself until she wastes away and joins him in oblivion, their kind erased for all time. Hunted out of existence."

Molly felt bad for the poor feline but knew she could do little to salve its hurt. She glared at Cain, so content with himself, his special hobby. So, what if he saved a few animals? He was a monster.

"What's my part in all this?"

"Don't you see?" He took her by the shoulders, inching his gut boldly close to the tip of her spear. "With your blood, your power, I would walk again in the sun as Evilyn did. Together, we could defy, nay, defeat Yhwh—make him bow before us. And, my mother, we could defeat her together, restore you to your true self. My gift to you as my bride. What say you, El Shaddai? Shall we rule this world arm in arm, side by side, king and queen of all that is?"

Molly looked at the lion, then at her spear. The poor thing deserved a better fate than what lay before it—as did all who'd ever had the misfortune of encountering this vile abomination smiling at her with his hand held out.

"I don't know if you deserved what you got for killing your brother—that's a pretty shitty thing as shitty things go. But man did you lean into that curse. I mean you sure worked to earn it out in spades, buddy. So, fuck you, fuck your stupid loser nerd castle, fuck your would-be king and queen nonsense, and fuck your shitty mom. I'll kick her ass too if I see her."

Cain rose, drawing out his height far above her, his face darkening, the horn on his forehead growing long, jagged as his eyes became black dots, his teeth frothing fangs.

"You dare mock me as they did?" He seethed and spat as he raged at her. "I am Belial Qayin Gallamu, the Ever-Living!"

"And I'm Molly from the Bay, and you can kiss my ass."

VI
"YOU'RE THE BEST"
–JOE ESPOSITO, 1984

MURPHY CARRIED BUCKETS, one on each side of an ox-yoke she hefted across her shoulders, down the winding steps toward the village in the valley below the temple. Down was never the problem. It was the buckets filled with water and the climb back up that got her. They'd woken her before the sun her first day, handed her a bowl of steamed rice with milk, then sent her down the mountain—and back up.

Hǔ Quán worked her harder than he ever had—or was going to—she couldn't wrap her head around it, seeing him as he was now, young, vibrant, full of life and energy. The man she had known had been terrified, shell-shocked, a burnt-out veteran of a war he never spoke of, only mumbled about in his sleep or when he got into his wine.

She sweated through the cold, this far up the topmost rim of the world, all was ice and biting wind. The pain in her back, shoulders, and legs ached her each day by noon. Another bowl of rice, some fruit. Then stances, breathing. Like it was her first day of kindergarten all over again.

"Show me Horse," he said. Murphy planted both feet, dropping to a squat and holding her stance just as he taught her years ago, or would years from now. "Now Crane." She raised one leg parallel to the ground, bent at the knee, foot ready to strike, tucking one arm and presenting her fist forward with the other.

He worked her through all her stances, correcting her where she had gone rusty in the years since...since he died—would die. She shook away the memory and focused on the now. Horse, Forward, Cat, Twist, Crane. Breathing steady, slow, fixating on the forms and the process. Hǔ Quán called out their movements calmly, quietly—gentle as could be. He had been louder when she was a girl, but he wore more intent on his face now.

By sundown, she collapsed into sleep as though she were dead. Then up again before the dawn. Rice. Yoke down. Yoke up. Rice. Forms. Rice. Sleep. Repeat. Soon they added more. Several monks piled in a heavy cart she had to lift upward, pivoting on its wheels. Every week another monk jumped in the cart till it could hold no more. The way her body responded to it frightened her.

Then came the horses—plural. Two heavy draft horses—how they got them up the mountain was a question she wanted to ask but didn't expect a straight answer.

"Hold them back." Hǔ Quán ordered her as he handed her the ropes attached to their harnesses. Makoto and the other monks looked down, all taking a break from their training and chores to watch her look like a fool.

"Do what? How the hell would I hold one, much less two?" She held the rope limp in one hand while looking at her young father's face for some clue, some reasoning as to the sense of any of it.

"Kai shi!" He slapped one on the back and set them trotting. Murphy's end of the rope jerked her along with it. She tried planting her feet but instead planted her face in the snow. They dragged her twenty yards before another command from Hǔ Quán stopped them.

"Again." He called out.

More humiliation as they dragged her around in circles, the clothes they'd given her—the same ones the other monks wore—muddy and filthy from the sludge.

"Again."

And so, it became the new part of her daily ritual. Up before the dawn. Rice. Yoke down. Yoke up. Rice. Lift cart. Dragged by horses. Forms. Rice. Sleep. Repeat.

Within a few weeks, Murphy couldn't name a part of her body that didn't hurt. One day a week, she rested, only practicing forms and some light sparring with her father. He was good, better than she remembered, not that he'd ever gone full metal on his ten-year-old daughter. But this one fought her back as an equal, as a peer. She'd lie if she told herself she didn't enjoy it. She barely remembered the old man's smile, but the young one smiled at her all the time. Every stance, kick, or maneuver she did to his satisfaction earned her a grin, a slap on the back, an extra bowl of rice, and each time, Murphy tried not to beam with pride.

"It's okay to feel it." He told her one afternoon after a blocking session. He and two other monks had thrown rocks, tools, buckets, anything they could pick up and tossed them at her in unison. Murphy had blocked, deflected, and knocked them away from her. A whirlwind of kicks, she had burst through buckets like balsa wood. "You have to believe in yourself first and most of all." He beamed at her. That was a good day.

"The horses, though." She moved to cat stance as they sparred. She circled her opponent, waiting for her opening. He jabbed and she slapped it away. He swept her feet from under her, but she flipped all the way over and put them right back where they belonged. That earned her the biggest smile yet. "What is that about?"

"To make you strong." He fired three kicks at her face, and she deflected them all. "To defeat the Prince of Darkness, you must find your Qi and use its power to hold him."

"What does fighting a man have to do with holding horses?" She feinted as he twisted and flung a leg at her from the side. She leapt into a spinning body twirl as his next kick landed in her grasping arms, flipping him onto the ground.

"But you are not fighting a man." He sprang back with his legs, then flew a punch at her, which she caught and pulled him off his balance. "You are fighting a beast. You are fighting *every* beast that ever walked the earth."

Like...all of them? Murphy didn't dare ask out loud. Because she didn't want to hear the answer.

The next day on the horses, she had another spectator—Victor, or Wukong as the monks here called him, looked on that day as she dug her heels into the cold, wet earth only to get jerked around like a doll. Her arms grew thick and taut as the months went by. How long had she been here? She hadn't kept count. She began to lose sense of where she'd been, the dark city and its demons, all of it a million miles and years from her.

"Close your eyes, Zuìzhōng." Victor's soft voice called to her.

She looked at him, then to her father. Makoto frowned. That lit something inside her. She was so tired of that sneering old prick. She closed her eyes, let her breath out slow, then back in. Out. In. She stood to her feet, eyes closed, breathing steady, calm, perfect.

"Hai!" her father slapped the horse.

The rope jerked tight. Her feet planted. Her breath steady. Her arms lithe and taut. She focused her breathing, her core. She waited for them to jerk her tight, pull her off her feet again. They didn't.

Whispers and wows echoed across the wind. She felt eyes on her even with hers shut. She let out one slow breath and looked. The two draft horses lurched forward, their hooves digging into the earth for purchase, hefting their mighty haunches. She held the rope steady, barely feeling the tension. She breathed, shaking her head, trembling, unsteady. She lost it.

She was back on her face in the snow. Victor's laugh both mocked and praised at once. When she got to her feet this time, Hǔ Quán's eyes looked at her as if for the first time all over again. The others gawked, mouths agape. They told her she had glowed—her whole body awash with blue and red light. Makoto retired to his chamber and did not return that day, nor the next.

The next few days, the other monks trained without him, going through their routines on their own, though with less energy. A strange crow lit upon the edge of the courtyard, watching them. Victor nodded to it, as it did him in return. It stayed and watched Murphy through her training.

At the bottom of the steps, taking her water buckets to the well, Victor met her—the way he just appeared places irked her, though she'd long since made her peace with it, and him, and what he was.

"Go this time without the buckets. Fast as you can." He smiled as he took her burden from her.

She smiled and shook her head, then lest he change his mind, she raced up the mountain. She felt the acid pump into her legs, then closed her eyes, focused her breath, and felt it, that same thing as with the horses, what she'd felt just for a moment on Canal Street when she knocked that sorceress three blocks into a brick wall.

Her legs bounded up several steps each time, the tips of her feet barely touching the edge of stone as they floated her upward each time. She felt like a feather dancing across the air as she fluttered up the last part of the steps.

"Qinggong." Hǔ Quán's eyes saw her feet licking the stones as she flung herself into the air at the top of the steps, her body gliding forward as she descended—as if the air beneath her bent to her will.

Victor smiled and nodded as he handed her the yoke with two full buckets of water, having long beaten her to the top. She smiled and cupped her hand to take a drink as she smiled at her daddy. Many of the other monks stood silent, staring. They put their fists into their palms at her and bowed.

Makoto didn't come again.

"What is the matter with him?" Murphy asked Hǔ Quán over their morning meal.

"It is clear now; you *are* the one who is chosen." He smiled through his own pain at her. It was the first time since arriving she saw the man she'd known as a kid.

"But isn't that a good thing? I don't get it." She searched his face, wanting to ease this new dread written across it.

"It means we have come to the end. Our best is our last. So it is, and was, and shall be. The crow has come with warning. Soon the Black Hands are upon us."

"Then we'll fight them. Together." She held her hand out to her father, desperate for him to take it. But he did not.

"That is not your destiny. Only ours."

* * *

The air high atop the world grew thin. Murphy came to know herself, her body in a way she never had. The trick she'd conjured with the stairs became routine as she did it now even with the yoke, never spilling a drop of water. She danced across the tops of high posts Hǔ Quán set up in the field behind the temple. He stood with her, both in crane stance, one foot balanced on a pole, the other held up, bent at the knee. Murphy flew to the next pole, then the next, kicking her leg high above her head.

The sky grayed as the monks sat longer in their prayers than before. Hǔ Quán grew fiercer in his attacks when they sparred. She feinted and dodged him easily now, and he knew it. She felt him, his angst, his unease at what the future—for both of them—held. He added force behind his attacks, putting all of himself into it, showing her how much he'd always held back. He kicked and punched and leapt at her, trying to knock her down, push her back, break her balance. She followed suit, slamming his blows away from her, parrying everything he had and thrusting palms into his chest, feet into his sides. She wanted him to stop, to tell him it was going too far. The last thing she wanted to do was... Then he roared a crescent moon kick, which Murphy butterfly-parried in return, slamming her leg against the inside of his knee.

She heard the pop before he felt it. He dropped to the ground, grabbing his knee and wincing from the pain.

"Daddy, I'm sorry I didn't mea—I mean—I..." Murphy lost her words. She panicked. She lost her breath. She hyperventilated, looking around her, waiting for Victor or the straw-hat guy to come take her away from this, to turn it all back like it was. "I meant to say I—"

"It's okay, little one." His voice, like it had been back then, like it would still become, soothed her trembling mind.

"You know?" Her eyes wanted to hold the flood but couldn't.

"As soon as I saw you. How could I not?" His face beamed at her.

"Daddy, I'm sorry. I'm so sorry. You were right. You were always right." Her words fired at him like a machine gun, dumping everything unsaid for the last fifteen years, pouring out all her guilt, her shame, her sorrow, all onto the back of this poor twenty-year old kid who wouldn't father her yet for another decade to come. "I love you. You must know that. I do. I promise, no matter what I'm gonna say back then, or later, or, I—I love you, Daddy. I promise."

"I know." His eyes lit for her. "And I will *always* know."

Murphy grabbed her father so hard she worried she would crush him. She never wanted to leave him again.

VII

"I STILL BELIEVE"
—TIM CAPELLO, 1987

LYDIA MARCHED THROUGH the doors of Dave's Occult Bookstore in Jackson Square. D watched her walk over the salt line like she was any normal person and breathed the heaviest sigh of relief. Mama's ritual had worked—so long as the kid held true and never drank the life of another human. In some ways she had the best of both worlds, their strength, cunning, changing abilities, but also walking in the light, going where she pleased, immune to silver. It had been Evilyn's grand plan, the first of many best laid. But Evilyn fell to the Beast's charm in the end—his pull, his sinister allure too strong even for her dominant will. D feared for the kid, more so for the redhead in the devil's den that very morning.

The day faded as night rose again over The Quarter. Lydia went straight for the same grimoire she'd bought her first night in the city—a novelty purchase that saved her life on the other side—some of which she'd explained to D, adding in details he'd never heard from Evilyn before—but Evilyn had always preferred her secrets. He wondered how many died with her.

"Sure I can't interest you in some other stuff? I got some real interesting finds in the back." Dave the shopkeeper pushed his glasses up as he read the cover of the book she had in her hand.

"Someday maybe. But I already learned this one." Her eyelids flitted as they'd done more than once since the sun set. D knew it meant she heard *His* call, the whispers on the night, a dark language shared by those who had felt his teeth. "And we're a little pressed for time."

* * *

They holed up at Buck's shotgun house off Esplanade now that the Scrapyard was burned. D hadn't yet gone back to see about the Falcon, if it could be flipped and would still run. The kid's Chevy dually rolled them fine for now.

Buck and Callum watched Lydia flip through her new book, taking a permanent marker and writing down the gibberish from the pages onto the fading ink on her skin.

"Is that Old Irish?" Al Davenport squinted at the marks on her forearms.

"Welsh, actually." Lydia flipped the book shut as she finished the work on her arms. Then she grabbed the phone.

"What's all this about?" Boudreaux looked to D.

"She wants to go get her friend back." D shook his head.

"That ain't happening. That shit's locked down tighter than Knox, hell, more than the damn Pentagon. That's Hanoi times a thousand, Sergeant. We're damn lucky to have lived through last night."

"Ain't asking y'all to come with. Ain't your fight this time."

"Hell it ain't." Colonel Carthage stood up, his eyes clear and awake for once.

"D's right." Buck hung his head, handing the revolver to D butt first—the one that still held the magic bullet—their one shot to kill a god.

"What's this?" D didn't take the gun. Buck held it out all the same.

"She can't let him have her blood—her power. He'll be unstoppable after that. If it comes to it, D..." Buck's eyes watered.

"It won't come to that." Lydia glared at the old soldiers making their plans without her. She cranked the dial on the wall phone next to the kitchen. "She won't let him. I have faith in her."

"This is crazy." Boudreaux swore.

"She brought me back from that frozen hell. I'm bringing her back from *Him*." Lydia held the receiver to her head. "Hello? Ms. Clair? ... Yeah, it's me, how are you? ... Yeah, is, um, Molly there?"

D stared in confusion as the other men mouthed the name *Molly* back to him with a question mark at the end of it.

"What do you mean she's on a *date*?" Lydia shouted into the phone. "Oh my— nevermind. I'm sorry, Ms. Clair, I'm sorry. I know. Look, can you give her these numbers when she gets back? Tell her it's really, REALLY, important." Lydia called out her numbers twice, then hung up the phone and sighed. "Guess it's just us."

"So, what's the plan?" The Colonel asked.

"Simple. We march right in and get her." Lydia popped her neck.

"Simple." D blinked at her.

"The night whispers say there's to be a black wedding. All the creatures of the night, the strange and unusual are commanded to attend." Lydia smiled as she then whispered in Welsh, her fingertips alighting themselves in dim blue flame. "I also happen to be strange and unusual."

VIII

"DANCING WITH MYSELF
—BILLY IDOL, 1981

THE GOD STARED at the girl in the mirror as she fixed her hair how she wanted it—how she thought it should look. She studied her features, this face, this image, the one they called Molly. Molly Slater. A name as good as any other, but the god knew it was not hers, had never been truly hers. Somewhere beyond, out there in the chasms of this world and others lay buried the truth—her truth. Who she was. What she was. She thought she had made her peace with it the night of prom, as her enemy lay beaten beneath her pink boots. But it gnawed at her now as the girl in the mirror touched up her face, making ready to go into the atrium for the ceremony—though that had yet to be decided. *Could he be telling the truth? Could he help her find her true self? Was it worth the price?*

"He makes *some* good points, doesn't he?"

The girl in the mirror looked back into the room with no one else visible. The voice, so much like her own, yet so very much—not her own, spoke back. "If you say so." She went on fixing herself. She looked into the mirror at the black dress hanging behind her. His new sorceress, Chélicère, had brought it by earlier.

"Should you accept his offer," the sorceress had said. The redhead took the gown and smirked at the conjurer who was clearly jealous of The Beast's choice of bride. Perhaps she had ambitions of her own.

But here, in the final hours before the ceremony, she lingered on the dilemma. She knew what she *wanted* to do. But what of her own life? Would she ever reclaim what was lost, taken from her? Blake's last words haunted her mind. *The bringer of sorrows,* he'd said. *The mother of demons.* Cain spoke of his mother, the serpent, the demon, the mother of monsters. How she'd come to him again in his exile, made herself his wife, bore true abominations from their unholiest of unions.

Surely, he had such intentions from *their* union. Even if she were to...would they come out...? She shivered at the thought.

"Why is everyone always trying to marry you?" The girl at the mirror asked her.

"I don't know, but it really sucks." The god's voice echoed through the room, everywhere and nowhere both.

"The dress is pretty, though, isn't it?" She looked at it again, hanging there. A black bliaut—it was long, stretching to her toes. Its high, stiff, aggressive collar rose above her head. Its ruffs at the shoulders puffed out thick. It had lace down the front, a triangle cut in the back.

The girl at the mirror reached to touch it, but it rose as if by its own will, though she knew better than that. She knew exactly what force held it as it mimicked a dance, twirling and waltzing, mocking her, enticing her, charming her.

"I've never worn a wedding dress." She told the other voice.

"Would you like to?" the voice said back to her. Her voice. But not her.

She curtsied to the flowing gown, the two bowing to each other as they began their own rendition of the courtly ritual. Would there be dancing at this ceremony? The girl from the mirror so loved to dance. But, she wasn't sure of that part. There would certainly be blood. He'd said as much. There must be a blood sacrifice. Each must taste the fresh blood of a living thing. The last great lion would cease its lonely suffering for *Her* to drink. He, of course, would drink of his bride, so long as she provided the open wound which only her Eldritch spear could produce, a thing that never left her hand. The others in this wicked castle gave her a wide berth as she travelled about the halls holding it. They knew what she was, and what it would do to them. Many had seen firsthand what happened to the Jester Queen. All others had heard the tale.

They danced and twirled, the girl and the dress with the invisible hands moving it, consumed in the moment with their own passions, hopes, fears, uncertainties. The music she loved echoed in her head, music she'd once imagined herself playing to packed bars. Was that still a thing she saw herself doing? No, she'd given that life away in the otherwold. She knew she had another destiny. Was this it? Was she to be the great destroyer, the Queen of Darkness to his Prince? Surely, he didn't imagine himself Lord over her? Or perhaps he did. She would soon cure him of that delusion.

The innocent girl and the dress danced on, one song bleeding into the next as she watched them, separate, outside it all. That's what she was—outside them. That sweet girl dancing made her so happy. She wanted nothing but joy for that child. She'd earned it. But the one watching her could never be truly like them. Nor should she be. She was a god. Perhaps even *the* God.

The girl twirled once more to gaze in the mirror, only now she wore the dress on herself. Her hair hung in ringlets down each side of her face, her body filling out the dress, its darkness wrapping around her, becoming part of her.

"So, we're doing this?" She asked the invisible one.

"I suppose we are." Her voice said back to her.

She walked to the door and opened it. A servant stood sentry in the hall, lest she tried to slip away—not that he could do much against her. But Cain would sense the death, and he would know.

"Tell him I said okay." She motioned him closer. "But under one condition."

"What be that, my lady?" The servant's voice cracked as she smiled at him, their faces, her spear's tip, both too close for his comfort.

"Tell him I want to kill the lion."

IX
"THE EAGLE LANDS"
—PAUL HERTZOG, 1989

MURPHY TOSSED IN HER BUNK, her body drenched in a cold sweat. She hadn't had a night like this since she first got to the temple—which felt like a year ago, maybe longer. They didn't keep time in this place. She still didn't know what country she was in. Not that it mattered.

In her studies, she'd learned some of the first cities had been started by Cain, the son of a mortal man and an Eldar god. *He* was the reason the order formed. He'd long worked in the shadows, only free to walk the world at night. He'd set up so many puppet demagogues, kings, emperors. And when they dared defy him, think themselves above him, he cut them down. He'd raised up empires only to tear them down again. Legends and tales of him and his acolytes were written on the various scrolls here in the temple, some of which she'd read during her few quiet moments.

But tonight, her mind would not quiet. She got out of bed, put on her own clothes again for the first time since she couldn't remember. Her jeans were both tighter and looser at the same time. Her jersey shirt stretched its seams at her shoulders and across her back, but it held well enough. She tied the laces on her Converse and went out for a run. She wanted to feel normal again, to taste some bit of the memory of her life before...this.

She ran into the courtyard. She leapt off the ground and flew to the tiled rooftop. So much for normality. Her Qinggong was second nature now. She floated down the other side of the temple. She ran to the treeline toward the high peak of the mountain looming over them. They'd never taken her to this side of the grounds before. She felt like exploring it.

The cold nipped at her ears, but nothing like it had that first trek up the long steps. She ran at a tree trunk and all the way up it, bounding atop the branches, lifting herself off them as she floated from one to another, flinging herself from tree to tree through the woods. She reached a clearing just at the foot of a tall cliff in the mountainside and crane-floated to the ground.

She saw Victor and her father sitting in front of a cave in the cliffside—sitting, talking—as if they'd been waiting for her.

"I told you." Victor patted Hǔ Quán on the shoulder, standing to meet Murphy. Her father's sad eyes—the ones she knew too well—stared back at her through the dim light of the moon.

"What's this?" She looked at them. Hǔ Quán approached her and bowed with respect. "Someone tell me what's happening. Please?"

"Your destiny has led you here. It's time, Tu di."

"No. I can't go in there. I can't... I'm–" She looked in her father's face for reassurance, for him to tell her it was okay, that she didn't have to go. Like when she'd been sick and didn't go to school. Like when her mother went through her religious phase, wanting to talk about saints and devils, and Hǔ Quán told her she shouldn't worry about any of that–*yet.* "I'm not ready, Daddy. I'm not."

"You are, Zuìzhōng."

"No, I can't–I can't fight him. I can't fight The Devil–he's like the actual damn Devil. I can't do it."

"You're the only one who can." Hǔ Quán hugged his daughter for his first and her last time. "Our best is our last."

She gripped him hard, not wanting to let him go.

"It's time." Victor touched her on the shoulder. He pointed at the cave.

"What–" She looked into the dark entrance, then back to her father and Victor. "What's in there?"

"Your final test."

She stared into the void, then back at her father. "I love you, Daddy!"

"I know. I will always know." His pride flowed from his face into her, making her stronger than she'd ever felt in her life.

Murphy nodded him a final goodbye and stepped into the darkness. She crept through the dank, rocky footing of the narrow cavern. Soon the faint light from outside faded to pure black. She felt with her feet, put her hands against the wet, craggy walls.

"I can't see," she said, though to whom she wasn't sure.

"There is light when you want it." Victor's voice echoed through the corridors.

"Victor?" She looked around but couldn't see a lick. "Are you–what light?" His voice didn't offer any additional help. "Thanks."

She went on, relying on touch and sound to guide her. She worried any second she'd step off in a hole to nowhere. She struggled to figure out what he meant by light when she wanted it. Then her foot set down and found nothing beneath it. She crouched and felt with her fingers–a ledge, whatever lay beyond it a mystery.

"What now?" She felt along the walls, hoping for some other hint from her mysterious non-guide. She racked her brain, listened around her, looking for any clue as to what to do next. Then she remembered. She reached in her back pocket and pulled out a book of matches she'd put there once upon a forgotten time back in New Orleans. She struck one, praying they still worked. Its tiny fire lit the chasm before her. A series of wooden posts loomed across the long empty space between her and the next corridor.

"O-kay..." Murph sighed, looking at the long, crooked line of posts. "Guess I just hop across then, huh? Here we go."

She jumped to the first post. A cry rang out to her left. A ghostly form shrieked at her, knocking her nearly off balance as the match blew out. She fumbled to strike another as more wails and howls came at her. Then the post beneath her gave way, the wood splintering under her foot. She leapt for the next one, taking it on faith she remembered where it had been. She exhaled when her foot landed. She felt her heart beating, erratic—her breath all over the place.

The second post crumbled. *So, it's gonna be like that, is it?* She swore and jumped again, blind into hope. She dropped the matchbook into the nothingness beneath her. Ghost shrieks tore at her mind. She caught her breath, put it back in rhythm. She closed her eyes. Her mind focused, remembered where each post had been—and she ran across them, her feet barely whispering to them with each step. She floated through the air just as she'd done across the treetops. When she got to the end, she flipped onto the ledge into the next corridor.

"That all you got?" She cocked her shoulders.

She followed the dark corridor into nowhere. This one inclined—she felt herself climbing higher into the bowels of the mountain. The shrieks of whatever demons or spirits lay behind her grew faint, only to be replaced by a pounding growing louder above her.

Next time just shut your mouth, Murphy, she told herself, knowing whatever made that noise was waiting for her—and would be terrible.

Light whispered back into her eyes, showing the outlines of the rocks and the path before her. It came in waves, flickering every few seconds, leaving glimmers as she followed the path upward until she came upon a large round chamber. Sparks fell from holes in the ceiling, extinguishing themselves as quickly as they appeared. She saw armor stands placed all over the room, dozens of them from all over the world. She recognized some—Crusaders, Romans, Greeks, Samurai, Vikings, Conquistadors, Persians. Many more she didn't know, but all were impressive—ornate, well-crafted, beautiful. They glimmered as the sparks illuminated them.

"Now what?" She squinted to peer through the throng of metal and leather suits.

"Only the one who is chosen may put on the armor of the gods. Only with the armor of god may she face the burning staff of the stone guardian and claim the Dǎkāi yīgè, the Open One." Victor's apparition came from nowhere, flickering as the sparks fell through his ethereal form.

"Which one is it?" Murphy stared back at Victor who she knew was an illusion.

"You must choose. And then you must face him."

Murphy looked around again, all the armors, all the different styles, so impressive, all of them. One rack stood empty. "I'm guessing that person chose poorly."

"None has ever made it this deep into the mountain." Victor's form faded.

"None?" Murphy shouted, trying not to panic. She steadied her breathing again, the pounding above her growing louder, stronger. "None?" She looked around the room, studying each piece. Which one? How would she even get it all on? Most of them looked like they needed a team of servants to bolt on and tie down. *Come on, Murphy, think. Armor of gods? What gods? Like what does a god even need with armor?* Murphy laughed to herself as she remembered Molly pulling out her denim cutoff jacket with the rainbow stripes. Just any old off-the-rack Jordache from some no-name mall. *Molly! Molly's a god. She doesn't wear armor. Why would she?*

"It's none of them." Murphy told the empty room. Victor was already gone. She heard her father's voice in her head again from when she was a girl. *Remember, Murphy. You're the weapon. You have the power.*

She ran up the next leg of the cave, this time curving as it climbed, taking her in a half-circle to another vast open room above the armory. There stood a massive, hulking stone monkey statue. Or maybe it was an ape. Murphy hadn't studied her primates enough. Either way it was big, twice her height. It held a massive iron staff in one hand, pounding it onto the cave floor beneath them. The ground shook with each slam, sending sparks everywhere like dancing sprites across the air.

The great ape roared as she entered its domain. It held up its staff in both hands above its head, lighting it up with flame as it bore down on her. Murphy didn't think. She threw her arm up in a block as she knelt to the ground to absorb the blow. The room lit up around her. Light burst in all directions, bright glowing blues and reds flickering off every surface in the room. She looked above her. Her arm had stopped the flaming rod. The iron monkey shrank to her size, laughing as its form altered into one she'd come to know.

"Victor?" She stared at him, then looked at her arm blocking his staff. It glowed. Her fist, bright as the sun, flowed with red and blue energy down her arm, into her shoulder, her chest. She stood, looking down—the light emanated from her whole body.

"Now you understand your power?" Victor turned, leading her to the far end of the room. Another smaller rod—barely a foot across with a fierce, barbed hook at each end—lay across a rack on a stone table. "Take it."

Murphy lifted the weapon, lighter than she thought from its size. She took it in both hands, turning it over. "I don't understand. How will this stop him?"

"Before the oceans drank Atlantea, there was an age now long forgotten. Unto this, a great beast was born who would swallow the Godking whole in one bite. And so they bound him—with this. But when the Twilight came, the beast's mother set him free, casting his bond into the aether. It fell to this world, and so became the Order of the Dragon its keeper. For as it held one great beast, so will it bind his brother, that cursed son of Mother Night, for she is the bringer of sorrows and the mother of demons."

Murphy pulled the weapon apart, revealing a thin length of finely crafted chain. It grew out as long as she stretched the handles at either end, shrinking back as she closed her grips again.

The man with the straw hat flowed into the room, a door into the void left open behind him. Victor nodded and bowed to Murphy.

"I get the feeling you're handy with that stick, Vic. Want to come with?"

"I stand guard here, at this gate. But when the horn blows, I shall join the fight." Victor nodded.

"More riddles." She shook her head, joining Legba.

"It's time," Legba said.

"Let's rock and roll."

X
"POISON"
—ALICE COOPER, 1989

LYDIA LED HER FURRY FRIEND along the root-woven path arranged for the creatures of the night as they arrived en masse for their master's ceremony. Many of them greeted one another by flashing their fangs under the light of the moon. Lydia flashed hers in return, signaling herself as one of their own.

The Copperhead sweated despite the chill on the moor. Lydia knew he doubted her spell giving him the guise of a northern sasquatch; the illusion of all that bristling hair shrouded the armored knight underneath it, fingers licking the pistols at his shoulders, even the one tucked at his belt—the one Lydia asked him *not* to bring.

Lydia believed in Molly.

"This is beyond insanity."

"Keep walking. Nothing out of the ordinary. Just two hell-creatures no different than any other." She whispered through her teeth.

She led them into the castle, through the gothic archways, along the hallways. Goblins scurried about—up to the master's business. Armor-clad higher vampires patrolled the corridors, stopping some of the more gangrel beings to inspect them.

A floating head with a hundred eyes hovered beyond them. Men with pig's noses shoved their way through as the hallway opened into the great arcade. The moon shone down on the gathered array as the black mass was set to begin.

Human-shaped beings with tentacles growing from their heads congregated nearer the center. Another sorceress entered the arcade. Lydia sensed her, they each other. This one was weaker than Evilyn, who'd cast her into the land of mist. Lydia's memory had returned, recalling how the two-tone-haired witch sent her into that tundric realm the night of the gala. Evilyn had seen the bite marks on her wrist and opened the doorway. "It's a better fate than becoming his slave—as I did," she had said and pushed Lydia through the portal. Now both sets of memories fought over the real estate of her mind. She looked to her arms, studying the words written on them—her primary set of spells she remained confident she could cast, most of them defensive or evasive. Right now, it took all her concentration to hold D's disguise. Everything depended on finding Molly fast and getting out before they were discovered.

"What is your name, caster?" The other witch approached them, her eyes suspicious.

"I am Oona." Lydia glared back at the vampire witch. "This is my companion, LaGaffe."

The two sorceresses looked over each other a moment longer, Lydia sensing the jig was up and wondering if she was up to the fight. The clang of a heavy gong burst the tension as the other witch faced the sound.

A sad roar echoed through the arcade. A mongrel trio led a giant white lion as big as a horse. They brought it to an altar in the center of the arena. The boom of leaden hooves reported Cain's entrance. His horn protruded above all others present for the dark ritual. His thick, wine-red arms ended in dark claws as his ferocious fangs bore his laughter into the choir of voices. They quieted before him. Somber music played from the bone horns of a demonic band along the high arches—their sound bouncing off every surface in the arena.

The Beast gestured his hand toward the dim hallway he'd come from.

"Rise!" He commanded his minions. "For the Queen of the Dead comes! Behold, my bride."

Lydia's eyes blinked three times as the black-clad Molly strode into the room. Her gothic gown trailed behind her, its high collar rising above her crimson hair. Her eyes masked themselves behind thick shadow and mascara. Her lips black, she wore a flat expression. Her eyebrows furrowed as she entered the arena, scanning the room.

"Bow to your queen." Her voice boomed louder than *His* had. Lydia saw the beast wince at her metallic sound. All knees bent as she marched forward, taking her place at Cain's side. Her right hand gripped her weapon.

"That's your friend? In that?" Copperhead whispered through his false face.

"Not her usual style, I admit. Though I'd rock that dress all day."

"I can't let her give him her blood. I can't." Copperhead touched the butt of his revolver with the magic bullet. Lydia's gut turned over. She couldn't believe her own eyes.

"Trust your heart, not your eyes." She put her hand on D's, nudging him away from the godkiller gun. "We have to believe in her."

The beast stretched his form higher than everyone in the room, even the cyclopes that had not gone unnoticed by the pilgrims in the unholy land.

"Hear me." His voice bellowed, bouncing all over the great arcade. "You creatures of the darkness, sons and daughters, all—by blood or by ritual, my acolytes. Descendants of our Mother Night—may she accept you in her dark embrace. For she has come unto us now, bringing forth her cold death. But we offer her this sacrifice." He waved his talon at the whimpering lion with little will left to live. "And through this matrimony, the union of our houses, along with the blood of the last of this breed, may her fierce appetite be sated, our realms spared this icy doom. I pray you, Mother, accept our sacrifice. Bless this union with cessation of your assault on this mortal realm and its stock, our fodder!"

Nervous laughter emanated from the congregation as Lydia studied Molly's face for some sign, some clue as to what to do—something to hang her faith on. Molly's eerie gaze rose toward the arches. Lydia followed her eyeline, looking for...anything. But she saw nothing save the moon's light.

"Do you, El Shaddai, the great destroyer, take me, Belial Qayin, as your Lord and husband?" He leered at Molly, baring his fangs in hungry anticipation of their next drink.

Molly's eyes found Lydia's across the room, lasered right to her. Lydia felt them see her. Molly's face twisted, sticking her tongue between her teeth as she flashed the sign of the beast with her empty hand.

"She's gonna do it." Copperhead gripped the pistol.

"What do you mean, Molly?" Lydia's face wrinkled from the clue. "Alice? Alice Cooper? What? I don't get it—"

"I gotta take the shot. I'm sorry."

"No, wait. Alice Cooper. Wait. *Rhew.*" Lydia commanded as she gripped the muzzle of D's pistol, turning it too cold for him to touch. He jerked his hand back from the pain.

"I do." Molly's sweet face looked up at Cain and smiled.

"Let it be sanctified, then—" He licked his grim lips. "In blood."

Lydia watched as Molly took her spear and carved a line across her forearm, letting her blood run red down to her fingers, dripping to the ground beneath her. She presented it to Cain, an offering of herself. He took her arm, greedy, eager, her face winking back across the distance at Lydia. And Cain drank. He sank his teeth into her open wound and took heaping gulps from her warm, red liquid.

His eyes rolled in his head. His teeth smoked, cracked. He opened his mouth wide to scream but only gasps came out. He clutched his throat as his knees buckled to the floor. His acolytes shrank in fear, none eager to challenge whatever power had rendered their master prostrate as she laughed. He clutched at her feet, down on all fours like the wretched beast he was.

"I was told you don't like a certain kind of metal." Molly's face smiled, glanced to Lydia once more then back at the beast beneath her. She absorbed the decoy spear into her arm, then transformed into a figure of gleaming metallic skin. "Well, I'm metal-est chick who ever lived!" She shifted back into classic Molly—blue jeans, tank top, Jordache cut with the rainbow emblem on the back.

"Andi!" Lydia shouted, unable to stop herself.

A blade flashed from the sky, slicing off Cain's head. Another Molly appeared from under a hood—the invisibility cloak from the otherworld, a souvenir she'd brought back along with them.

"Clever god." Lydia smiled at the stunt.

"Sister." The Copperhead dropped his jaw at the twins.

"Burn him!" Molly screamed to her doppelganger. The metal Molly formed both her arms into flamethrowers and blasted the corpse into ash. The god sank her spear into the severed head of the cursed creature. The flames kept the armies of the night at bay as the two finished the job they'd come to do. Cain's head erupted into spider legs as it pried itself off the searing, poisonous, silver-laced Eldritch weapon. It mutated and ran slick with its own goop as it pulled away from her. "The head! The head!"

Andi turned one fire cannon onto the crawling face of Cain and burnt it too. It screeched as it sizzled and popped.

Eyes from the arena turned to the intruders, their cover blown as Lydia's focus fell and The Copperhead's true form, bronze helmet and all, lay bare to the vast ensemble of evil.

"*Fflam!*" Lydia threw her hands forward and sent a blast of blue flame into the throng. Chaos erupted as they ran in all directions to escape the fire. The Copperhead wasted neither time nor bullets as his Berettas sang their song.

Molly kept the head pinned as her robotic ally poured fire into his corpse and head. Lydia and D fought their way to the center to join them. The pinky finger of Cain's left arm ripped itself from the rest, forming into a snake and shooting through the clamor of the arcade.

"Shit, no!" Molly reached for it but was too late. "There went the whole plan. Fuck."

"It was a shit plan." D shook his head as he popped another creature. "You got one now to get us out of this?"

"Well, I did until you showed up."

"You're welcome, by the way." Lydia sneered as she impaled a goblin with her own dark spire. "But seriously, what now?"

The throng regathered, licking their fangs for the fight. The Cyclopes wielded heavy clubs, and halberds populated the ranks of the guards marching in.

"I guess we fight our way out." D shoved in another mag.

"Time to shout at the devil!" the android grinned.

"Oh gods, not you too." Lydia sighed and drew a rune-shield around them. "There's other bands, damn."

XI

"SHOUT AT THE DEVIL"
—MÖTLEY CRÜE, 1983

LYDIA'S RUNE-SHIELD held against the slamming clubs of a cyclops. Molly's spear fired like a gun into its gut and slit up to its chest, spilling its innards onto the floor. The handle shrank back to a sword in her hand as she handed off the cloak to The Copperhead.

"Here, you need this more than I do." She took the legs out from under a charging centurion, then his head.

"We need to make an exit strategy and now." Copperhead put in his last two mags. 34 more shots and he was down to his knives and fists.

"Get him out of here." Molly looked to her friends. "I'm going for Cain. I have to finish it."

"Kid, no!" D reached as she broke through Lydia's barrier.

"I'll be okay. Besides, I know where he went. He needs fresh blood."

Molly took off down the north corridor, carving a trail of rotten corpses in her wake.

D slid on the cloak, pulling the hood over his head and vanished. Bullets sang through the air into the skulls of their enemies as the trio moved within the energy cage toward the front of the keep.

"I thought you were on a date." Lydia stabbed another goblin through the heart with her darkspire.

"Yeah, this is it." The android hammered into a cyclops, crushing its skull with her battering ram arm.

"This isn't a date. This is not how dates are."

"Oh. Well, I've only been on one other one."

"What other one? Who did you date? Oh my god."

"Girls?" Copperhead fired into the army between them and freedom. "Maybe now's not the time." He just knew he was about to die amidst bubble gum and prom stories. "We need to clear a path to the exit. Any ideas?"

"I got this. Let's see how they like a rhino coming at them." Lydia dropped her arms and concentrated, remembering the Loa said she'd be able to change her form like the other vamps could. She did change—into a nutria rat. "Wait what the?" she squeaked out.

The Copperhead holstered a pistol and scooped her up before she was trampled. Their shield down now, Andi shifted both her arms into silver-bladed chainsaws and mowed down anything that came near them.

"You can only change into what you've drank. And you only drank a rat so far." He cussed and let her go as she shifted back to normal.

The other sorceress got between them and the corridor. Copperhead covered their back as Lydia conjured another spire and drew a shield over them again.

"Pathetic little witch. I'll drink your very souls." She changed form, her hands becoming snapping claws, her back stretching, a giant scorpion tail growing behind her. She lashed the stinger at them as Lydia prepared to counter it. The lion burst free of its chains and charged at them, coming right at Lydia.

Andi lopped off the scorpion's tail with a chainsaw and morphed her other arm into a cannon. "I don't think I have a soul. But you can take a swig of this." She blasted the head off the scorpion-witch, leaving a smoldering nub.

Lydia cast the heavy cat off her with a word, blood dripping from her teeth. "Dude, I was totally going to have an epic witch-battle with her."

"Oh, sorry." Andi shrugged. "You can get the next one."

Copperhead, invisible to them, shook his head and decided, odd as they were, they would do fine without him. He needed to find the one they came for. She may be a god, but she still didn't know what she was doing. Not that he ever had either.

* * *

The god ran down the corridor, butchering anything stupid enough to get in her way, and soon nothing did. The night creatures fled in her wake as she burst through the rock walls into Cain's bestiary. There, the snake fed itself on a woolly mammoth—no more of its kind to come now as he drained its life to regrow his vile self.

Molly ran to cut off his lifeline before he could replenish himself to his full strength.

"Daughter," he cried out. "Protect me."

Before Molly's blade met his neck a second time, a colossal tentacle burst through the arched window into the room and wrapped around her body, flinging her out into the night.

* * *

Lydia and Andi made their way out the front gate of Cain's castle. They ran toward the clearing before the ground got soupy again in all directions. Their pursuers halted for the moment as many licked their wounds in the forms of severed limbs or holes in their bodies. Being what they were, only a killshot with silver or sunlight would end them fully. Lydia shifted one hand to a lion's claw while the other cast a shield as Andi covered them.

Lights burst from above, their hovering getaway vehicle appearing from its cloaking device. Ropes fell from the open bomb-bay. Seeing only the two of them, Buck Kobayashi slid down one of the lines, his particle accelerator strapped to his back. Captain Boudreaux followed behind with a pair of M4's and a slew of grenades on bandoliers across his chest.

"Where's D?" Buck sprayed a beam into the amassing throng at the castle gate.

"He's right here." Lydia stretched the energy field larger to cover them all. "D? He's got an invisible shroud on. He was right here with us. D?" She waved her arm in the air, feeling for him.

"We can't leave a man behind." Callum prepped his rifle to head into the devil's den.

"Two behind." Lydia's face sank. This whole rescue had turned to hot garbage. "Two?"

"Hi, I'm Molly, by the way." The android shrank her chainsaw into a hand, offering it to the two men.

"No, you're not. *She's* still inside. You're not Molly."

"Oh, right. Sorry. It's just I've been saying that all summer. Force of habit. I'm Molly's sister." She extended her hand again.

"What's the situation?" The Colonel's voice called out over the radios on Callum and Buck's suits. "I can only hold her a sec before they're on the ship."

"Pull off for now, Colonel. We gotta get D." The Captain called into his radio. The ship flew higher into the air.

More grim figures appeared. These plodded in front of the others, their legs hobbling, a gangly, gruesome horde, arms dangling at their sides, the flesh rotting from their faces. Eyes bulged, teeth bared. Their hands, little more than bones, reached out as they amassed into an army of foot soldiers moving toward the band of four.

"Draugr." Boudreaux put a round into one's chest, but it kept trudging forward.

"What?" Andi said. She was still not up to speed on all this quite yet.

"The ones they fed on but never turned. Eventually, they rot. Mindless, walking corpses who never quite die, but aren't alive either." Buck put his words to the test with a blast from his particle beam and sent one of them to the nethers.

"Whoa that's cool. Can I inspect that? I'd like to learn how it works." Andi elongated her neck to look at Buck's power pack.

"Gladly, once we're ever clear of this."

"Oh no, it won't take but a second." She stretched her fingers into liquid metal coils all through his device, learning its construction in 1.21 seconds. "Got it, thanks."

"What the?" Buck's eyes bulged as she formed one arm into a particle cannon three times the size of his.

The undead host marched at them while their vampiric masters stood ready to finish whatever their ghoulish pawns left behind. A whirring on the wind grew louder into the area as Lydia blinked into the darkness to make out shapes moving toward them.

"What in the hell now?" Boudreax swore.

"It's—" Lydia stared at the shapes—not believing her eyes—airboats, several of them, coming in fast. Two men jumped off the first one. Another boat landed, and a third. "My Daddy. And my brothers." Lydia couldn't believe her eyes. More boats floated up, their passengers jumping off, all armed with shotguns, crossbows, hunting rifles, and anything else they had. "My uncles. And even my aunt Janice." Lydia shivered her head at the absurdity of it.

"Baby girl, what in the damn hell?" Her father and two oldest brothers ran to her, the rest already aiming long guns at the contingent of corpses moving at them.

"Daddy, what the—how did you—what are you doing here?" Her face was more lost now than it had ever been since the first time she saw her best friend bounce bullets off her chest.

"Ms. Clair done called me and said you was in some kind of trouble and gave me them damn numbers. I know coordinates when I see 'em."

"Hey, Mr. Stiles!" Andi shrank her gun arm into a hand and waved at him, even giving him a hug.

"Why'd you come?" Lydia thought her brain would break.

"The hell kind of shitass daddy wouldn't?"

XII
"THE LAST DRAGON"
—DWIGHT DAVID, 1985

THE COPPERHEAD SHOT his way through the corridor. The fleeing vamps couldn't see where the shots came from since he wore the shroud. They ran through the hall, stumbling over each other, several shifting form into wolves or leopards or some other vicious beast so they could flee faster.

He spent his last round into a brown bear's skull, it slashing its claws blindly, hoping to get lucky. He watched it rot into the corpse of what had once been a man. He loathed them, the weaklings that fell to Cain's call—those who bore the mark. How many more waited out there in the wide world still? There were so many familiars Cain put in positions of power with the promise to turn them in due course. How many corporations did he control? How many world leaders were his pawns?

D took his knives from their sheaths. He sank one under the collarbone of a younger vamp that tripped, still trying to stand up. He twisted the blade to be sure he'd done the job. They were resilient, these abominations. But he'd taught himself their weak spots. The silver did its job before he took it out again, wiping the black blood of the damned on its own clothing.

He'd tried to follow the kid, the god, and shook his head at his folly. Always trying to be their hero. Now all it had got him was lost. He must have gone down the wrong path at some point. More of them came, stopping at the slew of bodies he'd made, sniffing the air—smelling for him. The cloak wouldn't hide him much longer. This was it, he decided.

"Fuck it." He gripped the knives tighter. Vamps came at him from both ends of the long hallway, sniffing, finding him with their animal senses.

Light burst into the hall from the far end behind him. Screams, shrieks rang out as what looked like blue and red flames burned beyond the fleeing beasts. They ran past him, no longer interested in ferreting him out. The ones on his other side fled. Then he saw what terrified them.

Murphy Long flung a length of glowing chain, barbed like hell at the end. It wrapped around the leg of one of them as she jerked it back, taking the leg with it. The creature fell and crawled forward as she flung her chain again, this time bursting through the skull of one, searing a hole into it. She whipped and flailed that burning weapon around her like a whirlwind. Her body glowed with red and blue energy surrounding her. She never saw him—charging right past as she burnt through the pack of hellspawn on her warpath.

She twirled her chain all around her, turning and spinning her body along with it, wrapping it over and under her legs, whipping it around her body to build more speed and control its path. She grappled one around his waist and jerked him to her. She seized his head with her empty hand and burnt his face off, tearing the skull and spine from the now empty vessel and tossing it behind her. She lashed another across the back, leaving a fiery gash still aflame as it engulfed the rest of him.

The Zuìzhōng Lóng burnt her way through the bowels of the dark castle. Every beast, creature, and demon fell to her lash. She made her way into the mighty arcade, the scene of the aborted nuptials. A sluggish brute slithered its heavy form away from the arena. She sent the chain into it, whipping it over and over again, leaving sear-marks across its wormy carcass until it collapsed into rot.

Winged gargoyles and armored vamps flooded into the arcade. The footsoldiers of Cain presented their spears as the winged demons hurled sharpened missiles at her. Murphy took the chain's ends in each hand and whirled them in arcs, lashing at her enemies with twin whips of godly fire. She pirouetted and gyrated the chains in criss-crossing arcs, popping and flogging them as they came at her. She flipped into the air, lashing one around its armor and using it as a club against the others, smashing and crushing her way into their drove, scattering their ranks. Soon, few remained as they fled her chaotic destruction.

Then *He* roared.

Murphy turned to face her destiny. Belial Cain stormed into the arena, his acolytes fleeing him as much as they did her burning chain. He stood a dozen feet tall, hooves stamping down on the stone floor. His arms, the size of trees, culminated into bear claws, each the length of a sword on its own. His massive hairy chest pulsed with his power and blood, his hate for all mankind—and most especially the gods they prayed to.

The Beast roared again, its hot breath bristling through her puffed-out hair. Murphy stood fast, flinging her chains in arcs on either side of her again. She steadied her breath, focused her Qi. The glowing energy radiated off her body. Nothing could touch her so long as she held. And she would have to hold.

"Come on, you goddamned son of a bitch. Let's go." She whipped one end of her chain at his chest, but he burst into black mist and reformed behind her. She'd already whipped her other end around as he appeared, wrapping it around his arm as he slashed his claws at her. "Saw that coming a mile away, *Jack*." It occurred to her this thing had once signed her paychecks.

Cain flinched, clenching all his muscles, tugging, pulling away, straining to dematerialize—as he always did. He tugged, and raged, and roared. But he couldn't break free. He was bound now to a single place and body. He couldn't tear apart or burst into bats, or anything. He was singular. Trapped.

"I got you now, boy." Murphy held her chain, planting her feet. *You're not fighting a man.* She heard the voice echo in her mind. But this beast was stronger than any herd of horses the Order had in its stable. He stretched even bigger. Bound as he was to only one body, there didn't seem any limit on what he became.

And what he became was terrible.

* * *

Above them, in the upper channels of the labyrinthine towers of Cain's castle, The Copperhead took out the strays. Using his invisibility, he slit the throat of every lingering centurion and guard still stupid enough to stand their duty. As a soldier, he almost felt for them—almost. But vamps got what they deserved.

A hand grabbed him from behind, pulling the hood from his head, rendering him visible under the flickering lights. He turned to slash whatever dared touch him only to face the dread figure of a dark knight bearing upon him. The black-iron plates interlocked themselves all over the enormous figure. The shadowy armor left no crevice uncovered for D's knife to slip into. His arcane shell protected every inch of him, a demonic copy of D's own chemical-sprayed, utilitarian armor.

"Stupid man in a tin can." Sandor picked up Copperhead and hurled him into the stone wall. D got up slower than he liked and caught a kick to the ribs. His body armor buffered the blows but not enough. This demon knight had at least double his strength. The older they were, the stronger they got. Another perversion of the natural order. And Sandor was one of the oldest generals Cain had.

D faded and dodged the next blows coming at his belly. He caught one to the helmet that jarred him and did worse to the Count's hand—but, of course, the vamp would heal a lot faster than he could. D had to dance if he was going to walk away from this one. He stuck and jabbed, knocking his opponent off balance but not enough. He caught one full fist the chest, rocketing him backward down the corridor.

* * *

Cain writhed and jerked at Murphy holding the other end of her chain binding him, burning at his wrist as it dug into his cells—melting his dark armor built to withstand even sunlight if it had to, but not whatever foul new thing had arrived. His black eyes stared their hate into Murphy's glowing face, her body alight with red and blue flame. He wrenched his arm, jerking her off her feet and slung her into the far wall.

Murphy kicked off the wall, hurling herself back into him, pulling the chain to her as she flew forward. She thrust her palm into his chest, knocking him back, stunning him. His head shook. His free hand grew tusks, horns, heavy and hard as stone. He slammed it down onto her like a club. Murphy caught it in a high block, holding him with her energy, her Qi. She kept her breathing steady. Always. There were no mistakes now. One slip and she was dead.

She crouched, bent her knees into a full squat, then launched herself upward, breaking through his attack. Cain jerked her toward him as she crested in the air, just like she wanted him to do. Murphy breathed, focused all her energy down into her free hand, made a fist and shattered it into the stone floor as she landed. Thunder boomed beneath them as the shockwave blasted him to the far end of the great arcade.

Dazed, disoriented. Cain struggled to his feet, his form shifting out of control now. Wolf. Deer. Bear. Leopard. Rhino. Jackal. His face and body ran the gamut of the lives he'd drank. He shifted through a dozen human faces or more as he tried to regain himself. He stood, raging, and charged at Murphy. She held fast, sure of her footing and herself.

Cain bore down on her. Murphy leapt into a backflip kick to his chin. She reversed it into a spinning aerial roundhouse to his temple. She yanked herself to him with the chain and landed a hook to his jaw, leaving a searing burn where her glowing hand struck.

Cain roared, pounding the ground with his fist, cracking the stone.

"Enough of this!" He bellowed and bones erupted from his back, molding and shaping themselves into massive, lanky appendages. Webbed skin grew from the tendrils stretching from each joint of the new limbs protruding off his back. A massive pair of wings took shape, flapping at full force into the arena. Murphy held tight as his mighty, bear-faced form rose into the air. She held her chain, pulling back against him with all her strength.

Still, he rose, thrusting with each flap of the mighty bat wings higher into the arches, shattering through the ceiling with his tusked fist, raining stone down on her. She lost her grip on the chain, seizing it again as he broke through and flew off into the night sky. She held on tight, trailing behind him into the dark clouds.

XIII
"NEVER SURRENDER"
—STAN BUSH, 1989

LYDIA STRETCHED HER FLEDGELING magic to her limits, holding a rune-shield all around her family and D's teammates. Buck sent blast after blast from his energy pack into the undead that kept coming, more and more from in and outside the castle. Winged ghouls and vamps flew overhead, trying to break through her energy, but she held. Her daddy and them fired everything they'd brought with them at the hellspawn. She didn't know what he thought he would find when he got to her, but she couldn't imagine it was anything close to this.

The other Molly blasted her cannons into the sky to counter their winged enemies. She walked outside the energy shield and cut them with her silver-blade chainsaw arms. Dogs, wolves, jackals, slobbering predators of all types ran at her, biting, chewing, tearing into her semi-fluid metal body. She sliced and mulched into them.

"Get back in the circle," Lydia shouted at her. She backflipped into their sanctum, revving her saw-hands for another wave as her body reshaped itself. "Where'd you even get the silver for those anyway?" Lydia fired a blast with a word, burning a winged wolf scratching at the top of her shield.

"Oh, I took Clair's forks and stuff, the ones she kept put away."

"She's gonna kill you when she finds out."

"Does anyone have anything like a plan?" Captain Boudreax emptied another M4 magazine, down to his last two. He looked to Lydia, as did Buck, her father, and Andi. *Who died and left ME in charge?* She cast another fireball. *And where the HELL is Molly?*

*　*　*

Meggoth, the quarter-Eldritch swamp-demon bearing a hundred writhing tentacles from her waist, hurled The Sledgehammer across the vast bog. Molly jumped up, gripping her spear to throw it into the fiend's eye. Meggoth jerked Molly's feet from under her, casting her throw wild as she tossed the godkiller spear into the murky void. Under the dim moon, the two great forces fought.

Molly slammed her fists into the slimy skin of the tentacled hag. Her piercing, evil laugh boiled Molly's blood as each blow only sank into more squishing tentacles. More of them slapped at her, wrapping around her legs, wrenching her arms back, pinning her to the wet, sloppy marsh. Meggoth pounded her into tree trunks and heavy root clusters, shattering them to splinters, raking Molly's body through the muck. Far in the distance, she saw and heard the reports of a battle—her friends fighting without her. They needed her. She heard them, felt them—*their prayers.* Buck crossed himself but called Molly's name under his breath.

Lydia's heart ached for her friend to arrive and save them. Inside the castle, D's pain wrenched her, though he would call no name. He was too stubborn, too proud to call on any gods, even the ones he knew were real. And she heard her own voice, the same she'd spoken with in her waiting room before their "wedding." Her android twin. Could a robot pray? Did she have a soul?

Meggoth shoved Molly's face into the grime. She sensed another cry, this one much closer to her. She hefted, trying to pry the oozing tentacle off her, rip it from the creature's body if she could. Then she saw it, the mighty lion Cain had meant to sacrifice.

"Yes, see her?" Meggoth's shrill voice poisoned Molly's ears. She would tear the throat from the hag's neck when she got the chance. "See how she struggles. As do you. The mire will claim her, as it claims all foolish enough to venture into my swamp. See how she drowns. As you drown."

"I don't need air, demon." Molly grit her teeth, pushing more force into the gorgon's writhing extremities.

"I know you don't. But there are ways to drown a god, aren't there?" She smiled her jagged, rotten teeth, raising one bony, gangly hand in the air, calling forth— *something*.

Molly felt them before she heard them. Anguish punched at her gut, buffeted against her soul. She felt a weight so heavy, she didn't know if she could lift it off herself. She'd felt this before. Back in the woods outside Easton's cabin—those cold, lonely voices on the wind. She'd never gone back to see to them. She'd felt it again in in the otherworld—at the Sea of Souls. There, she'd learned what it was.

Their apparitions appeared to her, wandering lost in these crags and cypress trees. Souls of the dead, those who hadn't crossed over—still waiting to be claimed. They moaned, wailed, sang songs of desperation. How long had they wandered here? Many of them wore blue uniforms. She could make out their insignia— soldiers and freedmen, all veterans in the righteous fight against the bastard slavers.

"They too drowned in my bog. Destined for better than this, but some never find their way, do they? Now they belong to me. Their sad souls weigh on yours, do they not? Yes, I see it."

Molly looked to the lion up to its neck in mud, its struggle almost over. Soon it would find whatever peace awaited it. But those behind her would not. She felt them, clawing at her mind, tearing her soul—their sadness, their need more than she thought she could bear. They wanted, needed at her. They thrust their hopelessness into her as she felt her strength slipping. Meggoth pushed her further down into the glop.

The ghost soldiers advanced, gathering their ranks, their sadness pulling at her. An army of them, a full platoon amassed. One floated at her from the rear ranks, their legs fading into the mist beneath their knees. His face, hollow, sunk-eyed, a century and more in this limbo. In his hand, he clung to something—something Molly recognized.

"Or perhaps I won't need to drown you after all." Meggoth curled her bony fingers toward the marching soldier. He held forth his prize, a guitar-shaped spear forged from Eldritch steel in the land beyond the veil—the weapon that could kill a god.

"There's just one problem, *Megs*." She turned to the hag. Molly's eyes burned a bright, hot green as Meggoth retracted from her. Molly gripped the spear *Her* soldier returned to her. Her voice deepened, twisted, reverberated into a booming echo through the drooping trees—the voice of God. "The dead are *mine* to command."

* * *

Inside the castle, its last two combatants raged against themselves—one an immortal son of Hell, the other an aging war veteran with a bad back and worse knees. There was no chance for D to win, and he knew it.

Sandor kicked him through an oaken door into a dressing chamber. He pummeled D in the chest, the ribs, the arms and shoulders. D blocked everything he could, but the demon was too fast, too strong, too armored to do anything against it. The vampire slammed him across the room, smashing him into the long mirror near the four-post bed. Its glass shattered across the floor.

The shards spat back a dozen different glimpses into D's weakness, his failure. He bled from his nose, his lips, at least three cracked ribs by his count. One knee had quit and the other not far behind. A shoulder needed relocating. He gasped, panted. Just one drink of water, and he'd hang it up.

Sandor straddled him, lifting him by his helmet, tearing it from his head. D saw his own bloody face, gray hairs in his beard staring back at him from the mirror shards. He squinted at the images, the reflections. But one of them was different. In it, he wore a weathered top hat, his face painted sugar white. A cigar jutting from his lips.

"You are pathetic. You dare challenge me?" Sandor stretched his fangs to tear into D's throat, ending the battle for good. "You're but a man. I am *Count* Sardo Sandor."

"I never was good at those damn fancy titles." D coughed out. "Remind me, does a Count beat a *Baron?*"

"What?" Sandor stared at his prey, then looked to the shards. But it was too late. D had already called the name, a whisper on his lips. The first prayer he'd ever uttered in his adult life. Three times, he called the name. *Baron Samedi. Baron Samedi. Baron Samedi.*

He felt the energy come into him, from outside, all around him, flowing into him. His knees, his shoulders, his back, all the pain gone, stronger than before.

He gripped Sandor's hands, breaking his fingers as he wrenched them off his neck and stood to his feet.

"It's showtime." D's mouth with the Baron's deepened voice spoke at the struggling demon.

D knocked him to the ground. He kicked his jaw, cracking it. He sent another fist into the belly of the armored vampire, bursting the plates at their joints. He battered and crushed the hellion with each strike. He felt the Baron inside him. Whispering to him. Aiming his strikes as they grew fiercer, faster. Sardo struggled to his feet, knocked back further with each blow from the man who only seconds ago lay prostrate before him. D slugged, boxed, and clobbered a full war's amount of damage into his enemy. Every terrible thing he'd ever witnessed, lived through, suffered—he poured it all into the creature that deserved every ounce of it. He fought him back into the hall, the building shaking, crumbling from the sound of something crashing through the ceiling in the arcade.

The floor beyond Sardo cracked, weakened, giving way. D jerked up the Count, put one arm under his armpit, stretching it across his enemy's chest, gripping him so tight he couldn't move, could barely breathe. He stared at the weak spot in the floor, and he leapt. He held the vampire lord's body in his massive arms, and he crashed them both through the floor. Falling through the air, D held onto his opponent, and slammed him into the very rock bottom of the great arcade beneath them.

Every bone in the sadistic thing's body burst. His black blood ran across the stone floor. D tore the helmet from the head of his enemy, pulled his knife from his boot—and plunged it through the eye of the damned.

"You're welcome, old friend." The Baron's voice trailed away into the vastness of the arena. D breathed and sat. Just for a minute.

* * *

Outside the front gate, the war raged on. Lydia's energy taxed, she knew the shield would fail any minute. Andi and Buck blasted anything that came anywhere close to them, Callum and Lydia's kinfolk now empty of ammunition and down to blades and sticks. They saw a winged beast crash through and fly away from the castle, someone dangling from a rope or something beneath it as they flew off into the night.

A booming, hollow screech tore through the air, stopping even the vampires and draugr in their tracks. The creatures of the night cowed, retreated beneath the even darker shadow that loomed above them.

Two arching, dinosauric necks stretched high above the castle's towers. The heads they supported growled and snarled as they bawled their deafening scream again. Giant, clawed arms gripped the castle turrets as one of the heads lurched toward Lydia's group. Her shield held, but wouldn't survive one more blow like that.

More titanic monsters appeared, cascading from the darkness, each as big or bigger than the last. Beings that stretched the limits of even the wildest imaginations among them. Only Lydia had seen such beings—in the otherworld. Cain's children had arrived.

"Ladies, Gentlemen," Captain Callum Boudreaux saluted them all. "It's been an honor."

Lydia looked to the only Molly she had, that sweet, innocent android's face staring back at her.

Then came the sound of hooves.

"Y'all hear horses?" Buck turned his head behind them.

The galloping hooves grew louder, nearer. But even those gave way, drowned out by the ear-splitting roar of some tremendous lion. Lydia saw it coming right at her. A screaming god of war, holding a dreadful spear before her, charged forth at the head of a ghastly army, the glimmering souls of those long dead.

El Shaddai rode her battle-lion into the draugr, tearing and clawing and making its way toward their larger enemies. The spectral cavalry charged with her. Soon the throng that had beset Lydia's troupe lay butchered across the moor.

But God was not done.

The colossal being with two heads bellowed. She flung her spear through its left skull and blasted herself into the sky. She caught the spear as it flew through the other side of the beast's neck, then flipped and sank it again into the second head, tearing a gash downward as she fell to the ground again. She ran up another gargantuan monster's body, using her spear as a claw to grip her way atop it. She leapt off its shoulder, extended her handle as long as it would go, and swiped across the giant's neck, raining its blood down on the world below.

From the chaos, The Copperhead appeared from under the shroud, definitely the worse for wear but alive. He stared amazed with his comrades as they watched the deity rain her wrath into the sons and daughters of Cain the Cursed.

In the shower of hot red rain, a parapet of Cain's castle exploded into flaming rubble. A bolt of white-hot energy surged from thin air at the walls and burst more brick and mortar into glassy shards.

"Guess what I finally found, boys!" The Colonel's voice cackled over Buck and Callum's radios. The spaceship de-cloaked and burned laser-fire into the foundation of Cain's stronghold, sending blast after blast until little remained but bubbling rock and tar.

"I swear." Callum's war-torn face stared into the chaotic scene as a vessel from some unknown world razed a building while a god leapt and stabbed her judgement into monstrous terrors from the void.

Molly flung her blade into one's face as her fists slammed another to the ground. Cain's greath behemoths, his miscreations, abominations before Molly, things her fellow gods had never intended to be born into the world—they all fell before her. And then she felt it—a surge across her whole body, tingling through the skin she knew wasn't her own. This. This is what she was supposed to do. This was her sacred duty. *This* was who she was. She was The Destroyer.

XIV
"THE HERO"
—QUEEN, 1980

THE VAST BLUE DARK of the night sky stretched endless before Murphy as they flew above the clouds. She trailed behind the soaring beast of a thousand species. His membrane wings flapped every few seconds, keeping them where the air grew thin. Her glowing, burning *armor* protected her from everything, even this. She breathed inside her energy field just fine, but for how long she had no idea. She was still new to this *chosen one* business.

The land beneath lay dotted with specks of light, but soon those gave way to a vast emptiness. They flew somewhere over the great desert to the west. Cain, demon that he was—*could he have ever been anything close to human?*—fled in the vain hope he'd find a way to release her consecrated chain. But Murphy would never let go her grip.

Her mind scattered across a hundred miles and as many memories of the life she'd had, the person she'd been. She had settled her guilt, her conscience with her father, dead these many years but somehow very much still alive—in some past she'd just come from, trained with him, ate with him, sat with him, laughed with him. That man who lived in that time would still go on to America. Meet her mother. Fall in love. Raise the child that would become her. She would then betray and abandon him, only to go back to him again. As she had. As she still would. *Was time one big circle?* She felt the emptiness of the dark climbing into her mind.

But she couldn't falter. She couldn't fail. She reached with her other arm, putting both hands on the chain, trying to pull him toward her. She slipped, dropping one hand from its grip while the other tightened. *She* had to do this, somehow. Her mission. Her destiny. The why of it, she'd asked as many times to as many gods as she'd met. But they seldom offered any answers that made any sense. *Gods.* She could sure use one or two of those right now. She closed her eyes, tried to summon her strength. Somehow, she had to bring this monster to the ground. There, she could finish him. She felt it. Knew it. She would.

Twisting in the howling winds, she looked behind her where they'd been. The clouds beneath them masked the world below. Bursting through them came a figure she breathed a heavy relief to see—one she'd missed more than she'd known. Even through the darkness, she saw that red hair in the moonlight. The spear-god crouched on the air itself as she rose higher.

The ship revealed itself. The metal of its fuselage glimmered as Molly stood atop it, reaching her hand to Murphy. They clasped their fingers together. Molly pulled Murph close. Murph's feet touched the ship.

"I can't bring him down." Murphy shouted at Molly's face.

"Yes, you can." Molly smiled at the one who was chosen to end the terror of Cain, cleaning up the mess of some older, less wise of her peers. "Now do what you came to do. Finish it."

Murphy nodded to Molly, narrowing her eyes, gritting herself for the fight, the fall that would precede it. She turned, feet planted—just like the draft horses at the temple—breathed, and she whipped the other end of the chain at him, making it as long as she needed it to be. She grappled it around his flapping bat wing, jerked the line tight, and yanked. She saw the skin tear. His wing ripped away at the joint, spraying his black blood upon the world. The wing fell away and turned to dust in the wind.

Murphy breathed, readied herself, and fell away from the ship. They plummeted. Cain's agony at his wound, spiraling down through the sky, distracted him—the pain of the chain's burning grip on his arm dug deeper into him. They fell, both of them. Cain's beastly form crashed into the white, hardened sands. Bones burst and shattered. He soaked the dry ground with his blood.

Murphy, holding her crane pose and focusing all her Qi, floated to the ground behind him, her end of the chain held firm. She rested her feet on the sand, wrapping the line tighter around her forearm, her other fist cocked.

He gathered what remained of himself. Nothing here to feed on, no fresh blood to renew him. Only what remained of him now, shaping itself into a man—a man once called Germain.

Behind them, a spacecraft of unknown origin hovered. The passenger atop it bounded to the ground, walking toward her ally's battle with the Prince of Darkness. She pulled out her spear, lengthening its handle enough to prop her arm on its hilt and lean on it, a mere spectator to the fight. Joined by The Copperhead, he took a swig of something pulled from his belt, offering it to his redhaired comrade. She drank, enjoying the cool water more than any she'd ever had.

Cain hurled a claw at Murphy's face. She swatted it with her palm, then fired another length of chain, spinning and twirling its hot energy. She lashed him across the face, leaving a burning scar. Then she licked it across his chest, bursting his skin, maggots falling out of him and rotting to dust as they fell. He winced and turned from her, her whip thrashing his back. Each piece of him torn off was erased from the world, all of him becoming dust.

Cain lunged, but Murphy dodged, parried, and sent him to the ground again. He snarled, and barked, and roared, and screeched, made every sound of every animal he'd ever consumed. Ten thousand years of genocides came to an end in a moment as Murphy grappled the other end of her chain around his other wrist. She twisted her body, wrapping the lines around herself as she moved closer to him. He struggled and fought and tugged, but she had carved too much of him away. He was no more now than any other man—barely enough mass left in him to rival her own height. He tried to lunge, baring his long fangs, going for her throat. They burst against the glowing energy that covered her skin. His mouth sizzled, his face catching flame from the contact. He screamed so loud and shrill, it was heard by every creature for miles.

Murphy wrapped the chain around him again and again, yanking tight with each jerk of her wrists. It burned and baked him everywhere it touched his skin. His roars tore through the stillness of the desert, but he was a long way from any allies. Even had there been, Murphy's ally watching her hogtie the beast would make short work of any who dared come to his aid. Murphy didn't mind having a god at her back. She didn't mind that at all.

"So now what?" She took a drink Molly offered her as Cain lay bound and sizzling at their feet. Molly kicked his ribs, breaking one for the fun of it. "Leave him bound for all eternity, guarding him night and day lest his kind ever find him again?"

"I guess." Copperhead stood behind them, looking down at the enemy who'd so long held his city under an evil thumb. Molly and Murph both saw the weight fall off his big shoulders. He looked an inch taller from the relief alone.

"He doesn't love the sun, right?" Molly took another swig of the water and spat some on Cain's face, sizzling and burning him as she sprayed it. "Hey, that's neat. Holy water, ha."

"Yeah, but it doesn't kill him, just hurts him something awful." The Copperhead chuckled at Molly's water trick, which she kept doing.

"What if we got him even closer to it?" She finished torturing him with her water and handed it back. She looked at both their quizzed faces, then behind them at the Colonel climbing down the gangway of the ship. "We have a spaceship." Molly smiled.

"We have a spaceship." Murphy raised one corner of her tired mouth.

"We have a spaceship." D sighed.

* * *

Out the corner of the cockpit windows, Molly watched a planet go by. Had to be Venus, she figured. They'd passed the moon a few hours before. Once out of the atmosphere, this thing really moved. D had crossed himself a good thirteen times as they'd first broke through the gravity field into dead space, never having had the guts to risk it before.

"No offense." He shrugged at Molly as he crossed himself again.

"No worries. I don't get jealous." She kept watch, as did Murph still holding one end of the chain. Cain's burning form had baked to almost nothing but charred cinder.

As they drew nearer the sun, its vibrant light threatening to blind all but one of them, it was time to end it. Molly and Murph sealed themselves in the second chamber, so the oxygen would stay in the pressurized cabin. The Colonel spoke to the ship with his mind, opening the bay doors beneath them. Molly kicked the charred form of Cain out into the cold of space. The Colonel quickly closed the doors. Murphy held the chain tight as it fed through the closed doors. The Colonel gunned it, building speed as they rocketed closer to the sun, then spun into a 180-degree turn. Murphy retracted the chain from Cain's corpse. Its momentum flung him speeding toward the fiery, gaseous orb where he would burn for ten billion years.

Molly smiled and hugged Murphy as the air came back in their chamber. They looked over each other, laughing at the absurdity that had become their lives. Molly pointed up and down at Murph's clothes—her worn jeans, Converse sneakers, and her faded Detroit jersey shirt.

"This your super suit?" She smirked. "Needs work."

XV

"PARADISE CITY"
—GUNS & ROSES, 1987

GOD SAT IN THE CORNER of the bar once called Tipitina's as the girls danced and sang with the karaoke machine. She smiled at Lydia and the sweet girl who wore her own face maybe better than she did. They looked so natural up there, back in normal clothes—well, as normal as Lydia ever got.

They'd done her proud, two heroes in their own right. Lydia got them all away from the chaos on her family's airboats. She'd have a long night of explaining all of it to her father and brothers sometime soon, but El Shaddai envied her old friend that closeness, that sense of home.

She looked to the balcony, where she'd first seen the witch Evilyn who would change all their lives forever, that poor lost soul who fought her own doomed war against Hell itself. For some reason her sad fate gnawed at Molly. Is this what being a god was, caring even for her worst enemies? That would suck.

The Copperhead—Boscaux Maximilien St. Michel Chevalier DeBrousse—or just D—took a well-deserved quaff from the biggest beer mug in the place. Murphy clinked hers against his, and they bent their elbows.

If it were at all possible to truly annoy another person all the way to death, that was very clearly and fully Buck Kobayashi's plan with his friend Callum Boudreaux. She laughed a heavy, booming laugh as the Lieutenant regaled the tired old Captain with *yet* another wild tale of heroics at which the good captain had been literally present himself.

"I was there, Buck. We took that hill together." Boudreaux drank another shot of whisky, glaring at his howling companion. "I swear."

"You know, I think I might buy this place, what you say to that D? New Copperheadquarters?"

"Don't expect a bar makes much sense as a hideout, now does it, Buck?" D shook his head. Murphy laughed and raised her pint to the sirens on the stage belting out some Clash. Lydia loved The Clash.

"No, reckon not. But there's an old fire station down the street might work. Huh? Huh?" Buck nodded his head.

They could all tell from his expression D didn't hate the idea.

"What about you?" D turned to Murphy. "Lot of Cain's kind still running the streets to be cleaned up. Could sure use you and that handy whip."

"Well, those masks your old buddy Ev gave out makes it hard for them to hide. I think y'all will do just fine now that *He's* gone for good. Plus, I've got a few loose ends up north to tie up."

"I'll drink to that." Buck clinked her glass, spilling some out of both. He was pissed up a tree already. Callum shook his head, got up and brought a drink to The Colonel who sat in the back near Molly. She felt whatever swam around in his mind bothering him again, and she leaned down and kissed him on the forehead.

"You'll get through it, Colonel." She couldn't heal them, per se, but she could help them heal themselves, she'd learned. And the dead soldiers, long due their peace, she'd sent into their next lives, those who chose to go. The Baron had asked for some to keep behind, to watch the city. But she insisted the choice be their own. Some stayed and now guarded the annals of this old city built on a far older world. It would always be a doorway to the other realm. But it had good watchmen.

Somewhere across town, a church bell clanged in the waxing hours of the dawn. Eyes turned to The Copperhead, already searching for his bronze helmet.

"Oh, come on, let the cops get one. You deserve a break, hoss." Murphy tugged his shoulder.

"What cops? You took out the better half of them last night." He put his helmet on.

"They can't all be vamps." Murphy pondered it for the first time all the way through. "But then even the ones that weren't covered for those that were. Damn." She closed her eyes.

"One quick question." D looked to her before he made for the door. Molly fell in with him. He might be fighting who-knows-what out there. But he wouldn't fight alone. "You say your mama's people's from down here? What parts, what's their name?"

"Beaumont," Murphy said. "Why?"

"Just wondering."

* * *

Lydia and Molly's twin walked down the gangway of the invisible ship hovering above the corner of Elm and E Street. A Volkswagen Rabbit sat parked against the curb. Few lights flickered across the still-sleeping neighborhood. The Slater house's garage opened and a very perturbed but smartly dressed Becky LeCroiseur stomped toward them.

"I've only been waiting up all freaking night. Do you have any idea how worried I was. And oh my God—" She gawked at the big Molly appearing over half a foot taller than she had been at the start of the summer, clad in her handmade Amazon tassets and her spear across her back. "What happened to you?"

"They'll fill you in." The god smiled at her old friends, trying not to show her pain as she gulped, closing her eyes.

"Uh..." Lydia looked back at her. "What are you doing?"

"I'm not staying, Lyd. I mean what do I even say about this, anyway?" She gestured at her body, her size not easy to explain to her parents, neighbors, the town around them. "Besides, more of Cain's children are still out there. And this cold, it isn't natural. I need to look into that too."

"But why is that your j—" Lydia stopped herself because she already knew the answer.

"So, it's just me and Becky and Andi now, I guess?" Lydia moped, but they all knew she had to go.

"Oh, right, that—" The android spoke up. "Yeah, I was gonna say I don't really like that name, either." She shrugged at Lydia.

"That's just as well." The god walked down the invisible gangway. She pulled her spear from her back sheath and lay the blade flat on one shoulder of her twin sister, then the other. "I hereby dub thee Molly Slater. Wear the name well. And be good to each other. Take care of each other. You've each got your abilities, help who you can, but stay safe. Okay?"

Their eyes leaked and made hers do the same.

"Wait." Lydia called out, her lip quivering. "Will you come back? Sometimes?"

"Yes. I will. I promise." She took one last long look at her friends, then turned up the gangway, calling out to the others inside. "Buck, I've got some thoughts on this wingsuit thing."

The door shut, concealing her with the rest of the ship. Becky, Lydia, and *Molly* felt it fly away from the little town on the bay.

"Wait, did she say 'abilities?'" Becky glared at Lydia.

"Oh yeah, I'm a witch now." Lydia shrugged.

The new Molly Slater stood, still processing her official name change—as if she were scared to accept it.

"Oh, and I can change into animals." Lydia added.

"So, you're telling me—" Becky fumed, breathing hard and fast, trying to calm down. "That out of this whole group... the only one who *doesn't* have superpowers... is me?" She blinked several times at each of them.

"You're rich." Molly patted her shoulder.

"That doesn't count. That's not a power. That's a really stupid power. Only an idiot would think that's a power by itself. That is so dumb. I mean you would have to be a complete asshole—"

"Thank you, Becky." Lydia sighed. They were definitely back home.

* * *

Wind sharpened the crisp air in the wee hours of that Detroit morning. Dawn crept above the horizon as the city this far north rarely had a warm night these last years. So many had left. The empty buildings—entire skyscrapers abandoned as their capital and personnel fled south, many to the Crescent City on the river.

But some remained, stragglers, the poor, the desperate, those with nowhere else to go. They struggled to make a home among the ice—the winters unbearable. But to make it all the worse for them—as though the bitter chill and war for warmth weren't enough to endure, The Company had taken over planning, administration, and policing from the now dissolved city government. The brilliant plan of AllCorp—a division of Volund-Yöndemoni InterGlobal. And now their dread machines pounded their steel feet across the frozen blacktop as they *patrolled* the city, keeping its chilly peace.

A pair of kids no more than thirteen scurried through the cool July morning. They each carried handfuls of firewood no doubt chopped from one the few remaining parks with trees left. They ran as fast as their load-bearing bodies could get them, but not fast enough. The red lights spun as the machine roared to life, standing to its full ten-foot height, presenting its already primed and chambered guns on either side. The company had given it guns, plural, instead of anything resembling hands.

"Freeze, perpetrators." It uttered without any semblance of irony in its directive. "Release your stolen property and face the wall with your hands spread. You are under arrest."

The kids did as ordered—they'd seen the fates of those who tried their luck.

"Release your stolen property and face the wall with your hands spread." It repeated. "You are under arrest." It glitched, repeating itself another time, slurring the words the third go-round. Sometimes their wiring short-circuited. The Company always cut corners.

"Face the wall with your hands spread." It called out again, aiming its guns.

"Hey, bolts for brains." A voice came from behind the machine.

The turbo-cop spun on its turret, engaging its tripod spider-walk toward the new threat. She stood, bathed in glowing red and blue light. A burning hot chain dropped from her right hand.

"You are interfering in a lawful arrest and are obstructing justice. Drop your weapon now and—"

She didn't let it finish the rest and lashed its body, slicing it diagonally in half. The wires sparked as its circuits fried, the severed top half sliding into the street as the legs walked in a circle for a few seconds, then fell down.

"Get on home and stay safe. It's gonna be a bad night out tonight." Murphy winked at the two kids, then turned in the direction of the sound of another cop-bot a block away and smiled.

End
"Stir It Up"
—Patti LaBelle, 1985

Molly Slater *and* The SledgeHammer
will return in:

Made in the USA
Columbia, SC
05 October 2021